Kiss Carlo

Also by Adriana Trigiani

FICTION

All the Stars in the Heavens

The Supreme Macaroni Company

The Shoemaker's Wife

Brava, Valentine

Very Valentine

Home to Big Stone Gap

Rococo

The Queen of the Big Time

Lucia, Lucia

Milk Glass Moon

Big Cherry Holler

Big Stone Gap

YOUNG ADULT FICTION

Viola in Reel Life

Viola in the Spotlight

NONFICTION

Don't Sing at the Table

Cooking with My Sisters (coauthor)

SCREENPLAY

Big Stone Gap

Kiss Carlo

A NOVEL

Adriana Trigiani

HARPER

An Imprint of HarperCollins*Publishers*

KISS CARLO. Copyright © 2017 by The Glory of Everything Company. All rights reserved. Printed in the United States of America. No part of this book may be used or reproduced in any manner whatsoever without written permission except in the case of brief quotations embodied in critical articles and reviews. For information, address HarperCollins Publishers, 195 Broadway, New York, NY 10007.

HarperCollins books may be purchased for educational, business, or sales promotional use. For information, please email the Special Markets Department at SPsales@harpercollins.com.

FIRST EDITION

Interior photographs courtesy of Anthony Trigiani and the author's private collection.

Designed by Fritz Metsch

Library of Congress Cataloging-in-Publication Data has been applied for.

ISBN 978-0-06-231922-7
ISBN 978-0-06-266052-7 (International Edition)
ISBN 978-0-06-274332-9 (BAM Signed Edition)
ISBN 978-0-06-274174-5 (B&N Signed Edition)

17 18 19 20 21   LSC   10 9 8 7 6 5 4 3 2

In memory of Michael A. Trigiani

A Note from the Author

This novel is set in 1949 after World War II, a time of jubilation in America, following a victory won by the brave women and men in our families who courageously fought for democracy with our allies around the world. Attitudes regarding matters of personal freedom, work, art, family life, religion, and the role of government as described were of their time. Use of specific language to describe women, girls, citizens of color, and immigrants is now considered outdated and offensive. The words we use to describe one another have evolved. I hope.

Kiss Carlo

Overture

A cool breeze shook the old wind chimes on the balcony outside the ambassador's bedroom. The peal of the delicate glass bells sounded like the tings of crystal after a wedding toast.

The stone palazzo had been grand before the war, with its terra-cotta-tiled roof, marble floors, and carved monastery doors. Positioned on the highest peak in Roseto Valfortore, it was also imposing, like a bell tower, save the bell or the tower. It was named Palazzo Fico Regale because the hills that cascaded down to the road that led north to Rome were speckled with fig trees. In summer the trees were lush and green, loaded with purple fruit; in winter the barren branches, wrapped in turbans of burlap, looked like the raised fists of Mussolini's blackshirts.

Inside, the official consort, Signora Elisabetta Guardinfante, packed her husband's dress uniform with care. Elisabetta was small and dark, her eyes like thumbprints of black ink, more iris than whites. Her fine bones and lips were delicate, like those of her relatives of French descent from the north of Italy.

She rolled the red, white, and green sash tightly into the shape of a snail shell, so that when he unfurled it, the silk would lay flat across his chest without a crease. She pinned the chevalier ribbon and the gold satin braid across the breast of the royal-blue jacket before buttoning the beaded cuffs to the sleeves. She hung the jacket on a hanger padded with cotton batting and placed it in a soft muslin dress bag, as though she were laying an infant in his bunting. She turned her attention to the trousers, folding them over a wooden hanger and straightening the military stripes that ran down the outside of each pant leg before slipping them into a separate muslin sack.

The wife hung the garments in an open standing trunk, took inventory of its contents, and counted out six pairs of socks, including three she had mended before packing. She checked the black patent dress shoes, each in its own chamois bag, and pulled out the left one. Finding a smudge on the toe, she buffed it with the hem of her apron until it shone. She rolled a wooden shaving cup and brush, a small circle of soap, and a straight razor tightly in a linen towel, then tucked the bundle into the dress shoe before placing it inside the trunk.

Elisabetta examined the impeccable stitchwork on the hem of her husband's undershirt, where she had used the silk trim of her own camisole to bind the frayed fabric. Satisfied that her husband had everything he needed for the journey ahead, she hung a small net pouch filled with fragrant lavender buds and cedar shavings inside the trunk, securing it tightly with two knots. The little things she did for her husband went unnoticed, but she did them anyway, because she knew they mattered.

She snapped the lids shut on a series of velvet jewelry cases containing regulation Italian Army gold cuff links, a matching tie bar, and two medals awarded to the ambassador's father from World War I, *al valor militare* and *merito di guerra*. She left the solid gold *aiutante* medal from World War II on the nightstand. It had been a gift from the previous ambassador, who was eager to unload it, as it bore the profile of Benito Mussolini etched on one side, with the symbol indicating a rank of major in the Italian Army on the other.

The winter of 1949 had been the worst in memory. A mudslide caused by a flash flood of the Fortore River marooned the locals high in the hills for several months. The Italian Army had dispatched a rescue party to bring supplies and medicine up to them, but the burro and cart regiment failed to reach the town because Via Capella della Consolazione, the only road with access to the village, had been washed out. Instead of saving the Rosetani, the regiment nearly lost their own lives as they slid back down the steep incline in a gloppy trough of deep mud.

The people of the village had lost all hope until spring arrived. The sun, which had disappeared for most of the winter, suddenly exploded in white streams over the town like the rays of gold on the monstrance in the tabernacle inside the church of Santa Maria Assunta.

"It's time, Bette." Carlo Guardinfante stood in the doorway of their bedroom wearing the only other suit he owned, a brown wool custom cut with wide lapels, his best pale blue dress shirt, and a rose-and-cream-striped tie. His wife fixed the knot and slipped his round-trip ticket and the telegram confirming his arrival into the breast pocket of his jacket.

Carlo was a southern Italian, typical in temperament but not in appearance. He possessed the passionate disposition of his neighbors but did not share their dark Mediterranean coloring. He had the freckled face of a farmer to the north, the large hands of a man who could handle a plow, and the height that gave him, at six foot two, the stature of a general. His broad shoulders had earned him the nickname Spadone.

"Everything is ready for you." Bette looked into her husband's eyes. In the bright morning light, they were the color of the soft waves in the port of Genoa, more green than blue. His reddish brown hair had flecks of white, too soon on a man of thirty-eight, and a reminder of all he had been through. Carlo had spent the last few years worried about the citizens of his province, frustrated by the lack of progress on their behalf, and the anxiety had taken a toll on him. Carlo was so thin, Elisabetta had punched two extra holes in the leather of his belt and attached the grommets herself. She'd adhered a small brass bar to the long end of the loop, so it wouldn't look as though she had made any adjustments.

"How's the belt?" She tugged on the loop.

He patted the brass plate and smiled. Carlo's front teeth had a space between them, known in the village as lucky teeth because, in theory, he could fit a coin between them, which meant good fortune would be his all his life. But Carlo didn't feel lucky, and any hope of prosperity had washed away with the road to Rome.

So Carlo looked for luck wherever he could find it.

"Am I supposed to pass this off as a new Italian style?"

"Why not?"

Carlo kissed his wife on the cheek. He picked up his billfold, opened it, and counted the lire. "There's more here. Did you club the priest?"

"The smart wife puts aside money and doesn't tell her husband."

"Your mother taught you well."

"Not my mother." Bette smiled. "Yours."

Carlo patted his wife on the fanny. "Pack the Il Duce."

"Oh, Carlo. Americans hated him."

"I'll show the symbol side. His *faccia* will face my heart. Maybe the brute bastard will finally do some good for us."

"He'll do better melted down and sold."

"The more gold I wear, the more important I seem. My chest should rattle like a tambourine." Carlo snapped the case shut and handed it to his wife. "*La bella figura.*"

"*Va bene.*" Elisabetta picked up the medal from the nightstand

and placed it in with the others, locking them into the safe box of the trunk.

Carlo pulled his wife close. "When I come home, we paint the villa."

"It needs more than paint." Elisabetta looked around the suite. As the lady of the house, she saw the failure to meet her obligations. There were the cracks in the plaster, rusty streaks where the ceiling leaked, frayed hems on the damask drapes, and most disturbing to her, squares of plywood covered the windows to replace the glass that had shattered in the heavy winds. Elisabetta sighed. The windows had been the most dazzling aspect of their residence, their rippled glass carted from Venice, but now the missing panes looked like teeth long gone from a lovely smile. "Our home needs a miracle."

"Put it on the list, Bette." Carlo embraced her.

"We won't live long enough to fix everything that needs repair."

Carlo did not take his appointment as *Ambasciatore da Provincia di Foggia e Provincia di Capitanata da Apulia* lightly, nor did he see his role simply as a figurehead. He wanted to do some good, but there were no funds attached to the honor and few favors. All across Italy, from the Mediterranean to the Adriatic and from north to south, reparations went to replace waterlines, restore electrical plants, and rebuild essential factories.

There was little concern for Roseto Valfortore and small villages like it. Stranded during the winter months, Carlo had not been able to go to Rome and plead for help. The letters that had made it through had been met with the curt response that there was greater need elsewhere.

The Holy Roman Church advised him to rally the townspeople to do the work themselves, but Roseto Valfortore had been deserted by the young; some had died in the war, and the rest migrated to Naples to find jobs along the Amalfi coast or east to the Adriatic to work on the trade ships. Most Rosetani, however, emigrated to America, where there were plenty of jobs in steel mills, factories, and construction. The families that stayed behind were too poor to take a risk, and too old to want to. Everywhere Carlo looked, life was bleak. He had hoped for a sign that their luck would change, and when none appeared, he hatched one final scheme to save his village.

The sun bathed the town in white light as Carlo, in his suit and fedora, and Elisabetta, who had put on a straw hat, linen coat, and her best black leather shoes, emerged from their home. The polished couple inspired confidence against the backdrop of the ravaged village where the tile roof tops had been mended hastily with mismatched planks of wood, ancient stone walls had crumbled to rubble, and deep potholes pitted the stone streets.

As the old houseman followed them out, he kept his head down and chewed on snuff, balancing Carlo's trunk on his back with ease as though it were light and he were still young.

The townspeople filled the winding streets for the ambassador's send-off, waving long green cypress branches high in the air like flags. Carlo tipped his hat and bowed to the people, taking in their cheers and affection like sips of cool water for his parched soul. Women rushed forward holding letters in sealed envelopes, which Elisabetta collected for her husband, promising them he would deliver them in person once he arrived at his destination.

The houseman placed the trunk in the cart, freshly painted in bright yellow partly to draw attention away from the decrepit donkey hitched to the carriage. The animal, too, was decorated in honor of the important passenger, his bridle festooned with colorful ribbons in pink and green. Carlo smiled, reflecting that the decorations on the donkey were a lot like a new hat on an old woman, a temporary distraction from a permanent problem.

The ambassador hoisted himself up into the open bench of the carriage. A cheer of great jubilation echoed through the streets as

Elisabetta handed her husband the stack of letters, which he held high in the air. Carlo leaned down to kiss his wife good-bye.

The crowd parted as the cart lumbered down the street followed by Elisabetta on foot. The Rosetani fell into place behind her as the cart moved through the village. A small contingent of girls threw rose petals chanting "Kiss Carlo!" as their mothers ran alongside the cart, reaching for him. The women were thrilled when Carlo chose them, took their hands, and kissed them.

Father DeNisco, wearing a black cassock, stood on the white marble steps of the church and made the sign of the cross as the carriage passed. The driver and Carlo bowed their heads and blessed themselves.

As they reached the entrance of the town, a new mother stepped forward and lifted her baby up to the carriage. Carlo reached for the infant and gently cradled the bundle swaddled in white in his arms. He pulled the baby close and kissed his cheek.

Elisabetta brushed away a tear at the sight of her husband holding the baby. It was the picture of her highest dream.

There was a time in Roseto Valfortore when the streets had been filled with prams. There were a hundred babies in the village before the war; now, they were as rare as this one infant. The thought of that galvanized Carlo to move forward with his plan.

As the carriage went through the gated entrance of the town, the throng stopped and cheered.

"The people love you," the driver said.

"They love you when they need you."

"And when they don't?"

"They find someone new." The ambassador pulled the brim of his hat over his eyes. "How's the road?"

"If we are careful, we'll make it."

"On time?"

"I think so. The car is waiting for you in Foggia."

"Does it have enough petrol?" Carlo asked wryly.

"Depends on his gratuity."

"And yours." Carlo smiled.

"I don't work for fun, *Ambasciatore.*"

"No one does."

"Italy forgot about us. All the money goes to Roma. Milano. Even Bologna took a slice of the reparations."

"For railways." Carlo was not interested in talking politics with the driver; he knew all too well that his people had been forgotten. "The station in Bologna is important."

"Of course. But so are we. The farmers feed the people, but they starve us. They forget the villages and save the cities."

"Can you pick up speed?"

"Not if I want to keep the wheels on the carriage. Your road is the worst I've seen."

"I appreciate your assessment," Carlo said, and checked his pocket watch. "I can't miss the boat in Naples."

"How's your luck?"

"The sun is shining, when I thought it never would again, so I would say my luck is good."

The ambassador was on his way to America, and he would need it.

Carlo turned to take one last look at his village. The hillsides were mounds of wet black mud, smattered with a few hopeful sprigs of green. The spindly trunks of the fig trees had survived, stubbornly pushing up through the earth like markers of hope itself. The clutter of stone houses on the hilltop stood against the powder blue sky like a stack of cracked plates on a shelf. All was not lost, but what remained might not be enough to save his home.

Carlo watched as his wife pushed through the crowd to get a final glimpse of the carriage. Carlo waved to her. Elisabetta placed her hand on her heart, which made him feel more pressure to return a hero and gave him an ache in his gut.

Elisabetta's face was the final image Carlo would take with him on the road to Naples to board the ship that would take him to America, where he would make his way to a small village in Pennsylvania that he believed held the key to saving Roseto Valfortore. He had heard that in America, all that was broken could be mended; there was a solution to every problem, and money flowed like the sweetest wine at a party that had no end.

Ambassador Carlo Guardinfante was about to see for himself what was true, and whether the land of hopes and dreams would provide either for him so he might save the village and the people he loved.

Prologue

MAY 1, 1949

PHILADELPHIA

Philadelphia est omnis divisa in partes tres.[1]

All of Philadelphia was divided into three parts because Dom Palazzini and his brother Mike had not spoken to one another since March of 1933 (or thereabouts, the date was fuzzy on either side of the vendetta). As a result of their argument, they split the family business, the profitable Palazzini Cab Company, down the middle, and with it, the city they served.

Hoc est bellum.[2]

Dom lay claim to Montrose Street and all blocks south, while Mike took the tony territory of Fitzwater and Center City to the north. It was decided that Broad Street, both north and south, would be neutral territory. Pickups and dropoffs could be made on either side without censure. The flip of a coin determined that Dom would keep the name Palazzini Cab Company, while Mike would call his new venture the Pronto Taxi & Limousine Service.

The brothers severed ties over money, the cause of every split in every Italian family since the Etruscans, but the details behind

---

[1] A reference to Julius Caesar's *Bellum Gallicum*.

[2] "This is war."

the rift changed depending upon whom you asked and which side of Broad Street they lived on.

The inheritance of a small plot of land on Montrose Street had been verbally promised to Dom by their father but left to Mike in his will. Mike intended to sell the parcel to Dom—who had purchased Mike's half of the family homestead upon their father's death—but Dom felt the land parcel was part of his rightful inheritance and should have been included in the buyout of the house at no additional cost to him. Dom believed Mike should have simply done the right thing and handed over the deed. After all, their father had lived with Dom and his family in the homestead for many years, and Dom's wife had cared for the old man until his death.

Unfortunately, what should have been a gift came with a bill. Insults were hurled. Dom accused Mike of being ungrateful, and Mike accused Dom of stealing. Money had gone missing from the petty cash in 1932—where was it? Who took it? Why did it matter now? There had been an incident one evening where the bank bag didn't make it to the night drop. What happened to the cash?

What had festered like a boil for years was lanced—true sentiments were exposed. Mike told Dom he was "a cut-rate manager who ran the place on the cheap," while Dom called Mike "a big-hearted Charlie" who was wasteful down to the lavish soap-to-water ratio used in the buckets when the fleet of taxicabs was washed and waxed. Dom wasn't flexible with fees and lost customers to competitors, while Mike, who was charming and a better negotiator, was muzzled by his older brother, a hardheaded know-it-all.

The grievances stacked up, one upon the other, like soggy layers of wedding pastries on a Venetian table. Then it got personal.

Mike took too much time off to play cards and frolic in Atlantic City while Dom stayed behind and covered for him. Dom was an old-fashioned off-the-boat Italian immigrant, while Mike was a flashy *Ameri-gan* who had forgotten his roots. Mike had taken loans from the business, built a grand home on Fitzwater with an above-ground pool, and lived extravagantly with a marble fountain in the front yard, while Dom never borrowed a penny, lived within his means, and made do with a birdbath that he filled with a watering can. There was tumult. But then it got worse.

The wives got involved.

Dom's wife, Jo, and Mike's wife, Nancy, were like sisters until they weren't. Jo was a martyr: she cared for her father-in-law until his last breath and cooked and cleaned and hosted Sunday dinner for both families without complaint, while Nancy put on airs, wore a leopard coat with a red satin lining, and dreamed of a Main Line life with servants. Jo wore a cloth coat, sewed her own clothes and curtains while Nancy went to the dressmaker, ordered her draperies from Wanamaker's, and drove a cobalt blue Packard.

As the business prospered, Jo saved, while Nancy spent. Jo's simple gold wedding band remained on her hand, but Nancy traded up. The prongs on Nancy's modest quarter-carat diamond engagement ring were stretched to accommodate the glitzy three-and-a-half-carat upgrade. The delicate gold chain around Nancy's neck was replaced with one as thick as a strand of pappardelle, from which dangled a new medal more miraculous than a pope's.

Jo kept to the old ways, holding on to the traditions of her Sicilian family. She was happy to stay home and take care of Nancy's boys along with her own, while Nancy went out on the town wearing the latest Mr. John hat to soirees, where the closest thing to anything Italian, besides her, was the cut lace on the tablecloths. Nancy, ever the climber, walked all over good-natured Jo on her way to the top, leaving bruises behind. Dom stepped in to defend Jo, and Mike did the same for Nancy.

Dom and Mike were so furious with one another that they brought their battle into the street, making it public, which no Italian family had done since Romulus and Remus called the wolf

Mama. Outsiders were happy to fuel the fight with gossip and innuendo, deepening the rift.

The truth grew spikes and became a wrecking ball, severing the families.

Every Italian knows that once the gravy is burned, there is no saving it. The only solution is to throw it out, all of it, every drop, along with the pot. Dominic and Mike threw one another away and did not look back.

A division within families was nothing new in South Philly. The neighborhood had at least two of everything, so it could accommodate any family schism. A family could split and survive, move into a new half of a two-family home, tithe in a different church, send their children to another parish school, and even get their haircuts at competing barbershops without running into each other on a regular basis. Life could go on as normal in a state of rage for years on end against one's own blood family without repercussion.

Vincit qui patitur.[3]

Mike and Dom would live a street apart without acknowledging one other, and so would their wives. Their children, a small army of boys, were mystified by the break between the two heads of their households, but quickly learned to abandon their relationships with their cousins to appease their parents, as they lived within the fault lines, careful not to upset the ones whose approval they most craved. Years later, the vitriol flowed fresh into the hearts of new family members who married in, the young brides taking sides easily as part of their oath of loyalty and proof of love to their new husbands.

If you wanted in, you had to recognize the sin.

The break didn't seem to bother Dom and Mike, even though they were the only two men in the world who remembered the

---

[3] "He conquers who endures."

port of Naples on the cloudy morning of April 29, 1901. Domenico, twelve years old, and Michele, eleven, stood together aboard the ship that would bring them to America, to their father, who had emigrated to Philadelphia to work in the Naval Shipyard as a welder. Their mother had died suddenly of a fever, and no relative in Avellino had enough room to take them in or the resources to provide for them, so their father sent their passage.

The boys mourned their mother desperately. They were grief-stricken and frightened. Clinging to one another, they held hands (which they had not done since they were three and four years old) on the deck of the *Argentinia* as they bid *arrivederci* to their home, without any idea what lay ahead. Only Dom would know that Mike wept in his arms, and only Mike would know that Dom whispered "*Non ti lascero mai.*" Dom may have promised to never leave his brother but all of that was forgotten years later, when one brother was certain the other was cheating him over a parcel of land whose value was negligible and which neither would have wanted had their father not left it behind, callously favoring one son over the other, or perhaps for another reason entirely.

Their father, Domenico Michele Palazzini, was a talented iron-worker but also a gambler, turning everything in his life into a contest he could bet on. He took particular pleasure in pitting one son against the other. Without the tender influence of his wife, he was a bully, and his sons knew that the only way to survive was to please him.

After the old man's death, the gold ruled, and the Palazzini brothers became loyal subjects. Dom didn't want to talk about their father, and Mike wanted to become him. Their kingdom, including their booming taxi business and their modest real estate holdings, was now divided in two, like the pot in a high-low game of lowball poker.

The brothers learned that half of something wonderful is just half, but their animosity was so deep, neither cared about what had been lost. They would live a street apart from one another, close enough for Mike to catch the scent of Jo's gravy on Sunday and Dom to hear Mike's hi-fi playing Sinatra in the wee hours, yet far enough apart to allow their anger to fuel their ambition to outdo the other and win. Sixteen long years had come and gone, but the wound was fresh.

Alea iacta est.[4]

[4] "The die has been cast."

ACT I

A young man married is a young man that's married.
—*All's Well That Ends Well*

1

MAY 2, 1949

PHILADELPHIA

Elsa Palazzini moved through the Ninth Street Market hastily, past the fishmonger, the farmer, the baker, the butcher, and the fruit vendor. The merchants' banter with the delivery boys filled the air, drowned out occasionally by the thuds of wooden merchandise boxes as they hit the ground, the squeaks of the rubber wheels on the trucks as they nosed in behind the stands to make deliveries, and the deafening crash of an avalanche of ice as it was poured into a metal bin. Out front, deals were made *sotto voce*, vendor to customer, with only their body language giving away the terms.

The sun was not yet up; the only light in the open-air market came from the headlights on the trucks and the bare bulbs that dangled underneath the red-striped awnings. Elsa pushed through until she found the peddler selling fresh flowers. An overnight rain had left a cool mist in the air. She shivered and buttoned her jacket.

A lone bulb on a wire swayed lazily back and forth in the breeze, throwing streaks of light on the display of gray buckets filled with fresh flowers. Elsa surveyed the selection of purple lilacs, yellow daffodils, pink peonies, puffs of blue hydrangea, and bunches of daisies until she found what she was looking for.

She lifted a cluster of baby roses tied with a string from a bucket jammed full of them. The fresh, icy water ran down her hand as she examined it. She put it back, choosing another, and another, until she found a bunch whose petals were closed so tightly the buds resembled pink flames.

"May Day celebration?" the peddler asked as he wrapped the flowers in waxed paper.

Elsa nodded.

"I ran out of white roses yesterday. Our Lady of Good Counsel decided all white this year."

Elsa smiled at him. "Luck is with me. All my girls are wearing pink. Except the queen and the statue of the Blessed Lady. And I've already made those crowns with white roses." Her accent, a combination of her native Polish and proper English, along with her willowy stature and innate elegance, gave Elsa an aristocratic air.

"The Queen of Heaven comes first," he said.

"Of course." Elsa unsnapped her change purse and fished for seventy-five cents. As she paid for the flowers, a woman joined them.

"Very pretty," the customer commented as the peddler handed Elsa the roses.

"Thank you. This is the best stand for fresh flowers." Elsa winked at the peddler.

"Then maybe you can help me. I don't know whether to choose the peonies or the daffodils."

"What is the occasion?"

"A wedding."

"Why not both? And add the laurel leaves." Elsa pointed to the bundles of waxy green leaves gathered with string.

"That would be lovely. I don't know what the ladies at the temple would say."

"What temple do you attend?"

"B'Nai Abraham," the woman answered. "Do you know it?"

"On Lombard Street?" Elsa heard the tap of her husband's horn and waved to him before turning back to the woman. *"Mazel tov* to the bride and groom. *Shalom.*"

"*Shalom.*" The lady watched after Elsa curiously.

By the time Elsa reached the car, Dominic Palazzini III had jumped out and opened the bright yellow taxi door for her. He was tall, like his wife, and matinee-idol handsome, with dark hair and eyes, a patrician nose like the movie star Robert Taylor, and expressive dark eyebrows. Elsa kissed him on the cheek. "Did they have what you needed?"

"Exactly what I needed."

Dominic helped her into the front seat of the cab. "You only get what you want if you get here early," he said as he closed the door behind her.

Dominic climbed into the driver's seat. Elsa scooted next to her husband. She laced her arm through his. "Let's take a drive on the river," he said. "We'll have the road to ourselves."

Elsa checked her wristwatch. "The baby is getting up soon."

"Ma's there."

"I don't like to miss the morning."

"You don't like to miss anything, Elsa."

Elsa smiled and placed her head on her husband's shoulder as they headed toward home.

A few blocks away, a low fog the color of pink champagne floated over Montrose Street.

The south side of Philadelphia glistened. The dingy row houses had the patina of seashells, as the blouse factory's gray entrance turned to polished silver in the morning light. The open trenches that scarred the street where the city had recently dug deep to install pipes weren't gulleys of mud but moats, ancient rivers to protect the kingdom the city planners had named Bella Vista.

Nicky Castone tucked his lunch bag under his arm as he stood on the steps of 810 Montrose Street, where he had lived with his uncle Dom and aunt Jo and their sons since he was five years old. His first cigarette of the day dangling from his mouth, he closed the brass buttons on his uniform jacket with his free hand. The fresh menthol in the Lucky Strike stung his throat, filled his lungs, and woke him up. A storage tube hung from his shoulder on a wide leather strap. He adjusted it to tilt to the side, like a rifle.

Nicky not only noticed the sun as it rose over the neighborhood but reveled in its serene splendor. He saw beauty in the world, even when there wasn't any. A certain kind of light, he figured, was like a veil on a bride at the altar of an arranged marriage: it obscured any defect while presenting mystery as potential. There was nothing wrong with that.

The air filled with the sweet scents of basil, lemon, and fresh earth. The Spatuzza boys, Nicky's farmer cousins on his mother's side from across the river in Jersey, had made their annual delivery during the night, dropping off the essentials for spring planting. The bounty was displayed on the porch steps like statues in a Roman atrium. There were pots filled with tomato plants, and urns holding fig trees, lemon trees, and boxwood topiaries. Crates of budding vegetable plants were arranged around wooden flats spiked with shoots of green herbs. It looked like Aunt Jo had ordered a sample of every plant that grew on the Eastern Seaboard. Their tags fluttered in the breeze like petals. Their official names written in Latin conjured memories of serving high mass as an altar boy: *Nasturtium Gloria. Aster laevis. Specularia perfoliata.*

As Nicky navigated his way through the dense foliage, he marveled at the Spatuzzas' aesthetics. Italians make anything artful, including the delivery of manure.

Soon, under Aunt Jo's supervision, the backyard, the rooftop, and the patches of earth that anchored the front porch would be planted. In a few weeks there would be *mille fiori*, explosions of color as flowers bloomed along the walkway. Come August the harvest from the garden would fill their al fresco table with Italian peppers, arugula, fennel, and cucumbers. Nicky could taste the zucchini blossoms already.

The tomato, the essential ingredient of any Palazzini dish, would multiply by the bushel on the roof garden. Close to the sun, they would grow red, plump, and sweet as they ripened. Eventually the women would pick them and place them in wooden baskets, which the men would haul down to the basement kitchen. There, the entire family was put to work as the tomatoes were cleaned, crushed, and canned, preserving enough jars of sauce to last through the long, gray Pennsylvania winter.

Nicky crossed the street to the garage, unlocked the rolling gate beneath the red tin sign: THE PALAZZINI CAB COMPANY AND WESTERN UNION TELEGRAPH OFFICE, and pushed it off to the side. He lifted the iron staff from its hiding place over the door, hooked the loop, and unfurled the awning out over the sidewalk. Nicky reached up and gently smoothed the fabric, which had been patched in places, worn thin where the rain had beaten the supports and the elements had faded the stripes, once military bright.

He remembered when the canopy was new. Eight years later, the war was won, and everything had changed. There was the big stuff: families reconfigured, men lost forever, others' futures uncertain. There were the small things, too, such as the welcome return of silk stockings and sugar. Some aspects of life on the home front had ended, including the government bond drives that brought beloved entertainers like Jimmy Durante to places like Palumbo's in Philly to raise money for the cause. There would be no more sacrifice in victory, no need to collect scraps of metal to drop off at Army Surplus to make wheel spokes and bombs. It was all over.

When the boys had left for the war, Montrose Street had exhibited patriotic polish and pride. Flags were displayed on every building, and storefront windows were dressed with photographs of the soldiers whose families lived in the neighborhood. The Palazzinis' awning, a blaze of red, with bold stripes of blue on a field of spotless white, looked like the flag. By the time Nicky returned, those hues had faded to gray and mauve and beige, the colors of the old men and the women who stood by them. Nicky talked to Uncle Dom about replacing the canopy, but he had gotten nowhere. "Does it keep you dry when it rains?" Dom had barked. "Canvas is expensive." Uncle Dom put a price on beauty, and no matter the cost, it was always too high.

Nicky wished that Dom were more like his estranged uncle Mike, who did care about appearances. The awning on Pronto Taxi was replaced every year, whether it needed it or not. The red, white, and green stripes remained pristine, in snow, rain, and sun. There were extras, too: the flap that faced the street was embroidered with a cursive *P* in snazzy gold thread, and the poles that anchored the canopy to the sidewalk were made of polished brass.

Uncle Mike was as smooth as a Mariano Fortuny bed jacket. He wore Italian-cut suits, silk ties, and oxblood loafers while Uncle Dom dressed like an undertaker, regardless of the occasion. Dom owned one black wool suit and one black serge, and paired both with plain white cotton dress shirts and a black tie. His dress shoes, black leather lace-ups, hadn't changed since the flapper era.

When Uncle Mike entered a room, women tingled as they got a brisk whiff of exotic patchouli and Sen-Sen. When Uncle Dom entered a room, he brought a different bouquet entirely. He reeked of Fels-Naptha soap, Listerine mouthwash, and the occasional trace of bleach.

Nicky was only twelve years old when he was no longer allowed to speak to Uncle Mike, Aunt Nancy, and their sons, Richard, Michael, and Anthony, whom their father had nicknamed Ricky,

Micky, and Tricky. Nicky missed his cousins, but out of respect to
Jo and Dom, he never mentioned how much.

Inside the garage, Nicky inspected the fleet of cabs that he had
washed the night before. Even in the morning gloom, they gleamed
like butterscotch candy under the work lights. Dominic III had already picked up No. 1, so there remained three yellow cabs in their
spaces. No. 2 was driven by Gio. No. 3 was driven by Nino.

Nicky drove No. 4. He gave his yellow cab a pat as he passed
it on the way to the stairs. The jewel of the operation, a glistening black 1947 Buick Roadmaster four-door sedan, covered with
a beige chamois cloth, was tucked in the alcove. The sedan was
the formal patent leather shoe in the fleet of casual loafers. Nicky
adjusted the cloth before making his way up the steps to the dispatch office, an aluminum box with a window giving a clear view
of the garage below.

Through the open door above, he heard the staccato taps of
Morse code as Hortense Mooney, the dispatcher, sent a telegram.
Hortense's hand, Nicky knew, was on the lever, her head bowed,
eyes closed, as she remitted the code across the wires. She maintained a somber countenance when she received any message,
whether it was a classified missive or a Kiddiegram. Careful not
to disturb her, Nicky tiptoed into the office, hung the gate keys
on a brass loop, placed his lunch quietly on the service desk, and
slipped the tube off his shoulder. He snapped off the end cap and
removed the long roll from inside. He unfurled the latest highway
and interstate road map of Pennsylvania and pinned it over the
outdated version on the corkboard.

Hortense Mooney had a routine. She arrived at her job every
morning, Monday through Saturday, at 4:00 a.m., having taken
the bus from her home to Chestnut Street. She climbed the long
metal stairs of the fire escape at the back of the garage, unlock-
ing the emergency door, and crossing inside through the upper

bridge and into the dispatch office, she would remove her green felt hat with the long brown pheasant feather, place it on the file cabinet, and hang her tan corduroy car coat on the back of the door. Her lunch bag was deposited into her private drawer in the file cabinet, while her thermos of hot coffee went onto her desk. She was the only person, outside the Palazzinis themselves, who had keys to the garage. This wasn't simply a matter of convenience; Dom trusted Hortense with his business, which meant he trusted her with his money, which meant he trusted her with his life.

Hortense Mooney was sixty-three years old. She had been hired as the dispatcher when Mike Palazzini was still with the company, and stayed on after he left, but it wasn't an easy decision, as she got along fine with both brothers. Mike offered her the same position at Pronto, but Hortense had her reasons for staying with the operation on Montrose Street. She figured she'd stay until she retired. Her smooth skin, the color of dark chocolate, had not a wrinkle to indicate age nor a line that mirrored tragedy. She had a wide, white smile, all her original teeth, a fact she mentioned casually to strangers when they complimented them. Her sleek pageboy was done professionally every Saturday at Mrs. Johnson's Curls & Q in the Negro section of northwest Germantown.

In her youth, Hortense had been known for her long, well-shaped legs that tapered at the ankles, though they were on the thin side by most standards. Her feet were also long and narrow in the extreme, and combined with her legs, they made her body look like it was perched on double L's when she waited for the bus. This morning, she tapped them mindlessly on the floor as she worked, as though she were keeping the beat to a song only she could hear.

Hortense sent the telegram with three quick, staccato taps of the lever. She rolled her chair over to the typewriter and began to type, her long fingers stretching across the keys with ease. Nicky enjoyed watching Hortense type. She was quick: the ding of the bell meant that she was about to sling the carriage with force, which he found hilarious because it looked like she was slapping Jimmy Cagney across the face in a fight picture.

Nicky cleared a space on the desk, opened the brown bag, emptied the contents, and, using the bag as a placemat, laid out his meal upon it. He anchored the bag with his drink, a mason jar filled with cold apple cider.

Hortense looked up at Nicky briefly as he unscrewed the lid on the jar and the squeaks of the rivets broke her concentration. Nicky smiled apologetically at her before quietly unfolding the waxed paper around his sandwich as though it were velvet, the contents were emeralds, and he was a jewel thief.

Aunt Jo made a good sandwich. Not too much meat. There were three thin layers of spicy capicola, a glaze of sweet butter on the fresh egg bread, and a dill pickle wrapped separately so as not to make the whole meal soggy. The sandwich would fill Nicky up like nobody's business, and before he ate it, he whispered a prayer as he placed a starched linen napkin over his uniform jacket. On the corner of the napkin, embroidered in blue, were his initials.

Aunt Jo still made Nicky's lunch, did his laundry and mending, and would continue to take care of him in this fashion, as she had her own sons, until the day he married. Nicky was her sister's only child; she favored him because he had lost his mother so young and was left an orphan. She couldn't imagine how any of her boys would have endured such a loss, so she tried to make up for Nicky's. Plus, Jo couldn't resist her Italian nephew, with his all-American coloring—thick reddish-brown hair and blue eyes— and a smile that flashed like high beams on a Caddy as it passed on a one-way street at midnight. Besides, Jo was already raising three boys. What was one more, especially if he was good?

Nicky Castone had never been a bit of trouble.

He took a bite of one of the soft triangles, closed his eyes, and chewed, savoring the flavors of the sweet ham rubbed in hot spices. He hadn't been an orphan who gobbled or hoarded; he was the opposite, moving slowly, as if to tempt anyone who shared a meal with him to take his food because it took him so long to eat it. It appeared he wasn't interested in eating at all, but he was, he just never made his hunger obvious. Nicky accepted his portion and never asked for seconds. He felt sorry for people who didn't know when to get up from the table.

As Nicky slowly sipped the sweet apple cider from the mason jar, he thought again about time. It had been on his mind a lot lately, when he'd realized that the years were flying by and taking him with them, as they'd taken his parents. At twenty-eight years old, Nicky had outlived both of them. Since his mother and father hadn't been given the luxury of planning for a future and seeing their son grow up, Nicky decided to build his own life before it was too late.

It was time to set a wedding date with Teresa "Peachy" DePino, his fiancée of seven years. He had grown weary of the blistering looks from Peachy's father when he casually put his arm around his daughter and her mother's overly solicitous inquiries whenever he picked up his fiancée or dropped her off after a date. The extremes of hot and cold from her parents were giving Nicky a kind of South Philly fever that could only be broken by Father Schifalacqua signing them into the book at Our Lady of Loreto Church after a high nuptial mass.

Peachy had not pressed Nicky for a wedding date, but he knew how she felt about it. Whenever they went to Echo Lake for dinner and dancing, after she'd slurped down a couple of Mai Tai cocktails in coconut shells through a straw, she'd toy with the green plastic monkey decoration and wonder aloud about a home of her own with an artful aluminum C monogram on the screen door. She longed to collect the tiny paper umbrellas and circus animals that decorated her drinks and take them home to her children after a night out with their father, to show them that they were never far from her thoughts.

Nicky knew she had her dreams. But before he gave Peachy what she wanted most in life, he also knew he must come clean with her about where he spent his time when he wasn't driving a cab for the Palazzinis. He had to. Honesty was the most important virtue to Nicky, not because he was intent on being good, but because the truth made life simple. He had seen what lies left unchallenged had done to his uncles, and he swore none of that would be visited on the family he would create with his own wife someday.

Dominic III tapped the horn lightly as he entered the garage below and Car No. 1 coasted into its spot. Nicky stood and looked out the office window and watched as his cousin opened the car door for his wife, who emerged from the cab with a bouquet of flowers.

"Elsa got her roses," Nicky reported. "She ran out of them last night and was crying about it."

Hortense shrugged. "Maybe she's having another baby."

"Or maybe she was crying because old man Sabetti didn't remove all the thorns from the stems and she was stabbing herself into a stigmata." Nicky watched as Dominic took Elsa's hand. "Dominic and Elsa are still in love."

"Those two are a good match."

Dominic waved up to Nicky. "Ma's making breakfast," he called. "How do you want your eggs?"

"I'm good." Nicky smiled and waved them off. He sat down at the desk and took a small bite of the pickle and another of the sandwich.

Hortense made a face. "Why don't you go across the street and let Mrs. Palazzini fix you something proper to eat? There's no reason to eat your lunch at breakfast." She adjusted her posture to upright as she sat. Her desk was cluttered with small bits of paper, a stack of black leather ledgers, an adding machine, and, in the center, a telephone system, consisting of one deep burgundy receiver, a board with four buttons that flashed, a hold button, and another to hang up. Hortense was the only thing in the office that didn't light up, and the only thing that moved. "You have the strangest eating habits. The rest of the Palazzini boys eat regular. Why don't you?"

Nicky shrugged. "Maybe 'cause I'm a Castone."

"You have an answer for everything. Tell me this." She fed paper into the roller on the telegraph machine. "If you eat your sandwich at breakfast, what do you eat at lunchtime?"

"I don't."

"You don't eat between six a.m. and six p.m.?"

Nicky nodded.

"That isn't good for your organs."

"Who says?"

"Everybody from your doctor to the men that run the United States Army. How did you win the war with such terrible eating habits?"

"Courage."

"More like luck. Three meals a day. It's what the body requires."

"Not mine."

"It's not going to end well for you."

"Don't worry about me, Mrs. Mooney. It's worse on the body to be pressured to submit to some arbitrary schedule than it is to deprive it of food on some general one."

"You eat like you're four years old. It's time to eat like a man."

"Maybe I need a wife to look after me."

"You need something. That's all I know."

"Ever since Nino got married, the house is packed like a stuffed cabbage. And it's only going to get tighter. Mabel is expecting, Elsa has little Dom, who will soon be walking, and any time now

Lena will make an announcement. My cousins are replenishing the earth, and they need the space to do it."

"Where will you go?"

"There's a new development on Wharton Street. They built a whole city block of two-family houses. Real nice too. Two floors. Linoleum on the kitchen floor and wood parquet in the living room. Bay window in the front. You get a porch and a backyard and a basement. There's a space in the street to park out front. "

"But you don't have a car."

"Not yet. But I'll get one."

"And just where are you going to get the funds to purchase all of this?"

"I saved up. Aunt Jo banked my rent since I got back from the war. I've already got the down payment and I'm gonna get a loan from the bank for the rest. First National has a low rate for vets."

"You don't say."

"Good deal, right?" Nicky said.

"Your Aunt Jo's very smart, saving up that money for you. Not many aunts would start a house fund for a nephew."

"She wasn't saving it for me to move out, she was hoping I'd move Peachy in. But there's no way Peachy would live with the Palazzinis. She's an only child. Can't see her living in the basement. She wants her own place."

"So it's all settled."

"Once we set the date."

"You've been engaged so long, that proposal almost turned from a promise into a pipe dream. You know, I've been wondering if it was ever going to happen."

"Well, it will. Peachy DePino will be my wife. "

"It's none of my concern."

"Your opinion matters to me, Mrs. Mooney."

"Then take my advice. Keep your business and pleasure separate. Have you met Mr. Mooney?"

"Only once."

"And that was an accident."

"Because you keep your business and pleasure separate." Nicky toasted Hortense with his apple cider before taking a sip.

"Now you're learning. You would have never laid eyes on him if he hadn't had to come and get me when I fainted that time. I'd probably still be lying on that greasy floor down there if it wasn't for you."

"Somebody would've noticed," Nicky said.

"Maybe," Hortense said, not meaning it. "Eventually somebody would have noticed the phone wasn't answered and the telegrams weren't sent or received and then and only then would there have been a search for my mortal body."

"Mr. Mooney was very nice."

"He can be," Hortense said, though it had been years since she had a warm feeling for her husband. He had good qualities, but over time he'd become critical and occasionally unkind. Hortense had learned to tune him out like the office radio when the boys switched the station from her favorite blues to pop.

"Did Mr. Mooney change?"

"Every husband is nice at the start, if that's what you're asking. Everything is fine until you disagree or start asking questions when prior to that, you didn't have any. So being agreeable when planning a wedding or a honeymoon isn't an achievement, that's just somebody behaving a certain way to get what they want from you. A person's true nature emerges over time."

"I've been seeing Peachy since before the war," Nicky said, rearranging the pencils in the cup on the spare desk. "We've been true blue for seven years."

"That doesn't mean you have to marry her."

"Don't have to. *Want* to." He pulled his wallet from his back pocket and flipped it open to a picture of his fiancée.

Hortense felt for the reading glasses that dangled around her

neck on a silver chain. She held them up to her eyes, peering critically at a cheesecake shot of a very slender Peachy—too skinny, in
Hortense's opinion—on the beach in Wildwood Crest. Peachy was
so thin, the leg openings on her one-piece bathing suit stood away
from her scrawny thighs, which looked like two straws floating in
a vanilla milkshake.

"That's my Peachy," Nicky said proudly.

"I remember. She came in here once, a few years ago, with her
parents. They rode in the sedan."

"That's right. They went to visit relatives up in New Haven.
Wanted to impress them."

Hortense nodded. "She had her own mind. Told everybody
where to sit in the car."

Nicky put the wallet back in his pocket. "I like feisty."

"Until you don't."

"What does that mean?"

"You'll get tired of the very thing you love about her."

Nicky was used to Mrs. Mooney's pronouncements. This time,
however, he wasn't going to let her ruin his mood. "I'd like you to
get to know her. I'll bring her over to your house sometime."

"The last thing I need is a couple of Italians disrupting my
street. Folks would run around in circles like Henny Penny."

"You could make us dinner."

"Not going to happen, Mr. Castone."

"Even when we set the date?"

"Not even then."

"I want you to come to the wedding."

"We'll see." Hortense made the possibility sound like a flat no.

"You never come to our parties."

"It wouldn't be comfortable for me or for you."

"Because you're colored?"

Hortense nodded.

"You use that as an excuse for everything," Nicky said.

"Well, look at me. It happens to be true. Besides, boundaries make a life. Rules make a day. Structure matters in three arenas: society, architecture, and girdles. Anything worth building needs bones."

"I'm not asking you to build the Main Line Bridge, I'm asking you to come to my wedding."

"And I told you I can't."

"I consider you part of my family."

"Well, I'm not."

Nicky laughed. "You're a heartbreaker."

"I was once," she said wistfully. "I know a little bit about romance and marriage. I wouldn't stay away from your wedding just because of my color, though that's a factor. And it's not because you all are Catholic and I'm not, though that can be a factor."

"What is it, Mrs. Mooney?"

"I won't say."

"Why not?"

"I only go to weddings when I believe they'll stick."

Nicky's face fell. After a moment, he asked, "Do your feet hurt?"

"Why do you ask?" Hortense looked down at her shoes.

"You must be in some terrific pain, or you wouldn't be taking your bad mood out on me. If I didn't know better, I'd say you didn't want me to be happy." Nicky rolled up the napkin, catching the crumbs, and dusted the desk with the napkin before putting it back into the lunch bag.

Hortense didn't see a grown man before her, but the boy she remembered in his youth. Nicky Castone was her favorite of the Palazzini bunch, even though no one had ever asked her to choose. She sighed. "It's not that. Forgive me. I *have* been surly lately. I don't know what it is, I find fault with everything. I got a malaise. It just showed up unannounced like the bunions that arrived on my forty-second birthday. If you must know, everything hurts. I'm at that age. It's probably a good idea not to tell me any happy news because I'll find some way to pull it apart thread by thread until you're left with nothing but an old rag where you once had a yard of fine silk. That's just me. I've seen too much and I know too much, so I'm a little bitter, I guess."

"Just a little," Nicky said quietly.

"Love, well, that's a fragile romantic dream, a journey that begins in a humble rowboat for two. You set sail when the water is calm, and later it turns choppy as the wind begins to blow and a storm kicks up and you realize there's a big hole in the bottom of the boat that you didn't see when you got in, but now you're out in the middle of the ocean and you've started to take on water and it's dark, there's thunder and lightning, you didn't pack any food, or a flashlight or a horn, all you got is love, and it's not enough. You're going to sink. You turn on each other. You forgot why you got in the boat in the first place. All you saw in the beginning was the endless blue and the bright sun and each other and you were blinded. Love is a doomed journey with all the good stops up front."

"Maybe you're growing new bunions. Ever thought about that?"

"I forget that young people still want to take the trip, so I come off a little skeptical sometimes. I don't ever want you to think I don't want you to be happy. But if you think Peachy DePino is going to make you happy—"

"I do!"

"You may want to get down on your knees in a dark room and pray to the sweet Lord Jesus in heaven that He shows you a different path, because the road you're about to go down is not going to take you home. And everybody wants to get home."

"I want my own life. My own home."

"Of course you do. But you also have to be careful. Contemplate, Nicky. Contemplate."

"Seven years is not long enough to make a cautious decision?"

"Fifty years may not be long enough in some cases! You see, I can spot compatibility. It's a gift. I know, on sight, who should go with whom. I can pair off people who belong together. I envision a kind of Noah's Ark, except it's for people looking for love, not animals seeking shelter. I can be anywhere—walking down Thompson Street, sitting on a bus going local on Broad—and I can look into any crowd and find two people who've never met but should."

"Peachy's a good girl."

"For someone else."

"She waited for me. Through the war. And ever since."

"Patience demonstrated is not a good reason to marry a man, and guilt is not a good reason to marry a woman. You need to come up with something better, or all mysteries will be revealed on that wedding night and there's no turning back. You're a Catholic. There is no divorce. There's only widowhood or sainthood."

Hortense Mooney was right about that, Nicky reflected. Marriage was for life. Years ago, when Father Chiaravalle came to talk to his confirmation class about the sacraments, he told the boys that the church looked at marriage like permanent internment in one of Houdini's steel boxes, dripping in chains, with five padlocks dangling like charms on a bracelet whose keys had been swallowed by an alligator in the Congo halfway around the world. You couldn't get out of it once you were in. The finality of it all may be why Nicky had taken so long to marry.

Nicky would be certain about his wife, and there would be no disasters on his wedding night. He was not going to be one of those suckers who rolled the dice on a pretty girl he just met and ended up with snake eyes on the honeymoon. Nicky had heard awful stories of girls who wept through their wedding nights, and raced home to their mothers the next morning, vowing never to return to their new husbands. He'd heard tales of brides who were not pleased with their grooms: it turned out their veils weren't to suggest virginity but to hide experience. He had heard plenty, with

the moral of every story the same: find a good girl, because goodness would take care of any problems, financial, familial, mental,
or sexual.

It had been Nicky's observation that every girl who hoped to
marry was a good girl; it was one of the requirements to secure
the engagement ring in the first place. As soon as Nicky had given
Peachy DePino a diamond, she'd been willing to be intimate in
a certain way, which was reassuring. It showed Nicky that she
wasn't like Veronica Verotti, whose name filled every young Italian American male in South Philly with dread.

Veronica, the story goes, was so traumatized by what she saw
on her wedding night, she abandoned her sleeping groom in the
double bed at the Blue Lagoon Hotel in Atlantic City, left her rings
in the ashtray on the nightstand, took the night bus to North Hale-
don, New Jersey, and the very next morning, joined the order of the
Salesian nuns of Saint John Bosco, where she'd lived ever since as
Sister Mary Immaculata.

Nicky admired Peachy's fine qualities: she had demonstrated
loyalty and trust over the years that he'd known her. But he also
knew that no woman would have all the attributes of character
and physical appearance he dreamed of. Nor, he knew, could he
fulfill all the hopes a woman might hold for him. Peachy was an
honest, ambitious girl with common sense and a warm smile. She
had a steady job as a bookkeeper at a Wanamaker's department
store, she was handy, she could repair small appliances and stuff a
nut roll with the same precision, and in Nicky's mind, she was not
only quick to learn, she was versatile. Even if all of that hadn't been
true, he loved Peachy, and she loved him.

Hortense folded a telegram neatly and placed it in an envelope,
which she handed to Nicky. "Take this to Mr. Da Ponte on North
Second Street."

Nicky placed the Western Union cap on his head and went down into the garage, which was now in full sun. Soon his cousins would finish breakfast, jump in their cabs, and begin their shifts too.

As Nicky got into the No. 4 car, he remembered the milliner Da Ponte. He had bought Peachy a green velvet hat in the shop, and she'd loved it so much that she asked Mr. Da Ponte to make her wedding veil when the date was set. Nicky smiled at the thought. This might be what he loved most about South Philly—you didn't have to go far to find anything you desired. Nicky couldn't imagine ever living anywhere else.

As he backed out of the garage, he looked up and saw Mrs. Mooney standing in the window of the office, watching him. She had her hands folded at her waist, in a pose that reminded him of the statue of Saint Ann behind glass in the crypt of Saint Rita of Cascia. A shiver went through him as he remembered waiting on the kneeler for his turn to enter the confessional when he was a boy. Nicky wondered if that was a sign. Wasn't everything?

The row of bachelor's buttons, pansies, and daffodils that were planted along the porch in front of the Borellis' home on 832 Ellsworth Street looked puny. The father and daughter who lived inside had planted them exactly as the lady of the house had always done, but since her death last summer, the garden looked sad.

Sam Borelli didn't have a green thumb, and neither did his daughter Calla, even though she had a name that would indicate otherwise. Their skills lay elsewhere, but they did their best to keep the sky blue clapboard two-story as Vincenza Borelli had liked it, and that included maintaining the flowerbeds.

Calla Borelli peered into the mirror of the medicine cabinet as she lifted a section of her hair that fell across her forehead in a feathered black fringe. She twisted it just so, snipped the ends with her nail scissors, and stood back to survey the results. Satisfied, she ran her fingers through the short layers that framed her face.

"Calla!" her father called from the bottom of the stairs.

"I'm coming, Pop," Calla hollered back. She swiped bright red lipstick onto her mouth, smacked her lips together, and as she blotted them, ran water in the sink to rinse away the tiny black slashes from her haircut. She took a final look at the model in the *Harper's Bazaar* magazine propped in the windowsill. The photograph of the long, lean Parisienne with a cigarette and an attitude whose chic, cropped hairstyle Calla had tried to copy had little in common with the Italian American woman in the mirror, but it didn't matter. Calla wasn't fussy and she certainly wasn't French. She flipped the magazine shut.

The morning sun drenched the Borelli kitchen like a stage in full light. The air was filled with the scent of sweet tomato sauce simmering on the stove.

Sam Borelli stood over the skillet with a spatula, watching two fresh eggs poach in the bubbling sauce, Venetian style. A moppeen was slung over his shoulder. At nearly eighty, age may have robbed him of his height and hair, but his intense black eyes and Neapolitan features, especially his thick black eyebrows, were as sharp as they had been in his youth.

Calla twirled when she entered the room. "What do you think?"

"I like it all right."

"I cut it myself."

"You shouldn't cut your own hair. That's like building your own car."

"Don't have time to go to the beauty parlor."

"Make the time." Sam worried about Calla. She wasn't like Helen or Portia, his other daughters, who made their appearances a priority, as well as marriage and motherhood. Calla seemed to skip over steps when it came to being a woman. It came naturally to his youngest daughter to be selfless and put herself last. But while he couldn't believe it, Calla was twenty-six years old, and he knew that the years burned away quickly like morning fog, and she'd soon be beyond the age of marriage. Sam thought it was time that Calla found someone to love, someone with whom she could build a future. But it was the father within him who worried about her, not the fellow artist. The fellow artist believed she was right on track.

"Where do you get the nerve to cut your own hair?"

"I style the wigs at the theater, so I figured, how hard could it be to do my own hair?"

"Wigs are not real hair."

"An even better reason to do the job myself. If I make a mistake, it'll grow back."

"Wish I could say the same." Sam rubbed his balding head.

"This is the rage in Paris. It's called the French Cap."

"But we're in South Philly."

"Maybe we need a little of the Left Bank on the banks of the Delaware." Calla picked up the newspaper. "How was the review?"

Sam didn't answer her. When he directed a play, he couldn't sleep the night it opened, nervous about the reviews that would come the following morning. On her opening night, the previous evening, Calla had toasted the cast with champagne in paper cups after the show, swept the lobby, cleaned the restrooms, returned home, and gone to bed.

Calla flipped through the *Philadelphia Inquirer* until she found a short review of her first directorial effort at the Borelli Theatrical Company. "Talk about burying my lede. This is harder to find than an Italian American at the Philly Free Library." She read aloud, "Mr. Carl Borelli . . ." She looked at her father. "Carl Borelli?"

"Strike one." Her father sighed. "I should have named you Susie."

"You should have had a son who became a director, not a daughter."

"I only make girls, you know that."

Calla continued to read aloud, "Mr. Borelli . . . ugh . . . attempts a grand feat with *Twelfth Night*, one that hits with the comedy occasionally, less so with the farce—" She looked up at her father again. "Isn't farce comedy?"

"Of a stripe." Sam flipped the eggs in the pan.

"He didn't understand what I was doing with Feste at all. I used him as a narrator." Calla plopped down into the chair and continued to read. "Who is this dolt?"

"That fellow likes his Shakespeare as it was at the old Globe." Sam ladled the over-easy eggs onto two pieces of Italian bread toasted to a golden brown, then smothered them with the tomato gravy he had cooked them in, finishing the dish with a pat of butter, which melted over the fragrant mixture. He placed the dish before his daughter, who placed a napkin on her lap. "Don't worry about the critics. Remember what Verdi said. He let a bad review ruin his breakfast, but never his lunch."

"Thanks, Pop," Calla said, not looking up from the paper this time. "If this wasn't so ridiculous, I'd be furious. And I'd be even angrier if this were a good review. Some guy named Carl would be getting all the credit."

"But you're fine with him getting the blame?"

Calla threw down the paper. "I'm not going to read another word." She picked up her fork and began to eat her breakfast, savoring every bite.

"Good idea." Sam poured her a cup of coffee. "Are you all right?"

"I wasn't expecting a good review."

"Yes, you were."

"How did you know?"

"You're an optimist."

"Not anymore."

Sam laughed. "It's your first show. And you did a fine job."

"You think so?"

"You created some inspired stage pictures."

"I learned that from you."

"You cast the show well. You directed the actors with sympathy. You got a performance out of Josie I never could have gotten."

"Less ham and more mustard, I told her. It worked."

"It all worked. The actors related to one another with an ease. That's all you up there."

"I think they were open to me because of their relationship with you over the years. You built the company, and they're loyal to you."

"No, you know what you're doing. And I'm proud of you."

"Yeah, well, we needed to pack them in, and a great review in a big newspaper would've done it. So much for high hopes."

"How's the house for tonight?" Sam sat down at the table and poured himself a cup of coffee.

"About half full and we're really short for the matinee tomorrow."

"You have to cut staff."

"I know."

"What are you thinking?"

"I figured I can do the accounting myself. I can lose the costume assistant."

"You can do the wigs."

"I can cut the prompter, too."

"That's too bad. I like that Nicky Castone. He's a good employee."

"I know. But I don't have enough money to pay him." Calla looked out the kitchen window as though the answer to the theater's financial problems lay in the gnarl of branches that covered her mother's grape arbor. "I have to find creative ways to make budget. Maybe I can get Mario Lanza to be in a play."

"Every time somebody needs something in South Philly they ask Mario Lanza. How much can one man do?"

"He's loyal to the old neighborhood. I'll write him a letter," Calla said, placing her dish in the sink. "I can turn this around."

"Maybe you don't have to. Maybe the place has run its course."

"Don't talk like that, Pop. What would this city be without Borelli's? It's your legacy. Have a little faith." Calla kissed him on the cheek. "I'll be home for supper. Now don't do anything crazy."

If Calla noticed that her father's color was off and that he was not himself, she didn't let on. She was worried about his theater, the troupe he founded, and not so concerned about the man himself that morning.

"No ladders. No step stools. No heavy lifting. Wait until I get home."

"Yeah, yeah, yeah."

"I mean it, Pop."

Calla grabbed her purse and keys before leaving the house. "I'll call you at lunchtime."

"You don't have to."

"Want to," she called out, before closing the front door behind her.

Once Calla was outside, she went down the porch steps at a clip, even though she wasn't late for work. When she reached the gate at the end of the walk, it wouldn't open. She yanked on it, becoming more frustrated when it wouldn't budge. She jostled the handle again, then kicked it, loosening the rusty latch.

Her neighbor, Pat Patronski, a petite Polish beauty around her age, was on her way to work when she saw Calla struggling with the fence. "I guess you read the reviews," Pat said apologetically.

"Only one. And that was enough."

The gate opened. Calla went through it, turned out onto the sidewalk, and began to walk quickly toward Broad Street. Her feet were moving too slowly for her liking, and soon she broke into a run.

Calla had lied to her father. She was devastated by the review. The paper had told her press agent they wouldn't be running it until the weekend, so she believed she had time to brace herself for the worst. Calla had planned to scan the paper and, depending upon whether the review was good or bad, either leave it in the kitchen for her father to enjoy or burn it in the marble birdbath in the backyard—something her father had done through the years whenever he received bad press. The only way for her to cope with the humiliation now was to outrun it.

Calla had done her best directing her first play, but of course she had ideas about how she might have done better. She had her own style, but she was very much her father's protégé, in that she had devised a concept, created an approach, and cast the play, directing it beat by beat, moment to moment, making each scene as visually interesting as she could. She helped the costumer build the costumes stitch by stitch and assisted the set designer as he painted the sets. She had even helped build the island of Illyria with chicken wire, burlap, and buckets of real sand. Had the critic built anything but a tower of bad adjectives to describe what he obviously did not understand?

As Calla ran, her flat shoes began to flap against her heels, and the bottoms of her feet began to burn. She felt like she was in some kind of hell now, consumed in flames of rage, that began at her feet. She was a failure; she had directed a lousy production of a good play. At the library, historians called *Twelfth Night* foolproof. They hadn't met this fool, who proved them wrong. Calla's debut wasn't a triumph, it was a soft landing, bringing with it nothing more than her name misspelled in the city paper and her gender revoked to dismiss her.

She couldn't bear the idea of looking into the sad eyes of her crew and actors, who would need reassuring that it wasn't their work that had caused the negative ink. She would get them through it, she had to, that was also her job. But who would get *her* through it? Her father wasn't joking when he said that directing was the loneliest job in the theater.

Worst of all, and this is what stung the most, the bad review meant any hope for advance ticket sales had evaporated. Calla could handle the pummeling of her ego, but not at the expense of the box office. Her father had given her the keys to the theater creatively, but he'd handed her a mess financially. Her eyes were burning at the thought of it when she heard a wolf whistle. Why was it that men always chose the worst possible moment to get a woman's attention? Calla ignored the whistle and ran faster still.

"Hey, Miss Borelli!" The man shouted as Car No. 4 glided slowly along next to her. She slowed down to a brisk walk when she recognized Nicky Castone behind the wheel.

"Need a lift?" he asked.

"No."

"Why the sprint?"

"I'm late."

"Then you need a lift. Get in."

"No thank you."

Calla sped up her pace to ditch Nicky, but her shoe flew off her foot when she tripped avoiding a gap in the sidewalk. She stumbled and fell forward onto the concrete landing on her knees.

Nicky pulled over and jumped out of the cab. "I'm sorry," Nicky said as he retrieved her shoe. "I distracted you."

Calla sat on the ground, her stocking ripped at the knee. "I told you I didn't want a ride."

"Okay. All right. Okay." Nicky handed her the shoe. He put his hands in the air. "Just trying to help."

"I don't need help." She stood, placed the shoe on the ground, and slipped her foot into it. As Calla walked away from Nicky, he noticed her fine figure, her curves in the simple skirt and sweater. He hadn't noticed Calla Borelli before, not in this way, or in this light. Maybe his single-minded fidelity to Peachy DePino had kept his eyes in his head, or maybe they had stayed there because before this morning, he had never seen Calla in a skirt and wasn't even sure she had legs. Besides that, she wasn't exactly girlish. Calla was either bossing people around, or covered in paint, or struggling to keep a grip on the double-brush buffer on the terrazzo floor in the theater lobby, which bounced like a jackhammer with a short in its cord. She was in constant motion, less like a ballerina than one of the Pep Boys at the service garage.

"Hey Calla," Nicky called after her.

She turned to him, her impatience clear in her rigid posture. "Yes?"

"Cute haircut."

She forced a smile. "Thanks." She waved him off, more a salute than a good-bye.

Dom and Jo Palazzini's middle son, Gio, paced nervously back and forth in the garage below, gingerly peering out the open door from side to side without stepping out onto the sidewalk on Montrose. Gio, in his early thirties, was short and shaped like a packing box; the thick wool of the Western Union uniform did him no favors. What God took away in height, He gave him in hair. His black waves were shiny and thick, tamed twice a day with Wildroot.

Gio stopped long enough to fish the Pall Malls out of his breast pocket, give it a shake and pull a cigarette out of the pack between his lips. It dangled from his mouth as he patted down his pockets in search of matches. When he couldn't find any, he left the cigarette unlit, buried his hands in his pockets, and continued to pace.

Hortense watched the familiar scene from her office and shook her head. Gio was in trouble again. No matter what measures were taken, the man couldn't shake his gambling problem. Nothing cured him—not a stint in the seminary in Spring Grove, where he was thrown out for taking bets on who would be elected pope; not his exemplary military service in the Battle of the Bulge, where he'd fought valiantly but postvictory was caught point shaving in intramural softball and confined to quarters; and not even his love for

Mabel, who, as a condition of their marriage, made her husband meet with a priest once a week in hopes a force more powerful than the lure of winning the pot of a random pickup game would force him to change.

Every manner of rehabilitation had been offered to Gio, but none of them could keep him from poker, pinochle, blackjack, bingo, and other games of chance. If the swallows were intent on Capistrano, the green felt on the tables of Big John Casella's Social Club called for Gio Palazzini to return every payday.

Nicky pulled into the garage as Hortense appeared at the top of the stairs with a telegram. "Don't cut off the motor," she hollered, waving the envelope.

"I'll take it," Gio offered.

"Nicky will take it."

"I said I will take it, Mrs. Mooney," Gio insisted.

"You're not good off the grid, Gio."

"I can read a map as good as anybody."

"Since when? You get lost in the garage on the way to the men's room," Hortense said impatiently.

"I need to get out of town," Gio admitted as the tic over his left eye began to pulse.

"Not again." Nicky looked at his cousin.

"It got away from me. I was at Casella's—"

"I don't want to hear it." Nicky put his hand in the air.

"Who is delivering this telegram? I have a duty," Hortense bellowed from above.

"We'll both go. Get in, Gio."

"Swell," he said, climbing into the passenger seat of No. 4.

Nicky took the steps two at a time to retrieve the envelope from Hortense.

"You're out of your mind," Hortense whispered. "What if you get tailed?"

"I'll hand him over."

"If only that were true. Be careful, Nicky." Hortense gave him the telegram and the folded map of the Pennsylvania interstate. "I mean it. Gio is chock full of nuts—you don't have to go down with him. In fact, don't."

Gio ducked down in the front passenger seat, his face on his knees, as Nicky tooled through the streets on his way out of the city. As the cab cleared the circle outside the Philadelphia Museum and Nicky turned off onto the highway, Gio sat up.

"What kind of trouble are you in now?"

"Ah. Nothing to worry about." Gio rolled down the window and inhaled the fresh air.

"You're on the lam again."

"It will pass."

"There's a comfort."

"When I hit it, I'm Caesar. When I lose, it's a problem. It's a simple equation."

"You lose a lot more than you win."

"I don't brag when I win."

"Gio, you have to stop. The day will come when some thug isn't going to be willing to wait for the bank to open on Monday morning so you can pay your marker and they'll hurt you."

"Nah. They wait."

"You have a baby on the way. Think of your child. And Mabel."

"Mabel's all right."

"For now. But you're testing her patience."

"Don't talk to me about patience. You're not even married yet."

"I'm almost there."

"You want some free advice?"

"Sure."

Gio shook the cigarette pack until one emerged. He offered it to Nicky, who took it. He shook the pack again and pulled one out with his lips. He lit his cigarette with the car lighter, then offered the lighter to his cousin. "Don't do it."

"Don't do what?"

"Marry Peachy."

"Why would you say that?"

"I'm looking out for you."

"How?"

"I know what it's like on the inside. Stay where you are. Stay in your room in the basement with your radio and your freedom. You got a cocoon. A cocoon is nice for one. For two? Not so much. It gets cramped."

"I want to get married, Gio."

"So did I."

"Don't you love Mabel?"

"It would be a little late not to."

"I agree."

"I love her. And she's having our baby. This is how life goes. And I go with life."

"You have some say in the matter. Life doesn't just unfold like a stack of baseball cards."

"Since when?"

"Since always."

"That's not been my experience. I've been told what to do since I was born. If it wasn't my parents ordering me around, it was my brother Dominic, and now it's Mabel."

"Or the bookies."

"Them too. Somebody's always after me for something. I'm pecked at from morning until night."

"Because people want their money."

"Regardless. It's my natural state. Pecked like a seed stick by a flock of starving canaries. That's me." Gio ran his hands through his thick hair, then pulled at it, as if dollar bills could have sprouted from his head if he yanked hard enough. "You can't change nature."

Nicky looked at him. "You could change. You could stop gambling."

Gio's neck snapped so quickly in Nicky's direction, both of them heard Gio's vertebrae crack. "I can't stop. It's in me."

"You have to fight it."

"I do. Sometimes. I try. I keep the urge at bay for a while, and then it comes roaring back worse. It's almost better if I sit in on a few games a week, blow a few bucks and a little steam. It evens out the need. If I hold back, it's all I think about, and then I give in, and it's like a levee breaks, and I'm back at the table, consumed to the point of drowning."

"That's horrible."

"Tell me about it. I'm a prisoner of my own thirst to win at all cost. I disgust myself. But it also thrills me, and that's the rub, cousin." Gio flicked the stub of cigarette out the window. He leaned back in the seat, pushed the brim of the Western Union cap over his eyes, and fell asleep so quickly, it seemed like a hypnotist's trick.

While Nicky marveled at Gio's ability to sleep while he owed God only knows how much money to the most nefarious characters at the Casella Social Club, he also pitied him. Gio was depleted; his emotional resources were shot, and his bank account was drained. He and Mabel only fought behind closed doors, but the doors at 810 Montrose were so thin everybody knew when Gio had a bad week—and, for that matter, when he had a good one. Nicky imagined it must be devastating to crawl home penniless after losing a week's pay at one of Casella's tables instead of rushing home a winner, flush with cash, into the arms of your wife. No wonder Gio didn't want Nicky to marry; he himself found no comfort in it—at least not when he lost.

Nicky found nothing on the radio that he cared to listen to as he spun the dial like a safecracker, so he rolled down the window and let the fresh air wash over him as he drove. Nothing woke his cousin, not even the sharp curves Nicky took at the base of the Pocono Mountains.

Signs with arrows pointing to the cluster of small villages in the folds of the foothills of the Poconos, including East Bangor, Bangor, and Roseto, were lined up on a single pole outside Stroudsburg. Nicky took the turn onto the road over the mountain toward his delivery destination.

Nicky came upon Roseto suddenly, a wishbone-shaped street taking him right to Garibaldi Avenue, the village's main drag. An orange sun burst through pink clouds, its rays of gold and fuchsia illuminating a town decorated to welcome an important visitor. The porches of the homes were dressed with hanging baskets bulging with flowers, flags blew in the breeze, the Italian standard next to the American one, and twists of red, white, and green silk crisscrossed over the avenue as far as Nicky could see. There were hand-painted signs everywhere:

WELCOME AMBASSADOR GUARDINFANTE!
CHE BELLO AMBASCIATORE!
VIVA ITALIA!
ROSETO VALFORTORE ETERNA!

Nicky drove slowly up the street, stopping at the top of the hill at Our Lady of Mount Carmel Church, the obvious architectural crown jewel of the town, which had a bell tower, an intricate rose window, and walls of stately gray granite, split with inlays of stained glass in swirls of ruby, emerald, and deepest blue. The church plaza was decorated for a celebration, the steps flanked with topiaries and more baskets of flowers, the handrails braided with ribbons.

As Nicky parked outside the entrance, the tires grazed the curb, waking Gio.

"Are we here?" Gio asked, startled.

"Not yet."

Gio looked out the window and squinted at the enormous church and its imposing granite facade. "Did I die?"

"No, this is just a church. I'm going inside to say a prayer."

"Why?"

"Are you serious, Gio? One of us is in dire need of spiritual intervention."

"Sorry to hear you're going through a tough time." Gio pulled the cap back over his eyes and went back to sleep.

Nicky stood inside the vestibule of Our Lady of Mount Carmel. The scent of beeswax and incense hung in the air, reminding Nicky of his own church, and of the comfort he found there. Inside, the sanctuary was a baroque showpiece of gold marble with red velvet accents. Pale ivory pillars lined the center aisle. The pews were bedecked with more ribbons, the altar with sprays of red roses, white carnations, and fronds of green. He looked over at the statues of the saints, mounted on the walls along the side aisles. They hovered over the pews like umpires on a baseball diamond.

Nicky knelt in the last pew. He made the sign of the cross and sat back on the bench, and on to a stack of commemorative booklets for the town Jubilee.

Nicky opened one and read the story of Roseto, falling into the story of the place as though it were a fairytale. A lot happened in this little burg. There were photographs of the women who worked in the town blouse factories, the priests of the parish, and the Monsignor from nearby Nesquehoning, the nuns of Saint Joseph and the men of Roseto working in the local slate quarries. He tucked the booklet into the breast pocket of his uniform before genuflecting at the end of the pew. On his way out, he picked up a flyer listing the Jubilee's events by the door, thinking it might be fun to take a drive back to Roseto with Peachy and attend the carnival. It was just the kind of date she enjoyed.

When Nicky returned to the cab, the slam of the car door didn't wake his cousin, so he nudged him. "Time to deliver."

"Yeah." Gio sat bolt upright.

"You never get a decent night's rest, do you?"

"I'm a spotty sleeper at best."

"Because you stay out too late."

"I got a lot on my mind."

"It's a lot of pressure, thinking up new places to hide."

"You are correct, cousin."

Nicky took the turn onto Truman Street, a cozy block of two-story clapboard houses painted pastel colors, separated by two-family brick homes with colorful striped awnings. Nicky pulled up to 125 Truman, a single-family home, and handed the telegram to Gio.

Gio adjusted the official cap of the Western Union telegraph service as he sauntered up the sidewalk and rapped on the door. The house's red-and-tan-striped awning looked sharp and clean against the brick. Nicky made a mental note to purchase awnings for the house he'd picked out for Peachy on Wharton, as they gave the exterior of a house a real flair.

"We're good," Gio said as he got back into the car.

As they drove to the top of Garibaldi Avenue to take the road out of town, Nicky took in the field roped off for a carnival. There were empty stands with signs advertising torrone candy for sale, sausage and pepper sandwiches, and zeppoles by the bag. Streamers decorated with small triangles of Italian flags flapped in the breeze. An empty Ferris wheel spun slowly in the distance, the sun peeking through its bright blue spokes.

"Cute town," Gio said. "Must be celebrating something."

Nicky stopped the car at the stop sign and pointed up, not wanting to miss a chance to educate his cousin beyond his expertise in the world of craps. "It's a Jubilee, Gio."

"How do you know?"

Nicky pointed to the banner that read WELCOME TO ROSETO'S JUBILEE.

"Hey, that guy looks like you."

"What guy?"

"The guy on the banner. The *faccia*. What do you know?"

Nicky peered up at the banner stretched across the street, welcoming Ambassador Carlo Guardinfante. The painted image of the ambassador, framed in a laurel-leaf medallion, was impressive. Gio was right, the man's face had the unmistakable shape, forehead, lips, and nose of a Castone.

"He has your hair. Your *Ameri-gan* hair."

"He does, doesn't he?" Nicky didn't have any brothers or sisters, so he was fascinated to see a picture of anyone who resembled him.

"Everybody's got a twin. Well, we found yours, didn't we?"

"I guess we did. And mine wears an impressive uniform. I'm glad if somebody looks just like me; he's a man of substance."

"I wish I had a twin," Gio said wistfully.

"So you'd have someone to cover for you when you were on the lam?"

"That's one consideration. I'd also like a twin to run things by. Talk to him—see if what I'm thinkin' is what I should be thinkin'."

"You already have a guardian angel."

"If you say so."

"Who do you think gets you out of your scrapes?"

"Mother luck." Gio shrugged.

Nicky drove down Garibaldi Avenue slowly taking in the quaint houses. At midmorning, the streets were empty; the men were at the quarries busting rock, the children were in school, and the women were working in the blouse mills.

"Cute little place," Gio commented. "I could never live here."

"Not enough action?"

"Nowhere near enough."

"I'm sure they have poker here. They have cards everywhere, you know."

"Yeah, but do they make their own cheese? I don't know if I could live in a place where they don't make their own cheese."

The girls of Saint Mary Magdalen de Pazzi's eighth-grade class were lined up in rows of ten across on Broad Street, leading the annual May Day procession. They wore pink eyelet ballerina-length dresses and carried bright blue prayer books in their white-gloved hands. On their heads, they wore crowns made of pale pink baby roses woven with white satin ribbons that cascaded down their backs, fluttering in the breeze as they walked.

Father Perlo walked behind the girls, moving from one side of the street to the other, dipping the sprinkler into the holy-water pot and blessing the crowd as he went.

The May Queen, Carol Schiavone, a fragile thirteen-year-old beauty selected by the nuns, stood proudly with one arm around the statue of the Blessed Mother, under an arch of red paper roses on the flatbed truck the class had decorated for the occasion. Beneath their feet was an Aubusson rug, in rich shades of ruby red, coral, and green borrowed from the convent entrance hall.

The Schiavone girl wore a formal white gown with long sleeves, a fitted bodice, and skirt made with layers of white tulle that were fluffed to look like a dollop of whipped cream. Anchored atop her deep brown curls, she wore a crown of white roses woven into delicate strands of gold wire, identical to the one on the statue. The Blessed Mother, her plaster robe freshly painted ice blue, loomed against the fawn-colored sky speckled with tufts of clouds.

The best-behaved boys of the eighth-grade, crisply dressed in black slacks, white shirts, and light blue ties, walked along the sides of the slow-moving float single file, while the rest marched in rows behind the flatbed. They carried black rosary beads; some bunched them in their hands while other boys laced them through their fingers.

Vinnie Matera, the class troublemaker with a flair for comedy, swung his beads, in a long loop, the tip end of the crucifix almost grazing the ground, until Sister Robbie Pentecost jogged up beside him and snapped her fingers. Vinnie quickly reeled his rosary back into his palm to safety and joined the rest of the class as they recited the sorrowful mysteries.

Broad Street was lined with onlookers who had taken their lunch hours to watch the procession. For the devout, it was a holy day. The priest would bless them, they would ask the Mother of God to intercede for their needs in heaven, or pray for their own mothers, grateful for their sacrifices on behalf of their families. For everyone else, it was the official kick-off of summer: with night games at Shibe Park cheering on the Phillies, days spent at Willow Grove Amusement Park on thrill rides like Sir Hiram Maxim's Captive Flying Machine, and enjoying a week of rest during the annual union vacation over the Fourth of July holiday.

Holy water spiked through the air like a shower of diamonds as the priest blessed the crowd. The old-timers genuflected as the priest passed, while the younger people bowed their heads. Calla Borelli pulled her scarf up over her head to cover it as the holy water touched her face in drops like soft rain. She made the sign of the cross, whispering along with the drone of the crowd, "*In nomine Patris et Filii et Spiritus Sancti, Amen.*"

Dom Palazzini stood on the corner of Broad and Montrose as the procession passed. As the float turned the corner, he went down on one knee and a pain ripped through his leg. He winced but did not make a sound, though he did make the sign of the cross on his way up to standing. He felt old, everything hurt, even though he had just been to Dr. Schrenker, who told him he wasn't in terrible shape, but admonished him to smoke less, eat less, and walk more. At sixty years old Dom wasn't going to start listening to doctors. Defiantly, he pulled a Tiparillo out of his shirt pocket, unwrapped it, and lit it with the swanky monogrammed silver lighter his kids had given him on his last birthday.

A block down the route, Mike Palazzini knelt on the opposite side of Broad Street, feeling the cool drops of holy water on his face as the priest sprinkled the crowd. He made the sign of the cross, stood with ease, and dusted off the knees of his fine wool trousers before replacing his Borsalino fedora on his head. He slanted the brim over one eye before turning down Broad Street.

Mike walked against the crowd as it dispersed, nodding his head when recognized, flashing a bright white smile that matched his thick hair. He was fifty-nine years old and didn't look or feel a day of it. He was strolling along thinking about the order his wife had placed at Paulie & Gloria Martines' Cheese Shop, wondering whether Nancy had ordered enough parm and scamorza, when his brother Dom ran into him, almost toppling him. At first Mike didn't recognize his brother. Mike's instinct was to apologize and extend his hand, but Dom's red face looked like a cartoon drawing of a bull galloping at full charge toward a matador. Mike could almost hear the snorting. All that was missing was the nose ring.

"Whoa," Mike said under his breath. "Excuse me."

"Hmph," Dom grunted before moving past him.

"Not going to say anything? Not a hello?" Mike said sarcastically as Dom walked off. Mike noticed Dom's limp. Too many baba au rhums, Mike thought to himself. His brother overdid the sweets. Dom had gotten heavy.

It had been at least ten years, probably eleven, since Mike had last run into his brother. He couldn't remember. Dom appeared to be wearing the same suit he wore the day the brothers parted. Looked like the same shoes too. It wasn't just Dom's clothes that were old; he moved like the elderly. There was the protruding stomach, of course, but Dom had lost height as his knees had given out, heck, curved out, so his legs were shaped like two half-moons that would never connect to make a full one. But it was Dom's face etched with anger lines and the deep wrinkles that develop from expressions of chronic annoyance that Mike noticed the most. Dom reveled in anger, it was as if holding a grudge held him together. The passage of time had obviously taught him nothing. After all these years, Dom had not yet learned how to live; he had not figured out that spending money should be more fun than making it. That was too bad. Mike shook his head in disbelief and entered the cheese shop.

Dom fished his handkerchief out of his pocket and mopped his forehead. He figured it had been two or three years since he had seen his brother on the street. He couldn't remember. Curious for a second look at his banished sibling, Dom turned around to look where Mike had gone. The Martines Cheese Shop. Of course Mike shopped there. Only the best imported cheese brought in aged barrels from Italy. And Mike's clothes! Only the most expensive lid, suit, and loafers for his fancy kid brother. Where had he gotten a suntan in May? Did he sit out on the sidewalk over on Fitzwater with a tinfoil foldout at high noon? Probably went to Bermuda. Of course Mike looked sharp—his idea of hard work was kibitzing with the customers and taking plenty of time off. As Dom remembered the argument that had severed their relationship, a fresh wave of resentment coursed through his veins.

Mike had been right about one thing—Dom liked being angry. Dom had been right about one thing, too—Mike looked good.

Around the corner, in the parking lot of the school, four members of the sodality of Saint Mary Magdalen de Pazzi, the social club and service organization for the ladies of the church, carefully lifted the statue of the Blessed Lady off the float, handing her off to the school janitor, who carried her in his arms like a bride over the threshold and back into the building.

Elsa stood at the base of the steps, holding a box, collecting the rosebud crowns she had made as the girls, in their pink dresses, filed back into the school for the reception. Elsa wore a simple beige wool coat over a day dress and a Breton hat of navy straw with a beige grosgrain ribbon at the crown, which set off her auburn hair.

"Where's the cake?" Dom barked as he walked up the sidewalk.

"Inside, Pop. In the cafeteria."

Dom gripped the metal banister of the stairs and worked his way up the steps.

"Are your knees bothering you?" Elsa asked him.

"The sun is shining, of course they are," he groused.

"Look for Mabel. She saved you a seat," Elsa called after him as he went inside.

"Thank you for your hard work, Mrs. Palazzini." Sister Theresa, a young nun in a crisp black-and-white habit, placed the crown from the statue in the box. "I let Carol keep her crown. I hope you don't mind."

"Not at all."

"You made the day special. I heard so many wonderful comments as the procession passed. The Blessed Mother will protect you always." Sister Theresa squeezed Elsa's hand before going into the school. Elsa looked down into the box of crowns she had so carefully constructed. It had taken hours to anchor the fresh flowers and weave the ribbons through the wires. Once assembled, she had spritzed them with cold sugar water, wrapped them in muslin, and stored them in the refrigerator. She had taken such pains with each crown, making them works of art. What had been so lovely was now a tangled mess. The circles of wire intersected one another in the box like magician's loops. The ribbons were knotted. Elsa's eyes filled with tears.

"It's a shame. One parade, one day, and it's all over," Mabel said, standing above her on the steps. "I could weep too. And I might. All your effort. All those thorns. All those crowns." Gio's wife wore a black maternity coat with a white collar. Her blue eyes looked lavender against the sky. "Hey, Elsa. Pop's inside, having cake and coffee with the priest. And I got a newsflash. The sky over South Philly hasn't fallen."

Elsa smiled. Mabel always managed to cheer her up.

Mabel joined Elsa at the bottom of the stairs and took the box of crowns from her. "Come inside and hear the compliments. Your crowns made the May Day. They're all yakking. All the mothers said so."

"They did?"

"Every single one. And these Neapolitans are a fussy bunch. Don't say I said it."

"I won't."

"You and me have to stick together. We're the outsiders. The Irish and the Pole in the middle of all this marinara. You know what I mean." Mabel winked.

"I know exactly what you mean."

"Now, come on inside. I want my sister-in-law to get her due. Let them fawn. The nuns included."

Mabel turned to go back up the steps. Elsa stood still, looking off in the distance.

"Are you all right?" Mabel asked.

"It all goes by so quickly. There's something sad about it."

"It won't be sad when our kids are in it. Your Dominic will march when he has his Confirmation. And you never know, maybe I'll have a girl and she'll be the May Queen someday and you'll make her crown. Won't that be something?"

"That'd be nice." Elsa followed Mabel into the school. She wasn't thinking about the parade, or the roses or the crowns. On this holy day of remembrance honoring mothers, Elsa was thinking about her own, and how much she missed her, and how it never hurt any less to know that she would never see her again.

2

The night air had a nip as Nicky pedaled through Bella Vista on his bicycle. He'd had a nourishing supper of pasta fazool with a heel of bread washed down with a glass of homemade wine before heading out to his second job. He stood up on the pedals and swerved onto Broad Street, feeling the breeze on his face as he skimmed past the childhood homes of his friends, where he had spent time as a boy when he wasn't with his cousins.

Nicky shifted his weight as he grabbed the handlebars, lifted his feet off the pedals, and jumped the curb, landing on the sidewalk as though the bike were a horse and he were a jockey. As he pedaled past the old houses, he sang the family names of the folks who lived inside like lyrics from an aria:

DeMeo, LaPrea,
　Festa, Testa, Fiordellisi, Giovannini,
　　Ochemo, Cudemo, Communale,
　　　Larantino, Constantino,
Imbesi, Concessi, Belgiorno, Morrone! Spatafora!
Cuttone, Caruso, Micucci, Meucci,
　　Gerace, Ciarlante, Stampone, Cantone,

> *Messina, Cortina, Matera, Ferrara,*
>   *Cucinelli, Marinelli, Bellanca, Ronca,*
> *Palermo, Zeppa! Ferragamo!*
> *Ruggiero, Florio, D'iorio... Sabatine, DeRea, Martino!*

Nicky peeled off the macadam and onto the dirt alley behind the Borelli Theatrical Company as he sang out one last name:

> *Sempre Borelli!*

He parked his bike on the loading dock next to the stage door and walked around to the front entrance of the theater, whistling as he went.

When Nicky entered the lobby of Borelli's, he walked into the vestibule of his own cathedral. The lobby was gloriously Belle Epoque—that is, if the belle had been through hard times, come out the other side, and survived. The vaulted ceiling, papered in gold leaf, was peeling from age but still shimmered. An impressive set of double-arched staircases swirled up to the mezzanine. Upon close inspection, the velvet rope that draped to the top and served as a banister was worn in places and the treads of carpet on the steps were thin, but from a distance, the rich red velvet and wool remained regal.

A hand-painted mural of a landscape of Pennsylvania horse country provided a backdrop on the landing that had appealed to the fancy orchestra patrons. The luster of the paint had faded over time, leaving behind a soft patina in shades of butter mints.

Overhead an opulent Murano glass chandelier with hand-blown horns of white milk glass twinkled over the polished terrazzo floor, causing the gold flecks in the black-and-white stone to sparkle. The lobby's flaws might be obvious in daylight, but at night, when the chandelier was dimmed, the soft glow made everything look lovely, including the patrons.

Sam Borelli's parents had founded the theater seventy-five years before. The company staged Italian operas, which were popular with Neapolitan immigrants who longed for the music and stories that conjured home. Sung and performed in their native language, a night at Borelli's made them feel as if the turquoise sea off the Amalfi Coast and the white beaches of Sicily were as close as the Jersey shore. But as these Italians became more American, their tastes changed as their memories faded. Soon, they preferred Broadway shows, plays and movies that featured stories about shop girls, men in uniform, and the swell set, young people with ambition and dough. No longer did they seek entertainment that reminded them of where they came from; they bought tickets to shows that dramatized where they were going: to the top, in Main Line style.

The Borellis were a show-business family, so instead of giving up, they adapted, forming an acting company. They dropped the opera, leaving it to the Academy of Music farther down on Broad Street, and instead began to produce classic plays, knowing anything British had appeal for their aspirational, working-class audience.

The company was semi-professional. Actors and staff were nominally paid, but locals often volunteered in exchange for ticket privileges. Nicky Castone found a community at Borelli's where he was welcome. There wasn't a job in the theater beneath him. As prompter, he ran lines with actors, helped them into their costumes, assisted the prop master, and placed and moved scenery during shows.

Nicky performed any task asked of him. He polished the brass on the staircase, washed the windows in the lobby, and swept the sidewalk. Sometimes he helped out in the box office, where they typically ran out of change on show nights. Latecomers knew that since there were always plenty of empty seats, they were let in whether they paid for a ticket or not. The first rule of show business is that everyone in it would do it for free but as a professional company, the artists were paid, which meant that the second rule of show business—you must charge for performances—was essential to survival. But the second rule was often waived at Borelli's, which is why the books showed the company was in the red.

"How's the house tonight?" Nicky asked, stopping at the ticket window.

Rosa DeNero, a round woman with a full-moon face, looked up from the pulp novel she was reading. "Could be better. Orchestra is sold about three-quarters full. Mez is empty. Might as well break a hole in the ceiling and rent the place out to pigeons." She held her place in her book with her thumb and looked at him. "You'd sell some tickets if you did a musical."

"We're a Shakespeare company."

"There's your trouble. Shakespeare is for snobs."

"What are you reading?"

Rosa held up the paperback. *Sin Cruise: She Was Tired of Being Good.* The busty woman on the cover looked anything but.

"Shakespeare is a very lusty writer, if that's what you're looking for."

"I can't understand what anybody on the stage is saying," Rosa said and sat back on her rolling stool.

"He wrote for the people. People like us. You ever heard of the groundlings?"

"Not interested."

"But you work in a theater."

"Don't care."

"Something must have compelled you to work in the oldest art form on earth."

"Twenty bucks a week called my name. That's what brought me to Borelli's. I'm saving up for a washing machine. I'm sick of the wringer."

"It can't just be about the money. There's more to you than that."

Nicky tried to flirt, but his charm didn't land on Rosa, rather circled around her like an annoying housefly. "How about it, Rosa? Surrender to the make-believe."

"I might think about it if you people would come up with something I'd want to see. *Warm for May* or something good like that. Something with sizzle."

"*Twelfth Night* has sizzle."

"Yeah. That's what the patrons say on the way out," Rosa cracked.

"You don't have to be mean about it."

"Nobody has the crust around here to tell it like it is." Rosa went back to her book.

"Will you put a ticket aside for Teresa DePino?"

"You paying?

"Put it on my tab."

"Half the world is on a tab."

Nicky ignored her jab and entered the theater. The scent of walnut oil, fresh paint, and stale perfume hung in the air, dense as the heavy green velvet curtains that were hoisted high in half-moons that draped the proscenium arch. As Nicky made his way down the aisle, the work lights cast full circles of light onto the stage floor. He was on his way up the stage-left steps when he saw Tony Coppolella, the leading man of the troupe, leaning against the upstage wall, studying his lines.

"We've already opened. You're still on script?"

"An actor never masters Shakespeare. 'If you take your eyes off the page, you'll never put it on the stage.' Sam Borelli taught me that." Tony puffed on a cigarette before tucking the script under his arm.

Had Tony been born anywhere but South Philly, he would have been a star. Tall and lithe, with black eyes, a strong jaw, good diction, and a limber body, he was a natural for the stage. But it was not to be: his father had died when he was a boy, and he helped raise his six younger sisters and brothers. Now, at forty, he had a family of his own and ran the shipping department at the A-Treat soda plant. For him, it was too late for a life in the theater beyond Borelli's.

Tony joined Nicky at the prop table. "What's with the suit? Somebody die?"

"I have a date later."

"We're never gonna meet your girl, are we?"

"You will tonight."

"No kidding."

"She's coming to the show."

"The first time. She really exists." Tony squinted at him. "How long you been engaged?"

"I gave her a ring seven years ago."

"Seven years. Very nice attenuation." Tony took a slow drag off his cigarette and exhaled slowly, the white smoke snaking into the air. "I wasn't so lucky. When I gave Sharon a diamond, she set a date six months from my proposal. Said she didn't like long engagements. Once I married her, I figured out why."

"Sharon is a wonderful girl."

"Yeah," Tony replied, unenthused. "How old are you?"

"Twenty-eight."

Tony smiled slyly. "No wonder you made it through the war. You're good at dodging bullets."

Nicky went backstage and checked the lectern at the stage-left entrance. He opened the script and turned on his small reading light. As he did, he felt the tingle of ten long fingernails down his back.

"You're tight," a woman's voice whispered. The fingernails worked their way back up and grazed the back of his neck until every hair on Nicky's head stood up like the fur on a frightened cat.

"My fiancée is coming to the show tonight." Nicky reached back to remove Josie Ciletti's hands from his neck, but they were gone, having moved down to the small of his back.

"I don't believe you," Josie whispered.

"She'll be sitting in the orchestra."

Josie wrapped her arms around Nicky's waist and dropped her head between his shoulder blades with a thud.

"Would you like to meet her?" Nicky asked.

Josie released her grip and came around the front of the lectern to face Nicky, unhappy that he'd broken the spell of their pretend game. She wore a flimsy red satin robe, tied tightly at the waist. Her breasts were hoisted so high in the bodice of the Elizabethan bustier that they wrinkled her neck. Josie was a looker from the last row of the mezzanine, but up close, at fifty-three, she was a Picasso. She had close-set slate-blue eyes, jet-black hair, and a feverish mouth. The work bulb on the lectern did her no favors, casting shadows where she most needed light.

"I'm not your girl anymore?"

"Josie, you're married."

"Oh, him."

"Yes. Him. Burt Ciletti? Your husband."

"But what if . . ."

Nicky had played this game with Josie since he began working at the theater.

"If you weren't married . . . ," Nicky droned.

"Go on," she purred.

". . . and I weren't engaged—"

"Ugh." Josie couldn't resist repulsion, followed by a dramatic pause. After all, she was a trained semi-professional regional theater actress.

Nicky continued, ". . . and if you weren't old enough to be my moth—"

"Drop that line."

"My nurse?"

"Better."

"Of course, you would be a lovely date, and who knows where it might lead."

"Nicholas, you are so right." Josie inhaled deeply, forcing the entirety of her rib cage to rise so high her breasts almost touched her chin, but she exhaled before they hit the dimple. "Timing is everything. In the theater. In life. In love. You and me? We live with the broken hands of time."

Calla Borelli, in a white party dress and pink ballet flats, yanked the pulley to release the stage curtain, which fell to the floor with a loud thud. She called out to the cast and crew, "Rosa is opening the house."

"I better get dressed," Josie purred in a way that told Nicky this wouldn't be the last time he'd feel her nails on his chalkboard. Her satin mules clopped all the way back to her dressing room like she was a pony in need of new shoes. Nicky shook his head and organized his script. Leading ladies needed so much reassurance.

"You look lovely," Nicky said to Calla.

"Thanks."

"You're welcome," Nicky said, then murmured, "Frosty."

"Who, me?"

"Yeah. You've been giving me the stink eye. The cold shoulder. The first day of winter. I guess because I made you fall."

Calla had to think. "Oh, that. No, that wasn't your fault, I was distracted."

"So was I."

"Why?"

"Doesn't matter. Why the dress? Something's up. A skirt. Then a dress. Did the fire department ask for their overalls back?"

"You're a real cut-up. If you must know, I have a date."

"Lucky guy."

"You think so?" Calla's eyes narrowed.

"It's finally been confirmed that you have legs. The young men of South Philly are rejoicing."

Calla closed her eyes and smoothed the space between her eyebrows. "Nicky, I need to talk to you."

"I'm only one man. I have a fiancée, and Josie is next in line. You'll be sixty-two before I get to you."

Calla folded her arms and looked down at the floor. "I can't afford to keep you on staff. I'm afraid this is your last night."

Nicky swallowed hard. "You're firing me?"

"I wish the financial situation around here were better and that things were different."

"I make seventy-five cents a night."

"I can't afford it."

"It's not the quality of my work?"

"You know the play better than the actors. I like you. You do anything we ask. But we're not making box office. Something has to go."

"You mean somebody."

"I'm sorry." Calla placed her hand on the lectern as if to soothe the situation. "If it helps, I hate this part of my job. Hate it." She turned toward the stairs.

"Calla?"

"Yeah?"

"I don't like your haircut after all."

"You and my dad." Calla went down the stairs.

Nicky was stunned. He had never been fired, and certainly not by a girl in a white piqué cotton dress. Granted, his only employers had been his uncle and the United States Army, and while family would never put him out of work and he had earned his honorable discharge, Calla's cold and abrupt canning of his position stung. Nicky was hurt, but he had a job to do, so like all theater people, he put the bad news out of his mind and got on with the show. He would deal with his feelings after the final curtain. For now, he would savor what was left of his time at the theater and stay in the moment. Nicky had heard Sam Borelli give this bit of direction to the actors many times in rehearsal, and while his job as prompter was strictly behind the scenes, it would only help to remain focused on the task at hand.

Of all the wonderful aspects of working in the theater, Nicky's favorite moments were spent standing in the wings before a performance, watching the audience take their seats. Over time, he had come to make certain assumptions about the patrons based upon their pre-curtain behavior.

Occasionally there was a tussle between an usher and a patron over the seat assignment. Women wore their best outfits to the theater, which often meant their biggest hats, with the widest brims decorated with enormous silk flowers and large satin bows. A big hat worn by a woman sitting in an orchestra seat could knock out an entire act of Shakespeare for the patron unlucky enough to sit behind her. Try asking the woman who was proud of her Agnes of Paris creation to remove it. If the woman wouldn't remove her hat, and the usher couldn't make her move her seat, she'd leave in a huff, and if she stayed, the patron with the compromised view demanded a refund.

When a group bought seats in a cluster, they would enter the theater with their stubs and proceed to engage in a version of musical chairs until everyone was satisfied with their particular view of the stage. The long-legged, claustrophobic, and hypochondriacal always fought for the aisle seats. Nuns never cared where they sat. Priests wanted center orchestra. Politicians wanted the front row while bookies, gamblers, and other players of the street stood in the back. As a director blocked the actors, Nicky could block the audience.

Nicky observed the single-ticket buyer with keen interest. This was usually a man who came alone, paid close attention to the action, and laughed and cried through the show, only to return the following night to repeat the experience. He related most to that fellow, the audience member who felt the production spoke directly to him.

Audiences were similar night after night, but onstage, the world of the play was never the same.

Theater was the volatile, dangerous, and restless sea in the world
of all art forms. Depending upon mood and context, emotion and
delivery, the play, as written and directed, could change night to
night, it could transform, in color, shade, and meaning; it could die
or explode, dazzle or fizzle, surprise and delight, anesthetize and
bore, same script, same actors, didn't matter, you never knew. That
mutability was the very thing that had hooked Nicky Castone. He
loved being near the danger, observing it from the wings. Even
though curtains, a podium, the script in a binder, and a small bright
desk light separated him from the thrill of what was happening onstage, he was grateful to be close enough to the fire to feel the heat.

Nicky's real life was predictable. After his mother died, his life
fell into place as he fell into the world of the Palazzinis. Army training wasn't that different from the drill on Montrose Street. Life,
when he returned home, was one of order and routine: at work,
pick up, collect the fare, drop off; at home, macaroni on Tuesday
nights, fish on Fridays, and Sunday dinners after ten o'clock mass.
But inside Borelli's, he reveled in uncertainty, shifts of mood, and
displays of emotion. Nicky ran on the highs of adrenaline, the lows
of disappointment, and the moments of triumph, and he didn't do
it alone. He had a company of actors and a crew of artisans to share
it with, a theatrical family. They relied on one another, as he had his
fellow soldiers in the war. A working life in the theater was harder
than one in the military in his estimation. As a soldier, he'd worried about being killed. In the theater, death came if you were dull.
Working at Borelli's forced Nicky to ponder where feelings origi-
nate, and to watch as the director coached the actor to challenge
the audience with that discovery through the story. It was the only
place in his life where that pursuit was even possible.

Peachy DePino wandered into the theater, holding her ticket. She
looked up at the ceiling, squinted at the stage, while she waited at

the top of the vom for the usher. The usher took her ticket and led Peachy to her seat. She sat down and wriggled out of her Easter coat, a light pink voile swing number with a ruffled collar. Underneath, she wore a white cotton blouse and dark pink cotton skirt. She adjusted her pink silk cocktail hat, with a large organza camellia over one ear, and smoothed her hair.

Peachy was a feral Philly girl, thin from the war and nerves. Her black hair was rolled under in marcelled waves, her brown eyes were so large they took up half of her face. Her nose was Calabrian in length and Roman sharp, a combination of her father's and mother's prominent features. When she smiled, anything within a block inside Bella Vista lit up. Nicky had fallen in love with Peachy because of that smile.

Nicky watched his fiancée as she read the program. She was a fast reader who went to the library once a month and picked up the latest bestsellers; she called herself *somebody in the know*. However, on this particular night, she wasn't. Peachy had no idea why Nicky had invited her to the theater.

Sitting in the seat and trying to appear as if she belonged, she looked around for a clue that might help her understand why Nicky had left a single ticket for her at the box office. She removed her wristwatch and gently wound the gear with her thumb and forefinger as she waited for the curtain to rise. Nicky's heart filled with feeling for her as he observed her all alone, as if warm pancake syrup flowed through his veins.

"Hey, I'm going to get into place." Tony turned and pointed to his back. "Give me a zip, will ya?"

Nicky zipped up Tony's costume, a gold tunic he wore over pale green tights and brown boots.

"How's the house?"

"Orchestra is full," Nicky told him, fudging a bit. But Tony was just nearsighted enough to believe him.

"Great."

In character as Orsino, the Duke, Tony strode onto the stage and took his position on the set, a castle on the island of Illyria. The trompe l'oeil windows and doors painted on the flats gave the illusion of dimension while hues of gold and soft coral suggested opulence. Tony jumped up and down on his toes and shook out his hands. He rotated his head on his neck to loosen up his vertebrae.

The cast drifted up from the dressing rooms, taking their places in the wings to await their cues, bringing with them the lingering scent of last cigarettes, talcum powder, and Jack Daniel's straight in a paper cup.

Hambone Mason swore he only needed liquor to bolster his confidence onstage at night, but evidently he also needed it to get through tax season at his accounting office during the day. The bald sixty-year-old leaned forward and touched his toes, reached his arms high above his head, inhaled, and exhaled, misting the stage-left wings with his tap-room breath.

As the actors joined Tony onstage, Calla manned the pulley for the curtain and Enzo Carini took his place on his mark downstage right. When the house lights dimmed and the curtain rose, he held a trumpet up to his lips. The follow spot found him as he blew a stately flurry of notes before he announced to the audience:

"Twelfth Night, or What You Will."

The stage lights pulled on until the set glistened. Tony turned downstage and walked into a puddle of intersecting pale blue beams and began to perform the opening speech. Nicky followed the lines in the script using a ruler to keep his place.

The pace of the play that evening was brisk. The actors were on top of their cues, the backstage crew was prepared, and it seemed all was well in Illyria and Borelli's.

As the scenes progressed, the actors and actresses moved like the gears on a large set of gang mowers, coming on and off the stage left or right into the wings with precision. By the first intermission, Nicky had finally caught his breath. He helped the crew move the flats, flipping the castle around to reveal a pastoral setting of rolling hills. Nicky was so consumed with the details of the production that he hadn't had a chance to gauge Peachy's reaction to the play, but he couldn't wait to hear her thoughts.

"How's it going?" Calla whispered behind Nicky as he assumed his stance behind the podium.

"Might be the best performance yet."

Calla nodded in agreement.

"Homestretch, kids," Nicky said softly to the actors in the wings.

The company took their places for the final scene of the fourth act, which left the last act in the capable hands of Tony and the great Norma Fusco Girolamo, the leading lady of the company, who was playing Viola.

Nicky did a quick head count. "Where's Menecola?" he asked.

"Yell down for Menecola," Tony turned to the prop master.

Josie, who was playing Maria the maid, clopped up the steps. "Peter Menecola left."

"What do you mean? Is he outside?" Nicky asked.

"He's gone. His mother's knees locked on her at Novena. She tripped on the choir steps, wiped out the tenor section like dominoes, and broke her hip in the fall. Here." She handed Calla his costume.

Calla turned to Enzo.

"I can't go on for him. I'm already covering for Paulie Gatto as the priest in this scene. Remember he's out? Gall bladder surgery." Enzo pulled the black cassock of the priest over his head.

"Cut the scene," Hambone suggested.

"We can't cut the scene. It's the marriage of Sebastian and Olivia." Nicky was frustrated as he flipped through the script.

"Nicky, you do it," Tony proposed.

"From here?"

"No, onstage. Act. You know the words. Play Sebastian."

"I couldn't."

"Good idea," Calla said.

"I'm not doing it."

"You have to."

"I'm not an actor."

"We're all actors," Tony said wryly.

"You're all we've got," Calla said with authority.

The next few seconds flew by quickly because Nicky was numb. Enzo handed him the costume. It seemed like a flock of birds descended upon him, pecking away his street clothes, but instead of winding up naked, they were replaced with the costume pieces.

"Let me help you into that tunic," Josie purred as she began to unbutton Nicky's shirt. He pushed her hands away.

"Give him privacy," Calla ordered. The cast turned away—Josie reluctantly—as Nicky slipped out of his trousers and into Sebastian's with Bonnie's assistance.

It felt a lot like the moment he was assigned his army uniform at Fort Rucker. If clothes make the man and a uniform makes the soldier, it must be true the costume makes the actor. Did this sack of dyed broadcloth have magical powers? Nicky adjusted the collar and yanked down the hem, hoping the tunic would give him courage, and transform him into the character.

Beyond that, Nicky wanted to save the show. He had never been a hero, but like all men, he aspired to it. This may very well have been the moment where fate and skill collided to give Nicky Castone the opportunity to show the world what he was made of, even though he resisted the notion of being an actor. In his deepest soul, Nicky had the urge to act onstage, but dismissed it. For one thing, the theater didn't fall in line with his regimented life; for another, he didn't believe he could rise to the talent level of Tony Coppolella. But now, whether he liked it or not, Nicky would find out. Sam Borelli believed the audience tells you if you belong onstage. Nicky was eager to find out if he agreed with them.

Norma ran up the steps two at a time. Her lustrous brown hair, curled into sausage waves, bounced down her back as she sprinted. "We have a problem!" she whispered. "Cathy went with him."

"We lost Cathy Menecola, too?" Calla was exasperated. "Couldn't one person in that family handle a broken hip?"

"Evidently not." Norma was half dressed herself, wearing only the top half of her costume for Act 5.

"Get her costume," Calla ordered.

Bonnie, the costume assistant, whose mood usually matched her name, bounded down the steps with the gown. She thrust it at Calla with a sarcastic "Who needs a costume crew?"

"I guess I do," Calla grumbled.

"You got fired too?" Nicky asked Bonnie.

"I sure did."

"This is no way to run an arts organization," Nicky huffed.

"You're telling me," Bonnie agreed.

"Can you two wait to rip me to shreds until the show's over?" Calla ordered. "Everybody turn around."

"You're going to play Olivia?" Tony asked.

"Who else we got?" Calla reached back to unzip her dress.

The men's necks snapped in unison in Calla's direction, anticipating the fall of the cotton piqué.

"Don't look," she barked.

They looked away.

As Calla stepped out of her dress and handed it to Bonnie, Nicky peeked. Calla's tawny skin shimmered in the low golden cross-beams of the backstage special lights, revealing her lovely shape. For a simple girl who wasn't prone to fussing, primping, and evidently wearing a girdle, he observed that, out of her clothes, Calla was anything but ordinary. Her neck was long, and her arms were graceful. Her breasts were exquisite, but he didn't want to miss the rest of her in the short amount of time he had, so he took in her small waist, the curve of her hips, the derrière a little more ample than it appeared in clothes, and, most exciting of all, the pale pink garter snapped onto silver mist stockings, which banded around her thighs like ribbons on a package. The stocking color was familiar—his cousin-in-law Lena hand-washed and line-dried hers in his bathroom every Saturday night in preparation for Sunday mass.

Bonnie formed a circle on the floor with Cathy's velvet gown, as Calla stepped into it. It was as if the Birth of Venus had sprung to life before them as Bonnie slowly lifted the bodice of a pink velvet gown off the ground like a clamshell and higher around those full breasts before slipping Calla's arms into the mutton sleeves. The gown was too big for Calla, but it didn't matter how the costume hid her assets now that Nicky had seen what was underneath.

Calla caught Nicky looking at her, and glared at him. "Really?" she admonished him.

Nicky looked off quickly, directly into the lights, which temporarily blinded him.

Bonnie zipped Calla into the gown as she moved toward the stage, following Enzo the priest. Nicky moved to join them.

"You peeked!"

"It was an accident," Nicky said apologetically.

"Like driving a cab into a brick wall in broad daylight," Calla shot back.

"Yeah, something like that." Nicky was glad he'd seen her almost naked body if she was going to be such a hatpin about it.

"Maybe you'll rethink my job?" Bonnie whispered to Calla as she flounced the skirt of the gown.

"Not now, Bonnie," Calla snapped.

Calla pushed Nicky onto the stage and shoved him into position before slipping behind a flat and joining Enzo.

Nicky knew the blocking because he had not missed a rehearsal. He knew the lines because he knew everyone's lines—the truth was, he could play Olivia or Viola if he had to.

Still, even with all that knowledge, he didn't have the experience to understudy the role. He could hardly count his performance as a shepherd in a nativity play at Saint Rita's when he was a boy or his stint as an animal-sound maker in a radio play at WPEN when he was a teenager as theatrical experience. Nicky was about to be in the glare of the spotlight, his skills, however meager, on the line. He had to act the part of Sebastian, but his body was in revolt. He was a tunic full of nerves. His knees began to shake so violently that when he looked down, he could not see his feet, just waves of wool where his joints shook under the costume. His throat closed, his mouth went dry, and his left eyelid began to twitch like a Morse Code key. Calla had shoved him onstage into the dark, and for the first time since he was a boy, he felt unmoored, abandoned, and frightened, his definition of what it meant to be an orphan.

Sebastian had the first speech of the scene in Olivia's garden, so there was no way to ease into this job. Nicky had to grab the role by the neck and throttle it, squeezing any meaning he could out of what he did not yet understand.

With nothing to lose, he reached deep into his own well of memory and thought of how he felt one night in France, in the town of Tours during the war, when he and two of his fellow infantrymen, separated from their platoon, couldn't find their way out of the woods. He remembered looking up into the black night sky and finding a slice of white light in a shard of a quarter moon. Taking it as a sign, he followed it, trusting it was the path to safety.

In this moment, Nicky stood in different darkness, this time on the stage, but just as he had claimed the ground beneath him as his own in the forest that night, he planted himself on the stage floor with all the confidence he could muster. There was something in the physical act of raising his eyes upward to the heavens as he had that night that motivated him. He allowed his body to hold him up, to lead his spirit. His spine fell straight and caused his shoulders to square, opening his chest, which expanded his lungs, which provided the oxygen to give him the breath to fuel his racing heart.

The stage lights pulled on slowly.

Peachy, thumbing through the program in her seat, looked up. She spotted Nicky onstage, but at first she didn't trust her eyes, having left her glasses in her desk at the office. But she would have known the shape of her fiancé's head and the line of his lean physique anywhere. She squinted, bewildered; she confirmed it! It was Nicky! She couldn't imagine her future husband getting up and talking in front of a small group, let alone a large audience. He hadn't exhibited the nerve. What was he doing up there?

Nicky stood in position, heard the rapture of chimes, followed by the fluttering of newspaper, which the crew used offstage to imitate the flapping of bird wings in the garden.

Nicky looked out into the theater. Light from the stage spilled out into the house and onto the audience. From Nicky's perspective onstage, the dark pit of seats ruffled by the gray ripple of heads in shadow resembled a turbulent night sky. A few patrons wore eyeglasses. Their lenses caught the stage lights like small mirrors, giving the illusion of the occasional sparkle of a star peeking through the dark.

"This is the air, that is the glorious sun," Nicky began, as he turned and looked up to the grid of lighting instruments attached to the balcony in a cluster of black metal boxes, bulbs, and wires.

The theatrical sun pulled on in a special spotlight, covered in a gel the color of the pulp of a pink grapefruit. The circle of light was resplendent as it illuminated Nicky before falling into a filmy shadow.

A woman in the audience sighed at the beauty of the tableau, a sound that motivated Nicky to press on, so he directed the line that followed in her direction. "This pearl she gave me, I do feel 't and see 't; And though 'tis wonder that enwraps me thus, Yet 'tis not madness. Where's Antonio, then?"

"Right here, buddy," he heard Hambone whisper from backstage. Nicky resumed the speech with confidence.

> *I could not find him at the Elephant;*
> *Yet there he was; and there I found this credit,*
> *That he did range the town to seek me out.*

Nicky flailed his arms, caught himself, and pulled in his performance before it went straight to Hamville. He lowered his voice to a whiskey timber and continued.

> *His counsel now might do me golden service;*
> *For though my soul disputes well with my sense*
> *That this may be some error, but no madness,*
> *Yet doth this accident and flood of fortune*
> *So far exceed all instance, all discourse,*
> *That I am ready to distrust mine eyes*
> *And wrangle with my reason, that persuades me*
> *To any other trust but that I am mad.*

Nicky slowed the cadence of his delivery and stepped forward, engaging the audience.

> *Or else the lady's mad; yet if 'twere so,*
> *She could not sway her house, command her followers,*
> *Take and give back affairs and their dispatch*
> *With such a smooth, discreet and stable bearing*
> *As I perceive she does; there's something in 't*
> *That is deceivable. But here comes the lady.*

Nicky turned upstage. Calla playing Olivia emerged from behind the flat, followed by Enzo, playing the priest. In the haze of pink light, her skin glistened, her cheeks dewy. The gown of soft coral velvet took on a silvery patina, as though she'd emerged from the sea.

As she moved toward Nicky, opening her hands, imploring him, a thick lock of her hair fell forward into her eyes, as naturally as it might in life. When she reached Nicky, he instinctively brushed the hair away.

The intimate gesture caught her off guard. She blushed, or maybe she burned with rage. Nicky couldn't tell. It didn't matter. He was in the moment.

The audience was still, except for Peachy, whose coat rustled underneath her as she shifted and craned to see what was happening between her fiancé and the strange princess with the uncombed hair in the big dress. Two deep furrows like matchsticks formed between Peachy's eyebrows as she observed the sparks between Nicky, wearing a bulky mustard-colored tunic and shrunken pants, and the woman with the kooky haircut. Where in Shakespeare's England did anyone have that kind of hair? In an instant, what Peachy had assumed to be a surprise from her fiancé turned into something else entirely. Was this a setup to tell her something he couldn't say in person? Was Nicky breaking up with her and this was his artful way of giving her the brush-off? Peachy began to perspire. She fanned herself with the program.

Enzo stepped back as Calla took a step forward. Calla remembered her blocking well, but now that she was center stage, she realized she should be farther downstage for the speech. Her thoughts were tumbling over one another. Why was Nicky looking at her so intently? Why was Enzo slightly nodding, as if to prod her? She began to speak.

Blame not this haste of mine. If you mean well,
Now go with me and with this holy man
Into the chantry by: there, before him,
And underneath that consecrated roof,
Plight me the full assurance of your faith;
That my most jealous and too doubtful soul

Peachy coughed at the mention of jealousy and doubt. The patron sitting in front of her turned around and glared at her as
Calla pressed on, repeating the line:

That my most jealous and too doubtful soul
May live at peace. He shall conceal it
Whilst you are willing it shall come to note,
What time we will our celebration keep
According to my birth. What do you say?

Nicky looked at her. He turned away and took a few steps as if
to distance himself from the decision, but then returned to Calla's
side. "I'll follow this good man, and go with you . . ." he announced.
    There was a collective sigh in the audience looking forward to
a happy ending.
    Nicky, squeezing the moment dry like a sponge in the rinse
bucket at the garage when he washed the cars, looked down at
his hands, almost as a reflex, and in so doing, realized they were
empty, therefore Sebastian knew he had nothing to offer Olivia, so using all his breath, and all the emotional power he could
summon, he delivered the line that offered the greatest gift a man
could give a woman, the promise of a faithful heart.
    ". . . And, having sworn truth, ever will be true."
    The diehard Shakespeare fan sitting in front of Peachy applauded
with one clap as the rest of the audience cooed.
    Enzo had thought the scene was dying, but now he knew from

the reaction that it was very much alive. Calla's eyes filled with tears, but Nicky wasn't sure if they were from relief that the play had been saved, or the emotions of the scene that had been conjured with authenticity. Whatever the truth, Calla couldn't look at Nicky, nor at Enzo. Out of the corner of his eye, Nicky could see Josie in the wings trying to feed Calla her next line. But their director was lost.

Enzo twirled in front of them in his cassock with his back to the audience, prompted her, whispering her line, "Then lead the way . . ."

A look of recognition crossed Calla's face. She took Nicky's hand and said to Enzo, "Then lead the way, good father, and Heavens so shine, That they may fairly note this act of mine."

Calla and Nicky exited hand in hand stage left. When they reached the dark pool of the wings, Calla released his hand and went to the prop table.

"Good work, Nick," Tony said before he rushed onstage for placement in the blackout between scenes.

Nicky was tingling from head to toe, and it wasn't from the pilling of cheap wool of the tunic. He was enraptured, electrified from within. Nicky had a sense of being in his body, but he wasn't; for the first time in his life, he felt his spirit take precedence over his physical state. He brought himself back into the present by gripping the lectern, afraid that if he didn't hold on to something, he would float away. The play continued onstage but Nicky was numb to it.

Norma pushed past him to enter the scene, followed by Josie, who mumbled something, but he did not hear them. His senses were shot. It was as if he were underwater, and they spoke to him from the surface. All Nicky heard was the movement of his own blood in his body; every nerve ending pulsed.

Calla said something to him and he nodded, agreed to it, whatever it was. She rushed behind the scrim, on her way to her Act 5 entrance.

In the wings, the fanfare of the finale and curtain call chaos erupted as props were grabbed, wigs yanked, girdles snapped, cigarettes were extinguished, and actors rushed past and into place. Onstage, the errant set piece was rolled into proper position before the final scene—and while Nicky observed the action, he was somewhere else entirely, in another place and time, in the chancery of a good priest by the side of his true love, as Sebastian in *Twelfth Night,* in a state he would know as bliss.

Nicky splashed water on his face at the sink in the men's dressing room.

"That was some scene," Hambone commented as he hung his costume on the rolling rack.

"Thanks." Nicky fixed his tie, smoothed his hair, and checked his teeth.

"You weren't scared to death?"

"At first, terrified."

"Acting is like kissing a girl for the first time. The idea of attempting it panics you, but once you do it, you never want to stop."

"Very astute of you." Nicky pulled on his jacket. It would take him a long time to try to explain to Peachy what he was feeling. He felt deeply content. At long last he owned the quiet confidence that comes from mastering a challenge after taking a risk.

Peachy was waiting for him outside the dressing room in the hallway. She leaned against the wall like a wilted daisy until she saw Nicky and revived. "Wow!" Peachy threw her arms around him and kissed him. "Wow. Wow."

"I was a last-minute replacement."

"It took me until the end of the play to get it. There was another guy in your part in the beginning, and then you were there and the pants were definitely not made for you. On you they were medieval clam diggers." Peachy was talking fast, which either meant she was nervous, uncomfortable, or horrified.

"There wasn't any time to find a costume that fit."

"The slacks were fine. No one noticed. I think it's sweet that you came up with a way to surprise me after seven years together. Some girls get a bouquet of flowers, or a box of candy, but who wants that stuff from her fiancé; one dies and the other gets eaten which means neither of them lasts. But me? I got something to hang on to. I got a memory. I got a wedding scene in an actual play by William Shakespeare performed by my future husband. Who gets that?"

Before Nicky could explain his role, Calla emerged from the women's dressing room, pulling on short white gloves to go with her dress.

"You're the actress." Peachy turned to Nicky and pointed at him, then at Calla, and back at Nicky again. "From your scene."

Nicky stepped forward. "Calla, I'd like you to meet my fiancée, Peachy DePino."

"We had a little crisis, and Nicky and I had to fill in. But I'm actually the director of the play." Calla smiled at Peachy warmly.

Peachy and Nicky felt awkward with Calla for different reasons.

"Calla takes care of her dad," Nicky blurted. "Sam Borelli. This is his theater. Or was. When he ran it."

"That's nice." Peachy's mind was elsewhere. She began to hatch scenarios of Calla—such a strange name—with Nicky onstage, beyond the footlights. She couldn't tell in the big dress, but now she could see that Calla had a nice shape. Her nose wasn't too long, and she had soft brown eyes. No myopia. If Peachy saw her in Wanamaker's going through the racks, she'd think Calla Borelli was a beauty. Peachy felt her gut churn with envy.

"Calla!" Frank Arrigo walked down the hallway towards them, almost filling it with the span of his broad shoulders and height. Frank was a robust Italian, in the pugilistic bent. He had the look of the hardworking men of the heel of the boot of Italy. His small nose had been broken a couple of times, but he had a winning smile and a gregarious manner, and there was, of course, the attractive element of his height. In any nationality, that was a plus.

"You were a knockout," Frank said, kissing Calla on the cheek. "I guess you have to be able to act if you direct."

"Only in an emergency. And tonight was an emergency. Right, Nicky?"

"Strictly a five-alarm theatrical situation," Nicky agreed. "The show must go on."

"Whether the pants fit or not," Peachy joked.

No one laughed, so Peachy covered with a low whistle.

"I thought you were going for Elizabethan knickers," Frank offered.

"No, they were supposed to hit my ankle."

"Well, they didn't and it doesn't matter now because you did such a swell job no one was looking below the tunic." Peachy clapped her hands together. Relieved that Nicky and she were almost free of this stilted small talk, in this strange situation she had been forced into, unannounced and without explanation, she unsnapped her purse, reached in for a handkerchief, and delicately dabbed the perspiration off her face. "And what do you do, Frank?"

"I'm a contractor."

"But he wants to be mayor of Philly someday," Calla added.

"Years from now. You know, when I learn every pipe and joint and grid in the city."

"Have you mastered the plumbing in Bella Vista yet? We have a problem over on Montrose you need to address," Nicky complained. "They've been digging trenches for months. And we've had some backup in the basement. I should know. That's where my room is. Maybe you can come over and do some pumping."

Calla laughed. "He's not a plumber."

"But he probably has a snake. You have a snake, Frank?"

"Sure."

Nicky looked at Calla. "See? He has a snake."

"We get it. He has a snake." Peachy pinched Nicky to get him off the subject. Nicky had no instincts when it came to knowing the difference between important people and regular people, and what's appropriate to say to one group as opposed to the other. Frank Arrigo obviously was on his way to being important, but Nicky would be the last person to figure that out. It was one of the little things about her fiancé that annoyed her, but Peachy was confident she could fix his poor social instincts after the wedding.

Nicky was sizing up Frank Arrigo, like an older brother might have if Calla had one. Frank seemed all right. Calla's feelings toward Frank, however, were hard to read, and Nicky wondered if she knew something he didn't.

Frank Arrigo sat on the worktable in the costume shop at Borelli's as Calla prepped and organized a few pieces for the next day's performance. Frank fiddled with the dial on the freestanding radio until he found a clear station playing Perry Como.

The costume shop was a large room in the basement of the theater, as much a museum of memorabilia of past shows as it was a factory for the important work of the designer and her crew.

A large flat table surrounded by metal stools took up the center of the room. There was a bin with large bolts of plain beige muslin, next to another filled with bolts of cotton cloth in shades of turquoise, yellow, orange, and deepest blue. Shelves were stacked with sheaths of fabric remnants, and boxes marked buttons, zippers, and thread. The walls were decorated with photographs of actors in all manner of Elizabethan costumes.

A floor-to-ceiling corkboard held the sketches of the costume designs for the current production. Next to the sketches, Bonnie had posted a list of the stock pieces from the inventory closet including gowns, tunics, cassocks, skirts, and knickers used in *Twelfth Night.*

A large round clock with a constant tick hung over a three-way mirror and standing stool. There were clocks in every workroom in the theater to encourage the crew to press through to hit their deadlines, or perhaps because a wealthy patron had died and left all her clocks to Borelli's, and Sam's philosophy was anything donated was used.

Frank picked up a cloth tomato stuffed with fitting pins and examined it. "Do you do everything around here?"

"Sometimes I have to. Don't get me wrong, I have a lot of help. But things have changed. We used to have big crews, but not anymore." Calla turned a velvet tunic inside out and placed it on the worktable, smoothing it flat. She misted it with a solution before hanging, tagging, and placing it on a rack marked "Chorus."

"Do you do this every night?"

"Once a week. The actors are great about taking care of their costumes. But we can't afford to send them out to be dry-cleaned until the end of a run, so we maintain them ourselves." Calla shook the glass bottle with a mister nozzle on the end. "Vodka."

"Usually on a date, the vodka's in the lady's cocktail I've bought her. She isn't spraying it on costumes."

Calla laughed. "Sorry, Frank. Welcome to the theater. This is an old trick my mom taught me." Calla turned Viola's finale costume, a sumptuous purple silk taffeta gown with a train and gold Edwardian braiding, inside out. She gently laid the garment on the table. "This costume has been used in our shows for as long as I can remember. Every leading lady has worn it. Every Luciana and Desdemona and Ophelia. We change the trim or add a different collar or a new sleeve. The audience is never the wiser." Calla carefully misted the lining without making the fabric too damp.

"You know I don't know anything about theater."

"Would you like to learn?"

"Do I have to?"

Calla laughed. "That's honest."

"But I am interested in you."

Calla blushed. "How could you be interested in me and not what I do?"

"Do you like cleaning septic tanks?"

"No."

"And I wouldn't expect you to—but it's part of my job."

"Fair enough."

"We have enough in common to keep us interested in one another."

"You think so?"

"I'm sure of it. See, you have exactly three freckles on your perfect nose." Frank jumped off the table and, catching Calla off guard, swept her into his arms. "My folks fell in love at the Saint Donato Dance in 1917 before my dad went to fight in the Great War. Do you dance?"

Before Calla could answer, Frank spun her around the costume shop, accidentally stepping on her toes.

"Was that lead foot mine or yours?"

"It's your fault. You were leading."

"I was not!"

"It couldn't have been me. I took lessons," Frank said proudly.

"You should ask for your money back."

"No refunds."

"That's unfortunate for your bank account and my feet." Calla curtsied and went back to working on the costume.

"How old are you, Calla?"

"Twenty-four. How old are you?"

"Thirty-three."

Calla whistled.

"Too old for you?"

"No. That's the age my dad was when he took over the theater."

"And he retired from here?"

"He worked here all his life."

"How did it make it?"

"There were times when we didn't have a lot. A flop can set a family back. But Dad would figure out how to turn it around. Usually it involved mounting a comedy."

"People like to laugh."

"They do. And they used to go to the theater."

"I just bought a television set."

"Really?" Calla was intrigued. "What's it like?"

"I'll have to show you sometime. It's fascinating. Now, maybe that's because it's a new gizmo. But you can see Martin and Lewis and all sorts of entertainers that you'd have to wait to see in a club or in the movies—but now you can sit at home and see them. I'm thinking it could take off."

"I was hoping it would fail."

"So your business would pick up?"

"So the world wouldn't change so fast."

"What's wrong with change?"

Calla shrugged. "What's wrong with holding on to a ritual that's been around as long as people? There's something sacred about an audience coming to see actors tell a story. It used to be enough just to tell the story well. But audiences want more. I wish I knew how to bring audiences in to see the shows. I think if they saw one, they'd want to come all the time."

"Maybe the theater is too old-fashioned," Frank suggested.

"Maybe the theater is just fine but people would rather stay home and watch their television set."

Frank leaned across the worktable closer to her. "Or maybe people are idiots and don't appreciate quality when it's offered to them."

"I think you just said that because you want to kiss me."

"No. I would just kiss you because life could not go on if I didn't."

"You should definitely run for mayor. You know how to play to the bleachers."

Frank came around the end of the table and stood next to Calla. He folded his arms, mirroring hers as she looked at the rack of costumes. "I would only kiss you if you wanted me to."

She turned to face him and smiled. "I'd like that."

Frank kissed Calla tenderly.

"Are you hungry?" he asked her.

"Always."

"Me too. But where does it go on you?"

"I leave it on the stairs between the mezzanine and the basement. If I had one wish . . ."

"Yeah?" Frank said, hoping she was thinking of him.

"I'd put in a lift. A platform elevator."

"Okay." Frank nodded.

"I saw a lift at the Philadelphia Opera Company, and I don't like to think I'm an envious person, but it made me feel that way. I do a lot of hauling around here." Calla returned the vodka bottle to its hiding place in the cubby of the Singer sewing machine. If she left it out, Hambone Mason would help himself to an intermission cocktail, not just a misting. She turned off the lights in the shop. "Where are we going?" she asked.

"I thought we'd go for a drive."

"I have my car."

"We'll drop yours at home and take mine. Then we'll go to Palumbo's for a late supper. Sound good?"

Calla liked that Frank was decisive; she spent her days and nights at the theater making decisions about everything from lighting to costumes to sound to how to remove gum from the lobby floor. It was nice for a fellow to make a plan, and it was even better when she knew in advance that he was a good kisser. Frank Arrigo had potential.

Nicky balanced Peachy on the handlebars of his bicycle across South Ninth Street. Peachy held on to her hat with one hand while gripping the bar with the other as Nicky navigated through the traffic.

When they reached Pat's Steaks, he gently braked to a stop. Peachy jumped off and waited as Nicky leaned the bike against a table. He put his arm around her as they got in line to order their sandwiches.

"I saw you make a friend in the audience."

"Yeah. Very nice lady. Works at Wanamaker's too."

"In accounting?

"Nope. She's in sales. She gave me her card. Never saw her before, but get this. She's in Bridal Registry. Is that fate or what? I figured we could go and see her together."

"Anytime you want."

"Well, you can't really make an appointment until you have a wedding day, otherwise they just have a bunch of random people on file who may or may not actually ever marry which makes a lot of paperwork for the department without the benefit of sales. You need an actual guest list to register our china, English Chintz by Royal Albert—"

"Let me guess, it's pink."

"Naturally. Then there's our silverware, Williamsburg by Towle, and the rest of the stuff a young couple on the move needs, like an ice bucket and a cocktail shaker and lead glass beer steins. We need six. But I can't do anything until we know what we're doing."

"Peach. You know what you're doing," Nicky teased her.

"Everything hinges on the date."

"I understand." Nicky leaned into the window and ordered two cheesesteak sandwiches, hers without peppers, his with peppers, and both with mozzarella, and two bottles of cold birch beer.

"I was thinking October twenty-ninth for our wedding day," Peachy said gently.

"That's fine with me."

"It is?"

"I like the fall."

"It's cooler then, and the wedding party can wear velvet. Velvet is my favorite fabric."

"Whatever you want, Peachy."

"You know my mom. Her only request was that we marry at a time of year when sleeves are required."

"Really? That's her only request?" Nicky joked.

"Let her have some fun. God knows she's waited long enough."

"I went over and looked at the houses going up on Wharton," Nicky admitted.

"You did?"

"I think you'd like them a lot. Nice and new. Backyard with a lot of room. You know, for kids and cookouts. A strong wooden fence. You can paint it whatever color you want, or stain it—a wood finish, pine or mahogany. You could even grow morning glories on it. There's room enough for a cutting garden. Do you have a green thumb?"

"My tomatoes grow tomatoes," Peachy assured him.

"Good. And I bet we'd get good neighbors on the other sides."

"Probably newlyweds like us."

"Probably."

Peachy threw her arms around Nicky. "I'm so happy." Their order appeared in the window. He placed each cold soda bottle in one of his pockets and grabbed the bag of sandwiches. Peachy jumped back on the bike as Nicky pedaled across the bridge to the Fairmount Park and swerved through the Azalea Garden to the Fountain of the Sea Horses.

The Art Institute, a majestic white sandstone building with rows of large windows overlooking the gardens, was fully lit from within, throwing light on the green lawn.

"Hey, our bench is free," Peachy said, taking Nicky's arm. "That's a sign. This is the very spot where I said yes."

Nicky kissed her. "Everything is going our way."

"I hope so."

"Hey, it's true."

"I get these black feelings of doom sometimes. I don't know where they come from—they just move in. You know?" Peachy picked a loose thread off her skirt.

"Well, get rid of them."

"Not so easy. I worry about us. You're a flirt."

"What are you talking about? You're my girl."

"I know. I got the ring to prove it." She held up her hand and wiggled the ring finger fitted with her diamond. "But you, Mister, are very chummy with the girls."

"What girls?"

"That Stella Corelli."

"Calla Borelli."

"Yeah, her. There are some sparks there between the two of you."

"There are no sparks." Nicky was glad that Peachy wasn't a mind reader, because if she was, she would have just seen Calla Borelli dance across the front lobe of his brain in her underpants. He opened the soda bottles and handed one to his fiancée. He took a swig from the other. "No sparks."

"Better not be. My father was unfaithful to my mother once, and it left a scar."

"On her or on you?"

"Both of us."

"I'm true, Peachy. True to you."

"I have no evidence to the contrary. But don't test me. I did not come all this way to have you blow us up like a stick of dynamite in a sewer pipe."

"There will be no explosions. I had enough of those in France. But I hope you take comfort that your mother and father made it through their dilemma."

"Barely. No charges were filed, but it was close."

Nicky unbuttoned his collar, feeling the air cut off from his windpipe. "Charges?"

"My mother may appear demure—"

Nicky sipped his birch beer. The last word he would use to describe his future mother-in-law was *demure*; in fact, she wasn't *de* anything, not light, or airy, or even French. She was a pile driver.

Peachy continued, "But when you challenge my mother, she will fight you like a wild alligator. She will lie in the depths and then when you least expect it, she opens wide and chomps."

"What do you mean?" Nicky's voice squeaked.

"She found out where the woman my father was seeing lived, and she went for a little visit. When the woman opened the door, my mother took off her shoe and began to beat the woman about the head."

"My God."

"She didn't die."

"Thank goodness."

Peachy shrugged. "She almost lost an eye, though."

"What?"

"One of Ma's heels came close to the eye socket. Whacked her nose instead. It didn't break completely, but she got it good enough that the lady had to have it reset. That's when the cops showed up."

Nicky stood up. "Your mother has a police record?"

"She still votes." Peachy pulled the sandwiches out of the bag. "So the moral of that story is—"

"Don't open the door when your mother is holding a shoe?"

"You're funny. No. The moral is: Don't cross us."

"I have no intention." Nicky sat down.

"You know I'm looking into the Art Institute for our reception? Who needs the old catering halls? Let's be original! I love this fountain so much."

"I saw the original fountain in Rome, you know."

"You did?"

"During the war. At the end of it. Same artist made both of them—Bernini. But this one was given to the city by Mussolini."

"And we kept it?"

"It was gifted to Philly before the war. Nineteen twenty-eight. It's not the fountain's fault it was commissioned by a fascist. Besides, it wasn't from him, it was from the people of Italy. He happened to be in charge."

"I guess we had to accept the gift. That's where we come from, those are our people," Peachy said wistfully. "I wish we could go to Italy on our honeymoon."

"We're getting the house."

"And that's fine. I can't be greedy. Atlantic City will do for our honeymoon."

"How about Niagara Falls?"

"We'll freeze to death, but if that's your desire, we'll freeze together. I'm starving," Peachy said as she opened the bag of sandwiches. "You must be. You worked in the car all day."

"And then I pull double duty."

"So, did you get my ticket for free in exchange for helping out tonight?"

"Not exactly."

"They want you to come back another time?" Peachy tucked the cheese that had oozed out of her sandwich into the bread.

"Peachy, I've been working there for about three years."

"What do you mean, working?"

"I've had a second job at Borelli's since I came back from the war."

"All this time?"

"A couple nights a week. Sometimes more. "

"Why didn't you tell me?"

"I don't know. I was a prompter, mostly. I didn't know how to explain what I did. I feed the actors their lines from offstage when they forget them. It didn't seem like something I could explain."

"Three years is a long time not to explain where you go and what you're doing and that you've taken on a second job. That's not a hobby. That's a commitment. It's almost like a career. How did you get the job?"

"I wasn't looking for it. Aunt Jo gave me a ticket to see a play one night when I got back. The sodality had a group going, and she wasn't up to it, so I went in her place. They performed *As You Like It*. I had never seen a Shakespeare play, but I liked it right away."

"A show can do that to a person. When I saw my first ice show in Atlantic City, it was as if the world changed. Gretchen Merrill in person on skates! The figure eights! The jumps! The rink. The music. The costumes. All that handwork and beading and ermine fur." Peachy's eyes sparkled like sequins just thinking about it.

Nicky was encouraged that Peachy understood how he felt. "Yeah, those are important. That's called spectacle. And then there's the words."

"There aren't words in an ice show."

"Right. But in Shakespeare, it's all about the words. And they spoke to me. The words seemed familiar. The story held my attention. I felt I knew it. "

"Maybe you studied the play in school."

"No, we read *Romeo and Juliet*, and that was it. Anyhow, I stuck around afterward and one thing led to another, and I could see they needed help, so old man Borelli gave me a job. I started out in the box office, and then I worked my way up to the crew—"

"Worked your way up?"

"Yeah. There's a pecking order in the theater."

"There's a pecking order in everything, Nicky. It's the way the world in general works. But you have to be in line in the first place to be promoted."

"I understand that. Then I became a prompter."

"Okay. Whoa. Hold on. You're going to Borelli's a couple nights a week, and you're working your way up in the company, and you forgot to tell your fiancée?"

"I'm telling you now. But, I think it's important to have things that are just for myself. I hope you have that."

"I don't. You know everything."

"Oh, okay."

"I mean, nothing I can think of."

"You never asked me where I went."

"I figured you were working an extra shift in the cab."

"But you called the garage, and I wasn't there. It happened a lot."

"I didn't leave a message on purpose."

"Where did you think I was?"

"I thought maybe you were gambling with your cousin Gio."

"Why wouldn't you ask me if I gambled?"

"I don't like bad news," Peachy said, then bit into her sandwich.

"So what did you think of the play?"

"It was cute. I still don't understand how you wound up in it."

"Peter Menecola, one of our actors, had to leave the theater, and we don't have a budget for understudies. Well, what usually happens is we have a guy named Enzo who understudies all the parts, but he was already in the scene, filling in for Paulie."

"Why did you have to do the love scene?"

"There was no one else to do it."

"And nobody but Calla to do the lover part?"

"Nobody."

"She was pretty good," Peachy admitted. "She cried. I would think crying is the hardest of all."

"I agree!" Nicky didn't know much about acting technique, except what he had observed onstage and picked up in rehearsals directed by Sam and now Calla, but he knew you had to be pretty good to weep.

"Honestly, Nick? A lot of the play went right over my head. The whole thing was very murky to me."

"It can be confusing," Nicky admitted. "I understand why you might get lost. The same actors play two or three different roles in the play, who's a man in one scene becomes a woman in the next, who's a woman dresses like a man, it goes back and forth." Nicky gave up trying to explain the plot of *Twelfth Night*. He would, however have liked to talk to her about his accidental role in it. He would have liked to share how panicked he was when he was yanked from his position on the crew as prompter from behind the podium and pushed into the play. Nicky would have liked to share what a thrill it was when the scene began and he felt a connection to the words and the other actors, but Peachy wasn't a fan of the theater. So what? They didn't agree on everything. She liked pink, he didn't. She liked white sauce, he liked red. The sound of Jeanette MacDonald's voice made his teeth ache, while Peachy could watch her movies four times in a row. They were different. Men and women were different, and that was that.

"This was a one-time occurrence, right?" Peachy said gingerly.

"That Enzo couldn't understudy? I don't know."

"What I'm asking, this is a thing where you do it once and then you're done?"

"There's nothing to worry about. I got fired tonight."

Peachy tried not to show how relieved she was that Nicky's theatrical career was over. "Fired?"

"Calla fired me. There's your proof that there are no sparks between us. I don't know how long the theater can stay open. It's struggling. We're not selling enough tickets."

"Well, it's all for the best, Nicky. You won't have a lot of time once we're married. We'll be fixing our house and planting a garden and taking trips."

Nicky put his head into his hands.

"Oh, Nick, I'm sorry. You liked working at Borelli's." Peachy patted Nicky on the back and rolled her eyes.

"I did."

"I understand about the pushing scenery and prompting the lines, but the acting part—" Peachy's voice caught. "Do you want to continue such a hobby?"

"I don't think I'm any good."

"From what I saw tonight, judging from the rest of the cast, that's not really a criterion for participation."

"Tony is a fine actor. I could never be as good as him."

"Well, not to compare, but who could tell? You only had one scene."

"I know." Nicky didn't want to admit that he'd felt a charge go through him that he had never known before. And after Peachy's reaction to the play, his second job, and his having been fired, he figured this wasn't the moment to share his epiphany.

Peachy shrugged. "You're better off. Borelli's is a fleabag joint. It's on its way out."

"It needs renovation." Nicky took a sip of his birch beer.

"It needs more than that. Nobody thinks to go there. Nobody says 'Let's go to Borelli's on a Saturday night.' No, they say 'Let's go see a movie.' Or 'Let's go see Louis Prima and Keely Smith at Sailor's Lake Pavilion,' or 'Let's go into New York and see a Broadway show and hit the Vesuvio after for a nightcap.' Nobody says 'Let's go see *Twelve Nights*.' "

"*Twelfth Night.*"

"Whatever it's called. It's attracting moths. It's like the hair my nonna used to collect in a ceramic dish with a lid—now we backcomb. We don't save our hair. Things go out of style or become redundant. Like Borelli's."

"It is old-fashioned. I guess."

"Whenever a man wears leotards, it's not au courant. It's of a time when people rode horses and wore suits of armor. In the program it said 'Carriage arrives at 9:20 p.m.' "

"That's just a tip of the hat to when the theater first opened. They used to put that on the box-office window so patrons would know when the show was over."

"Okay, Nick, anything that you have to explain in that kind of detail is out of style. It's for the history books no one reads because no one cares. We're young. We can't live in the past, in an attic full of dust and trunks and musty pantaloons. We belong to the here and the now. When we get married, we are all about the future, about a life together. About our own kids and our own house with new appliances in the kitchen. We're living on the cusp of 1950. Everything is new. It's even called new. Think about it. Even the dresses—they're calling them the New Look. We are going to *be* the 1950s!"

Peachy took Nicky's hands into her own. "Do you really want to hang around a place like that? We'll have a car and go places. We're modern! On the move! We'll drive into the city and go to clubs. New York—there's another *new* for you, the city—is an hour and twenty minutes through Jersey and over the bridge. It's nothing for us to go to a museum and get culture and have dinner at Sal Anthony's and dance at the Latin Quarter! We can see the world top to bottom once we're married. You can see all the plays you want. Good ones. With real actors like Ernest Borgnine. Not with guys that deliver A-Treat soda to the International Ladies' Garment Workers' Union Labor Day picnic in Twelfth Street Park. You know what I'm saying?"

Nicky nodded.

"I mean, it's nice that you have a place to go after work, that you have extracurricular activities you enjoy outside of the garage and me. My dad plays cards. My mother? She enjoys the sodality meetings at the church. It's camaraderie. And I can see where Borelli's is a social thing for you, with people you wouldn't normally run into at work or at church. I mean, I'm sure they have receptions and you meet people and make friends and have conversations about interesting topics. But it's not real life. It's make-believe—there's that guy who is an accountant by day and by night he's in your play in a sword fight wearing tights."

"Hambone?"

"Whatever. Or that lady with the bosoms playing come-hither to a guy that clearly doesn't want to hither."

"You mean Josie."

"It doesn't matter. It's not authentic."

"*Legitimate*, you mean."

"Not that."

"Legitimate theater means professional."

"Then that's what I mean. This is not professional."

"But it is. We sell tickets. We're paid."

"Okay. So people pay to see it—that doesn't mean it's good. It's the Borellis holding on to a family business that's obsolete, clutching an old dream like some poor slob hangs on to a frayed rope when he's dangling over a cliff. Eventually that rope will break and he will plummet to his death on sharp rocks that will rip him into hamburger. But if he holds on, what has he got? Rug burn on his hands. That's it. Borelli's is hanging on but it's not going to be around much longer. That building is about to be condemned."

"Did you hear something?"

"No, I just went to the ladies' room and my foot went through the linoleum when I washed my hands."

"You really didn't like the play, did you?"

"I don't want to go back there again, if that's what you're asking."

"Never?"

"Not if I have a choice."

Nicky bit into the sandwich and chewed slowly. The tender steak, warm cheese, and hot peppers were delicious, but he wasn't enjoying the flavors. He was thinking about the possibility of never going back to the Borelli Theater again, and what that might mean to him, what that would *do* to him. He could imagine a life where he never drove a cab again, but he couldn't imagine his life without Borelli's.

"Nick, you take so long to eat." Peachy had finished her sandwich and wiped her hands on the paper napkin. The camellia on her hat had slipped to the back of her head, and she looked like a little girl, all eyes, no chin, just longing and need in her face, with her head framed by a halo of pink organza. "Did I say something wrong?" she asked. "I went too far. Ma says I go too far and pile on. I piled on."

"No, of course not."

"I don't know, sometimes I can't say anything right." Her brown eyes filled like fish tanks. "I can't do anything right either."

"Come on. Don't cry, Peachy."

"All of a sudden I'm bereft."

"Why?"

"Like I'm not supposed to say what I'm feeling. Like I'm supposed to hold it in."

"I never want you to do that."

"Good. Because I can't. We've been together too long to start acting with each other."

"You're right."

"Plus it will give me a migraine. And I don't need that. I got enough to worry about." She extended both of her hands to him. Her purse dangled from her thin wrist. "Come on. I gotta go to work early tomorrow."

"Should we hop a bus? They let me take the bike onboard at night."

"Nah, the air is good for us." Peachy kissed Nicky lightly on the lips. "It's swell. It's fine. As long as we're together."

Nicky wrapped up the rest of his sandwich neatly and handed it to Peachy. She put it in her purse. He hopped on the bike and put up the kickstand. She slipped up onto the handlebars, and Nicky centered her between them. She gripped the handles, and as he began to pedal, he leaned forward and kissed the back of her neck.

Frank Arrigo drove slowly across the bridge because he wanted to make the evening with Calla last. She was just what he was looking for, a gutsy Italian girl from South Philly, younger than he but not silly. He loathed silly. She was pretty too, but not in the way that he'd be afraid to touch her. She didn't seem to care about her hair, she just let it blow around. He liked that he could just leave the top down on his convertible. He liked that she ate everything on her plate and drank wine. She didn't order drinks with paper umbrellas in them. If he had to bet, he'd guess that she drank beer when the weather was hot. Calla slid closer to him in the front seat and took his hand.

Nicky and Peachy sailed across the bridge on the walkway, two silhouettes in the dark as they passed Frank and Calla.

"Those poor souls on a bike," Frank commented.

"What's wrong with that?" Calla watched as the two figures turned off the bridge onto the river road.

"I don't know. They don't have a car." Frank patted the dashboard of his Pontiac Torpedo.

"I think it's romantic." Calla watched as the pair on the bicycle dissolved into the black night.

"You leave the romance to me." Frank picked up speed and turned on the radio.

As Nicky pedaled his fiancée on the road, a tiny sliver of the moon came out, enough to guide him along the river.

Peachy closed her eyes and let the cool night air whisk away any worries and cares she may have had and blow them out of reach.

There weren't a lot of girls in the world who would settle for a sandwich in the park and a bike ride home, but Peachy DePino would, and she did. In Nicky Castone's mind, that made her a keeper.

AB.C 0123

TELEGRAM

Office Date Stamp.

T.

C.

B.

The time received at this office is shown at the end of the message.

PLEASE TURN OVER.

Office of Origin.   No. of Words.   Time of Lodgment.   No.

TO: E. GUARDINFANTE
FROM: C. GUARDINFANTE
    10 MAGGIO, 1949
VAGGIO PIACEVOLE. PIÙ DALL AMERICA ALL' ARRIVO.

The MS *Vulcania* had been sailing across the Atlantic for five days when a handwritten invitation was slipped under Ambassador Carlo Guardinfante's cabin door in second class.

The pleasure of your company is requested this evening
For dinner and dancing
At 8:00 p.m. in the Grand Hall

Carlo's eyes widened.

We will be joined by Captain Jack Hodgins

He nodded, impressed.

Mr. and Mrs. Joseph (Isabel) Scacciaferro
Mr. and Mrs. Attila Mario Seltembrino (Dorena Fata) Castellani
and
Mrs. Patricia Zampieri

The ambassador's heart began to race. The Scacciaferros, the Castellanis, and the widow Zampieri were titans of American industry, importers of Italian marble with family ties to the quarries in Tuscany. They provided American contractors with exquisite Carrara marble for use in buildings, churches, and monuments. This invitation presented the kind of company that the ambassador had hoped to keep on the MS *Vulcania*.

His eyes fell on one last detail.

Formal dress required

Carlo would dazzle them in his regimentals. Elisabetta had seen to it.

3

Concetta DePino placed neat stacks of hot-pink tulle in front of each place setting on her dining room table. She anchored the squares with a box of Jordan almonds tied with a pink satin ribbon and a tag bearing the name of each of Peachy's bridal attendants and her aunt-in-law Jo Palazzini. Two work baskets, filled with craft scissors, rolls of pink ribbon, and additional boxes of Jordan almonds were placed at either end of the table.

The mother of the bride checked the centerpiece, a large, white honeycomb paper wedding bell that folded out in three dimensions, which she'd borrowed from her neighbor, Dolly Farino, who had a closet full of whimsical table decorations on hand for every occasion.

Dangling from the cut-crystal chandelier over the table was the wedding date: October 29, 1949, spelled out in cardboard letters and numbers dipped in silver glitter. If Concetta DePino could have hung those digits in pavé diamonds etched in gold bricks, she would have, as the single highest achievement of her career as a mother was the confirmation of the wedding date of her daughter and Nicholas Castone.

Only the Second World War and Nicky's procrastinating had

stood between her daughter and the altar celebrating the DePino/ Castone high nuptial mass, and now, the path was clear. In a few short months, Peachy would have her dream, the paperwork filed, and the gold band on her finger. Mr. and Mrs. Nicholas Castone would be recorded in the chancery for all eternity. Concetta was as ebullient as she was relieved.

Connie looked into the mirror hanging over the bar cart and examined her changing face. It was framed by her hair, dyed a soft apricot to cover the white. Her eyebrows remained black and thick from her youth, nicely contrasting with her brown eyes, but her lips needed something extra. Concetta had taken to using three shades of coral lipstick, from light to dark, blotting in between applications to plump up what nature had taken away. She pulled the clasp from the back of her pearls to the front so that the pavé diamonds threw light, which Concetta believed gave her a glow. She stepped back, turned sideways, and tilted her face to the mirror as she pulled in her stomach and threw back her shoulders. Since her sixty-fifth birthday, Concetta's shape had shifted from that of a violin to a duck. Her small waist had broadened; it was shot, loose like elastic found in old underpants. It would be a longline girdle for her for the rest of her life. She hummed a sigh of surrender. At least she still had the face.

Small tea sandwiches made from thin white American bread, filled with either pimento cheese and bacon bits or cream cheese and red caviar or a mixture of fig paste with whipped honey butter, were arranged on a ceramic platter on the dining table by flavor. On a tiered silver server, snowball wedding cookies iced in pink coconut were arranged alongside cutout sugar cookies shaped in the letters D and C, which Concetta had been horrified to realize were not only the initials of the surnames of the bride and groom but shorthand for a procedure she had at Allegheny Medical a few years earlier. Concetta quickly flipped the letters to C and D until the tier was in alphabetical order.

"Why the damn fuss, Connie?" Al DePino, her husband of forty-two years, stood in the doorway in his thick white undershorts. Not since Humpty Dumpty sat on his wall had a neck, chest, and waist been so seamlessly connected.

"Criminy, Al! Get dressed. The Palazzini women are on their way over."

"So?"

"I don't want to scare them."

"It's the DePinos who should be scared."

"Why should we be afraid?"

"Castone is not a man of conviction."

"Don't talk like that."

"I don't like him."

"Well, I do."

"He's a shifty orphan. Couldn't she have picked one of the boys with parents?"

"She likes the nephew. Okay? The oldest one was never going to go for Peachy. Gio? I don't want a gambler in the family. That's a curse you can never crawl out from under. Besides, that one went for the Irish girl anyway. And Nino has loved Lena Cortina since grade school. That leaves Nicky Castone."

"We only got to pick from one family in all of Philadelphia?" Al put his fingers together in the formation of two beaks and pecked his words for emphasis. "We can't choose from the tri-state area? We're limited by geography? We're like a potted plant that can only grow in certain climes. Who made up these rules?"

"Your daughter likes what she likes."

"You spoiled her, and this is the result."

"No, you moved us here against our will from Rhode Island when Peachy was getting traction with some very nice young men, and she had to start over and then there was the war and here we are."

"What does all that have to do with anything now?"

"There were more marriageable young men in North Providence. Look around. Philly is a dustbin."

"Your opinion. I like it here. At least we didn't wind up in the internment camp."

"That's because of me and my connections. Your people are a bunch of followers. The DePinos put their hands in the air and marched right into the coops. If it weren't for my family and Joe Peters and his quick thinking . . ."

"I am not going to kiss your cousin Joe's coolie for the rest of my life."

"It wouldn't kill you. He kept us out of the camps."

"I send him a bottle every Christmas, what more do you want from me?" Al scratched an itch on his rear end.

"Not near the food, Al!" Connie pushed her husband away from the dining room table. "Please behave yourself. I can handle your glares and grunts and gas, but other people aren't obligated. You look like you could kill someone with your black-eyed stare. It's off-putting. It's ill-mannered."

"I'm not changing to impress people. You didn't marry Serge Obolensky."

"No, I did not. But you could have a little class. Show a little effort. Some couth! If not for me, for your daughter." Concetta went around the dining room table and straightened the chairs and adjusted the place mats and napkins. "I don't understand you, Alessio."

"What's to understand? I love my kid," Al said, his eyes filling with tears. He grabbed a paper napkin.

"Not my party napkins!" Concetta fished into her dress and under her bra strap, producing a pressed handkerchief, and handed it to her husband, grabbing the paper napkin out of his hand.

"Always with the decorations." Al dabbed his eyes with her handkerchief.

"It's what women do." Concetta fanned the paper napkin next

to the cookie tier. "We get tired of looking at the same old thing, so we decorate. Now go upstairs and put on your pants. And would it kill you to put on a tie?"

"It would."

"Do it for Peachy."

"Do what for Peachy?" Peachy entered the dining room, wearing a pink wool skirt and a pale green sweater. She had placed a small pink velvet bow and a matching green one in her hair.

"Whatever you want!" Concetta took her daughter's face in her hands and kissed her forehead. She reached down to her daughter's skirt and pulled at the loose waistband. "You're too thin."

"I'm all right, Ma."

"You're my Peachy *Piccina*, Skinny Minnie, Fattie Boom-ba-lattie, I don't care about your size. You're getting married and I'm so happy for you."

"The only time I've ever seen your mother this happy is never." Al popped a coconut cookie into his mouth.

"Al. Stop poaching the refreshments. Your pants."

"I mean it, Peach," Al said, hiking up his briefs to cover his belly button. "This wedding is your mother's life."

"Peachy *is* my life. So what? She will have the most beautiful wedding South Philly has ever seen."

The doorbell rang, sending Concetta across the dining room, arms akimbo, to shove her husband out of it. "Pants, Al! Pants!"

Peachy laughed and slipped a C cookie from the tier on her way through the living room to the front door. She chewed and swallowed quickly before throwing the door open to greet her wedding party. "Aunt Jo!" Peachy embraced Nicky's aunt, standing in for the mother of the groom.

Jo Palazzini had a small, muscular build and a chic, cropped hairstyle that showed off her thick black hair streaked with white. "Ma!" Peachy called out. "The girls are here!"

Jo's daughters-in-law filed on to the porch carrying gifts. Peachy welcomed them inside as her mother emerged from the living room carrying a polished silver bowl, which she shook as she greeted the women. "Prizes! I've got prizes!"

"This is going to be fun!" Lena said and clapped her hands together. Still young and newly married, she couldn't get enough of wedding hoopla. Lena was Sicilian, petite, and shapely, with almond-shaped Cleopatra eyes.

"Where can I sit? I've got a varicose vein in my left leg that's throbbing like a sump pump clearing out a root cellar after a flash flood." Mabel was bloated that afternoon, her wedding ring lodged on her finger, more a tiny gold tourniquet than an article of jewelry.

"Elsa, you're simply regal," Concetta said as she took in Elsa's crisp linen day shift.

"Thank you."

"Very Mainbocher."

"I'm afraid not. My mother-in-law made this dress for me."

"How I wish I was handy with the needle and thread," Concetta lamented.

"But you do all right, Ma. You don't have to sew as long as I work at Wanamaker's. You get a discount at the store off the rack," Peachy reminded her.

"Hey, do we get the discount once we're family?" Mabel barked.

"I'll ask," Peachy said, clenching her molars.

"Follow me, girls." Concetta led them into the dining room.

Concetta had made place cards for the ladies. As they found their names and took their seats, the Palazzini women fussed and commented about the lovely decorations and bridal spread.

Peachy took the seat of honor at the head of the table. Concetta poured tea as the ladies filled their plates.

Mabel didn't bother to use her plate as a way station between the cookie tier and her mouth, she simply popped the coconut snow-

balls like pep pills. "These are delicious," she said through a mouth-
ful of icing. "I have such a sweet tooth now that I'm expecting."

"I'm sure the weight will come right off after the baby," Concetta assured her.

"It doesn't matter if I get as big as a coal truck," Mabel articu-
lated through her second cookie. "I can't be in the wedding anyway in my condition."

"Can you keep the bride's book?" Peachy asked Mabel.

"Sure. Why not?" Mabel replied less than enthusiastically. "His-
torically that's what they do with the fat girls. They give them the
recording secretary position behind a table, practically out of the
public eye. It makes sense. In the official wedding album, you never
see their bodies, because they're sitting collecting signatures. You
just see their floating heads."

"Noooo!" Peachy, Jo, and Concetta cried.

"You don't want to flaunt the fatties. Trust me. I remember when my shape opened doors and when the same ones got
slammed in my face when I put on a couple of pounds. Just show
me where the book and pen are, and I'll get every signature in the
hall." Mabel sampled the caviar tea sandwich. "I'm switching to
savory, if that's all right."

"Fine, fine." Concetta began to worry whether she had made
enough food.

"What are we wearing?" Lena was unable to contain her enthusiasm.

"Pink," Peachy said definitively. "Ma, what color are you wearing?"

"Chartreuse silk with leaf-green piping. It's a dress-and-coat
ensemble."

"Aunt Jo?"

"You tell me."

"I thought yellow would be nice," Peachy suggested.

"Fine." Jo hated yellow, but she would do whatever her nephew's bride wanted.

"What dress did you pick out for us?" Lena relished being a bridesmaid. It was a job with a uniform.

"It's in the bridal shop at Wanamaker's. It's a Susan Poster design. Scrumptious! It's pink velvet, full circle skirt, square neckline. On your heads, a calot hat in matching pink with pink seed pearls."

"That's a lot of pink." Mabel helped herself to another sandwich. "You girls are gonna look like a box of candy cigars."

"Do you have a problem with pink?" Peachy asked Mabel.

"Not at all. I don't have to wear it. I can wear hedgehog brown, for all anyone cares. I'm just keeping the book."

"Pink is lovely," Jo said with a smile, defusing the situation.

Lena nodded. "You've thought this through."

"Since she was seven years old," Concetta said proudly.

"I was hoping you could do the altar flowers." Peachy looked at Elsa. "Father says no one does a more beautiful job with the flowers than you."

"I will be happy to." Elsa patted Peachy's hand to reassure her. "Thank you."

"I don't get a thank-you in advance for keeping the book?" Mabel asked, reaching for the cream for her tea. "You know I'll completely miss the cocktail hour waiting around for the latecomers and stragglers and men who couldn't find parking. No Swedish meatballs for me."

"Thank you for your sacrifice, Mabel," Peachy said tersely.

"Elsa has a way with flower arranging—better than the florist. Our garden has never looked better." Aunt Jo smiled at Elsa. "And the May crowns were lovely."

"What are you wearing, Peachy?" Mabel asked.

"Well . . ." Peachy placed her hands on the table and closed her eyes, conjuring the image of her glorious gown on the most important day of her life. "Duchesse satin. Illusion sleeve . . ."

"I love an illusion sleeve," Concetta said wistfully. "My side of the family has arms less than Greek, which Peachy did not inherit so she can show a little flesh."

"Most of those ancient statues don't have hands. You're lucky to have an arm at all. Forget two of them." Mabel reached across the table for a handful of bridge mix.

"You wouldn't want ours," Concetta assured her. "We have the flap up top and elbows like walnuts."

"That's why God invented the bishop sleeve," Jo commented.

Peachy continued, "Illusion lace over a sweetheart neckline, pointed cuff, buttons up the back, seventy-seven cut glass Venetian buttons—"

"We'll have to get a third-grader in here to button her into the dress. We need tiny fingers and hands. The buttons are minuscule!" Concetta said with delight.

"Tiara, lace veil . . . Mr. Da Ponte is creating the veil from lace—"

"That's been in the family since Torre del Greco," Concetta confirmed.

"And a train." Peachy stood up and modeled the imaginary train. "Like a princess of an Italian province, I will wear a train that will extend from the first pew to the last, just yards and yards of cut Italian lace, I don't know how many centuries old, worn by every bride in the Cuccamorsina family since the first girl was born."

"And one day your daughter will wear it, too," Aunt Jo commented.

"Of course. We are traditional," Peachy promised.

"And evidently excellent at avoiding silkworm and moth problems. Old lace is candy to bugs." Mabel cut a slab of coffee cake from the ring. "My grandmother's gown was eaten by boll weevils during the potato famine."

"That's too bad." Peachy cut her mother a look.

"Your dress sounds beautiful. We'll be sure to come over and help you dress the morning of the wedding," Lena said supportively.

"You will?"

"Absolutely." The Palazzini wives all nodded.

"With that train, you'll need the help." Lena smiled.

Peachy's eyes filled with tears. "I'm an only child and I wanted sisters all my life, and now I have them. I can't believe I've waited seven years for this day. I'll plan plenty of time to dress."

"You might want to start now. With that train, those buttons, and that veil, you'll need a fleet of Carmelites to put you together. I hear they farm out the postulates for a donation." Mabel cut a forkful of coffee cake and ate it.

Concetta clapped her hands. "I thought it would be fun to assemble some confetti bags. At each of your place settings are the tulle squares, the ribbons, and the Jordan almonds."

"My father broke a molar on the Jordan almonds at my wedding. Bit down. Howled in pain. They should come with a warning," Mabel commented.

The ladies filled the tulle with the almonds. Elsa tied a ribbon around the netting, making the pouch.

"Who is doing the dolls for the cars?" Lena asked. "It's my favorite wedding tradition in South Philly. I love to come out of the church and see the cars decorated for the wedding party with dolls dressed like the bridesmaids, and then of course, the doll dressed as the bride on the limousine. You'll have to be careful with your replica, though—that long train could flap in the breeze and blind the driver."

"Mabel, I was hoping you could make the dolls. The ones you created for your wedding were so pretty."

"Yeah. I can do them. How many cars?"

"Twelve."

"But you only have two girls in the wedding party."

"The family is coming from Canada," Peachy explained.

"Nooo. Out-of-town guests don't get dolls. You'll start a trend that will never be reversed. Dolls on the hoods of wedding party only."

"I thought it would be nice. Something special. Something different. They're coming from so far away."

"Why don't we just put dolls on all the cars? Including the ones for sale at Dotta's car dealership, while I'm at it?" Mabel complained.

"They wouldn't be special then."

"Exactly. They're not going to be very special when you see twelve pink dolls driving by on various hoods hauling a bunch of Canadians around."

Peachy looked as though she might cry.

"Just do the dolls," Jo said quietly to Mabel.

"We thought we'd have the bridal shower at Tarello's—" Lena began.

"Why Tarello's?" Concetta asked nervously.

"They have the nice garden in the back."

"Daddy choked on the squid there," Peachy blurted.

"But the shower is women only. Your dad won't be coming," Lena reminded her.

"How about Victor's Café?" Mabel suggested.

"I suppose," Peachy mused.

"Well, why don't you pick? Think about it." Lena forced a smile.

"I had mine at Echo Lake. Vacation Valley Inn," Mabel offered.

"The Poconos? That's a long drive." Concetta put her foot down.

"Not as long as it's going to take me to dress a fleet of dolls." Mabel sighed.

Elsa took the wheel of the sedan parked in front of the DePino home. Mabel sat next to her in the front seat. Lena gave a final wave to Peachy and her parents from the sidewalk before climbing into the back seat with Aunt Jo.

Elsa started the car and pulled out onto the street. After a few moments, Lena said, "Poor Nicky."

"They're all right," Aunt Jo said optimistically. "Peachy knows what she likes. Concetta is eager, and she's a hard worker. It will be fine."

"If you say so." Mabel sighed.

Lena searched for something positive to say. "They are very thorough and organized. I'm scared of Mr. DePino, though. He's a black bowling ball."

"Stay out of his way," Mabel advised.

"And not one word about Nicky," Elsa sighed.

"Yeah, that's not good, but you won the tongs when we played guess the jelly beans," Mabel said.

"You won a prize, too," Lena commented.

"Forgive me if I don't get excited about a can of foot powder."

"You guessed how many chocolate-covered raisins there were in the bridge mix. That's a talent," Aunt Jo said.

"I actually had the time to count each one while Peachy went into detail about the food at the reception. So many courses! And the Venetian dessert table. How many cannoli stuffings are there, anyway?" Mabel removed a few flakes of pink coconut from her collar.

"All brides are nervous and want every detail to fall into place as they dreamed it. And she's waited a long time for this. So let's give her some room," Aunt Jo said evenly. "Let's say only nice things going forward, shall we, girls?"

The women rode in silence for a few moments. Then Mabel turned to them and said, "The cream cheese sandwiches were quite tasty."

Calla stood at the entrance of the Palazzini garage and looked around. "Hello?" she called out. When no one answered, she went inside, where the scent of motor oil and cigar smoke hung in the air. She looked down on the floor, where the numbers 1 through 4

were painted in red, indicating parking spots. She heard the soft staccato of a radio show filter down from the office, so she climbed the stairs.

Hortense was sitting at her desk, studying the Burpee seed catalog, when Calla knocked lightly on the open door.

"Excuse me. I'm looking for Nicky Castone."

"What for?" Hortense asked without looking up from the delphiniums.

"Business."

"What kind of business?" Hortense raised her head and peered at Calla over her reading glasses.

"Theatrical."

"You selling tickets? If you are, he's too old for the circus."

"No. Nicky works for me. Well, he did. I fired him. And now I need him back."

"You got the wrong Nicky."

"I'm pretty sure I've got the right one. He says he works here during the day. He's a hack. Drives Number 4. About six feet tall. Hair brown on the way to red. Blue eyes. Nice smile. Excellent teeth."

"Not as good as mine." Hortense forced a smile.

"You do have beautiful teeth."

"I know. Can't take any credit. I come from a long line of hard teeth. And, I brush with baking soda and salt every night faithfully. Mornings too."

"It's the old remedies that work best."

"Don't you forget it."

"My name is Calla Borelli," she said, extending her hand.

"Mrs. Mooney." Hortense shook her hand.

"At night Nicky works at my theater."

"He's an usher?"

"Prompter. But now he's an actor."

"He's in the shows?"

"He understudied a part, and now I need him. The actor that was playing the role is out for the rest of the run. His mother broke her hip."

"That's too bad. A broken hip is one slip away from the dirt nap."

"I've heard," Calla said sadly.

"What do you do?"

"I'm the director."

"A girl?"

"Yeah. It's a family business. Not that I need an excuse. Do I need an excuse?"

"No, no. Women work. Look at me. Dispatcher. Morse code operator. That's right. Western Union. But look around. Rosie the Riveter. She made Sherman tanks. You can do whatever you want. The war changed everything for women. Well, for you."

"I think so."

"You may want to leave him a note. He's on a job. It's a round robin. He's taking a fare to New York International." Hortense handed Calla a pad. She wrote down her information and handed it back.

"Borelli. I wonder if there's any Italians left in Italy. Do you think they all came to America?"

"I don't know. Lots of us did. I haven't been to Italy."

"It's an interesting question, though, isn't it?"

"It is." Calla felt scrutinized under Hortense's intense stare. "Is there something wrong? I feel like my slip is hanging or something."

"No, Miss Borelli, your slip is fine. I'm just looking at you. I do that with folks."

"It was nice to meet you, Mrs. Mooney." Calla forced an awkward smile and backed out of the office.

Hortense went to the window and watched Calla as she went down the steps and out of the garage.

⫷

Nicky drove through Ambler, a quiet suburb of Philadelphia, its winding streets paved with fresh macadam and lined with sycamore trees. The green lawns that hemmed the stone houses were more carpet than grass. He let out a low whistle, imagining the price tag of a home in this neighborhood.

He slowed down as he counted the house numbers until he found 17 Mackinaw Street, the home of Mr. and Mrs. Gary Allison. Hortense assigned the airport runs into New York International to Nicky, knowing that the tips were generous and he needed the extra money to save up for his honeymoon. She had done the same for his cousins when they were engaged to be married. Hortense was considerate that way.

Nicky confirmed the Allisons' address when he saw three tan suitcases lined up on the walkway of a Georgian home whose front door gaped open.

Nicky jumped out of the cab and was loading the luggage into the trunk when a petite blond woman waved urgently at him from the porch.

"Hurry!" she shouted.

Nicky ran up the front walk and into the house.

"There's something wrong with my husband," Mrs. Allison exclaimed. Around forty, she wore a navy blue suit and held her hat, a small cloche with a bold white band, in her hand. Her husband sat in a chair, holding his head in his hands.

"Sir?"

The man looked up at Nicky. His eyes were clouded and unfocused.

"We'll be late for the airplane," his wife said nervously.

"Your husband needs to go to the hospital."

"What's wrong with him?"

"We should go right away."

Nicky helped the man to his feet, assisted him down the walk, and eased him into the backseat of the cab. His wife ran around to the passenger door and jumped in next to her husband.

Nicky put on the emergency lights and peeled through the streets of Ambler as Mrs. Allison shouted directions to the hospital.

Nicky could hear Mrs. Allison gently coaching her husband. "Gary, hold on, we're almost there," she said between commands.

Nicky checked his passenger in the rearview mirror. He was slumped over in his wife's arms.

"Please hurry," she pleaded.

Nicky pulled out of the line of cars at the red light and sped on the shoulder past them. He was making the turn for the hospital when the wife cried out.

Nicky pulled up to the entrance of the emergency room, jumped out of the car, and ran inside to find a doctor. He came back outside, ran to Mr. Allison's side of the car, and opened the door.

"Help is on the way," Nicky said to Mr. Allison, whose wife was crying and patting her husband's face and hands, trying to rouse him.

"We're losing him. Gary, wake up," she said desperately.

Nicky checked the man's pulse, as he had been trained to do when he was in the army. He touched the man's neck, one side and then the other, and with the other hand, his wrist. There was barely a flutter.

"Did you find a pulse?" his wife asked.

Nicky closed his eyes to concentrate, to try to feel a faint tap against his fingers.

"Out of the way," the medic barked. Nicky stepped away from the car as a flurry of hospital staff, including a nurse overseeing the maneuver, transferred the man from the cab to a gurney.

The wife jumped out of the cab, now frantic. She shouted at the medic, as though this turn of events was somehow his fault, asking if he knew what he was doing, as if his skill alone could change the outcome.

A nurse lifted a sheet folded into a triangle from the foot of the gurney. The wind kicked up as she unfurled the sheet in the air. It billowed like immaculate white angel wings against the blue sky.

Nicky heard the flapping of wings over the shouting of the medic, the creaky wheels of the gurney, the desperate pleas of the wife, and the firm orders of the nurse. The attempt to save the dying man seemed to be happening under glass. Nicky looked up, searching the sky for the origin of the sound of the wings, but there was nothing but blue.

The wife ran alongside the gurney as the staff pushed it through the doors of Abington Hospital.

Nicky stood in the spot where he had moved to get out of the way of the medic. He did not move until an ambulance arrived and needed the space. He closed the doors of the cab and parked in a spot near the entrance. He removed the Allisons' luggage from the trunk and carried the suitcases into the hospital. Once inside the hospital, he sat in a chair with a clear view of the doors to the examining rooms and waited. He wasn't sure how long he sat there, as he hadn't checked his watch.

All sorts of wounded people came into the hospital as he sat. A woman ran in with her hand wrapped in a bloody dishtowel. A boy around seven, holding an ice pack to his mouth where a baseball had split open his lip, was cradled in his father's arms. The boy's mother rushed alongside them, having remembered to put the tooth that was knocked out in a glass of milk, preserving the root. Later still, a woman arrived whose face had drooped with palsy. Her gray skin looked like it was made of wet clay, as though an artist had pinched her face into its odd shape on his way to sculpting something of symmetry and beauty.

The day shift changed to night at the admittance desk before Nicky's fare, Mrs. Allison, the woman who had not put on her hat, who had not made it to New York International Airport with her husband and suitcases, eventually emerged through the doors. She looked tiny, like a delicate bird made of blown glass, the kind that dangles from a chandelier, so fragile that light might go through it.

Nicky stood, holding his cap.

She went to him. "You waited for me?"

"To see if there was anything I could do."

"He's gone."

Nicky nodded. "I'm sorry. I wish I would have called an ambulance."

"It wouldn't have mattered."

Nicky was surprised. "I don't understand."

"When·he was a boy, he almost died from scarlet fever. When I met him, it was the first thing he told me. He said, 'I'm on borrowed time.' He told me he had a bad heart. We were at a mixer and the band was loud, and I thought he said he had a *sad* heart and I said I could fix that. He laughed and said, no, a *bad* heart. And through the years, he'd remind me. And one time, I got impatient with him when we were fussing about something and I said, 'Everyone is on borrowed time.' And he said, 'The difference is, I know it.' Why didn't I believe him?"

Mrs. Allison's sons and her family members pushed through the entrance door and spotted her. They encircled her as she wept and comforted her, and soon, they moved together to go. Nicky handed off the luggage to a neighbor. Mrs. Allison hadn't noticed, but Nicky knew she would want her husband's clothing. All of it would matter later. Nicky watched as Mrs. Allison, shored up on both arms by one of her sons, left the hospital. Family is essential; they scoop up their own to rescue them in tragedy, to bind them close, to shore them up and heal them. Those who don't share their name or their grief or their history are left behind. A witness is only that, a passerby who observes a moment in the landscape of a stranger's life story. But Nicky had heard the wings, and now the death of Gary Allison was part of his story too.

⟨⟩

Nicky drove around aimlessly in No. 4 after he left the hospital. He stopped for coffee and had a cigarette. Not ready to return to the garage or go home, he found himself on Broad Street.

He parked the cab behind the Borelli Theater near the stage door, climbed the steps, and tried the door, relieved when it opened easily. The theater was a lot like a church in that way: usually, no matter the time, you could find an unlocked door to enter. He flipped on the work lights and walked out onto the stage, where the set pieces from *Twelfth Night* were marooned in the circles of light. The rowboat that washed up on the chicken wire shore of Illyria had been propped against the flat, its oars tucked neatly inside. The forest, a collection of papier-mâché trees, flanked the wings. As Nicky stood at the edge of the pretend forest, he wished it would multiply and grow into acres, filling a painted landscape of mountains beyond it. He imagined walking into that world and never returning to this one.

But no such luck. After a time, he walked off the stage and up the aisle to the stairs that led to the mezzanine. He took a seat in the dark theater in one of the red velvet seats, worn from use and time, which suited his weary body just right. The scent in the air, of paint and chalk, stale perfume, and peppermint soothed him as he leaned back and stretched his legs out onto the mezzanine wall. The clutter of overhead lights, rigged on black, reminded him of a traffic jam, their metal shells layered one over the other, flaps open like the hoods of cars. He liked a theater in repose between performances, every aspect at rest; all that was needed were the actors, the crew, and the audience. Despite all he'd been through that day, the theater still gave him a sense of possibility.

Nicky had watched most rehearsals from the mezzanine over the past three years, and remembered them in detail. On the first day of rehearsal of every new production, Sam Borelli had a ritual. He gathered the company and crew on the stage to introduce them to one another for the first time. There would be forty or fifty of them, but Borelli knew each person by name, and when he introduced them individually, he'd give a quick snapshot of the job they did and why they were great at it.

A spear chucker was given the same deference as the leading man, the set designer as the costume assistant, the prop master as the director himself. Borelli insisted that the theater belonged to everyone, regardless of their role or position, and that came with a personal responsibility to be excellent, to be alert, stay focused, and do one's best work because each artisan's contribution had a direct effect on the outcome of the play and therefore the audience's experience.

Nicky remembered Mrs. Borelli observing rehearsals from the last row of the orchestra. Calla, he remembered, was in and out. He hadn't paid her much attention; she was younger than he and helped out on the various crews, but he had little interaction with her. He was surprised when it was announced she would take over the company. Evidently he wasn't the only person at Borelli's keeping a secret.

Nicky found himself drifting off to sleep, when he heard, "Anybody here?"

He sat up in his chair and saw Calla Borelli onstage looking around the empty theater for signs of life.

He waved, "Up here."

"Nicky?"

"Yeah."

"That was fast. Did Mrs. Mooney send you a telegram?"

Calla Borelli held a mop and bucket as she stood in a pool of light onstage.

"I don't know what you're talking about."

"Come down and I'll tell you."

Nicky joined her onstage. "Allow me." He picked up the cleaning supplies. "How can I help?"

"Put them back in the supply closet. Monsieur and Madame are now sparkling."

"Why do you clean the bathrooms?" Nicky followed Calla downstairs to the costume shop.

"They needed it."

"You could have the janitor do it."

"I had to cut back on his hours."

"Him too?"

"It's okay. They gave him more hours at the bank." Calla opened the doors of the supply closet. Nicky loaded the equipment inside before following her into the costume shop.

"Does it seem to you there are more banks in Philadelphia than ever before?"

"You know what my dad says. Better a cabaret on every corner than a bank. If there's a cabaret, at least you can sing about the pain." Calla buried her hands in the pockets of her work coveralls and looked at Nicky. "I went over to the garage to see you today."

"You've finally come to your senses and figured out that Frank Arrigo is never going to amount to anything, and you'd be better off with a cab driver?"

"No. I wanted to ask if you'd take over the role of Sebastian in *Twelfth Night*. Peter Menecola is out."

Nicky didn't know what to say.

Calla took his silence as the sign of a tough negotiation. "I know I fired you from the company, and that might give you pause."

"Why wouldn't it?" he said softly.

"But one has nothing to do with the other. Tony and Norma came to me and were impressed with how well you did, and they believe you could play the part. I believe you can too."

"Are you playing Olivia?"

"Cathy's back."

"Hmm." Nicky folded his arms and leaned against the work table. "I don't know."

"Five dollars a show."

"You're giving me a raise after you canned me?"

"You could look at it that way. So do you want to do it?"

"It's not about wanting to. I want to. Do you really think I can do the job?"

"I wouldn't offer you the part. We'll rehearse so you're comfortable. We'll have to work fast—and put some hours in. And Dad is around. He said he'd coach you if you needed help."

"He'd do that?"

"Sure. He's been meeting with Tony for years. Norma too. A couple other actors in the company stop by and meet with him for tune-ups."

"I didn't know."

"There's a lot more to acting than rehearsals."

"Now I'm scared."

"You should be."

"Are you the same director that just hired me?"

"If you weren't scared, you'd be a lousy actor. And if I wasn't scared, I'd be a terrible director."

Nicky sat down on the work stool.

"You okay?" Calla asked.

"This was the worst day, and now you've made it the best day. This sort of thing doesn't happen to me. I either have a good run or a bad run, but not something horrible followed by good news in the same day. This can only mean one thing. Doom."

Calla put her hands on Nicky's shoulders. He reached back and placed his hands upon hers. "May I tell you something?"

Calla sat down next to him.

"A man died in my cab today. A heart attack. I took him to the hospital. The doctor, the nurses, they brought him inside. I guess they revived him, and he lasted for a few hours. I stayed until the end."

"It was kind of you to make sure he wasn't alone."

"His wife was with him. She was with him the whole time. I stayed in the waiting room."

"Did she ask you to stay?"

"No. She was surprised I was there when she came out."

"Why did you stay?"

Nicky felt he might cry. He never cried, so he willed himself not to. "I'm not sure. What do you think?"

"Maybe you thought you could help."

"Do what, though?" Nicky looked at her.

"Have you ever been somewhere, like a party, and you thought, if I leave, this whole shebang will fall apart without me?"

Nicky laughed. "Maybe."

"Maybe you thought if you left, he'd die."

"But he did."

"But not right away. Have you ever been with anyone when they died?"

Nicky shook his head that he hadn't.

"I was with my mother. My sisters had gone out to get a cup of coffee. My dad had gone outside for some air. And something told me not to leave the room. So I didn't. So right at the end, her eyes opened, and the last person she saw on earth was me. And I made sure not to cry. I smiled really big, as big as I could, because I wanted her to have a happy end."

"I wanted Mr. Allison to live."

"But that's out of your hands."

"He didn't think so."

"What do you mean?"

"It's a small thing and I can't be sure of it. He didn't say anything, but he looked at me and the way he looked at me told me he didn't want to die. He wasn't ready."

"You can't worry about that now," Calla said softly. "It's not his decision any more than my mother's passing was hers."

"I couldn't save him."

"That's right. No one could."

Calla got up and went to the cupboard. She pulled a bottle of whiskey, hidden in a wooden box marked "bobbins," off the shelf. She picked up two clean glasses off the prop cart parked in the corner. She poured them each a shot.

"I knew it. You're a lush."

"Keep it to yourself."

She held up her glass. He clinked his glass against hers. *"Cent'Anni,"* they said in unison before throwing back the shots of whiskey.

"Calla? I'm going to need ten bucks a show. It's going to cut into my hours as a hack."

"I can only do five."

"What if I'm really good?"

"Five."

⌒

The walls, floor, appliances, and regulation moppeens in the Palazzini kitchen were white, and except for the streaks of gray in the Carrara marble on the countertops, the only color in the room came from the food as it was prepared. Whatever time, day or night, you walked in, the place was neat and clean.

There was a large window over the sink that overlooked Aunt Jo's garden in the backyard. The sill was lined with a row of small terra-cotta pots where she grew herbs year round. She grew basil, which she used liberally in her traditional gravy, or shredded by hand over fresh mozzarella drizzled in olive oil. There was mint, which she used for medicinal purposes, making a tea whenever anyone in the house was ill; but she also used it to make Nicky's favorite meal, spaghetti with fresh peas and mint. The garden was just like Aunt Jo's kitchen. Neatly plowed rows were organized by vegetable, her tools were kept in an orderly fashion in a covered potting shed, and the garden hose was coiled carefully in a circle on a hook. The entire operation was guarded by a weather-beaten scarecrow that resembled Peter Lorre.

Aunt Jo's kitchen could have been a professional restaurant operation. She believed in using the best appliances, utensils, and ingredients to get the best results. At his wife's request, Dom purchased the first icebox on Montrose in 1926, and the first dishwasher when it was available at Martinelli's in 1948. If Dom splurged, it was for Jo's kitchen.

A white linoleum-topped table and matching leather booth wrapped around the corner by the door to the mudroom. Nicky and the boys ate their lunch on this table on weekends when they were little. Aunt Jo also used the table as her office. She sorted bills, worked her crossword puzzles, and talked on the phone mounted on the wall behind the booth. The black telephone had an extra-long cord, so she might move around the kitchen as she talked with a friend.

The dining room, situated through the swinging portal doors beyond the kitchen, was the center of the home and the largest room on the main floor. Jo had enlisted the help of her sister-in-law, Nancy, to help her decorate it. The dining room was completed shortly before the falling-out, and it was sad to Jo that she'd never had Nancy, Mike, and their sons over to enjoy it.

The room was a copy of a classic dining room in a Main Line mansion that had been modeled after the original decorated by Colefax & Fowler in London. Jo might have wanted something formal, but for Nancy, that meant grand. In 1932 it was decorated with the best furniture the Palazzinis could afford, a polished Georgian-style cherry-wood dining table and matching chairs. The seats were upholstered in gold-and-white-striped velvet, which Nancy and Jo installed themselves. The walls were covered in gold-flocked wallpaper hung by Dom and Mike. *The Last Supper*, framed in gold leaf and carved out of hammered silver, had been given to Jo and Dom by Nancy and Mike as a gift, the final Christmas they were friendly. It had been blessed by the parish priest.

The table seated sixteen. The chandelier dripped daggers of crystal. Nancy had the same model in her own home, which meant she had gotten a two-for-one deal, which pleased the brothers. The crystals reflected the fine bone china Jo had collected through the years. Later on, Jo made the draperies, pale yellow silk jabots gathered off to one side with a thin braided cord. The single-panel draperies swept off to one side were inspired by Veronica Lake's peekaboo hairstyle. Nicky remembered when Aunt Jo unveiled them and Uncle Dom said, "I'd rather have Veronica Lake eating off my china than these curtains."

The gold-leafed sideboard was used to display desserts, and no matter when you passed through, the cookie jar was filled with biscotti and the cut glass candy dish was filled with bridge mix. When a meal was finished, the daughters-in-law cleared and washed the dishes, and Aunt Jo would set the table for the next meal. The tablecloths were pressed and hung in a linen closet in the kitchen on hangers. When Nicky was an altar boy, he noticed that the vestments of the priests got the same treatment.

That evening, Aunt Jo had left Nicky two stuffed peppers and a baked potato in the oven. Nicky pulled the hot meal out of the oven and placed it on the tray Aunt Jo had prepared.

In many ways 810 Montrose was like a boardinghouse, though Nicky had never stayed in one. The closest he had come was the barracks in the army in Alabama, where he moved through training with a group, sleeping and eating on a schedule set by the officers in command of the platoon.

Aunt Jo ran the Palazzini household with her version of military precision. She had to—with all her sons married, she had three daughters-in-law to help her, and three meals a day to serve.

There was laundry to do, cleaning, food to cook, the garden to tend, and the first grandchild to raise. And there would be more children.

Nicky balanced his plate, bottle of beer, and utensils on the tray and went down to his room in the basement through the kitchen.

Aunt Jo had painted his basement room a cheery yellow. The windows that ran along the ceiling were ground-level and let in very little light. But Nicky had a double bed, a rocking chair, a chest of drawers, a mirror, an armoire for his hanging garments, and best of all, his own bathroom, with a standing shower stall.

Nicky placed his dinner on the dresser and emptied his pockets before changing out of his work clothes. He placed his change in a tip jar and his cigarettes and lighter next to the ashtray. He almost threw the pickup order for the Allisons in Ambler into the wastebasket, but thought better of it and put it in his drawer. He wanted it to remember this day, even though he doubted he could ever forget it.

Nicky turned the dial on the radio and heard Dinah Shore's satin-smooth voice bounce off the concrete walls. He lowered the volume.

He hung up his suit, placed the shoe trees in his work oxfords, and put on his pajamas. Aunt Jo had placed his clean laundry on top of the dresser. The clean scent of borax and hints of bleach that made his undergarments bright white filled the drawer as he placed them into the dresser.

Nicky opened the bottle of beer and took a swig. He pushed the door to the basement kitchen open and flipped on the light. The daughters-in-law had made pasta that day, and the wooden dowels were draped with long, thin strands of linguini for Sunday dinner. Cavatelli, small hand-rolled pasta tubes resembling beads for stringing, were laid out on the enamel worktable on fresh white cotton sack cloths sprinkled with cornmeal.

Nicky took in the women's handiwork. He went to the table and studied the macaroni as though it were art. Flour and egg and a bit of water, kneaded and pressed into dough, was the only tactile memory he had of his mother. If he concentrated and used all of his senses, he could see her at the table in this room, wearing an apron with red pockets in the shapes of hearts. He could inhale the scent of the flour, touch the soft dough snakes on the cold table, pinch a taste of it, feel the sting on his hand when Aunt Jo lightly smacked it and the warmth of his mother's embrace that followed the smack.

Most precious to him was the laughter his mother and Aunt Jo shared as they gossiped while making ravioli in the presses or folding tortellini or standing at the stove and making the crepes for manicotti. If he closed his eyes, he could hear them as they bantered over the worktable. What he missed the most about his mother was surely the sound of her voice. He remembered when she spoke, it had a lovely timbre, light and clear, like the gold church bells rung by hand at the altar at Holy Communion. Nicola Castone's voice was soft when she read to him, and firm when she scolded him, but never brusque. He remembered she was tender and kind. A lady.

Nicky turned out the light and pulled the door closed. One radio show had ended, and it was Rosemary Clooney's turn to fill the air over South Philly with her velvet sound. Nicky preferred her to Dinah. Rosemary sang like she knew what it was to be alone, and in hearing her, Nicky felt less so.

He leaned back in the chair without rocking, the legs creaking under his weight. Nicky stared at the ceiling, filled with a nagging sense of guilt. The presence of guilt meant his conscience was reminding him to claim responsibility for wrongdoing, or so he had been taught on the eve of his First Confession by the parish priest. So, as he had done since his seventh birthday, he reviewed the day's events in search of the source of his sin. Whom had he offended, dismissed, disregarded, or treated poorly? Not for nothing, Nicky was proud of himself for sticking around for Mrs. Allison. He thought about the sound of the wings, thinking that might have been a mystical experience, though he couldn't be sure. Nicky sat up in the rocker and remembered. Peachy. He had forgotten his fiancée in all the turmoil. He hadn't called her, even though there was a phone booth in the waiting area of the hospital. Why hadn't he called her? Wasn't it Peachy who always said, "One thin dime. Take the time"?

It would have been so easy, but he hadn't thought to do it. Nor had he had the impulse to stop by the department store on the way back from Ambler to the garage. He could have picked up the phone in the office at the garage, but he hadn't. There were phone booths on every block when he delivered the telegrams that night; he could have easily slipped into any one of them and called her to see how she was, and, for his own part, for reassurance from her, support from the woman who loved him after a terrible day. But he hadn't done it. There was no good excuse. Peachy had slipped his mind. He felt worse knowing he had put seven dimes into his tip jar. Nicky even had the change to make the call.

Instead, he'd found himself at Borelli's, led there by something he didn't understand. It was just a feeling. He went where he found peace, where he could think. Nicky believed he had that kind of solace in Peachy, he really did. But that day, that belief hadn't led him to her. It had led him to the theater and his friend Calla Borelli.

Calla could be a smart aleck and she always had a comeback, but she was all right. She was cute. He thought about her body, how flawless it was in the beam of the work light in the wings— was it just the light and the way it fell across her like lace? It wasn't the light, it was *her.*

Her body enchanted him like the silver Pierce-Arrow hood ornament that had arrived at the shop in layers of padded brown paper when he was a boy. Knowing the contents, Nicky had carefully unwrapped the ornament and marveled at the sleek lines and smooth polish of the silver. He remembered holding the ornament and not wanting to put it down.

Calla's clothing, like the paper, was just fabric covering a work of art. He thought about where her body might take him, but before it became real, he shook his head, trying to erase the image of her from his mind. What kind of a guy examines his conscience to pinpoint his sin and then, without apology, throws himself headfirst into lust like he's bobbing for apples?

Nicky said a fast prayer to Saint Maria Goretti in hopes she might help remove the image of Calla Borelli's fantastic form from his mind's eye. But prayer was a weak bleach; it could not remove the stain. Devotion hadn't helped much—Calla came to him uninvited in a dream; nor did his spiritual habits protect him much when he needed to stay awake on a long shift. When he was exhausted behind the wheel, he'd think of Calla in the wings, stepping into the gown, and his eyes would pop open and the barely dressed image of her gave him a boost of energy to complete the run. It's not that he didn't imagine his fiancée in provocative ways too, here and there now and then—of course he did. But the Borelli girl was different.

Nicky didn't want to compare Calla to Peachy—well, he wouldn't. He was betrothed to Peachy. He had chosen her. She had said yes. They had made a deal. The banns of marriage had been printed in the church bulletin—in essence, page one of the final contract to be signed in the church book on their wedding day had already been negotiated.

He made the sign of the cross to ward off further impure thoughts of Calla Borelli, and any disloyal ones toward Peachy DePino. But he knew lusty thoughts were like waterskiing. It only took one distraction to loosen his grip on the bar, and once he did, the ride was over, he'd for sure go under and drown.

Occasions of sin of a sexual nature in the venial variety would unspool in his mind like a B movie, and soon Nicky would find himself in the capable hands of a faceless vixen with a willing body, who would make love to him in ways he imagined satisfying, reckless, and athletic, which in turn would lead to her ecstasy, his ruin, the fall of the Holy Roman Church, and the crumbling of all nations. And all of this mayhem and degradation triggered because Calla Borelli innocently placed her hands on his shoulders in the costume shop. He felt sick within himself.

Nicky couldn't finish the beer, and he didn't want his dinner. He'd lost his appetite entirely. He crawled into bed and flipped off the light, leaving the radio on, which he never did. But that night, he needed the company.

Calla sat on the straight-backed chair outside the Calabrese & Sons accounting office on Vine Street. The waiting area had two chairs, a small console table painted black, and a flower arrangement of blue plastic roses in a chinoiserie vase set upon a handmade doily.

She placed the box of ledgers from the theater on the floor beside her feet. She sat up, removed her short white gloves and placed them in her purse, patted the hem of her best skirt, and straightened the buttons on the jacket.

"Calla, come in," Joe hollered from inside his office.

Calla picked up the box and stood up tall and straight, mustering her courage. She smiled before entering.

"Anna sends her best. She wants you to come see her on the Jersey shore this summer."

"I'd like that."

"She has a place in Tinton Falls. You know it?"

"Nope. But I can find anything on the South Shore bus line."

Joe Calabrese was wiry and trim. He wore eyeglasses, and his straight black hair was thinning, but he was attractive for an egghead. "The cousins have to stay close. You know, with your mom gone, it's going to be a challenge."

"She brought everybody together."

"What do you have there?"

"The ledgers for the last two seasons."

Joe leaned back in his chair. "I took this place over from my dad, and I had to update everything. He had his ways, and I have mine."

"Dad did a good job with the theater."

"But he didn't make any money."

"He owns the real estate."

"Calla, the place needs a lot of work. Even to sell it."

"What are you saying?"

"You're burning daylight over there. I think you should shut it down. Try to rent the building out. And prepare to sell it."

"Joe, I didn't come to you to find a way to close the theater. I came to you to help me to find a way to make capital improvements and keep it open."

"I don't see any profit here. Not for years. "

"Because Dad plowed it back into the theater. We lived off it all my life."

"It's not a failure, then. That's good. But I'm telling you, based upon your numbers, your operating costs, your box office receipts, and your debt, you have no choice. Why are you saddling yourself with this?"

"It's my life."

"It's your father's life."

"So you can't help me."

"I'm an accountant. I do numbers, not miracles. What do you want me to do?"

"I was hoping you could take me to a bank and help me get a business loan. I understand that the banks are loaning money now that the war is over."

"How would we convince them that you could make money at the theater?"

"I could add shows. Advertise. I thought about a touring company. I don't have the resources to grow it. If I had help, I could do it. I know I could."

"The only assurance you can give a bank is past performance. Those ledgers show an occasional break-even at best."

The tone she heard in her cousin's voice was all she needed to know that he was not going to help her any further. "Well, thanks for taking a look at everything."

"I'm not going to charge you."

"Please do." Calla stood and picked up her box of ledgers.

"I don't want this to cause friction." Joe stood up to see her out.

"It won't."

"I'm glad."

Calla got to the door and turned to her cousin. "You know, Joe, there is something you could do to help that has nothing to do with the books."

"Sure."

"You could come see a play sometime. You never have."

"I'm so busy. You know. I got the wife. The kids. The job."

"My dad was your father's client all those years, and I believe my dad paid his bills on time."

"He did."

"Your dad never missed a show. See, I'm not inclined to take your advice as gospel truth this morning because it's coming from a place of ignorance. Now, if it was your dad telling me to padlock the building, I might think about it. But your free advice? What's the saying? Oh yeah, when it's free, you get what you pay for."

Calla walked out the door before Joe could see her eyes sting with tears. She was furious, and embarrassed that she hadn't seen it coming.

Frank was waiting on the sidewalk outside the Calabrese office.

He dusted a smudge off the hood of the car with his handkerchief as Calla came down the steps.

"What happened?" Frank asked as he opened the car door for her.

"He said that I should close the doors on the theater."

"Just like that?"

"He won't help me with the banks." Calla leaned her head on her hand. "Said it was impossible to get a loan. I thought there were all sorts of loans for small businesses after the war."

"How about lunch?"

"I'm not hungry."

"What can I do to make you smile?"

"Do you know J. P. Morgan?"

Frank took Calla's hand as he walked her up to the porch of a two-family home on Constitution Street. His side of the property was neat, with a simple set of two straight-back chairs anchoring the door. On the other side, a baseball bat, glove, and ball were propped by the door, a homemade cardboard dollhouse was set under the window, and the grass in the small patch of yard was trampled down to the dirt. "My sister lives next door. Four kids and one on the way."

Calla looked around Frank's living room, if she could call it that. His coffee table was filled with documents, a stack of papers anchored with a coffee cup with a handwritten note under it that read "BIDS." Propped in the corner was a survey kit, tripod sticks, a leveler, and a gauge. Tacked up on the wall was a map of Philadelphia, showing the pipeworks under the city, the grid unlike anything she had ever seen before.

As Calla moved around the room, she kept her hand behind her back as though she were in a museum. If she had a weakness, it was for experts. She appreciated anyone who understood a subject deeply and had mastered that subject in a profound way. A person with passion was endlessly fascinating, no matter the arena.

"If a pipe bursts on Wharton, I can name the joint," Frank said, handing her a glass of red wine.

"Thank you."

"Your friend Nicky should have his street patched up in no time," Frank said, pointing to Montrose, represented by a long, thin blue strand that looked like a linguini noodle on the map.

"I'll tell him."

"Come here." Frank led Calla to the alcove off the living room and pointed to a small settee covered in brown corduroy with white piping. "Sit."

Calla recognized the television set from the windows of Wanamaker's and the Sunday circulars. Frank's set was a Philco with a square screen of green milk glass that rested inside a walnut cabinet. On either side of the screen were two panels of gold-and-brown mesh fabric. A long, thin silver stick resembling a conductor's baton angled out from the back of the set, pointing directly toward the front door.

"That's the antenna. You have to position it just so to get the best picture." He pointed. "And these are the speakers for sound."

"It looks like a piece of furniture." Calla laced her arms around her legs and leaned forward as Frank sat down on the floor and opened a small panel that had three dials, an on and off button, a contrast button, and a brightness button with an arrow. "These buttons control the picture quality."

"What are you waiting for? Entertain me," Calla teased.

Frank turned on the television set. A series of black-and-white lines gave way to wider ones that vibrated, expanding into bold chevron-style zigzags that belonged on an argyle sweater. "Hold on, it's coming." In a matter of seconds, a moving picture appeared on the screen, a car riding along an open country road. "This is a commercial. An advertisement for the show. Ford is paying for whatever you're going to see."

"Why?"

Frank shrugged. "People will buy the car if they see it enough."

"People would just do that?"

"Why not? You'd buy it off a billboard or a magazine."

Calla watched Gertrude Berg appear on the screen. She appeared in a window on a set, and hollered down to the street below as if in a play. The audience's laughter was captured. They must be there. Calla was mesmerized.

"This is television." Frank kept his eyes on the screen.

"How do they do it?"

"The image is transmitted from the camera in the studio to a board that can reach every grid that is connected to it."

"Like electricity?"

"A little. The transmission of an image requires a cathode ray tube—which every one of these sets has inside. The man that sold it to me showed me the guts of this thing. I couldn't believe it."

"What will happen to radio?"

Frank shrugged. "Who cares?"

Calla sat back and watched the images. They weren't sleek like the movies, or colorful, like the lavish Hollywood productions in movie theaters that cost a quarter, but this was in Frank's home, which made it novel. The black-and-white images reminded her of photographs; the lighting made the actors fall in shadow and emerge in light that made them appear like puppets, more Man Ray than cinematic.

"Hey, what do you think?" Frank turned to her.

"I don't know what to think. It moves awful fast."

Nicky parked on the street two blocks from the Trinity Episcopal Church in Ambler. The lot closest to the entrance was full, and the street in front by the Matthews Funeral Home had been roped off.

This morning in May was saturated with so much color, Nicky seemed to walk in a Tiepolo painting. The sky overhead was peacock blue. A tangerine sun was fixed on a cushion of coral clouds, as Nicky passed azalea bushes bursting with fuchsia blossoms, and flowerbeds filled with yellow tulips and purple irises. He moved through this palette dressed in ceremonial black like a slash of ink. He tugged at the knot in his tie as he walked in his best black leather dress shoes up the steps of the church and into the vestibule.

A well-dressed lady in a hat and gloves, wearing two-tone spectator pumps, the dress shoe of choice of the Protestant class, handed him a program, on the front of which was printed:

Gary Bigelow Allison
1903–1949

An usher led Nicky up the aisle. Nicky stopped, choosing to sit near the back so that the seats in the front pews might go to a mourner who knew Mr. Allison, had worked with him, was related to him, or had loved him. Nicky had been his driver on that fateful day. That was all.

Once seated, Nicky looked up the aisle, surprised to see the casket in place in front of the altar, banked with a simple blanket of the waxy green leaves of the local mountain laurel that had yet to bloom. He had never been to a funeral outside his own church, so this would be a new experience for him.

The church was full, but not overflowing. The mourners were dressed in somber tones in fine fabrics, plain silks, light summer wool, the ladies wore simple hats and short gloves. They sat in white pine pews, facing a stained glass window of Jesus kneeling in the garden of Gethsemane. The windows along the sides of the aisles were clear beveled glass. The altar was plain, as was the lectern, covered in a white ceremonial cloth. The window featuring Jesus was all the adornment in the church.

At first, the austere interior threw Nicky, who expected the polish of brass or glint of crystal in this comfortable suburb. Where was the hand of a Michelangelo, even if it was a copy, or the flair of a Bernini, even if it was an imitation, or the genius of Leonardo, even if it was a smaller-scale reproduction of a sculpture? The scent of Madonna lilies wafted through the air, but he missed the incense of his Holy Roman Church and the sweet scent of the beeswax from the candles burning in the votive trays.

Nicky had learned to pray in ornate splendor; it was what he was used to, and what his faith provided, in exchange for his lifelong devotion. When Nicky prayed to earn his salvation, he pictured the magnificence of the art of the Renaissance, in jewel-toned oil paint, gold leaf, and silver-veined marble, awaiting him on the other side. From the looks of this church, his Protestant brethren could expect a Shaker bench and an oil lamp in their version of the promised "house with many rooms" when they reached the gates of heaven.

A minister in a black suit emerged from the sacristy as the choir sang. Mrs. Allison and her sons, guided by the undertaker, walked up the aisle, taking their seats in the front row. Nicky leaned forward as the minister talked about Gary Allison, what a fine man he had been, husband, father, and co-worker.

Gary's eldest son stood to eulogize his father. He spoke of a parent who taught him how to hunt and fish, throw a baseball, and camp in the woods. The words stung Nicky as he listened to the testimony of the life of a good man by a son who knew his father well.

Nicky had spent countless hours imagining what might have been had his own father lived. Would they have been friends? Or would he have had the other kind of father-son relationship, fraught with misunderstandings and pain and missed opportunities to connect? The thought made him weep. He hated himself for crying.

He found his handkerchief in his suit pocket and dabbed his eyes. He questioned why he had come to the funeral at all. But given that something had compelled him to attend, he was now forced to accept his portion of a grief that didn't belong to him.

Gary's youngest son rose to speak. Nicky thought about leaving in the moments it took the young man to walk from the pew to the lectern, but the usher had blocked him in, and he was reluctant to climb over the old couple on the end of the pew. Forced to listen, he sat back and was trying to think of something, anything, else when he heard Mr. Allison's son say, "Dad had never been across the ocean, and this would have been his first trip."

Nicky wanted to stand up and shout, "Your father knew he had a bad heart, he shouldn't have waited!" but then he remembered the man could hardly be blamed for that, and besides, travel is a luxury, and the man had a family. But now Gary Allison was gone, and it turned out that he had not done everything he had hoped to do. Nicky had seen the desperation in Mr. Allison's eyes that day. Though he knew he had a bad heart, Mr. Allison did not want to die, and he had not planned on dying that day. It was all taken from him, and he'd had no say in the matter.

Nicky felt a wave of claustrophobia so acute he could not breathe. He began to sweat profusely as his heart raced. Putting etiquette aside, he whispered a sincere apology, climbed over the couple at the end of the pew, and escaped from the church outside into the day that shimmered like a ruby. Once free, he inhaled the fresh air in huge gulps, savoring it, filling his lungs, feeling the space of the outdoors where there were no walls.

Nicky got his bearings. As he slowly walked back to his car, he heard the ticking of the big clock, the one that determines the exact moment of a man's birth and his death and is marked by every timepiece set by the sun. He saw the days of his life pass in the plain-faced round clock in the auditorium at Saint Charles Borromeo school, in the priest's small gold travel clock in the sacristy at Saint Rita's, in the cuckoo in the kitchen at the Palazzinis', and on the flashing counter on a grenade in France. Time flew on the ticker in the dispatch office, the flimsy tin one in the garage that also housed a thermometer, the wristwatch on his arm, and on the stopwatch that Mrs. Mooney used to remit a code. He heard it on the clock that rested on his nightstand with the alarm that sounded like a garbage disposal when it jumped, metal on wood, reminding him to get up and own the day that didn't belong to him.

Time dragged on the clock that hung in the lobby of the First National Bank when he went for the loan, the Roman numeral clock set in filigree in the dressing room at Borelli's when he waited between scenes, and the one in the train station in Rome with the mother-of-pearl face whose onyx hands had stopped and made him miss the train that would return him to the port city to catch the boat that would bring him home to America after the war. He heard every timepiece that ever ticked, rang, gonged, buzzed, chimed, and heaved Nicky toward the end of a life whose purpose he had surrendered to please everyone but himself.

Until he didn't. Soon the only sound he heard was the barking of a dog in the distance and a curlicue of laughter that trailed off as a cluster of girls skipped past.

It was time for Nicky Castone to live a life that mattered, where the long hours of the days of his life would be spent doing work he loved, that meant something to him, that brought meaning to the world that could only be delivered by him, where risk meant growth and the reward came in the doing.

Everything must go, he decided as he climbed into the car, and everything would—because he knew now, with a certainty that few men possess, that it would soon be him lying in a pine casket under a blanket of laurel leaves on a spring day of unspeakable beauty.

Nicky Castone decided he must not die until he had lived.

4

Calla's legs dangled over the lip of the stage as she flipped through the loose-leaf binder that contained the script of *Twelfth Night*. Nicky sat next to her, peering over her shoulder. She found the scene she was looking for, and as she read, without looking up, she took Nicky's cigarette from his hand, lifted it to her lips, and inhaled a puff. She handed it back to him and kept reading.

"I didn't know you smoked." Nicky ashed the cigarette into the company ashtray, an old tin can that used to house split pea soup.

"I don't."

"You just took a drag off my cigarette."

"It was one puff. It calms me down."

"Then you're a smoker."

"I've never bought a pack of cigarettes in my life."

"That makes you a bum."

"I'm not a bum. I've never smoked an entire cigarette."

"Over the course of your life, let's say since you were fifteen . . ."

"*Sixteen.*"

"Since you began bumming a drag off a cigarette, you're now, what, twenty-one?"

"Twenty-four, but thanks. I'll need those three years on the back nine."

"I don't think so but, you're welcome. Then you've had at least an entire pack of cigarettes in eleven years of bumming—maybe more."

"You could be right." Calla jumped up on the stage. "It still doesn't make me a smoker."

"What's wrong with being a smoker?"

"Nothing. It's not something I want to do on a regular basis."

"Why? Who cares if you smoke?"

"Frank."

"Oh, Frank." Nicky put his hand on his heart.

"Yes, Frank. Promise me you'll never put your hand on your heart when you're in one of my plays."

"I won't." Nicky put his hand down and into his pocket.

"He doesn't like when a lady smokes."

"Not a Bette Davis fan, I guess."

"He's not. Linda Darnell. Gene Tierney. Those are his types."

"Brunettes."

"Something wrong with that?"

"Not at all. Look at Peachy. Her hair is as black as a Firestone tire."

"I hope you come up with more romantic ways to describe her to her face, when the moment calls for it."

"She doesn't have any complaints." Nicky put out his cigarette in the can and jumped up onto the stage next to Calla. "Believe you me."

"Anything you say, Nicky."

"At least, she's never voiced her complaints. Where do I go when Viola is revealed?"

"I have you entering stage left. You stop downstage here. Cheat out just a bit and wait for the Duke." Calla gently put her hands on Nicky's shoulders and blocked him in the scene. She jumped off the stage and ran up the aisle, turning to face him. "Okay, Viola's cue is 'Hath been between this lady and the Lord,' and you say to Olivia—"

Nicky cheated out, turning ever so slightly toward the audience just as Calla had blocked him. He tucked the script under his arm and spoke:

> *So comes it, lady, you have been mistook:*
> *But nature to her bias drew in that,*
> *You would have been contracted to a maid;*
> *Nor are you therein, by my life deceived,*
> *You are both betroth'd to a maid and a man.*

"These particular lines delivered by Sebastian are the pith of the whole play."

"They're in *my* hands?" Nicky shook his head.

"*Your* hands. Sorry, pal. You have to let the audience know that you know that Olivia has fallen for Viola, who has been posing as a man. But you're her twin, and she has agreed to marry you, thinking you're Viola posing as Cesario. You have to tee this up for Viola."

"I get it."

"So when you tell us what's happened, let us in on what you're feeling."

"I'm afraid I'm going to lose Olivia when she finds out who I really am."

"That's a thought."

"Is it correct?"

"I don't know."

"You're the director."

"You're the actor," she shot back.

"You're the boss."

"You're the storyteller. They're paying to see you. I'm not up there when the audience shows up and sits in their seats. You have to make sense of it for them. Every play is an argument. You're stating your case."

"I'm following." Nicky nodded he understood.

"You bring the words to life and give them emotion and meaning."

"Fancy talk."

"You ever had a fare in your cab and the guy gets in and you don't know why, but you just like him on sight?"

"Yeah."

"You can talk to the person?"

"Yeah."

"And you're driving the guy where he wants to go and he asks you a question and you tell him a story. You don't think too much about the details, you just tell him what happened. It's natural. You just tell the story, the details, deliver the information. That's all acting is. Tell what's on the page like you'd tell a guy in the back of the cab something you heard that you thought was interesting or funny or even disturbing—or scary, which these lines can be if a man thinks he's going to lose the woman he loves when she figures out he isn't who she thinks he is."

Nicky nodded. "I know a little something about that."

"So use it," Calla suggested.

Tony Coppolella pushed the stage door open, and soon the actors filed in for the rehearsal Calla had added to the show schedule to incorporate Nicky into the play. He didn't hear the door open. He didn't hear Josie laugh backstage, or Hambone trip when he came up from the dressing room. All the while, he was thinking about what Calla had said.

Nicky had long suspected that there were two levels to life—the street level, where he drove the cab, upon which people lived and worked and shopped, ate and slept, made love, argued and settled their differences, and the other level, the depths, beneath the grid, the pavement and sidewalks, deep into the earth, under the rivers, through the silt past the stone and clay, under the layers of rock, deeper still to the magma, the tectonic plates, farther down and in, as far as one could go, to the center of things, where feelings were buried and could only be mined if a human soul bothered to dig.

Nicky had come to the knowledge of this duality of the surface and the depths early on in his life because he had grieved before he learned to read. He believed that anyone who suffered loss knew it was the only thing in the face of anything else in the human experience.

Grief was the alpha and the omega of all that resided in between thought and feeling, and between inertia and action. There was room for nothing else in the presence of grief except understanding. Understanding was the deepest level of empathy. Perhaps—and Nicky would have to think about this—this was what he had to summon within himself if he was going play a part, if he was to become an actor. He would have to show an audience what it was to feel what it meant for a man to go through something. He knew it was possible, because he had seen it from the wings when an actor, using the words of a playwright, told a story that belonged to the audience.

Calla had her theories about the theater, but Nicky had begun to have his too. He'd play the scene as she blocked it, listen to his fellow actors, and stay in the moment. If he did those three things, he might become Sebastian in *Twelfth Night.* If he didn't, Nicky was certain he'd lay the biggest egg South Philly had ever seen.

Nicky pulled the new No. 4 cab up in front of 832 Ellsworth Street and grabbed the brown bag off the front seat before making his way up the walk. He knocked on the screen door. "Mr. Borelli?" He knocked again. The interior door was open. Nicky peered in. He saw a light on in the kitchen. "Hey? Mr. Borelli?" He knocked harder.

Nicky had been around enough old people to know that one didn't hesitate to check on them. He pushed the screen door open and continued to call out to Calla's father as he made his way back to the kitchen. There, he looked through the window and saw Sam sitting in the backyard. He exhaled a sigh of relief.

Nicky had turned to go outside to join Sam when he saw a tool-box opened, with the contents in disarray, scattered on the kitchen table. "Mr. Borelli!" he hollered on his way out to the backyard. "Calla sent you dinner. Said to tell you she'd be late. Tony's wife made a platter of roast pork sandwiches."

"My favorite."

"So I heard. And there's a couple of pizelles in there."

"Thanks. How are you doing in the play?"

"I can't tell."

Sam smiled. "That's good. A man that thinks he has the world by a string ends up being choked by it."

"I was less terrified in France in a foxhole."

"You'll get past that. You have to fall in love with the words. When you do, you'll serve them."

"Good to know. Rehearsal was rigorous but the actors were really helpful. Do you want me to get you something to drink?"

"There's a beer in the fridge. I'll get it." Sam stood up. "You want to join me?"

"Sure." Nicky followed Sam into the kitchen. "You fixing something?"

"Tried. Something wrong with the sink. I was waiting for Calla's fella to come over and take a whack at it, but you know the old saying, a shoemaker's kid goes barefoot, well, the contractor's girlfriend's father doesn't get his sink fixed."

"I'll take a stab at it. But get me that beer. I'm not a professional." Nicky took the flashlight, got on his knees, and looked under the sink. "You need a new joint. The rivets are shot."

"That's all?"

"I think so." Nicky rummaged through the tool kit and found the pieces he needed to fix the pipe.

"I don't want to leave this place a wreck."

"Where are you going?"

"When I die."

"Okay."

"I don't want to leave Calla with a mess. The theater is enough of a responsibility. If I leave this house in pretty good shape, my daughters should be able to sell it."

"Where would Calla go?"

"I hope that she's settled soon."

"That'd be nice."

"It's what you want for your children. You want them to have security—even when you've lived the life of an artist."

"What's that like? To be an artist?" Nicky asked.

"All it means is that you did what you wanted with your life and you didn't make any money. Not a bad trade off. It's what *Twelfth Night* is about. Every character in the play is trying to find happiness."

"Love." Nicky peeked out from under the sink.

Sam nodded. "Or meaning. Shakespeare answers the question 'Why do I matter?' by the end of the play. That's a big freight for a comedy."

"I'll say. If you don't mind me asking, Mr. Borelli, why the impostors? Why all the disguises and mistaken identities?"

"I think Shakespeare was saying find truth however you can, put on a different hat, or suit or mask, and see where it takes you. It may lead you to the life you should be living. It will lead you to what is pure and noble."

Nicky emerged from under the sink. He ran the water in the sink, knelt down, and checked the pipe.

"You fixed it. Thank you!" Sam was impressed.

"Have Frank take a look anyway. I believe in experts having the last word. I better shove off."

"What about that beer?"

"I'll be back for it."

"Could you do one more thing for me? Could you take these tools back to the theater? I had Calla loan them to me from the scene shop."

"Sure." Nicky loaded them back into the toolbox.

Sam reached into the refrigerator, pulled out two more bottles, and handed them to Nicky. "My daughter likes a cold beer at the end of a workday. Would you mind bringing her one?"

The only entrance open at Borelli's was the stage door, which had been propped open with a brick. Nicky pushed it open with his hip. He carried the toolbox onto the stage, where Calla was sitting cross-legged against the proscenium wall, reading a ledger, with her prompt book opened and propped on the floor. The work lights were on full blast.

"Miss me?" Nicky sat down next to her.

"No."

"I fixed your sink."

"You did?"

"Your dad paid me with two beers. But he said to give you one of them." Nicky handed her one of the cold beers that he'd placed in the toolbox.

"He's a piece of work."

"He sure is." Nicky snapped the lid off Calla's beer and then his own.

"The man has no patience. I told him Frank would swing by tomorrow to fix it."

"Too late. Your father had all the tools out like a surgeon."

"But he has no idea what to do with any of them. I always wondered what it would be like to have a father who could fix things. The knob on our bedroom door fell off when I was eight, and it still hasn't been replaced."

"One man can't be everything. Can't *do* everything."

"It's worth the search, though, don't you think?"

"If you've got the time. And you've got the time. You have youth and beauty and that long list of unreasonable demands on your side."

"I've got time."

"You can't take a compliment."

"Yes, I can."

"Say thank you. I think you're pretty. What's the big tingle?"

"It's not a big tingle at all," Calla said defensively.

"Sounds like it. You almost curdle. You fold up. You recoil. You can't take a social nicety."

"I can!"

"You don't. You close your eyes halfway." Nicky demonstrated. "Your lids go down by half. Like garage doors."

"Lovely."

"I think so."

"Are you flirting with me?" Calla kept her eyes on the ledger.

"No."

"Good. Because you're about to get married to Miss DePino."

"You've heard of atomic bombs?"

"Yeah."

"The day I marry Peachy DePino, a giant pink gas cloud is going to explode over Our Lady of Loreto Church. It will burst forth from the heavens in a fireball made of lace and smoke and rose petals and Jordan almonds. No one will survive it. Not even you."

"Will you?"

"Nope. We're all going down for the cause."

"But a worthy one. A man. A woman. A sacrament. True love. Nothing like it."

"You've seen enough Shakespeare to know."

"I grew up with it. My parents. That was a real love story." Calla closed the ledger.

"You're lucky. That was the saddest part of losing my parents. And the worst part of being an orphan. I never saw a love story that I could say was mine."

"Forgive me. What a clod. Bragging about my parents."

"You should! Revel in it! What is better than hearing about two people who loved each other and made a life and a family. It's like something out of a play. Almost doesn't seem possible offstage. What I wouldn't give to have known my father with my mother in love—together, you know, just the two of them, in the kitchen, laughing, making a sandwich, or holding hands on the street, or seeing my father open a car door for my mother. The absence of those things are what makes you an orphan—it's the ordinary everyday expressions of love you miss."

Calla looked away.

"Hey, I'm boring you." Nicky nudged her.

"Not at all."

"You sure?"

"It's what everyone wants."

"Is it what you want?"

"Of course." Calla felt her cheeks flush.

"I remember your mother. She was a beauty."

"She was." Calla looked down at her hands because they reminded her of her mother's.

"You look just like her."

"I look like my dad."

"No. You look like her. You really do."

"Thank you. You couldn't pay me a higher compliment."

"That was it? I've been trying to figure out how to impress you and I stumble upon it blind. Go figure."

"That's it." Calla laughed.

"I'm sorry you lost her."

"It's been hard. And really difficult for Dad. I haven't been able to get him back since she died. The grief took him over, and he got sick. But I'm determined to get him well, and have him direct the next production. He doesn't want to do it, but I'm going to make him."

"You took all this on for him?"

"It's the family business." Calla smiled.

"I understand. I work in one, you know."

"But I love the theater. Maybe not as much as my dad, who sacrificed everything for it, but almost as much. He spent all of his time here when we were kids. Mom would pack his lunch and bring him his dinner here. I probably spent more time in this mezzanine than I did in my backyard at home."

"Did your mother mind?"

"Whatever made him happy made her happy."

Nicky's thoughts went to Peachy, who thought happiness was a joint venture, not a personal search. "They don't make them like your mother anymore."

"No, they don't. But she's gone—and maybe that has something to do with it. She worked so hard to make our lives comfortable and happy that she sacrificed her health and her peace of mind. Her whole life was my father and her daughters. We were her world. And I don't know if that's good."

"It was good for you," said Nicky.

"Yeah. But what about her?"

"Mothers don't think about themselves. When my mother was dying, she said, 'When you're happy, I'm happy, and I'll know it, even in the next world. So promise me you will always be happy.'"

"She guilted you into being happy."

"I didn't see it that way."

"My mother guilted my sisters and me into being good and working hard in school, really, everything. Guilt was her tool. But it was effective."

"It builds loyalty. You had her all those years. I'd have taken my mother, guilt and all, any terms set, I would have agreed to them just to have her around."

"How old were you when she died?"

"Five. Almost six."

"And you remember her?"

"I do. I like to think I remember every word she said, but that's just wishful thinking. I fill in whatever I can't remember like it's a scene in a play and then I watch it in my mind."

"I find myself doing the same thing with my mom."

"You have to. Who will remember her if you don't? Who knew your mother in the way you did? In my dreams my mother is young and full of pep and quite the beauty. I remember how she brushed her hair. And what she wore. And how she laughed. And her perfume. You know, whatever you wear reminds me of my mom."

Calla held out her wrist and put it under Nicky's nose. "It's called Bella Arancia. I get a big bottle at the feast every year."

"It's nice."

"Thanks. There's a Calabrian couple that have come over here every summer for years, and they make cologne themselves. Mine is made with Sicilian blood oranges. You should get Peachy a bottle next feast."

"I never buy her perfume. She gets a discount at the department store. So she wears Arpège."

"Fancy."

"Very. I like it. But she doesn't smell like an Italian garden in the summertime. You know, like my ma."

"Someday you'll have a daughter, and your mother will be back. That's how it goes, you know."

"You think so? I hope it's true. I'm beginning to forget the small details and I'm afraid the memories of her will eventually fade altogether when I move out of Montrose Street. I've lived in that house all my life, and it's the only house I lived in with my mother. I'm reminded of her every day when I come and go. When I walk out the door, I feel like I'm leaving her there somehow."

"What does that say about us?" Calla wondered.

"What do you mean?"

"We never left home."

"There must have been an important reason for us to stay." Nicky shrugged.

"I had to take care of Dad."

"And I wasn't ready to get married until now."

"How did you know you were?"

"You just know. How about that handsome devil with the delicate, upturned schnoz you're seeing?"

"Frank is very nice."

"The future mayor of Philly. Important man. That's some stature right there. The very definition. He's climbing the ladder. You better invest in some nice hats."

"I don't exactly fit the role, do I?"

"You can do anything."

Calla blushed. The only person who had ever said those words to her and meant them was her father. And those particular words had given her the confidence to direct her first play. "Not according to the *Philadelphia Inquirer*," she said as she gathered the pages from her prompt book. "We're done for today. You need to rest. You have Shakespeare to master—and I have accounting to do. "

"I heard this new actor Nicky Castone is going to turn things around. Take the old barn out of the red and put it in the black." Nicky stood, extended his hands, and pulled Calla to standing.

"That would be nice, because I heard from Mario Lanza's agent and he's gone to Hollywood. He won't be back to South Philly any- time soon to save us," Calla admitted.

Nicky held Calla's hands. "You don't need Lanza when you've got Castone."

"I have to lock up."

Nicky let go of her hands. "Work. Work. And more work," Nicky teased as he followed Calla to the stage door, past the prop table, where there were stacks of flyers and posters to advertise the production.

"That's how you get good." Calla picked up a stack of flyers. "Could you do us a favor and take some of these and hand them to your customers?"

"That's only about sixty people a day."

"It would help."

"Why not think bigger?"

"You want to take all the flyers?"

Nicky picked up the large cardboard posters advertising the show stacked on the table. "I'll ask my uncle if we can put the posters on the cabs. We're all over South Philly. I think that would get the word out faster."

"You'd do that?"

Nicky nodded and tucked the posters under his arm. "I'll see you Saturday night." He pushed through the door.

Once Nicky was outside, Calla could hear him whistling. She heard the motor turn in the cab, followed by the crunch of the gravel as Nicky drove off. She flipped the switches in the light box, stepped outside the door, and fished for her ring of keys to lock it. The key clicked in the lock, and when it did, her heart broke. She couldn't imagine closing the theater for good but she also was running out of ideas about how she might save it.

Nicky drove back to the garage slowly that night, taking his time. He needed to think about what he had learned in rehearsal before joining the family on Macaroni Night. His stomach growled. The thought of Aunt Jo, serving the spaghetti, lifting it with two long serving forks hot from the bowl, high in the air in a graceful movement like an orchestra conductor, made his mouth water. He yawned as he pulled into the garage and parked over the big red 4.

Peachy was sitting on the office steps wiping tears from her eyes. He jumped out of the cab.

"Are you all right?" Nicky said, running to her.

She looked up at him, her black eyes charcoal pits where her mascara had run. She looked like Theda Bara in a silent picture, forlorn, miserable, and all eyes. "Where were you?" She leaned toward him. "Beer breath. You've been drinking."

"I had one beer."

"We had an appointment at the bridal registry at Wanamaker's tonight."

"Oh, Peach, I'm so sorry! I forgot."

"Nobody could find you. Not your aunt, your uncle, or the colored lady." Peachy pointed up to the dispatch office. "Nobody knew where you were. Where were you?"

"I was at the theater."

She put her head in her hands. "I thought they fired you."

"I was cast in the play. I did pretty good the night you saw me and . . ."

Peachy cut him off. "You're *in* the play?"

"Yeah."

"And you didn't ask me?"

"It happened so fast."

"I'll bet."

"I'm sorry, honey. I didn't do this on purpose. I just forgot to tell you."

"Nick, we got to register. Silverware. Glassware. Goblets. Linens. Folderol!"

"Honey, you know what you want. The Lady Carmine plates."

"Carlyle."

"Just sign up for it. What do you need me for?"

"I didn't get engaged to do all of this alone. The point of engagement and marriage is to be one, to do everything together. That's the joy of life. The merge! I want you to see the stuff—hold it in your hands, because that's what you'll be eating from and drinking out of and using in our home for the rest of your life."

"But I trust your taste, Peach."

"Fine."

"I don't understand why we even have to register at all. Just let people give us whatever they want."

Peachy's eyes bulged out of her head in disbelief. "Stop right there, Nicholas. We will have three hundred and fifty guests including Canadians who won't know what to give us, and if we don't pick the stuff ourselves, we'll wind up with a pile of crapola from Woolworth's! We will be lowballed with pressed glass when we deserve lead crystal! It happened to Rosemary DeCara when she didn't register. She lives in house with a junkpile of dreck she didn't pick. And she kicks herself to this day for not making the effort."

"I'll go with you tomorrow," Nicky said wearily.

"You have to quit the play. You can't work and have that hobby and be a fiancé. It's too much."

"Let me take you home."

"I have my father's car."

"You're in no condition to drive."

"I can drive. I dried up. I wept like my aunt Shush who was put in an asylum because she couldn't stop crying. Okay?"

"That was the aunt with the goiter?"

"Yeah. The one with the neck of a linebacker. I was so traumatized I imagined you bludgeoned on the side of the road like an animal, hairless and abandoned, dead, nothing left but the carcass and that got me through."

"That doesn't make me feel better, Peach."

"I don't want you to feel better. I want you to feel lousy, so this never happens again."

"It won't."

"This is supposed to be the happiest time in my life." Peachy threw up her hands. "And it's been the bleakest. I walk in a vale of tears. Details eat away at my gut like carbolic acid. I can't eat. And I can't sleep, because I'm wondering about you. It's been a black and dismal period. And you are not helping me, Nicholas Castone!" Peachy dabbed away the fresh tears.

"It will change, Peachy."

"It had better." She dried her tears with the handkerchief that was tucked in the cuff of her coat. The white linen square was covered in splotches of black mascara. "Because I am not going to live like this."

"We won't."

"Kiss me."

Nicky kissed Peachy and helped her to her feet. "Are you sure I can't drive you home?"

"No, I'm okay. I'll call you tomorrow with the reschedule."

Nicky walked his fiancée out onto Montrose Street. He opened the door of the car, and she climbed in. She looked so small behind the wheel, with her tiny body and little hands. Even her head looked small. Her hat, a cluster of pink leaves, lay flat against her head. The hat had a green velvet stem protruding from the crown, which made Peachy's head look like a hazelnut.

Nicky stood on the sidewalk for a long time after Peachy drove off, thinking about what he had done. It was true. He kept forgetting Peachy. What was happening to him? What was happening to *them*? And why wasn't he putting Peachy first? She had never done anything but love him. Why wasn't that enough?

The Palazzini women were gathered in the family kitchen preparing dinner while the baby Dominic IV pulled himself to stand in his playpen in the mudroom. Elsa checked on her son through the open door. Nonna, Jo's mother, was asleep in a rocking chair under an afghan in the dining room. Elsa looked in on her before turning back to the stove.

As the Palazzini boys married, their wives folded into life inside 810 Montrose Street under the direction of Aunt Jo, who did her best to make them feel at home but was also clear that they had a stake in it, therefore the girls had responsibilities. Elsa, Mabel, and Lena had to cook, clean, garden, and do laundry for their husbands and themselves, as well as pitch in with the family meals.

The five-story house was assigned by age, with the oldest closest to the ground. The first floor held the common kitchen, dining room, and entrance parlor. The second floor had the most rooms, configured with four small bedrooms and one bathroom.

Aunt Jo and Uncle Dom were in one room; Nonna had another; and Dominic, Elsa, and the baby shared the other two. The third floor, where Mabel and Gio lived, had two rooms. Because Mabel was expecting, the second room was in the process of being turned into a nursery. They shared one bathroom with the fourth floor, where Nino and Lena lived in one large room. A staircase ran from the entrance parlor to the top of the house. Mail and messages were left on the steps, as were baskets of laundry to be carried up and down for convenience.

In the kitchen, situated in the back of the house on the main floor, the enormous black enamel pasta pot full of water was bubbling. Elsa added salt, which caused the water to crest into foam. "Lena, please tell Mom the water is ready."

Lena opened the basement door and hollered down to their mother-in-law, "We got a full boil, Ma."

"On my way," Aunt Jo hollered back.

"Look who's here. The phantom Nicky," Mabel said as she sliced the fresh bread and dumped it into a wooden basket lined with a starched cloth napkin.

Nicky took a seat as Lena prepared the crudités: olives, celery, fennel, and carrots in a cut glass dish.

"You look good, Mabel."

"I'm an ice truck."

"Don't say that, Mabel," Lena said supportively.

"Look at my face. It's like a wheel of Parm."

"You still have your cheekbones," Nicky assured her.

"Where? Who are you kidding? I picked up a book of nursery rhymes for the baby. He's going to have a mother that looks like the dish that ran away with the spoon."

"Don't be so hard on yourself," Elsa said quietly.

"You hardly gained any weight with little Dominic. You're long and slender like Dovina, like one of those exotic models from Europe. Probably because you are from Europe. They make them lean over there."

Elsa smiled and picked up the salad bowl to take into the dining room. She pushed through the doors gracefully.

"Plus she has an air of mystery," Mabel said softly. "War bride."

"We're all war brides," Elsa said as she returned, catching her sister-in-law gossiping.

"Sorry, Elsa."

"There's nothing to apologize for. We all married soldiers, so we're all war brides."

"That's a good point," Nicky said. "And now you'll all be peace-time mothers." He fished an olive out of the jar and ate it. "The family expands."

"Along with my waist." Mabel patted her stomach.

"It doesn't matter what size you are. You look sharp," Lena assured Mabel.

"Thanks to my wardrobe. My mother made me twelve maternity tops—all from the same pattern. Simplicity Number 512, if you're interested. One day you'll see me in gingham checks, the next day stripes, a few solids here and there, and even florals that will be easy to convert into table skirts when this is over. So far, I've only worn this one, and I'm already sick of them."

"They're cute," Lena chirped.

"You think so? I'll save them for you. Have you ever seen a collar this big? My mother said if you have a big collar on a maternity blouse, people look at your face and not lower. I say they look at the big collar."

"All the magazines are showing pilgrim collars and mutton sleeves," Lena offered.

"Gio thinks I look like one of the guys that signed the Declaration of Independence. But what does my husband know about fashion?"

"Not much," Nicky confirmed.

"Go easy. The man is color-blind. Anyhow, it's impossible to look stylish in this condition. They should sell graduation gowns in the maternity department. Save us all a lot of heartache. "

"And it would encourage you to have a smart baby," Nicky said, chewing a slice of the fennel.

"I'm not worried about that. Our baby will be very good at arithmetic. Have you ever watched Gio take bets? His mind holds more numbers than a bingo drum."

"How are we doing, girls?" Aunt Jo pushed through the basement door carrying a tray of homemade cavatelli. Elsa took the tray from her and carefully folded the pasta into the pot of boiling water.

"Call the boys," Aunt Jo instructed Nicky.

"Will do." Nicky moved to leave the kitchen.

"You don't kiss your aunt when you haven't seen her in weeks?"

"It's been a couple days, Aunt Jo," Nicky said, but embraced her and kissed her on the cheek. "You're very needy."

"You're her favorite," Elsa assured him.

"Yes, he is," Aunt Jo agreed.

"You love him more than your own sons," Lena teased.

"At least as much. Right, Aunt Jo?" Nicky gave her another quick hug.

"At least."

Jo went into the mudroom and lifted her grandson out of the playpen and brought him into the kitchen.

"He needs a bottle, Elsa."

"It's ready." Elsa lifted the bottle of milk out of the warmer and tested it on her hand on the way to handing it to her mother-in-law.

"May I feed him?" Jo asked.

"Of course."

Jo took her grandson into the dining room as Mabel, Lena, and Elsa worked in sync to bring Macaroni Night, always on Tuesday evenings, to the table. Elsa lifted the cavatelli off the stove and drained it in a colander in the sink. Lena prepared the pasta bowl with grated cheese, as Mabel arranged the meat platter with fragrant Italian sausage, delicate meatballs, and succulent pieces of pork smothered in the marinara.

Elsa ladled the thick tomato gravy onto the cavatelli in the bowl as Lena cranked fresh Parmesan cheese over the mixture. Elsa lifted the bowl and carried it into the dining room. Her sisters-in-law followed, carrying the platters of meat, bread, and salad. Dominic poured homemade red wine into the glasses. Jo leaned down and kissed her ninety-two-year-old mother on the cheek before taking her place at the head of the table. She cradled her grandson in her arms, and fed him a bottle.

Gio entered from the living room, dressed up in an Italian suit, a silk shirt, and a flashy yellow tie, followed by Nino, who wore the gray pants of the Western Union uniform, with his pale blue work shirt opened at the collar.

Nino was lean, with the sparkling black eyes, regal nose, and full lips of the Sicilian side of the family. The brothers took their seats at the table as Dominic poured them each a glass of wine.

"Elsa, can he try a little of the cavatelli tonight?"

"No. We started him on bananas today. We'll see how he does." Elsa kissed her husband on the cheek.

"You're starving my grandson," Dom thundered as he entered from the parlor. "Here," he said as he handed a small box to Lena. "I was on the turnpike today. Stopped at Stuckey's. Turtles for later."

"Thanks, Pop." Lena took the box into the kitchen.

"What, no ice cream?" Jo asked.

"I didn't have time to stop at Howard Johnson's."

"I like their saltwater taffy," Lena offered.

"Well, tonight you get turtles."

"Thanks, Pop."

Dom took his seat at the opposite end of the table from Jo. "I ate pastina when I was two weeks old. Jo, have your mother instruct Elsa on the proper way to feed Italian babies."

"My mother doesn't remember." Jo winked at Elsa.

"If she could, she'd tell you to give him pastina," Dom barked.

"Pop, he's half Polish, so we're going to wait to give him the pastina," Elsa said agreeably.

Nonna shifted in her chair by the server. Mabel tucked the afghan around her feet. Nonna sighed. Her health had been compromised by a stroke she endured during the war.

"Do whatever you want." Dom held up his hands in surrender,

not meaning it. "My own mother, who rests with the angels, mashed up whatever was lying around and added milk to it and put it in a bottle and fed it to me just like that. She had to make the nipple hole bigger with a safety pin, but you do what you got to do when it comes to building strong bones in a boy."

"Thank you, Pop." Elsa placed her napkin on her lap.

Lena shot Mabel a look. Lena was a newlywed who would do whatever Pop ordered. Elsa had a way of doing what she wanted without directly confronting their father-in-law. Mabel and Lena considered the way Elsa handled Pop an art form.

"Gio," Dom said, turning toward his son, "Jack Carrao came to see me today."

"What for?" Gio swigged his wine.

"I renewed the insurance on the shop, and he told me that you've been playing cards over at Casella's."

"It's strictly a leisure activity, Pop."

"It can be, if you're playing for pennies."

"I do a little wagering here and there. That's all."

"Jack said the pot went to twelve hundred dollars Saturday night."

"Gio!" Mabel sat back in her chair. "That's a house!" She threw her hands in the air, which made the collar on her maternity blouse flip up, nearly poking her in the eye. She patted it down. "You said you weren't playing cards anymore."

He shrugged. "I don't get in deep, honey."

"It stops today," Dom ordered. "We aren't the kind of people who work all day and piss away our profits at night. We work, we save, we live. Right, Jo?"

"That's right."

"So knock it off, Gio."

"Okay, Pop."

Mabel stared at her husband across the table. Gio didn't meet her gaze; instead he cut the sausage on his plate into thin circles before spearing them, putting them in his mouth, and swallowing without chewing as if they were pills.

"I made a deal with Fiore's Funeral Home today," Nino announced.

"You booked Gio's wake?" Dominic joked.

"That's only in the event Pop kills him." Nino played along.

"Or I do," Mabel said as she buttered her bread.

The family laughed.

"I'm not laughing," Gio snarled.

"What deal did you make, Nino?" Dom asked.

"He needs an extra sedan from time to time for his bigger funerals, and he's been using Pronto's."

"Don't say that name in this house. Who names a company after nobody?"

"You took the Palazzini name, Dominic. It's been sixteen years. Give it a rest already," Jo said calmly.

"Anyhow, Fiore told me the quality is not so great, and he'd like to use us. So I said we'd appreciate the business, and he's coming to see you."

Dom shook his fork at Gio. "See that? See your brother? He brings business home, not consternation. I want you to clean up your act, Gio. I grew up with my father the bookmaker, banging on the party wall, tapping out bets on Christmas Eve. I remember a raid at Midnight Mass that scarred me. When you see your priest hauled off in handcuffs, you question your faith, believe you me. And when God's replacement here on earth is parked in a prison cell next to your own father, your gut twists like a python. I don't want the future generations in this family to live with that shroud over their heads."

"Cloud, Dom. *Cloud*," Jo said softly.

"Pop, I said I'd quit." Gio looked at Mabel and back at his father. "It's enough now. I respect you."

"I agree. If this subject was braciole, the meat would be paper-thin by now." Jo glared at her husband. "If you want to reprimand, do it after we eat."

"In other business—" Uncle Dom began.

"I thought we were eating dinner. A peaceful, civilized meal. Is this a business meeting?" Dominic interrupted.

"It's called consolidation of time and effort," his father explained. "We have to sell Car Number Four."

"What will Nicky drive?" Gio asked.

"The sedan, until we procure a new cab."

"Why sell it?" Dominic asked his father.

"Perhaps you didn't hear. We had a dead body in there. You want to ride in such a vehicle?"

"It's not still in the car, is it?"

The boys laughed, and their wives joined in.

"No," Dom said curtly.

"So what's the problem, Pop? Things happen, you clean them up and move forward."

"In normal circumstances you can do that. This is not one of those times."

"Yoo-hoo," Hortense Mooney called out from the kitchen. "I'll leave the bag in the freezer."

"Mrs. Mooney, come in," Dom hollered.

Hortense appeared in her hat, coat, and gloves in the doorway. "I put the accounting sheet in the bank bag. Take it out before you do the night drop."

"How did we do last week?"

"Excellent, Mr. Palazzini. The boys are working hard, and for whatever reason, it was a big week for telegrams."

"Memorial Day coming up," Nino offered.

"Could be. I'd like to put in for the week of July fourth for my vacation."

"No problem, Mrs. Mooney," Dom agreed.

"Where are you going this year?" Jo asked.

"I'm going to paint my kitchen." Hortense smiled. "I'll see you tomorrow. Good evening."

Hortense left through the back door as quietly as she had arrived. Once she was outside, she looked back into the dining room window and observed the Palazzini family seated at the table inside. In her mind, it was the thing these Italians got right: not an evening went by that they didn't share a meal together. There was something about that, something good.

"Uncle Dom, you don't have to sell number four," Nicky said, then sipped his water. "I cleaned it up real nice. You'd never know what happened in the back seat."

"I'm not worried about you, the driver. I'm worried about the passenger that has to sit where that guy had a heart attack and then worse."

"What *worse*?" Lena asked. "What's worse than dying?"

"Dominic, don't say it," Jo warned him. "We're eating."

"The girls are about to clear."

"I'm having another meatball," Gio said as he stabbed the last one on the platter. "But go ahead, Pop."

"Haven't we had enough business tonight? Let's move on to a pleasant topic. Like Nicky's wedding. October twenty-ninth is the big day."

The cousins ribbed Nicky. He slid down in his chair.

"Settle down, boys," Jo admonished her sons.

"We can't wait for Nicky to get married," Gio said.

"So he knows what true happiness is?" Mabel stabbed a pork slab and placed it on her plate.

"Yeah honey. That's it." Gio rolled his eyes.

"Mrs. DePino assigned the cookie trays. We start baking after Labor Day. The girls are wearing pink, I'm wearing yellow, and Connie DePino is wearing green."

"Like a Christmas tree. She'll sparkle like one of those clowns in the Mummer's Day Parade," Uncle Dom promised.

"You're talking about Nicky's future mother-in-law."

"So? They're not blood."

"But she will be family to him. Watch what you say," Aunt Jo said firmly.

Nicky rapped a teaspoon on the table. "Uncle Dom, I need a favor."

"I don't believe you've ever asked me for one."

"I haven't."

"Well, make it a doozy, because evidently I owe you."

"Can we put posters on the cabs to advertise the play at Borelli's?"

"What kind of play?" Gio asked.

"Shakespeare. They do Shakespeare," Mabel barked. "Don't you have any culture?"

"Not presently," Gio retorted. "A cream from Rexall's cleared it right up."

"*Twelfth Night*. That's the play we're doing now," Nicky explained.

"I don't see why not. But no signs on number four. That car is going back as soon as I can make the arrangements."

"What's so terrible you're returning the car?"

"It's not important, Dominic."

"Ma, we're all veterans," Dominic said, and looked at his brothers. "We've seen the worst."

"Tell 'em, Nicky." Uncle Dom removed the napkin he had tucked in his collar from his shirt. It was sprayed with polka dots of red sauce where he'd dripped gravy from the cavatelli. "Go on, tell everybody what happened in the cab."

"I'd rather not." Nicky motioned to Nonna, asleep in her chair.

"She's out like a sack of chestnuts," Uncle Dom promised.

"It's unsavory," Gio said, picking his teeth.

"You know?" Mabel looked at her husband. "And you didn't tell me?"

"I don't like to burden you."

"You don't mind cleaning out my savings account when you want to gamble, but a stupid car story you keep secret?"

"It's not like that," Gio countered.

"See what you started, Dominic? Get the jelly roll, please," Jo instructed Elsa.

"Here's what happened, since my nephew is too schkeeved to impart the story. The fare gets in the cab—where were you?"

"Ambler."

"That's a good fare to the airport," Gio confirmed.

"The fare gets in the car. The wife is in the car. The man collapses. In a flash, Nicky drives him to the nearest hospital. The wife is unglued."

"Her husband is sick, Pop, of course she's upset," Mabel said, looking around the table for support.

"They get to the hospital, but before they can load him on a gurney, the man has a massive heart attack in number four."

"Oh, Nicky," Lena said, her hand on her heart.

"And he died," Nicky said softly.

The family murmured their regrets. Mabel made the sign of the cross.

"But they brought him back inside the hospital with the paddles. But it didn't take. He died anyway." Dom hit his chest with his fist.

"I went to his funeral."

"To collect the tip?" Nino joked.

Everyone laughed except Nicky.

"To pay my respects."

"You hardly knew the guy," Nino said softly.

"True." Nicky nodded.

"People come through your life and you don't know why, they have an effect on you," Aunt Jo said reassuringly.

"He happened to have an effect on me too. He ruined my cab," Dom added.

"I slept for twelve years in the bed Nonno died in, and you

didn't get me a new one. Why do you have to trade in a perfectly good car?" Nino wanted to know.

"Because the man died in my car, in my fleet, and I don't want that story rolling around South Philly connected to my cab company. Okay? We're a class operation, and that's the kind of story that kills business. Pronto gets wind of this, they'll embellish the story and steal our business and print money on our misfortune. I worked too hard to throw everything away on a fluke accident on an airport run. Now, I've made my final decision. Nicky, you're driving the sedan until I can get up to my buddy Lou Caruso on Staten Island and trade in number four."

"Are you going to tell your car dealer what happened?" Jo asked. "Why should he get saddled with a death car?"

"Now you choose to speak?" Dom looked at his wife. "There's nothing wrong with the engine. The car is three years old, hardly a clunker."

"It's like pawning a wedding ring when the marriage doesn't work out. It's bad luck," Lena reasoned.

"Or it's good luck for the person who buys a stone on the cheap and is ignorant of the origins of it and gets it reset and lives happily ever after with a big, hulking diamond on her hand," Dom chided his daughter-in-law.

"I just think you need to tell your dealer that something unfortunate happened in the car, so it's all out in the open up front," Jo offered.

"Okay, now you're forcing me to say the worst."

"That's not necessary, Dom," Jo fired back.

"What could be worse than dying?" Gio pondered.

"When the fare had the massive heart attack in my car . . ."

"Dom, I'm warning you." Jo meant it.

"He soiled himself."

"He what?" The meatball in Nino's stomach flipped like a softball. He put down his fork.

"You heard him." Mabel made a face. "I have a very weak stomach."

"I didn't. But I do now," Lena grumbled.

"Now you've upset the entire family!" Jo raised her voice to her husband.

"Jo, they need to know. As for Car Number Four: I'm going to do what I do the way I do what I do. Period. The facts: The customer had a pain, he had a heart attack, he died, and he shat. The car goes back. End of story."

Elsa entered from the kitchen, placing the dessert plates on the table.

"I'm going to break it off with Peachy," Nicky said softly.

Dominic turned to his cousin. "You like living in the basement that much?"

"What happened?" Lena asked.

"What did you do?" Mabel wanted to know.

"Nothing." Nicky leaned back in his chair.

"Are you all right, Nick?" Elsa asked gently.

"No, I'm not."

"See what you've done?" Aunt Jo glared at her husband.

"What do I have to do with this?"

"Selling his car out from under him. Upsetting the order of things around here. You caused Nicky to vacillate! This was a man who was certain of his decision, and now he's confused." Aunt Jo faced Nicky. "You can't break the engagement."

"Why can't he?" Dom interjected. "Cancel the cookie trays. Return the swatches to Connie DePino. She can wear her green sequins and her big hat to the Knights of Columbus Weenie Roast."

Elsa went into the kitchen.

"I don't care about the clothes," Aunt Jo told him. "I don't care about the desserts. I care about Nicky. He loves Peachy—he's loved her for seven years. That's not for nothing. You don't just throw all that away. That's something. He's at a time in his life when he should be married."

"I agree with you, Aunt Jo. But I'm having thoughts."

"What kind of thoughts?"

"Doubts."

"I had one this morning when I was shaving. You're going to have those," Uncle Dom said with authority. "I get doubts all the time. They tumble over one another inside me like Chinese acrobats. I get so worked up, I think I'm having a series of mini-strokes."

Elsa returned with the jelly roll. She placed it on the table and began slicing it, placing the pieces on the dessert plates and passing them around the table. Mabel reached for the wooden nut bowl on the server. She placed it in the center of the table. The men began to reach for handfuls of nuts in their shells as Mabel handed out the nutcrackers.

"Maybe it's that strange funeral you attended. Maybe you shouldn't have gone," Lena suggested. "It sent you careening down a path."

"Maybe."

"Don't do anything rash." Mabel reached across the table, stabbed the last bite of Gio's meatball off his plate, and ate it. "Sleep on it." Mabel cleared the last of the dinner dishes.

"I will." Nicky had stayed with Peachy for a reason, one greater than love. He believed that she was the right girl for him. But with all that had changed in his life, was she still the right girl? He wasn't so sure.

"Promise me you won't be hasty," Aunt Jo implored.

"Ma doesn't want you to break it off with Peachy because she already got the dishes from the bank," Dominic said, cracking a filbert with the silver nutcracker before popping the meat of it into his mouth.

"What dishes?" Nicky was confused.

"They're a surprise," Aunt Jo confirmed.

"How can they be a surprise when you get them for everybody?" Nino asked her.

"Those dishes from the bank are free." Gio poured himself a cup of coffee.

"They were?" Mabel was surprised.

"You and your big mouth," Jo chided her middle son. "Okay, Elsa, Mabel, and you too, Lena—I gave you each a set of dishes when you got married. I save up and get them at the bank."

"With stamps," Nino added.

"They're good dishes." Lena cared about all wedding rituals, including this display of gifts in the bride's family home after the ceremony. "They were the hit of my bridal shower."

"I thought so too. Of course, I got a set for Nicky and Peachy. They're in the basement. They're white with a daisy chain on the border."

"Very cheery for everyday. Ours are blue with cornflowers on the edge. If we ever get our own place," Lena said wistfully.

"So give the daisy dishes to somebody else," Uncle Dom said impatiently. "Or save them for when Nicky does get married to another girl he likes. Why are we going round and round about a box of free dishes from the bank?"

"I don't care about the dishes," Aunt Jo said. She spaced her silverware next to her plate evenly. "I care about Peachy. The DePinos have been through enough. Some of the family on his side were sent to New Mexico and put in an internment camp during the war. They rounded up the Italians in New Haven without an explanation. That's how the DePinos ended up here in the first place."

"I didn't know they were seeking asylum." Mabel cracked a walnut.

"Not exactly. Al got a job here shortly before the war."

"Any Italian with a boat was suspect. The DePinos had a skiff," Dom confirmed. "What they did to our people."

"Pop, not for nothing, but Italy was on the wrong side of the war." Mabel poured herself a cup of coffee.

"That didn't give them the right to round us up in America."

"This is another slap in the face to that family. Another disappointment. First they're estranged from their family because of the war, and now they lose Nicky. What did they do to deserve all this agita? They're good people."

Elsa took the baby from her mother-in-law and returned to the kitchen.

"Ma. Watch it, would you?" Dominic followed his wife out.

"Must I never mention the war ever again in this house?" Jo threw her hands in the air.

"No," Gio and Nino said in unison.

"I'm sorry. Nicky, I wish you'd reconsider. You're not thinking straight. I don't think you're well. You're pale. Maybe you have anemia. Your iron could be low. You're tired," Jo reasoned.

"Maybe he's tired of Peachy." Dom sampled the jelly roll.

"It's not that, Uncle Dom."

"Then why would you break it off?" Gio asked.

"Seven years—that's about the limit," Uncle Dom said with authority.

"What does that mean, Pop?" Mabel said defensively.

"It means what it means." Dom banged the table.

"It's not as if it was a true seven-year period," Aunt Jo argued. "Nicky wasn't here for half of it. Peachy went to business college in Albany for some of it—he went into the army. When you add it all up, they're practically a new couple, right?"

"He shouldn't marry Peachy if he isn't one hundred percent sure he wants to—he'll be miserable and that will make her unhappy and it will be a disaster." Lena stood up and put her hands on Nicky's shoulders. "I'm with you, Nicky. Do the right thing and the right thing will hold you in good stead. We need more cream for the coffee." She went into the kitchen.

"Peachy will kill herself," Mabel said as she picked at the jelly roll. "I have no personal interest in this because I am not in the wedding party. As an expectant mother-to-be, I'm in a pew with the general guests. I won't be asked to bring up the gifts at Offertory. Nothing. I'll be a face in the crowd with the rest of the onlookers until you see me at the reception parked behind a potted plant getting everybody's John Hancock in the guest book before they go into the hall. But I know a little bit about the DePinos, and they've been saving crates of champagne since the Spanish Civil War for this wedding reception, and they will show up over here with bayonets when Nicky breaks it off."

"Mabel. Don't pile on," Gio said softly.

"Who's piling? It's the truth. You can't yank a girl along for seven years and then cut the rope and leave her drifting out to sea like an old dinghy. Pirates do that, and if they're caught they have to walk the plank. Time is valuable. It has worth. Therefore when you squander someone's time, particularly a woman's, it's stealing. You steal her youth, you might as well steal her car."

"You're just making Nicky feel worse," Gio said tersely.

"He's doing the severing!" Mabel raised her voice.

"He doesn't love her!" Gio yelled.

"He doesn't know what he wants!" Mabel yelled louder.

"He doesn't want her!" Gio stood.

"He needs to grow up!" Mabel stood and leaned across the dining room table.

"He is a grown-up!" Gio stood, banged the table, and sat down.

"A man doesn't flail on the important decisions! He nails down the important things and does not falter! Right, Ma?"

"You're right, Mabel," Jo said weakly.

Uncle Dom poured himself a small glass of bitters. "Women always stand together, and it starts early. Don't ever play Red Rover at Sacred Heart School. Those girls form a line like a chain-link fence—believe me, the Four Horsemen of Notre Dame couldn't cut through it." He downed the glass.

Nicky got a whiff of the Fernet Branca, and it invigorated him. "She'll understand. I'm not doing this to be selfish."

"Oh, now it's a generous act of a loving heart?" Mabel was mystified. "Nicky, for the love of God, pick a side here."

"You'll ruin her life for sure by not marrying her," Aunt Jo said softly.

"How? Besides the ring, the new house, and the party, what is the big deal about getting married?" Nicky was exasperated.

A pall came over the room. Nicky could hear his Uncle Dom's heart thumping in his carotid artery.

Mabel raised her hand. "May I speak?"

"I wish you wouldn't," Gio said under his breath.

"Nicky," Mabel began, "I've been in this family for twelve months, and if I may, I'm gonna explain this to you once. So listen carefully. From the time she has thoughts, a girl dreams of her wedding day like a little boy dreams of becoming a famous baseball player, getting rich, conquering the world, and being important."

Gio groaned.

"A woman holds her virtue like a prize," she continued. "It's her way of securing her future with one man under one God in one house of her own design. In exchange for that life, imagined in her dreams, and promised by the man of her choosing, secured with a decent ring, the woman gives the man a joy he has never known."

Uncle Dom belched on his bitters.

Mabel went on, "Look at what the man gets. He gets a life! He is taken care of! He gets a house full of children, hot meals, the laundry done, waxed floors, clean sheets, and a foot rub every other Saturday night or whatever particular request the husband makes of the wife, that's for the couple to sort out in private. Now, let's look at what she gets. She gets a purpose. A woman aspires to be a bride in order to be a wife, which gives her a job, which gives her a place in this world that is indisputable, irrefutable, and wholly and uniquely her own in the eyes of God and the law. When you yank that away from a woman and you rescind a proper offer of marriage, you have fired her from her own life."

"She'll find somebody else," Uncle Dom interjected. "She's a pleasant enough–looking girl. She's a very lean tomato."

"That's not what we look for in a tomato." Jo didn't try to hide her annoyance.

"Doesn't matter. Won't happen. She won't find anyone else if Nicky wrecks the deal," Mabel assured him.

"How do you know?" Lena asked.

"Peachy waited too long for Nicky. Our group is married off. Whoever might have been a potential replacement died in the war. Only the odd duck here and there is available, and you don't want a specimen from that pool. Peachy is finished." Mabel dumped three teaspoons of sugar into her coffee.

"I agree with Mabel." Aunt Jo patted Nicky's hand. "You've never done anything wrong, Nicky, until now."

"Look, I want to be Joe DiMaggio, but I'm not angry because I can't throw a baseball. I'm not going to marry Peachy because she's wanted this since she was a little girl. I won't marry her because it makes all of you comfortable or because the DePinos want to use up the free champagne they won at a carnival or because they feel badly about their cousins who got thrown into an internment camp."

"Then don't." Aunt Jo removed her hand from Nicky's.

Mabel picked up the empty dessert plates. "Fine. Don't marry her, Nicky. But you will hate yourself for the rest of your life. At night, when you close your eyes, you'll see Peachy's face—like a martyr on a Holy Card. You'll think of those big eyes of hers that look like manhole covers and the image of her face will make you shake like a live electrical cord in the bathtub. I couldn't live with the constant reminder of the pain I inflicted. But of course, it's up to you." Mabel picked up the dishes and went into the kitchen.

"God almighty, she's like an anvil." Uncle Dom threw back the rest of his drink.

"I married a strong girl," Gio said with a shrug. "She can pick up a car with her bare hands."

"We have a lift in the garage for that," Dom reminded him.

"Gio, help with dessert. Daddy will want a dish of gelato. There's peach in the freezer." Aunt Jo motioned with her head, averting a father-and-son argument. Gio complied, and Dom sat back in his chair.

"Mabel is gigantic. I've never seen a woman that big." Dom ate a chocolate turtle from Stuckey's.

"Your mother."

"She was large-boned in her youth."

"So, Mabel is large-boned too."

"From sfogliatelle. Not from bones."

"It doesn't matter. Everyone ends up thin in the end. We all shrink. Bones or not. So knock it off."

"Mabel may have triplets in there. Nicky, we may have to camp a couple babies with you."

"No babies in the basement," Aunt Jo said to Nicky to reassure him. It reminded him that he had put a down payment on the house on Wharton. What a mess he had made, what a pile of details to untangle, if he even could. He hoped that he woke up in the morning having changed his mind and decided to marry Peachy after all.

"Don't marry her," Nonna said from her rocker, under her afghan.

The family turned to her.

"No good!" she said, then closed her eyes again.

"Or. You listen to my mother-in-law. When she's not senile, she's a seer." Uncle Dom cracked a walnut and fished out the meat of the nut and chewed. "To me? That's a sign."

"Pop, you need a sweater," Calla said through the screen door.

"I like the air," Sam told her. The breeze ruffled the leaves on the old elm that shadowed the porch as the blue night settled in around him.

Calla pushed the door open with her hip, handed her father a demitasse cup of espresso, and placed one for herself on the small side table on the porch. She reached into the pocket of her apron and pulled out a cloth napkin. "Biscotti." Calla offered one to her father, almond with glints of pistachio. He took one and sat down.

"You're getting to be a pretty good baker."

"You think so?"

"These are as good as your mother's."

"I'll tell the folks at the bakery you said so."

Sam laughed. "And here I thought you were going to tell me you're ready to get married to that nice Frank Arrigo and make a home of your own and start baking from your mother's recipe box."

"Come on, Dad."

"Don't you want to get married?"

"Someday, maybe."

"He wants to marry you."

"Did he say something?"

"He didn't have to. He circles you like a hummingbird. It's how men do."

"I like him."

"He seems like a nice guy."

"It's happening too fast."

"Your mother was eighteen years old when we fell in love. We got married when she was twenty."

"I know."

"I'd like to see you settled."

"I am settled."

"You look after me. That's not how a young woman should be spending her time."

"I have a say in the matter, and this is where I want to be."

"Helen said I could go and live with them."

"Helen? You'd last two days over there."

"I'd barely get through an afternoon." Sam chuckled.

"Nice of her to offer."

"I have three good daughters. Portia said she'd have me too. But I would never move to New York. Not at this age."

"You should live here in the house you love until the day you die."

"It doesn't always work like that, Calla."

"It will as long as I'm on the job."

"Why are you so determined? Who put you in charge of the happy ending of my life story?"

"I think you should have what you want. You've worked your whole life. Really hard too. And you didn't have a job where you went in and punched a clock, worked your time, and took a paycheck and went home. You had a job where you stuck your neck out—you had to create something that entertained people, that lifted their spirits or made them think. You made something that took them away from the drudgery of their jobs and made them feel like something more was possible. You never knew if there'd be enough left over to pay you and provide for your family. That had to be difficult. On top of that, you had to endure criticism in public. You had to take the beating from the critics, hold your head high, and go back into the theater the next night and pretend that the terrible things written about your best efforts didn't bother you. That's why I want you to live in this house until the end. You should, at long last, do what you want to do. You should choose."

"I did choose, Calla. And your mother let me. She wanted me to be happy at work, even if that meant a year or two would go by where she wouldn't have a new dress or go to the shore, or do the things women enjoy. She never made me feel like I was wasting time or squandering our future on a dream that couldn't sustain us. She just let me work. She just let me be. I hope there's an afterlife, because I want to see her to thank her. I didn't thank her. She gave up everything for me and for you girls, and it was as if we expected it. I had my purpose, and she had hers. It may have worked, but only one of us was selfless."

"When Ma was dying, she asked me to look out for you. She said that you would probably remarry. She thought that Monica Spadoni had an eye on you."

"She ended up with a wallpaper man from Metuchen."

"So Ma was wrong about that. But you're wrong about her. She loved you and admired your work and supported the theater. I almost think she enjoyed Shakespeare more than you do. So you are not to feel badly about what you did or didn't do. You did plenty, and it was enough. You gave up a lot too. And that's why you don't have to live with Helen and her husband and her noisy kids, or with Portia in New York. You will remain right here in your home where you have peace and a kitchen and a garden that doesn't exactly look good but grows in its fashion, the best it can. Okay?"

Sam Borelli nodded because he couldn't speak. He was afraid he would cry, and the last thing he wanted was for Calla to feel sorry for him.

"I'm going to do the dishes." She gave her father a kiss on the cheek. "You need anything?"

"Nope. Thank you."

Calla went inside the old house. The streetlights pulled on, pink beams streaked through the twilight as if to set a scene. Sam sipped his espresso and imagined what might play in the light.

Sam was reading Lear and Richard and the Henrys again, seeking the counsel of kings. He returned to the plays he had tackled in his youth, but now that history was tangible to him, he found wisdom in the verse, phrases that pinpointed his pain and identified his longing in the final act of his life. The monologues and speeches, once his greatest challenges to stage, were now literature to him, and he could read them solely for insight. Sam had always found clarity in the Shakespeare canon, but now he also found solace.

Lear tested his daughters, so Sam never did. Richard chose favorites on the court, which led to his ruin, so Sam was careful to treat all the members of his troupe equally. Henry IV convinced Sam to surrender the theater to Calla, to the next generation, so it might become hers and reflect a new vision. But there was nothing in all of Shakespeare, so familiar to Sam, the text having been his constant companion over many years, that could prepare him for the finale of his own life.

Sam Borelli was suspended in a state of disbelief that he had arrived at the destination. He never thought he would get old, but he had. He never thought he would outlive his wife, and he had. He hadn't foreseen a time when he wouldn't be working, directing a play, running the business of the theater, but now he wasn't. So he filled the moments reading the plays that had brought him pleasure and attempting, through them, to make sense of the experience of living in the context of leaving.

He doubted he would master the mystery in time.

It had been a Sam Borelli choice, and eventually a signature of his process, to stage the final scene of any play he directed on the first day of rehearsal. The actors never liked it, but it gave Sam a framework to build to the playwright's intention. And just as in life, if a man imagines himself on his deathbed and then works back through the years of his life, he will make better decisions along the way, knowing the end. Or at the very least, he'll spend his time more wisely.

The night sky over Bella Vista was violet, embroidered with ribbons of gray clouds obscuring the stars and the moon. From the

Palazzinis' rooftop garden, the neighborhood twinkled below, with strings of lights crisscrossed over gardens and orange embers glistening in the hibachis like buckets of gold.

Alone on the roof, Elsa reveled in the cool night air as she watered the tomato plants. Nicky pushed the door to the roof open.

"Sorry, Elsa." Nicky turned to go back down the stairs.

"No, no, come up. No clouds today, so they got a lot of sun. They need more water."

"Looks like it could rain tonight, though," Nicky said, looking up.

"It could."

"Good batch?"

"There will be enough tomatoes for two winters."

"Here, let me help." Nicky took the hose from her.

Elsa sat down in the chaise longue and put her feet up.

"Is the baby asleep?" Nicky asked.

"Always asleep by eight o'clock."

"You know my aunt Jo is in awe of you."

"Why?"

"Your boy is on a schedule."

"I remember my mother and how she ran our home, and that's how I do it."

Nicky nodded.

"Everyone is worried about you," Elsa said. "Are you sure about ending your engagement?"

"I'm more sure than I was when I asked her to marry me."

"Don't let anyone pressure you into doing something you don't want to do."

"It's not easy."

"If you marry the wrong girl, you'll have a very sad life."

"It sounds like I'm going to be sad any way it goes."

"Only at first."

Nicky turned off the hose and took a seat on the lawn chair. He offered Elsa a cigarette. She took it. He lit hers and then his own. "You have some experience with a broken engagement?"

"I do."

"No kidding."

"I was betrothed to a man before the war. He was a good man. His name was Peter. He was a professor, and he was driving home from a conference, and he was killed in an accident."

"I'm sorry."

"We were going to marry, and our plan was to come to America together and bring my family and his parents. He died, and the plan fell apart. His mother didn't want to leave his grave there. So she insisted on staying."

"And your family?"

"My mother and father thought it was all a terrible mistake and that the people in Germany would come to their senses and take back their government. We know now that didn't happen. I lost my family. My sisters. For nothing."

"And you had already lost Peter."

"In a way, that prepared me for the worst. I was already broken— the war just finished me off."

"But you met Dominic."

"He looks like Peter."

"No kidding."

"I thought Dominic was him. The war was over, and the Americans came in, and I was standing with a group of girls—we had been working in a hospital; spared, they called us—and he came in with the American officers, and he looked at me as though he knew me, and I felt the same when I looked at him, and that was that."

"Did you marry right away?"

"We were liberated, and as soon as he could, Dominic came for me."

"Based on one meeting?"

"He knew."

"And you?"

"I felt safe with him. For me, that's love. Nick, you have to decide what love is for you. Everybody does. And people are different."

"I'll say."

"You should find a girl who is the same as you are in the ways that matter."

"Peachy wants the wedding, the house, the kids, but I have a funny feeling she doesn't really want me."

"Why do you say that?"

"She could have everything she dreams of with just about any guy in the world. She doesn't really need me to have her dream."

"I'm sure she doesn't feel that way."

"I don't think she'd understand, even if I explained it."

"But you'll have to."

"I know. She's waited so long."

"Don't feel badly about that."

"Why not?"

"Because she didn't have to wait. No one made her wait."

Nicky thought about this, and it made sense. Never once did Peachy ever say, "I've had enough." She never forced an issue or took any side but his; she waited patiently, knowing that if she did, that Nicky would eventually do what she wanted, because he always had.

Elsa put out her cigarette and stood. "I'm going to check on the baby." She started down the stairs, but before she left, she turned back. "Nicky, of all the things I hope for you, I want you to know the joy that comes from watching your baby sleep. It almost makes up for everything I've lost."

"I believe you."

Elsa went down the stairs, and Nicky leaned back, took a slow drag off his cigarette, and wondered where he'd find the courage to change his life. He remembered sometimes valor just shows up. If he was going to do any praying on the subject, it would be to ask for the vision to recognize it when it did.

Calla listened at her father's bedroom door. When she heard his loud, rhythmic snores, she smiled and walked down the hallway to her room. She left her bedroom door slightly ajar in case her father needed her during the night, and climbed into her bed. Through the open window, a cool breeze floated over her. She heard the soft echo of laughter from the street below as a man and a woman walked by, laughing over a joke. She shivered and pulled the coverlet up to her chin.

Lately, Calla had gone off to sleep playing the same scene in her mind, Act 4, scene 5 of *Twelfth Night*. She felt the velvet gown stand stiffly away from her body, the heat of the spotlight on her brow, the grainy finish of the paint on the stage floor, and Nicky Castone's touch when he brushed the hair out of her eyes. Her mind would wander to the witnesses, the audience beyond the curved lip of the stage, watching the scene. She would remember the note she gave the actors about wedding scenes in Shakespeare's comedies. The characters commit to marriage in front of a crowd in order for the vows to stick. People are unlikely to break a promise when they have made it public.

Calla had a recurring dream whereby Nicky and she would pop up in other scenes in the play, sometimes as themselves. The scene would unfold, Nicky would say his lines, but when it came time for Calla to speak, she couldn't. Calla never spoke in the dream, and yet she knew the lines. She spent the dream frustrated, trying to get the words out, to explain that she understood, that she knew her lines.

Calla thought she might confide in Frank about the strange dream, but decided not to, even though, as they became closer, it was exactly the kind of thing she believed she should share with him. What she couldn't figure out is why she dreamed of that scene and continued to, and when she woke up, it stayed on her mind.

When she examined the memory of that night, she recalled that she was unable to control her emotions. She remembered that Enzo and Nicky were very good, and for reasons she could not name, she had lost control of the scene. It didn't matter, of course—she was a last-minute understudy with minimal acting skills. It wasn't that she had not hit the mark in her own estimation. It was something else entirely, something that had not yet revealed itself to her. In time, she hoped to crack it.

Ambassador Carlo Guardinfante woke up in a hospital bed, not knowing where he was or how long he had been there. He had a view of a small patch of gray sky from his window. When he tried to move, his midsection, bandaged tightly like a corset, would not allow him to bend, sit up, or breathe deeply.

The last thing he remembered was sipping champagne and eating lobster with the American Italians and the captain of the MS *Vulcania.*

Carlo panicked and cried out.

A serious nun, the sober nurse, Sister Julia Dennehy, wearing a full-length blue and white habit, pushed through the door. She helped Carlo lie back in the bed.

"You must rest, sir."

"Parli Italiano, Sorella?"

"Poco." She smiled.

The nun could speak a bit of Italian, and the Ambassador knew enough English, that the pair could cobble together a conversation, enough to assuage his fears.

"Dove sono?"

"L'ospedale. Saint Vincent's Hospital in Greenwich Village. New York City."

"Cosa mi é successo?"

"You collapsed aboard ship, you were very sick. They brought you here as soon as the boat docked. The surgeon removed your appendix."

Carlo looked around the room. His regimentals hung on the back of the door; his medals dangled off the sash, pulling away from the silk. His trunk stood in the corner of the room.

"I must go. *Sono un ospite d'onore di una festa a Roseto*, Pennsylvania."

"No. I won't allow it. You had surgery. You risk infection if you leave this hospital. I will send a telegram and explain the circumstances of your cancellation."

Carlo looked into Sister Julia's eyes. No matter where a man walked in the world, no good would come of arguing with a nun. He pointed. *"C'e una lettera nella tasca della mia uniforme,"* Carlo sighed. *"I miei piani."*

The nun wrote down Carlo's itinerary and the contact information in Roseto and left his room. She handed the message for the telegram to the nurse on duty.

"Telegram for Roseto, Pennsylvania."

"Where's that, Sister?"

"Send it through Philadelphia. They'll find it."

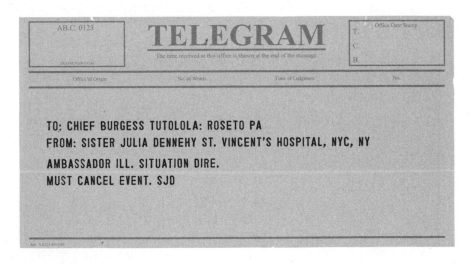

TO: CHIEF BURGESS TUTOLOLA: ROSETO PA
FROM: SISTER JULIA DENNEHY ST. VINCENT'S HOSPITAL, NYC, NY
AMBASSADOR ILL. SITUATION DIRE.
MUST CANCEL EVENT. SJD

5

The Palazzini family bought the entire Row H in the orchestra, straight across, for Nicky's debut in *Twelfth Night*. He had warned the girls about their hats, and they obliged him. Aunt Jo wore her chignon in a snood. Elsa wore a simple black velvet curvette that matched her church coat; Lena a brimless calot hat of peacock-blue satin that adhered to her head like a bandage; and Mabel wore a Scottie hat, the only small hat she owned. Made of emerald-green velvet, the Scottie was out of season, but it qualified as teensy, so it made the cut and was worn to the theater.

Aunt Jo had invited the DePinos, who sat in the center of the row, with Peachy, dressed head to toe in pink, sitting between her parents like a smear of raspberry jam. The trio sat upright like three pillars of granite in a Tuscan tomb.

Nicky wasn't shy about sharing the hat rule with the DePino women so Peachy wore a band in her hair with a flat pink bow, while her mother, attempting to keep within the bounds of restraint, wore a dark pink roller hat covered in ostrich feathers. The patron who sat behind Concetta in Row R of the orchestra sat on the Philadelphia phone book to see over the feathers.

Dom anchored the row on one aisle, his bad knee extended out into the aisle like a divining rod. Nino sat next to his father. Dominic the son took the aisle seat on the far end of the row, while Gio's seat remained next to his brother.

Gio stood in the back of the theater, tapping his foot on the floor as he rested his chin on the orchestra wall facing the stage. His face looked like an apple used for target practice in Sherwood Forest. Gio followed Nicky's rule about two bit hustlers who attend the theater, but his cousin also had claustrophobia in crowds, so whenever he entered a public space, he perspired, choked for air, and checked the exits, camping near one for a quick getaway.

Calla moved through the hallway outside the dressing rooms in the basement as the actors emerged in costume to go up the stairs to take their places onstage for the first scene. She wore a caramel-colored tulle skirt, upon which she had added layers in the costume shop, and a crisp white blouse paired with her mother's pearls. She ran a brush through her hair as she walked.

"How are we doing?" she asked the star of her company.

"We're good." Tony put out his cigarette in the ash can before going up the stairs. Calla pulled him into a corner. "Look out for Nick, will you?"

"He's got it."

"You think so?"

"He knows the show better than me."

"He seems awfully nervous." Calla wrung her hands.

"My first show—remember?"

"Yeah. You went out the stage door. We had to hold the curtain. Dad found you over on Pine Street in the alley."

"Terrified."

"I'll check on him."

Calla walked down the hallway to the men's dressing room and rapped on the door. "Everybody decent?"

She heard a rumble in the affirmative and entered to find Nicky sitting alone at the mirror. "You okay?"

Nicky nodded.

"You're going to be great," Calla said supportively.

"I'm shooting for . . . getting through it."

"You'll do just fine."

"My whole family's here."

"We have a full house. Your uncle invited everybody from the American Legion, and they paid full price. Rosa is beside herself. She never had to count that much money. She actually used the adding machine. Thank you."

Calla turned to go, but Nicky grabbed her hand. She looked at him, her heart filled with sympathy.

"You're ready, Nick. You really are." She smiled at him.

In that moment, Calla Borelli had the face of an angel. The light from the dressing mirror made her eyes dazzle like black spinel; her hair fell forward to frame her face as if it were a painting. She was golden and pure, hovering over him, protecting him. He felt safe, which meant he could be honest with her. "I'm scared."

Calla sat down next to him and took his hands into hers. "You know every word. And if you forget anything, Tony and Norma will jump in and cover for you no matter what. Enzo is your rock. He knows every role in the play, he has your back. Josie would like all that's attached to your back . . ."

Nicky laughed.

"There's nothing to be afraid of—unless you have a fear of success."

"I'm getting exactly what I want," Nicky said softly.

"What's wrong with that?"

"It's the first time it's ever happened to me."

"Well, it's about time. You deserve it."

Frank Arrigo stood in the doorway of the dressing room, observing his girlfriend holding hands with a guy in a leotard, their heads together, whispering, practically cheek to cheek. The moment appeared so intimate, it looked like they might kiss. Frank almost backed away to give them privacy until he remembered that Calla was his girl, and he didn't like what he saw. Jealousy roiled through him, pea green and nasty. "Hey," he barked, breaking them apart.

Calla jumped in her chair, and Nicky turned to face him.

"I have some pre-curtain jitters," Nicky explained.

"Have a nip, buddy. That'll help." Frank extended his hand to Calla. She rose and took it.

"You'll be fine," Calla assured Nicky. "See you after the show."

"If I'm feeling generous," Frank warned Nicky.

Rosa DeNero flickered the lights in the lobby, her mood bubbly for the first time since she'd begun working the box office at Borelli's. Show night didn't stretch in front of her like a penance; she actually had something to do. A full house meant a full accounting, which would be her pleasure after a run where most of the velvet seats had sat empty. Rosa returned to the box office to count the money.

Hortense Mooney pushed through the glass doors and walked up to the box office window. "One ticket, please."

Rosa looked at up her.

"Do you have a colored section?" Hortense asked matter-of-factly.

"The mezzanine, I guess."

"You guess?" Hortense smiled but her tone was pure annoyance.

"No one colored ever came to this theater."

Hortense chuckled. "Not a lot of us in Shakespeare. Forgive me. There's *Othello*. Do you have a ticket for me?"

"Yes, we do. It's the last seat in the mezzanine. Two dollars."

Hortense beamed as she reached into her purse. "Nicky Castone filled the house."

"Do you think that's the reason?"

"Absolutely."

"I wondered."

"He's special," Hortense said. She laid two crisp one-dollar bills in the money tray.

"Or he runs into a lot of people when he's driving a cab."

Hortense made her way up the stairs to find her seat. The usher was taken aback when she saw her, but nodded, checked her ticket, handed her a program, and gently lifted the velvet curtain so that she might slip into her aisle seat. No one noticed her when she did.

Sam Borelli walked through the lobby as Rosa DeNero was closing the auditorium doors. "Mr. Borelli!"

"I'm going to stand," he said with a grin.

"You look good."

"You sound surprised."

"I haven't seen you in a long time."

"I'm staging a comeback. What do you think?"

"We sold out the house tonight. I just sold the last seat."

"Tops my comeback."

Sam slipped into the theater. He looked over the heads of the audience from the rear of the orchestra. Rosa was right. There wasn't an empty seat. He filled his lungs with the air of the place, inhaling the scents of oil paint, lily of the valley, tobacco, and the fresh ink on the glossy paper of the Playbill. After all these years, the anticipation of the curtain going up still thrilled Sam Borelli.

Calla hiked up her skirt and took the steps to backstage wings two at a time with Frank following closely behind her. In the wings, the actors were stacked up in a row, like a deck of cards, ready for their entrance in the opening scene. Nicky stood behind Tony, his eyes focused on the stage and the task that lay before him.

Calla whistled softly before releasing the pulley and yanking the stage curtain. Frank took over the ropes, which allowed her to take one final look at her cast before the trumpet sounded. She was confident, but in this moment, she wanted success for Nicky more than he wanted it for himself. Nicky as Sebastian would not make his entrance until the first scene of Act 2. Calla slipped over to him. "You have time. Relax into it."

"I will," Nicky whispered without taking his eyes off the stage.

Frank was annoyed that Calla was paying attention to Nicky again. If he could have, he would have lifted one of the stage weights, the heavy sandbags that countered the pulley system that flew the flats up and down from the ceiling, and thrown it in Nicky Castone's direction. Instead, Frank gently took Calla's arm. He pulled her close and cinched his arm around her waist, making it clear to anyone who was curious that she belonged to him.

"Let's watch the show with Dad," she said.

Frank answered by kissing her lightly on the lips.

Peachy DePino had meant to ask Nicky for a copy of the play, so she might read it before his debut, but she had been so consumed with details of their wedding that she forgot. Besides, the theater had become a subject they avoided. She'd demanded he quit the play, but he'd ignored her request, so she in turn pretended she had not made it.

Peachy slipped her gloved hand into her mother's. As Connie turned to look at her daughter, she nodded, causing a few ostrich feathers to fly off her hat and dance through the air. The patron seated behind Connie sat up higher on her phone book to avoid the filaments as the opening scene unfolded.

Peachy was grateful to her mother, who was the rudder on the ship of her long engagement, guiding her daughter toward the safe harbor of a wedding ceremony. It was her mother who'd convinced her to ignore Nicky's weird obsession with the theater. Every marriage is a power struggle, Connie had assured her daughter, and even though she wished to protect her from any agita, Peachy and Nicky would have their struggles too.

Besides, Connie was happy when Jo Palazzini called and in-

vited them to the play; it showed that they were on the DePino
side and wanted this wedding to unfold without incident and be
as splendid as Connie had envisioned it. It showed that they loved
Peachy and wanted the two families to mingle socially. These positive steps were more than that; they were signs that the marriage
would be solid and supported on both sides by two good families.
Connie felt secure that night; her apprehensions about show business and Nicky's role in it were put aside as her husband, daughter,
and she were safely landlocked by Palazzinis in the center of the
row. Connie relaxed back into her seat, confidently if not smugly.

A series of lights rigged to the mezzanine wall were covered in
blue gels, the color of the water off the coast of Capri. The beams
pulled on behind the various shades of blue, casting a glow that
conjured the sea. Nicky followed Paulie out onto the stage, crossing to take his downstage mark. His senses heightened, he heard
whispers of *Break a leg* from the wings, the rustle of programs
from the audience, and the familiar murmurs of his family's chorus of voices as he crossed the stage.

Paulie, playing Antonio, turned and faced Nicky. "Will you stay
no longer? nor will you not that I go with you?"

Nicky looked at him. He knew he had the next line, but he could
not remember it. He breathed deeply. Paulie cheated upstage and
murmured, "By your patience, no . . . ," to cue him.

But the prompt did not help. Nicky stood still, engulfed in the
blue, untethered, unconnected, and floating.

The Palazzini family and the DePinos leaned forward in their
seats, uncertain what was happening but knowing something was
terribly wrong.

Sam Borelli mouthed the lines silently from the back of the
theater.

Paulie, thinking quickly, gave his next cue, hoping that it would
jostle Nicky into the moment. He knew that when an actor went
up and the line was gone, it might be gone in that performance

forever, so it was best to press on. "Let me yet know of you whither you are bound."

Frank propped himself against the back wall of the theater, behind the orchestra section, and folded his arms, secretly thrilled that the artichoke in tights was failing, as Calla moved forward, and stood next to her father.

Hortense leaned forward in her seat in the mezzanine. "Come on, Nicky," she whispered softly. "Come on."

Nicky turned toward the audience, and soon the blue lights became like waves of cool water that refreshed him and brought him back to life, into the play, the scene, this line, and to the moment:

> *No, sooth, sir: my determinate voyage is mere*
> *extravagancy. But I perceive in you so excellent a*
> *touch of modesty, that you will not extort from me*
> *what I am willing to keep in; therefore it charges*
> *me in manners the rather to express myself. You*
> *must know of me then, Antonio, my name is Sebastian,*
> *which I called Roderigo. My father was that*
> *Sebastian of Messaline, whom I know you have heard*
> *of. He left behind him myself and a sister, both*
> *born in an hour: if the heavens had been pleased,*
> *would we had so ended! but you, sir, altered that;*
> *for some hour before you took me from the breach of*
> *the sea was my sister drowned.*

Calla went up on her toes in victory as Sam nodded his approval. Hortense's hands went up in the air in a silent hallelujah, as the Palazzini family exhaled and relaxed back into their seats. Al DePino stayed upright, judging his future son-in-law with disdain. What kind of a man wears hosiery and why is that man in leotards marrying his daughter?

Connie looked around the theater. When she saw the audience

approve of Nicky, it made his victory her own. A smile crept across her face and would remain there through the curtain call. Peachy, who was perspiring so heavily she was caught in her own rain shower, pulled the wet fabric away from her skin under her armpits to air it out.

Onstage Nicky eased into the play, recalling his lines through the blocking. Careful not to exaggerate or primp, he listened and moved and spoke with clarity. Sam noticed his daughter's eyes follow Nicky in his scenes with particular interest. Calla caught her father looking at her. He didn't have to say a word; he knew something was happening; so did she, and so did Frank Arrigo.

After the show, the families and some of the patrons waited for the cast in the lobby. Rosa broke out the Dixie cups and a few bottles of cold champagne left over from opening night to celebrate Nicky's debut.

When Nicky entered the lobby, his aunt, uncle, and cousins surrounded him. Gio hugged him. "I can't believe you made it through the whole thing."

"So did you, Gio. Your first play. Right?"

"Yep. Unless you count *Gert's the Gal with Garters*. Saw that in the Poconos."

"Nothing but class, that's my Gio. How did you memorize all those lines?" Mabel marveled.

"I'm just relieved they came out of my mouth when they were supposed to."

"You were so handsome in the wedding scene!" Lena swooned.

"The language didn't put you off?" Nicky asked them.

"After a while you understand it," Uncle Dom admitted. "It's like going to a foreign country, you listen long enough, eventually people make sense."

As Rosa passed the paper cups filled with champagne, Nicky

reveled in his family's support. This might be what he loved most about being a part of a big family. The Palazzinis showed up for one another no matter the occasion. If any family member was receiving a sacrament, a diploma, or a driver's license, every member of the family put on their best hat and went to bear witness to the achievement. If Nicky had any sense of self-confidence, it had come from the circle Aunt Jo and Uncle Dom had created; even though he was their nephew and not one of their sons, Nicky had always been made to feel he was inside of it.

Peachy stood back with her parents and watched the Palazzinis fawn over Nicky, waiting her turn to do the same. Her mother stuck her finger in her daughter's back. "Get in there," she hissed.

Peachy moved into the huddle of Palazzinis like a pink streak in the whipped cream of a cherries jubilee. She squeezed through until she got to her fiancé.

"You were wonderful, Nicky," she said, throwing her arms around him.

"You think so?"

"I do. There was that awkward start where something happened, but then you bounced right back."

The Palazzinis grew quiet.

"I mean, it was nothing," Peachy covered. "No one noticed."

"Then why did you mention it?" Mabel said under her breath.

"It was a glitch. Just a glitch. The rest of the play—you were Palmer Method perfect."

Nicky put his arms around Peachy. "Thanks, honey. Your support means the world to me."

Al DePino stood back and rolled his eyes into the top of his head until there was nothing left in his eye sockets but the whites.

"Behave yourself. Don't say a word," Connie whispered to her husband.

"Maybe you want to throw another peignoir set into the wedding trousseau for the groom."

"I mean it, Al." Connie glared at him. "If you can't behave, go sit in the car."

Calla and Frank joined the group. "Mr. Palazzini, I'm Calla Borelli, and I want to thank you for filling the theater."

"It's the least the boys at the Legion could do. I think they enjoyed the show."

"We're very grateful to you."

"Mr. P? Calla's fella is going to be mayor someday," Peachy offered. "Mayor Frank Arrigo."

"Peachy is a visionary." Calla patted Peachy's shoulder. "I hope this vision comes true."

"Me too." Frank smiled at Peachy.

"Really," Dom said, looking Frank up and down. "You're out of your mind if you think this city will ever elect an Italian American mayor."

"Things are changing, sir." Frank shrugged. "We are making inroads."

"That's only because we built them," Dom fired back. "But good luck to you. You're a tall man, and that goes a long way in politics. Usually it's the only thing you need."

"That and the purse," Frank joked.

Dom nodded approval. "Hey, with that attitude, you may swing an election your way."

Nicky made sure everyone was served champagne. Peachy held the tray and stayed by his side as he thanked every person in the lobby for coming to the show.

"We should get going." Connie laced her arm through her husband's. "We want to say good night." She interrupted the small group Nicky was regaling with stories of the play. "We have a gown fitting in the morning. Can you get her home soon, Nicky?"

"Yes, of course."

"I'm really tired, honey." Peachy put her arm around Nicky's waist.

"Just a sec, and we'll go." Nicky continued with his story.

Frank helped Rosa collect the empty paper cups. Calla stood by the box office with her father. "You tired, Dad?"

"Not when I come to the theater."

"Who needs sleep when you're doing what you love?"

"That's right, Calla. Don't forget it. When you love your work, you never need a vacation."

"Is that true?"

"I think so."

"I thought we didn't go on vacation because we didn't have any money."

"Well, there was that too." Sam laughed.

Calla looked across the lobby. Peachy had her head on Nicky's shoulder. She looked over at Frank, chatting with Al DePino, then back at Nicky. She watched as Nicky took Peachy's hand and walked out the glass doors, followed by the Palazzini clan.

"You all right?" her father asked her.

"That's a big family."

"Nothing like it."

"I wish we had one, Dad."

"It's got its minuses."

"I'm sure it does. But it seems you get so much more of everything," Calla said wistfully. "More support. More love. Look at how they carry Nicky."

"Depends on the family. Sometimes a family can drop you too. I've seen that happen. Nothing is what it seems from the outside, Calla. There's always a story when the door closes or the curtain comes down."

Sam went to talk with the cast, who were huddled in a corner, smoking and laughing. He wanted to congratulate them too.

Calla leaned against the box office window just as Rosa DeNero raised the shade. The snap startled Calla.

"I have a question," Rosa said through the glass.

"Yes, we have a night drop at our bank. We've just never had to use it."

"I know all about that. I have it all set to go. I have another question if you don't mind. Do we have a colored section?"

"I don't think so."

"We do now. I sold a lady a ticket. A single. I put her in the mezz."

"Did she mind?"

"No, she liked it. Left during the curtain call."

"Hat with a long feather?"

"Yeah. You know her?"

"Nicky does." Calla beamed. Hortense Mooney had made it. Nicky had more than a big extended family, he had a world behind him, lucky guy, and it was in color.

Nicky leaned into the circle curve as he drove around the Art Institute to the lot nearest the Fountain of the Sea Horses. He parked the sedan near the Azalea Garden as the orange sun rose in a pink sky. The purple lace of azalea blossoms poked through the green along the winding white gravel path. In the morning light, the stones under his feet looked like gold nuggets.

He didn't hear the familiar whoosh of sheets of fresh water rushing over the fluted urn at the top of the fountain. He quickened his step to find that the shallow bowl beneath the pedestal was dry. The marble sea horses that held up the bowl were dry as well; no rivulets of water flowed over the carved scales of their smooth backs and tumbled into the pool beneath them.

Nicky walked around the base of the fountain and found a repairman working on the limestone lip of the pool beneath the sea horses, filing a small section of the stone with a wire brush.

"What's the problem?"

"There's a crack at the base. We went in yesterday and patched it."

"I thought this fountain was indestructible."

"Where'd you get that idea?"

"I don't know. Italian travertine. Isn't it the most durable of all stone? And it was carved by the great artisans."

"Great sculptors aren't God. They make objects of beauty, but they can't make them last forever. Well, I might have to include God in that group. Look at women."

"A woman's beauty is a matter of perspective, not age." Nicky shrugged.

"I'm just joking with you. The problem here is the exterior. The carving is superb, but the foundation is under stress from the weight of the sculptures, and then you add the water. Eventually we'll have to take the entire thing apart and shore up the central disc."

"That sounds complicated."

"And expensive. That's the problem with something like this— it's built to impress. Nobody thinks, 'How's it going to work over the long haul, how will it survive ten, twenty years in the elements?' They don't know from a Philadelphia winter in balmy Rome. You know what I mean?"

"I do."

"Anything that lasts has to be built with strength from the inside out. The veneer—"

"Is just a veneer?"

"The builder had to have a way in to work on the stone over time—you're not looking at one solid piece of stone on these dishes."

"I spend a lot time on that bench over there. It's interesting to know the facts. Thanks." Nicky turned to go.

"Were you going to make a wish?"

"I'm sorry?"

"Were you going to make a wish this morning? You know, throw a coin in the fountain."

"I just came here to think."

"You got the look of somebody who already made a decision."

"I do?"

The man laughed. "That, or you expected to meet somebody here."

"I'm alone."

"You came here to think." The man stood back from his work. "I wish I could tell you I'll have the water flowing soon. But as it stands, I'm behind. Even with overtime, I can't get the work done."

"Do you like your job?"

"I work so my wife can spend. I'm lucky. I have a good pension coming. I've been an engineer with the city since I was twenty-six years old. You married?"

"No."

"Would you like to be?"

"To the right girl." Nicky kicked the gravel with his shoe. Now that the sun was up, the stone path was back to gray, the gold lifted away with the morning light.

"When Bernini built the original fountain in Rome, a woman had just broken his heart. And the sea horse is the only male species that can reproduce without a woman. There was a message in the ravioli there."

"I'll say."

"Did you get your heart broken?"

"I'm afraid I might be the one doing the breaking."

"You want a piece of advice? Don't do it on her birthday, your birthday, or a holiday, or in a place she frequents."

"Sounds like you've been in my predicament."

"And back again. I made the mistake of choosing the wrong day, time, and place. It backfired."

"How did it work out?"

"Married thirty-two years in December."

"Congratulations." Nicky extended his hand. "Nicky Castone."

"Ed Shaughnessy. Everybody calls me Big Ed."

Uncle Dom leaned back in the driver's seat of No. 4 as though it were the flannel-covered club chair in the corner of the garage where he'd sit and nap or listen to the Dodgers games on the radio. He had one arm propped on the driver's-side door, the steering wheel nestled in the crook of his thumb and forefinger, and his other arm slung over back of the passenger seat. As he joined the line for the car ferry, Dom's stomach grumbled. "Nicky, root around in that basket your aunt packed, will you?"

"Sure." Nicky reached behind the front seat and pulled the picnic basket onto his lap. "She put all kinds of stuff in here."

"Like what?"

"Cavazoons. There's ham-and-butter sandwiches. Olives. Cookies."

"To drink?"

"Limeade."

"That's my girl. Nick, when you do get married, whether you marry Thin Melba—"

"You mean Peachy?"

"Yeah, the DePino kid. Peach Melba. Whether you marry her or not, marry a girl that can pack a basket for a car trip."

"What would you like?"

"We'll save the sandwiches and the savories for the trip home. Let's have a cavazoon. That'll tide us over. I like a little uptick of sugar before a negotiation."

Nicky unwrapped the large half-moon-shaped pastry, which Aunt Jo had cut in half. The flaky crust was filled with a fluffy mixture of whipped ricotta, egg, and vanilla. The uncle and his nephew bit into the delicacy and chewed. There weren't words for how light and delicious a treat the cavazoons were, so they ate them in silence.

"Uncle Dom, did you know my dad?"

"Yeah. I knew him. Not well. But I knew him."

"What was he like?"

"A fine fellow. Why do you ask?"

"I wonder about him."

"You never asked me about him before."

"I didn't think it was a good idea."

"Why?"

"You know how it is, there are things you can ask and things you shouldn't."

"You can ask me anything, kid. I'm an open book with torn pages. Your mother was a beautiful person."

"I remember her."

"Anyone that ever met her never forgot her. Your aunt still cries, she misses her so much."

"Do you miss your brother?"

Dom grunted. "No, I do not."

"He's still alive."

"Yes, he is."

"So it's different. If he were dead, you'd feel differently. Or maybe you wouldn't. I don't want to speak for you."

"I try not to think about it. I can't change the situation."

"You could. You could walk over to Fitzwater Street and talk to him any time you wanted."

"I don't go where I'm not wanted."

"If he came to you?"

"My door is always open."

"So you do miss Uncle Mike."

Uncle Dom swatted the crumbs from the front of his shirt. "Well, you miss the history. He knows things only he could know about me, and vice versa. That has value when you get to be my age. But you have to weigh it against the Sturm und Drang, the tumult and the agita. And when it comes to your uncle, it's obvious what teeters and what totters."

"If I had a brother, I don't think I could live so close to him and not see him."

"I know he's there."

"But you don't speak to each other."

"But I know he's there."

"And that's enough?"

"It has to be. You can't go out and fix it now."

"Why not?"

"Too much. Too much."

"And that's that?"

"It's something you have to accept. I went to see a priest about it. And he told me a story about the Renaissance. Funny, it always takes an Irishman to tell an Italian a good story about our people. Anyhow, I told him my troubles because I was guilty about the situation—I'm the oldest brother and I take responsibility, you know? Primogeniture is a concept that goes back to the Bible, Isaac and Jacob and Esau, it's the basis of law itself. The firstborn son gets everything. No fooling around there. So this priest says that Mike and I were rivals, like Michelangelo and Leonardo da Vinci. When we worked together, we went at each other, and there were problems. But when we separated, my business did well, and his business did well. The priest said, go talk to your brother and just be his brother. Keep business out of it. But I couldn't do it. It was too late."

Dom pulled into Lou Caruso's Cars New & Used on Empire Street and glided the cab next to the glass box in the center of the lot. "Take the basket," he said to Nicky.

Nicky waited outside with the basket as Uncle Dom went inside. He watched the men shake hands. Lou Caruso sat in his chair as Uncle Dom negotiated the return of Car No. 4 to the lot. Uncle Dom had his arms outstretched for much of the wheeling and dealing, looking a lot like the trapeze artist who walks the high wire between skyscrapers, holding a crossbow and wearing nothing but ballet slippers and a wrestler's tank suit. It was as if his uncle were balancing the return of the car with the value of a new one in his hands.

Fascinated, Nicky began to copy his uncle's stance, looking at his own shadow on the sidewalk. He remembered how Sam Borelli insisted his actors observe behavior, and how emotions move through the body. There was something about the way Uncle Dom held his body that made the men inside listen to him and do his bidding. Nicky could see Lou Caruso through the glass, mesmerized, or maybe entertained. It didn't matter. It appeared that Uncle Dom was effective. If there's anyone in the world who has seen the gamut of human emotion, from lust to greed to indifference and back again, it's the used-car salesman.

Uncle Dom emerged with a set of keys that he tossed to his nephew. "We're taking a lightly used 1946 Chrysler. This one's used less miles than old number four, if you can believe it, and it's got a posh interior. Lou Caruso is very particular. You'll be riding in style, Nicky." Dom took the basket and led Nicky to the spot where the newest addition to the Palazzini fleet was parked.

The mustard-yellow cab gleamed in the sun. Nicky peered inside. Uncle Dom wasn't kidding. Black leather seats, pin-tucked, with flat turquoise leather buttons and a shiny licorice trim, looked fashionable and chic, almost too upscale for a Philly cab. Nicky flipped the hood on his way to the driver's seat. The engine was an orchestra of tubes, wires, bolts, and boxes in mint condition.

"How is she under the hat?" Dom asked as Nicky climbed into the new used cab and turned the key over. Uncle Dom climbed into the passenger seat.

"What a stunner." Nicky grinned.

"And she's all yours. Say hello to the new number four." Uncle Dom pushed his seat back.

"Almost makes me happy to be a hack, Uncle Dom." Nicky turned the key. The engine purred like Eartha Kitt holding a blue note as Dom and his nephew headed for home.

Nicky waited for Peachy on the sidewalk outside of Wanamaker's. He took the final drag off his cigarette when he saw her coming through the revolving doors. She smiled at him through the spinning glass.

She kissed him. "Where's number four?"

"Uncle Dom traded it in."

"It was practically new."

"Yeah. But he had his reasons."

"You better watch him. You know he's getting to that age where their arteries harden and they go *stunod* and make stupid decisions. I'm not going to let that happen to you."

"It might be too late."

"What are your symptoms?"

"All kinds of them."

"Well, keep them under wraps until after the wedding. I don't need any aggravation. Ma wants us to go and see the priest this Sunday because the banns of marriage in the church bulletin lock in our date in the church calendar, and it's already packed—we are penciled in, of course, but we need to get it in ink—or, as my mother prefers, in blood. A lot of people get married at the end of a decade."

"I didn't know that. Why?"

"It's a hard deadline. A girl says, Look, you either marry me by the end of 1949 or there will be no us in 1950."

"Makes sense."

"I think so. Nothing worth doing in life ever gets done without a deadline."

Nicky took a turn to the parking lot of the King of Peace Church.

"What are we doing here?"

"Let's go sit in the garden."

"But it's not my parish. Or yours."

"But it's quiet."

"Can't we ride around and listen to WFIL? It's Mellow Night. They got the Cloone. You love the Cloone."

"I'm not in the mood for music. And I haven't seen you since you came to the play."

"I've been so busy planning the wedding. The details. My mother has so much to do. Samples everywhere. Cocktail napkins with our initials. Matchbooks! Our names and the date in silver—oh, Nicky, and you'll love this. When you open the matchbook, Ma put a surprise in there. There's a quote printed in there: 'Strike one for love.' How cute is that? Ma's doing all accoutrements in shades of blue. Tablecloths. Charger plates. I didn't know that 'ocean wave' was a color, did you?"

"Never heard of it."

"Me neither. I've heard of seafoam, but not ocean wave. It's a deeper blue."

"I did not know that."

"You're wearing a morning suit, by the way. The gray will look so good with your blue eyes. My mother says I cut a picture of the Duke and Duchess of Windsor out of *Life* magazine when I was in high school—this was before I knew they were Nazi sympathizers. Anyway, he wore a morning suit to everything, even the beach. He wasn't a looker like you, and let's face it, she had a face like an old hammer, but together, they were sartorially splendid."

Nicky pulled into the parking lot of the church.

"What is going on, Nick? A church setting? Something is up with you, or something is going down. It's either good news or bad news. You're either giving me a piece of jewelry, or you've got a brain tumor."

"It's neither." He opened the car door, helped Peachy out of the car, took her by the hand, and walked her to a bench.

"Thank you, Jesus." Peachy leaned back on the bench. She held her hands to the sky. Then she turned and looked up at the statue of Mary. "And you, Blessed Lady. Back me up here. I don't need any bad news."

"Peachy, we shouldn't get married."

Peachy turned to him. She placed her hands on his face and turned it toward hers. "What?"

"I've thought about this and prayed about this, and we shouldn't get married."

"Why not?"

"We're not right for each other."

"How do you figure?"

"Take away all the details of planning the wedding, and what have we got?"

"Each other?"

"We don't think about each other."

"When I'm picking swatches, I'm thinking about you. When I'm choosing which hors d'oeuvres to pass during the cocktail hour, I'm thinking about you. When I'm thinking should my dress have a round collar or a sweetheart neckline, I'm thinking, 'What would Nicky like?' When I'm choosing flatware at Wanamaker's for the registry, I'm thinking about you eating breakfast every day for the rest of your life and what fork would you like to eat your eggs with. I'm always thinking about you."

"I didn't come to this decision overnight."

"You've been carrying this around like a hump on your back?"

"No. Things happened, and I came to a place of understanding."

"Speak English."

"I'm trying. It became clear at the theater."

Peachy's legs went akimbo, and she slid down low on the bench. "You are breaking up with me over that stupid play?"

"Partly. It didn't help that you hate the thing I love to do. But I hated myself more for not telling you. I didn't share something that was important to me for three years. That's almost half our engagement. I worked there all that time, and I didn't tell you."

"And I told you I didn't care. My dad keeps girlie magazines under his mattress. My mother acts like she doesn't see them when she flips it. Everybody has secrets."

"Not me. Not anymore. It was wrong of me not to tell you. I kept it a secret because I knew it would make you unhappy or angry or I believed you would judge it. And when I told you, you were all three of those things."

"Can you blame me? What if I had a wooden leg, and on our wedding night I came out of the bathroom in my nightie and snapped the leg off and said, 'Hey Nick, oops. Forgot to tell you. I have a wooden leg.' "

"This is different."

"How? You chose not to share something with me for three years, and then you want to break up with me because I had a reaction to something I didn't see coming. That's not fair. But I don't even care about that. You blindsided me. But I got over it. I'm resilient. You took a part in the same play without asking me, and I didn't make a fuss. Instead I brought my parents and we toasted you with champagne."

"Your father told me he hoped I got it out of my system."

"Well, did you?"

"No."

"So for the rest of your life, you want to drive a cab all day and be in plays at night?"

"I don't know. I'm just sure I don't want to be married."

Peachy made fists with her hands, closed her eyes, and inhaled. "You are cutting a twenty-eight-year-old"—she said deliberately— "a thirty-four-year-old woman loose in 1949?"

"Thirty-four?" Nicky gulped. He had never questioned Peachy's age. Her family had moved to Philly right before the war. He had no idea she was older than he. It's so hard to tell the age of an extremely thin person.

"You're not the only one with a secret. That's right. I'm thirty-four, on my way to crashing into thirty-five, which is the death of everything when you're a girl. You might as well murder me by bludgeoning. Go ahead. Find a shovel and beat me into the ground like a nail until all that's left is my hat. I'm an old maid—worse, an old maid who waited for her soldier boy to return—and he comes back all right, he returns without a scratch, and he still waits three years to marry me and then decides right before the cake is baked that he has changed his mind? At least if you died overseas, I would've mourned you already. Three years later, I'd be myself again."

"I would hope so."

"Every girl that waited through the war is married except me!"

"We shouldn't marry each other just because everybody else is taken."

"Why not? You think there's a better choice out there? Open your eyes! I'm an exotic! What is wrong in that thick head of yours? You got goldfish up there? Is your brain an attic room of dry rot? An empty space with a For Rent sign? You break it off with me, and I have to live with the sight of you forever in South Philly like the sign over the zoo? I see you driving around in a cab, and I wave at what? Not my husband? Who? The man I went with for seven long years and then nothing?"

Peachy slid off the bench and dropped to the ground with a thud like a sack of flour.

"What will happen to me? I've run out the clock. How could you do this to me? You've thrown me away like an old tire. I'm like a knife without the blade. A machine whose purpose has been lost. Please just kill me, because I cannot face my parents. This will kill my mother! And shortly thereafter my father! They'll probably choose to go together! They'll drive off the Delaware Water Gap in the Ford Fairlane and burst into flames."

"You don't love me, Peachy," Nicky said calmly.

"How can you say that? What have I been doing all this time other than loving you? I make you happy."

"But what about you? What do I do for you?"

"You love me back. You're my man. You dance with me at everybody else's weddings. I don't know. What does a woman get from a man?"

"Think. You don't love me. If you loved me, you would want me to be happy."

"Is this about my job? About the fact that I have an office job and went to college?"

"I'm proud of your accomplishments."

"I didn't even tell you I got made assistant manager at Wanamaker's because I thought it would make you feel bad. My mother said to bury my promotion like a milk bone, because it would scare you off. Well, she was wrong about that. Something else scared you off."

"It's not your career at Wanamaker's, Peachy. It's about happiness. Personal fulfillment. See, if you loved me, you'd want me to do the things that bring me joy, and in turn, I would want to share those things with you, and those things would make you happy too."

Peachy got up off the ground, dusted off her wool work skirt, and stood in front of her fiancé. "Nicholas Castone. You live in your aunt's basement, and you drive a cab. I am your joy. Me. I love you, and my intent was to make you a home and give you children and, God help me, keep my figure in the process. I was going to quit my job when we got married, after we saved a cushion, not because I hate my job but because I wanted to take the burden off of you. What more can one woman do for one man? You tell me."

"She could support his dreams."

"Ugh. What dreams?"

"Borelli's."

"That bunch of nut bags? We're back to them again?"

"They're my respite."

"They're outcasts of society. The men are fruity and the women are loose."

"They're my friends."

"God, Nicky."

"I understand them, and they understand me."

"What's to understand? You're a very simple person."

"They don't think so."

"Oh, now they're a pack of intellectuals. Great thinkers in wigs . . . and . . . and leotards!"

"It's not like that."

"I went to college! New York State Business College. You didn't even go to college—where do you get these crazy ideas?"

Nicky was losing patience. "You can keep the ring."

"Do you think I was in this for the ring? I'd need more than a ring for a seven-year commitment, I'd require a diamond mine and Mr. De Beers himself bringing me breakfast in bed for the rest of my life in exchange for the time I've put in. I don't care about the ring. I wanted the life. You were it for me, the only one."

"Don't say that."

"It's true. Who would want me now? I'm a relic. I'm like some ancient talisman the nuns found in an old monastery and hung in the sacristy to pray to on Holy Days of Obligation. I might as well be made of rusted tin and hanging on the wall by a thumbtack with a piece of my sleeve in a glass box as proof I lived."

"You're still young and as lovely as you ever were."

"One hundred and fifteen pounds. Not since the Crusades has a female DePino been this thin. I can still fit into my fourth-grade Catholic school uniform. And you don't want me."

"It's not about want. You're a very desirable woman."

Peachy began to pace, as if the answer to her dilemma could be found on the ground, like the paper footsteps of the Learn the Lindy sequence in the Arthur Murray dance kit. She clapped her hands together. "It's because I didn't do the thing."

"You did enough."

"No, I held back. Donna Bonnani told me to do the deed, and I thought to hold out for the wedding night—give you the fireworks display after the nuptial mass. Something special. But Donna was right. She told me to submit."

"I didn't want you to submit." Using the word *submit* made Nicky feel sick.

"Oh, don't tell me, you're fruity like the theater people?"

"I don't think so."

"You don't think—that's something you *know*, Nicky. People know what they are. They know what they like."

Peachy was desperate. She climbed onto Nicky's lap and coiled herself around him like a garden hose. She placed her hands on his chest, traced the vein in his neck with her tongue, found his mouth, and kissed him, engaging her lips, tongue, and jaw like she was breaking down a tough piece of saltwater taffy.

The situation with Peachy's tongue became so moist that when Nicky closed his eyes, he thought he was in a car wash. "Peachy. Stop. Come on. The religious statues."

"Now you feel shame?" She wiped her mouth on her hand and removed the slash of coral lipstick from Nicky's mouth. "Am I repulsive?"

"No."

"What is it, then?"

"It's not right."

"You have enlightenment after I compromised my moral code for you?"

"You cannot guilt me into staying."

"I will guilt you into staying for the rest of your life. Think about what you're doing. We have to look at our years, accumulated like a Christmas Club at the First National Bank. I've got interest earned in this thing, and so do you. You can't throw that away. Besides, you made me happy. Don't I make you happy?"

"Peachy, no person can make another person happy. The person has to make him- or herself happy."

"You're out of your mind."

"Could be."

"That's what I'll tell my parents. I'll tell them you lost your mind—an undetected mass clogged your cerebellum, or you stood too close to a tank in Germany and you're having flashbacks, or you're a selfish bastard who got tired of me and dropped me for some mysterious reason."

"I will always regret my timing."

"Seriously? That's what you regret? Your timing?"

"I should have told you sooner."

"Who is she?"

"There's no one else."

"It will come out. Just tell me."

"It's not about another woman, it's about a man. *Me.* I was content, and it's not enough."

"Do you know how many poor slobs in this world hope for contentment? It's the goal—not the enemy!"

"I want to take a risk with my life—I want to do something that scares me."

"A German putting a machine gun in your face didn't scare you?"

"Not that kind of fear. The kind that you get when you take a chance."

"On what?"

"On me. On my life."

"Nicky, you sound like somebody who drinks."

"I understand why you would feel that way. It isn't rational."

"You can't wake up someday and snap your fingers and have a good wife and a nice family. You'll be like creepy Mr. Freggo who lives in the bus station. You'll be old and all alone, picking fleas out of your shorts."

"I don't think I want what you want."

"Who doesn't want a home and a family? It's un-American. It's inhuman. It's lonely!"

"It might be, and it probably is, but I can live with that."

"My mother warned me that an orphan has no ties. Who throws away the future like this?"

"Somebody whose future has already been written. Somebody who could predict everything that would happen between this moment and a spot on his lung at age seventy-eight."

"Did you go see a witch?"

"I'm just guessing, Peachy. I'm not living, I'm just in line. I do what I'm told. I've always done what I'm told. I joined the army, put on a uniform, and followed my cousins. When I got back, I put on another uniform, and I followed them from the house on Montrose right across the street into the garage. I'm a hack because they're hacks. I've done what is expected of me because it made everyone around me happy. I thought that's what happiness was—making sure everyone else is happy. Now all my cousins are married—"

"Which is normal!" Peachy shrieked.

"Yes, it's normal, but I said, how long will I follow them? How long do I do exactly as they do? Do I follow my cousins all the way to Holy Cross Cemetery?"

"Probably. The Palazzinis have a plot." Peachy threw her hands up in frustration.

"Interesting. Even that has been determined. Well, I didn't get that far in my thinking. I never thought about dying because I wasn't living."

"So what is this that we have been doing all this time, if it wasn't living?"

"Existing."

"Okay." Peachy put her head in her hands as though holding her brain would help it get around the idea of what was happening to her.

"You've been so patient. A smart man would've married you and given you what you wanted and worked hard every day to give you more as you dreamed it up along the way. But I'm not very smart. It's taken me thirty years to figure out I'm unhappy."

Peachy unsnapped her purse and fished out her handkerchief. "You couldn't have figured this out three years ago? Binny Falcone got a letter from Chi Chi Alzaro saying he was in a godforsaken trench in France when he figured out Binny wasn't for him. Turns out he never saw a trench—he was at a party with a French girl when he had his particular epiphany because it sat on his lap—but it turned out all right because Binny was young and had time to grieve the loss and get back out into the world to find a nice guy and get her dream. But it's too late for me. It's all over. It has passed me by—all of it."

"That's not true, Peachy."

"Isn't it? Look at me. I'm washed up like an old whore in a Laundromat who's out of soap and quarters."

"You will find happiness, Peachy."

"You can get everything back in this life but time. It's gone, Nicky, and there's no replenishing what has been lost."

"I'm sorry."

"This is what you do to a girl who had half her family locked up in an internment camp in New Mexico? Really? My family hasn't been through enough? They lived in a chicken coop for two years and ate beef knuckles and rye bread and wept, and all you can say to me is you're sorry?"

Peachy stood up and walked to the car, flung the door open, and got in. Nicky got into the driver's seat.

"Do not speak to me."

Nicky drove Peachy home in silence. He could hear the drip of her tears as they hit her patent leather purse.

Nicky pulled up in front of her house. "Peach."

Peachy opened the car door and swung her legs out before Nicky could open the door on his side of the car. She was halfway up the steps on her parents' porch when he got out. She had her key in the door before he could run around the front of the car. He was halfway up the walk when Peachy slammed the front door behind her from the inside. He heard the snap of the bolt.

Nicky stood back and watched, as he had many nights, under different circumstances, the lights going on inside the dark house as Peachy made her way up to her bedroom. As always, the light in the hallway flipped on and off as she climbed up to the second story; the overhead light upstairs turned on and off as she went into her bedroom. She turned on her bedside lamp. But this time, instead of going to the front window and blowing Nicky a kiss, she pulled down the shade and walked away, leaving a rectangle of light in the blue darkness.

ACT II

The course of true love never did run smooth.

—*A Midsummer Night's Dream*

6

Hortense bowed her head and tapped out the code, using the lever, as she took down the telegram coming in over the wire. She spun in her seat to the typewriter, typed out the message, and looked up at Nicky. "Those are the same clothes you had on yesterday."

"I had a bad night."

"You shouldn't go out when you have the early shift."

"I pray I will never have a night like that ever again."

"Then do yourself a favor and lay off the liquor. There's nothing worse than a young man with a sauce problem, unless it's gambling. Then you're both drunk and broke." She peeled the message off the Western Union ribbon and glued it to the letterhead. "You up for a ride to Roseto, Pennsylvania?"

Before Nicky could answer, they heard the thunder of footsteps on the metal stairs up to the office. Aunt Jo and Uncle Dom, followed by Dominic, Gio, and Nino, crowded into the office.

"You're in trouble, Nicky," Uncle Dom panted.

"Al DePino is on his way over here to kill you," Gio announced.

"You broke off with Peachy?" Aunt Jo took her nephew by the shoulders.

"Last night."

"You're lucky the old man didn't come over here and stab you in your sleep." Gio went to the window, as he was experienced at surveillance.

"I didn't sleep."

"It isn't going to matter to him," Uncle Dom said. "He's gonna take you dead or alive."

"You have to hide," Aunt Jo implored him.

"Good morning." Calla Borelli stood in the doorway, holding a bakery box of pastries. "I brought over a little thank-you gift for filling the theater. We closed the show in profit, thanks to you."

"Not now!" Dom thundered.

"We got a matter of life and death here!" Gio added, but took the pastry box from her.

"I can come back later." Calla turned to go.

"No, stay," Nicky implored her.

Mabel came through the door in her bathrobe, panting. "Nicky, you got to get out of here. You are dealing with volatile people. I have a cousin on my Polish side—"

"I thought you were Irish," Nino said, surprised.

"I have one Polish grandmother. That's why I can bake. Anyhow, my cousin crossed Al DePino—nobody's seen him since."

"We've got a telegram to deliver to Roseto, PA. Who is taking it up there?" Hortense said impatiently.

"You're not worried about this?" Aunt Jo turned to Hortense.

"I have a terrible anxiety. Inside, my organs are collapsing on each other, but somebody around here has to stay calm," Hortense said evenly.

"What's in the telegram?" Gio asked.

"I'm not allowed to tell you. All right. I'll tell you. The ambassador that was scheduled to attend the Jubilee is sick and can't make it."

"That's the guy you look like!" Gio punched Nicky's arm. "The guy on the banner!"

"I look like the guy who can't make it." Nicky looked at Calla. "I have a twin."

"I'm bonded by Western Union to make sure this telegram gets to Chief Burgess to alert him that the cat can't make it for their Jubilee. So who's delivering the telegram?"

"Mrs. Mooney, forget the telegram. We have to hide Nicky," Aunt Jo cried.

"Put him in a trunk. Ship him to New Jersey. The Spatuzzas have a farm," Gio offered.

"I saw that in a Van Johnson picture," Dom commented.

"Me too. I couldn't make that up." Gio sorted through the pastry box, choosing a cannoli.

"I can't do trunks. I'm slightly claustrophobic."

"So's a casket, if we don't hurry. And that's a permanent residence." Uncle Dom drummed his fingers on the wall.

"Take the telegram to Roseto," Gio said. "Or don't."

Nicky's eyes moved like pinballs in his head as he hatched the scheme. "I take the telegram, but I don't deliver. I deliver me. I become the ambassador. I perform the part, hiding in plain sight. The village gets their Jubilee and their honored guest, and I get the role of a lifetime, and save what's left of it. By the time I return, Al DePino calms down and realizes he doesn't want me for a son-in-law anyway, and life goes on as it always has."

"It's a terrible idea. It has more plot holes than *Cymbeline*. Don't do it!" Calla implored him.

"I have to do something."

"And somebody has to make this delivery," Hortense added.

"Take a breath. Stay calm. Think this through."

"Give me an alternative, Calla."

"Go back to Peachy. Tell her you've made a mistake. Beg her forgiveness. Buy her a piece of jewelry as a penance. Tell her you love her and the wedding is on."

"Thank you. That's what I think!" Aunt Jo clasped her hands together. "She's a nice girl."

"I'm not marrying her. I'm not marrying anybody. I'm going to be"—he opened the telegram—"Ambassador Carlo Guardinfante of Roseto Valfortore, Italy. I'll ride in a parade, kiss a couple of babies. How hard could this be?"

"You've only acted in one play," Calla reminded him.

"But it was the right play. Mistaken identity," Nicky said, feeling empowered by his own talent.

"He was pretty good in it," Dominic commented.

"I was, wasn't I?"

"Actors. Filled with hubris or self-loathing, nothing in between. Nicky. Listen to me. You were in a play with words and a plot. This crackpot plan you have—there's no script!"

"I'll improvise."

"You're stealing someone's life," Calla reminded him.

"From the sounds of this telegram, he's not long for this world anyway. He's doing me a kindness on his way out," Nicky rationalized. "He dies so I can live."

"But you're not an ambassador. You don't even know one."

"I drove the vice mayor of Philadelphia once."

"You're not an Italian from the other side."

"I can do an accent. I'll just do my impression of Nonna."

"It really cracks us up at the holiday dinners," Dom admitted.

Nicky tried it out for them, " 'I so happy to be in America.' See, I can do it. It's the role of a lifetime. It's three parts in one—it's *Two Gentlemen of Verona*, *The Comedy of Errors*, and *As You Like It*. I saw all of those productions directed by your father. I know them by heart. I know how to play a twin. I'll be in rep for the weekend."

"You're not experienced enough to pull this off."

"Timing is everything, Calla. And I don't have any. I have to get out of here. Al DePino is not nimble, but he owns a fast car."

"And bullets move at the speed of sound," Dom added.

"Are you with me or against me?"

"Against!" Calla folded her arms over her chest.

"Then you don't get to come. Mrs. Mooney, will you come and play the nurse?"

"I don't know anything about medicine."

"You can be the maid, then. Shakespeare was loaded with them."

"Why does the colored lady always have to play the domestic?"

"Be an attaché, then," Nicky schemed.

"A briefcase?" Gio queried.

"No, an attaché, a person who assists an ambassador. She is accompanying me as a representative of the US government. Mrs. Mooney worked for . . . Eleanor Roosevelt."

A collective sigh went up to the heavens from the dispatch office. A mention of Franklin Delano Roosevelt in this working-class household of New Deal Democrats was all it took to swing the vote to full support in Nicky's direction, except for Dom.

"He never did much for the Italians," Dom complained.

"He did fine by the Irish," Mabel countered.

"I like what I'm hearing. Mrs. Roosevelt does like the Negro race. Go on." Hortense rolled her hand like a hula dancer, as if to pull more information from thin air. "What's my part?"

Calla turned to Hortense. "You will make the ambassador's visit look official."

"Oh, now you're helping." Nicky gently punched Calla's arm.

"You're nothing without a director."

"Says the director," Nicky sniffed.

"He can take the sedan," Dom suggested.

"Do you have those little Italian flags from Columbus Day and the American flags from the Fourth of July?" Calla asked Gio.

"They're in the supply closet downstairs."

"Get them. That will make the sedan look official," Calla said, surrendering to the stunt. Nicky smiled at her. "What? The ambassador to Guam came to a play during the war. I remember flags."

"I'll need my suit," Hortense said. "My Sunday suit."

"Let's go," said Dominic. "I'll take Mrs. Mooney to her house. Nicky, pick her up in the sedan on the way out of town."

Hortense skimmed down the office steps like a dancer as Dominic opened the back door of the cab.

"Tuck in Hortense!" Dom instructed from the landing.

Dom had never called Hortense by her first name before. She shot him a look before she ducked low in the seat as Dominic started the engine and sped out of the garage.

"Fire up the sedan, Gio!" Dom bellowed.

"I need clothes!" Nicky cried.

"I'll get your suit!" Mabel clunked down the stairs.

"Don't forget my dress socks, Mabel! And my razor!" Nicky called. "I need a military uniform. An official military uniform. The guy on the banner had a uniform."

"I have the one we used for Prince Hal in *Henry the Fourth*. It's in the storage room in the costume shop."

"Thirty-four long?"

"It'll fit."

Nicky grabbed the telegram off the table and stuffed it in his pocket. "What are you going to do about Al DePino?"

"I'll take care of him," Dom said calmly.

"You're not going to kill him, are you?"

"Of course not." Uncle Dom cracked his knuckles.

Nicky and Calla raced down the stairs and jumped into the sedan as Mabel ran back into the garage with his suit and shoes and dopp kit. She threw them into the back of the car as though the items were on fire, stepped back, and rubbed her pregnant belly. Dom reached into his pocket and handed Nicky a wad of cash. "Stay out of Philly until you hear from me."

"Thank you, Uncle Dom. Don't cry, Aunt Jo."

"If something happens to you, I won't be able to bear it."

"If something *doesn't* happen to me, I won't be able to bear it." Nicky blew his aunt a kiss before peeling out of the garage.

Calla hung on to the door handle as Nicky sped through the streets. "What did you mean by that? If something doesn't happen to you—"

"You heard right. If something doesn't happen to me, this life is all for nothing."

"What's wrong with your life?"

"Everything." Nicky adjusted the rearview mirror.

"Why did you break up with Peachy?"

"I don't love her."

"Turn the car around."

"What?"

"You didn't mean it. Go to her. Tell her you made a mistake."

"But I did mean it."

"She's a fine girl. She fits in your big family. She looks at you like you're Marc Antony and you just parked the barge on her dock. Her love for you turned her into Cleopatra."

"I don't want to get married."

"Of course you do."

"How would you know?"

"You have cold feet. She can warm them up. She lights up like a three-way bulb on three around you."

"I'm going to be the ambassador." Nicky gripped the steering wheel. "And you can't stop me."

"You're not the ambassador."

"What is wrong with giving people what they want? Why ruin a perfectly good Jubilee?"

"You're deceiving people."

"How is that any different from playing Sebastian?"

"You got bit by the acting bug, and now you believe it's the answer to everything. Theater is your religion, and anyone who doesn't believe has to get out of your way. But this is a mistake! When the glow wears off, you'll realize Peachy is your destiny. You have a good job. You come from a family that loves you. You had a plan. You were excited about your new house and the parking space in front of it, and the wedding, and the Jordan almonds. It was an enterprise of true love for you. And now what have you got?"

Nicky skidded into the back alley of the theater, taking the curve so quickly, it threw Calla against the passenger door.

He turned to her. "You okay?"

She nodded.

He jumped out of the car. "Hurry!" he shouted to Calla.

They bolted through the stage door, ran through the wings, peeled down the steps, and burst into the costume shop. Calla unlocked the costume storage room, flipped the light, and began shuffling through the racks, flipping through the men's costumes on hangers.

"Faster, Calla. Faster."

"Here," Calla said, holding a Prussian-blue waistcoat with gold epaulets and long trousers with a white satin pinstripe on either side of the pant legs.

"It's a little flashy, but it'll do."

"You're not going to try it on?"

"No time."

Nicky grabbed a wide white satin belt off an evening gown to wear as a sash over the regimentals. "Thanks, Calla." He ran out of the shop.

Calla went out into the hallway and called out after him, "You could avoid all of this if you just made nice with your fiancée."

"It's over," he hollered back.

"It's a mistake!" Calla argued. She heard the stage door snap shut.

Nicky emerged from the theater, threw the uniform in the back seat, and jumped into the car, heading down the alley that connected Broad to Chestnut and would lead him through the backstreets to 103 Charlotte Street.

He had not felt this alive since he appeared for the first time onstage in *Twelfth Night*. He was desperate to take a chance, in a life that had been filled with decisions made for him. He was compelled to go to Roseto, to take the place of a dying man and assume his life as his own. Why not? He had the excuse, the guts, and the costume! Nicky was determined to be the dramatist of his future, to set in motion a series of actions based upon risk, not security. He yearned to build another character and play him, knowing that if he succeeded, he might be able to create the man he wanted to be.

Nicky Castone would break the cycle of expectations foisted upon every young Italian American man in South Philly. Becoming Carlo meant he wouldn't be defined by his community's markers of success: the steady paycheck, the nuptial mass, the two-family house, and the goal that gave him the chills: dying in one's own bed at the end of a life lived to satisfy others with a parting gift to his loved ones of a pre-paid funeral. Nicky would break free by playing an Italian from the other side.

The Roseto Jubilee was his first step out into the wider world, beyond the safety of Montrose Street. Sam Borelli's words to his actors in the rehearsals of long ago echoed in Nicky's head: *Stay in the moment. If you do, it will lead you forward.*

As Nicky drove down the block in the sedan, he saw Hortense waiting on her porch like a good soldier, dressed primly in black in a matching hat and shoes. He was pleased with his casting of the attaché.

Nicky pulled up in front, jumped out, and circled around to open the back door for Hortense. She climbed aboard for an adventure that had no itinerary, only a destination.

As they drove off, her next-door neighbor, the schoolteacher Jean Williams, peered out her curtains and shook her head. "Hortense Mooney. Black suit. Black car. Black day."

Frank Arrigo stood under the chandelier in the lobby of Borelli's while he waited for the engineer to come down from the mezzanine. He tapped his foot on the terrazzo floor, impressed with how well it had held up over decades. Frank appreciated quality, but he believed the standards for construction were changing. There wasn't a need for a floor surface to last for a hundred years when a modern design was implemented. He was open to new ways— cheaper, faster, better.

"She's an old beauty."

"Yes, sir," Frank Arrigo agreed.

Ed Shaughnessy came down the staircase and joined him. "We're looking at a serious renovation here. There are leaks in the upstairs restrooms. Pretty substantial plumbing issues. The theater itself is in pretty good shape. The mezzanine needs reinforcement. There weren't codes prior to 1916, so who knows if the structure can hold the seat allotment? I don't know. Roof is all right. The catacombs where the dressing rooms are aren't up to code either."

"So what would it cost?"

"It would be cheaper to tear it down and start over. Unless someone cared about the history of the place and wanted to fund a restoration."

"We're putting up an apartment complex over on Pierce Street. We're not done yet, and we already have them all rented to vets. We could do double the business building apartments on Broad. This is a great location. The loading dock behind the building would make great parking."

"I see how you're thinking. You could do a tear-down but you could save the facade," Shaughnessy offered.

"Why would I?"

"History."

"History never made anybody any money, Ed."

"No, but people are attached to these old barns."

"Yeah. But you'd be surprised. You put up something new, and they never miss what was here." Frank opened a small notebook he carried and jotted down a few notes. "I'd appreciate it if you'd keep this between us. Calla is a little emotional about this place, and it's going to take a little finessing to get her to understand what's best."

"I understand. Not a word from me."

Peachy DePino pushed through the glass doors of the lobby, wearing a full cotton skirt with bold red-and-white stripes, a cropped red shell, and a Venetian gondolier hat. She wore sunglasses.

"Good afternoon." She forced a smile.

"Peachy, right?"

"Yes. You're Frank. Where's Calla?"

"She's downstairs in the costume shop. Say hello to Ed Shaughnessy, engineer with the city."

"Pleasure."

"He's here to check the building for repairs."

"I almost fell through the ladies' room floor when I attended a play here. Maybe you can do something about that. Excuse me." Peachy gave them a tense smile before marching off.

"If that isn't an advertisement for a tear-down, I don't know what is." Ed chuckled.

Peachy burst into the costume shop to find Calla sitting cross-legged on the cutting table, sorting through swatches of fabric.

"Calla, I think we should talk."

"Are you all right, Peachy?"

"No. I am not."

"What's wrong?"

"Why do I have a haunting feeling you already know?"

"Know what?"

"Where is my fiancé?"

"I don't know. Is there a problem?"

"He broke up with me last night."

"He's an idiot."

Peachy was taken aback by Calla's response, so much so that she sat down on a work stool, pulled off her hat and sunglasses, folded her arms on the table, put her head down, and cried.

"He's an idiot to break up with you. You're a great girl, Peachy. I saw you with the Palazzinis. The only thing I can say is that he must be having a mental breakdown."

Peachy pulled a hanky from her bra strap and wiped her tears. "Maybe there's a growth. A fatty tumor. My uncle Jerry had one. One day he woke up and was fluent in French."

"Nicky is a fool."

"I did everything right. I kept quiet. I didn't pressure him. I waited. I tiptoed around, made sure he felt good about himself. And he drops me."

"Stupid, stupid man."

"I know. They all are, you know." Peachy blew her nose.

"We can't change them."

"My father's going to kill him."

"Not really?"

Peachy nodded. "He didn't like him to start with. He feels like he sacrificed seven years, too. He wants to wring Nicky's neck with his bare hands."

"Violence never made a dope think."

"True. But it will make my dad feel better."

The rolling green fields outside Philadelphia gave way to the foothills of the Poconos, thick with laurel, bursts of pink peonies, and wild orange tiger lilies. In the distance, the peaks and crests of the Blue Mountains filled the horizon with a stripe of deepest purple.

The air was fragrant with smoky pine that morning. Nicky was making good time on the road to Roseto. If Hortense weren't so nervous, she might have enjoyed the ride through northeastern Pennsylvania on the cusp of summer. Instead, she sat low in the back seat, and tried not to fidget.

"I don't like sitting back here."

"You'll draw attention if you're in the front seat."

"How much do you know about this ambassador?" Hortense asked as she flipped through the Jubilee booklet.

"Just what's in there."

"He looks wealthy." Hortense looked at the suit on the seat next to her. "Do you think this costume is going to fool these people?"

"It has to."

"What is a Cadillac Dinner?"

"It's a fund-raiser for the town. They raffle off a Cadillac at the end."

"Nice."

"I have to dance with the ladies. That's when I wear the regimentals."

"Lord, have mercy. What do I do while you dance and give away a car?"

"Stand there and look official."

"All right. I can do that. But know this. Small towns aren't very welcoming to colored folks. We don't like to be places where they can corner us."

"You'll impress them. There will be no cornering."

"That's what you think. I've gotten my hopes up before. When they find out you aren't a servant, all hell breaks loose."

"You stick with me, and nobody will give you any trouble."

"Mm-hm," Hortense grumbled.

"I mean it."

"Nicky, I've been colored all my life, and the only thing I know that remains true is that there are no surprises. I always know what I'm walking into." Hortense chuckled. "Well, not always. I got sandbagged once. You know, old man Rotundo of the trucking outfit tried to steal me away during the war."

"No kidding."

"Rotundo had heard Palazzini's had a crack dispatcher and a first-class operation. So he called the office and told me to name my price. So I did. He said, 'No problem. Come and see me.' When I walked in the door, his face went puce, and then the color left his face entirely, which took a while because he's southern Italian, so he's on his way to being as dark as me. Anyway, he took one look at me and said the position had already been filled. The very one he offered to me over the telephone. I kid you not. That money would have been nice, too. At the time I had both the girls at home, and we needed a new furnace. So I walked back to Montrose Street and straight to your uncle and told him about Rotundo and the offer and said I needed a raise. He gave me an argument, but I stood my ground. I got my raise. I wasn't ever going to be rich, but I got my furnace."

"Would you rather be rich or respected?"

"Both."

"If you had to choose."

"Respect is more important, of course."

"I don't care about money," Nicky said, and meant it.

"You don't?"

"I really don't. As long as I have enough to survive, that's fine with me. Peachy bought government bonds during the war, and she bought stocks, she saved up money. She's a saver. She'd talk about that stuff, and I was so bored."

"She's a very responsible young lady."

"She's thirty-four."

"She's a very responsible lady."

"You could look at it like that. Or you could look at it like once we were married she'd be waiting by the door every Friday with an empty jar ready to fill with my tips."

"She might have changed if you married her."

"She would have. For worse."

"You did the right thing, then."

"Do you think her father will kill me?"

"If every father killed every son that did a woman wrong, there'd be no men left to marry. Al DePino may slap you around a little. Loosen a couple of teeth. You may get your arm twisted and your nose broken. But you'll survive."

Nicky swallowed hard. "Thanks."

"I'm getting older by the day, and I've yet to see a couple bust up where both people wanted to leave at the same time. It's always one or the other. So one person always ends up irate at the end of a love affair. Why is that? Just move along. The globe is crawling with people, you mean to tell me you can't find somebody else who spins your wheels? I never understood it."

"I should have had you talk to Peachy."

"I would have talked plain. I have a feeling you puttered around. You can't putter around when you want to end something. You have to get to the point."

"She didn't want to accept it."

"There's that, too."

"She had everything planned. The future came with a recipe."

"That's too bad. You need wiggle room in life, because you don't know what you're going to get thrown your way."

"Look at my parents."

"That's right. They died so young, which means they went to heaven before their marriage gave them hell."

"Or maybe they were happy," Nicky countered.

"I'm sure they were."

"You're just saying that to make me feel good."

"Nothing wrong with believing in fairy tales, Nicky. Pretty pictures make pretty thoughts."

The pair rode in silence as Nicky drove along narrow roads that edged the Delaware River. After a bit he asked, "Why did you agree to come with me to Roseto, Mrs. Mooney?"

"Oh, I don't know. A little adventure never hurt anyone."

"I'm glad you did. Thank you."

"You're entirely welcome. I've worked at the garage for twenty-three years. And I've witnessed what I'd call an Italian opera. The battles. The dialogue. The ice-cold silences broken by the smash of glass on cement followed by more screaming and yelling. The choreography. The sight of a wrench whizzing through the air like a bird. The denouement. A cold cock to the jaw, followed by remorse, ending in forgiveness. Borelli's isn't the only theater in South Philly. There's always something going on in the garage. Must be what it's like to live on Mount Vesuvius. You never know when things are going to blow. But the Italians are good people, I do know that."

"How did you get the job with Uncle Dom?"

"I worked for both your uncles. I like them both. I graduated from Cheyney with a degree in teaching. When I went there, way back in 1905, it was called the Institute for Colored Youth. I came out of there and wanted to work in a business—I was done with classrooms, but I spent the next few years teaching. I was looking for something new. Your uncles posted the job with the city. They used to have boards back then at the Jobs Administration. I went for an interview and got the job."

"You must like it."

"I wouldn't say that."

"But you never left."

"Mr. Mooney has a job where they need him around the clock and then not much. My job always covered the not much. I'm half kidding you. I did like it when the telegraph office went in. That challenged me."

"I'm glad you're up for new challenges. We don't know what we're walking into here." Nicky adjusted the rearview mirror so he might look Hortense in the eye. "Mrs. Mooney, I learned a lot at Borelli's, but here's the most important thing. You have to commit to your role. You're in the play now. And that means you accepted the part, which means you have to do the job and stay in it until the curtain falls. You can't flinch. You have to stick with the story. You must not panic. You can't leave the stage."

"If anybody is going to be flinching and panicking, it won't be me. I've been put on the spot in my lifetime. I know how to wheedle."

"Good. Just follow my cues."

Hortense looked out the window and muttered, "Any fool can do that."

"What did you say?"

"I said I can do that."

It wasn't long before Nicky passed Easton and followed the signs north for Roseto. Finally they got to town, and he drove up the incline and took the turn onto Garibaldi Avenue. "This is it," he said quietly.

Hortense placed the black straw hat on her head. It had a wide brim and a tall crown decorated with a wide, grosgrain ribbon and a large, flat bow. She secured it in place with a hatpin, pulled on her formal white gloves with the scalloped wrist detail, and adjusted the collar of her black serge suit, her Sunday best. She straightened the cloth flag pin on her lapel that she had received as a free gift when she made a donation to the Negro Armed Services Relief Fund, hoping it looked official enough to get her through whatever Nicky had in mind for her, as she posed as a representative of the United States government.

Hortense reached into her purse and pulled out a small silver flask of Evening in Paris perfume. She pumped the rubber ball lightly on her neck, returned it to her purse, and snapped the clasp shut.

"That smells nice," Nicky commented.

"Mrs. Roosevelt gave it to me for Christmas." Hortense folded her gloved hands on her lap. "She's thoughtful that way."

Nicky grinned. Mrs. Mooney was ready for the Jubilee.

Nicky intended to drive directly to 125 Truman Street, the home of Chief Burgess Rocco Tutolola, but the sedan was met on Garibaldi Avenue by a hundred locals who had gathered to welcome the ambassador.

"What is this?" Hortense looked up at the streamers, the banners on the houses, and the welcome signs, feeling overwhelmed. "This was not in the booklet."

"I don't know."

"Are we in a parade?"

"No, that's tomorrow."

"Take me back, Nicky. I can't do this." Hortense felt trapped.

"It's only a weekend. You can do this."

"I mean it. Let me out of this car."

"That wouldn't be a good idea."

"I am going to call your uncle to come and get me." Hortense pulled the brim of her hat down over her face.

Nicky braked the car, while the Rosetani crowded around them, and turned to face Hortense. "Please, Mrs. Mooney."

Hortense kept her head down. Outside the sedan's windows, a sea of Italian Americans pressed forth to greet them. Hortense quickly realized that even if she was able to get out of the car, it was unlikely they would let her use a telephone. She accepted she was in deep. "Let's go through with this. But we're out of here first thing Sunday morning. Promise me that," she whispered.

"I promise."

Nicky drove the sedan slowly up Garibaldi Avenue. The crowd backed away and stood against the curb, forming a ribbon on either side of the street. As Nicky smiled and waved to them, the townspeople became animated, cheering and shouting words of welcome to the long-awaited visitor.

He pulled up in front of 125 Truman Street, followed by the throng, which had grown to fill the street from one end to the other. Before Nicky could get out of the sedan, Chief Burgess Rocco, with thick brown hair like pine needles, flinty black eyes, a pointed nose, and a warm smile, emerged from the house wearing a suit with an official sash across his chest.

Hortense peeked out from under her hat. "They followed us," Hortense whispered. "The whole town is out there."

"Pull yourself together, Mrs. Mooney," Nicky said, before getting out of the car to greet the chief burgess.

"My-uh Paisan! My-uh friend!" Nicky said in an Italian accent, a combination of his pal Ben Tartaglia's grandfather, who worked in a butcher shop on Wharton, and Nicky's grandmother.

"*Ambasciatore* Guardinfante, *come sta!*"

"No Italian. I learn-uh the English. We speak English please on this vee-zeet."

"Very good. But we were ready for you—one of our ladies is fluent. We arranged to have her by your side throughout your visit. Most of us in Roseto speak the dialect from your province."

"Not-ta necessary. I must-uh practice my English. So, I speak-uh the English for you."

"Bravo!"

Nicky wagged his finger. "Remember. No EE-talian!"

"No Italian. I am—"

"Rocco Tutolola." Nicky embraced him, disarming his host.

"Yes, did you receive my letter?" Rocco asked.

"I did not."

"It was sent to you. Your schedule and itinerary were included."

"It must have gotten lost. It's a big ocean, no? But I here now. I here now! We jubilee!" Nicky turned to the crowd and waved his arms high in the air, and they cheered.

"Yes, yes, we jubilee," Rocco agreed.

The crowd pushed forward, encroaching with enthusiasm. The thought that he might be discovered crossed Nicky's mind, and he began to sweat. The friendly throng could easily turn into an angry mob. He wished he would've gassed up in Easton in preparation for a hasty exit.

"How did you get here? You were to come on the train from New York, and I was to greet you in Easton in an hour."

"Change of plans. I wanted to see Philadelphia, the birthplace of freedom. I hope-uh you understand. *Capisce?* My first visit to America, a cause for excitement! And, independence. So, I drive-uh myself from the New York to the Philly to the Jubilee! The adventure! The experience! The Palazzini Cab Company of Philadelphia donated the sedan."

"They did?"

"Everything was paid for. Gas included." Nicky grinned, slapping Rocco on the back. "Petrol! Petrol! We-uh call the gas in Roseto Valfortore."

"Well, we'll have to thank them. Was your crossing comfortable?"

"The airplane was so fast. Zoom-uh. Zoom-uh," Nicky said, reaching into his grab bag of bad Italian and finding an impression of Louis Prima.

"What airplane? Are you sure you don't want to speak Italian? We have to work on your English."

"Crossing?"

"The boat. You know, the ship." Rocco spoke slowly: "Ocean liner."

"Oh yes, yes. It was *magnifico!*"

Nicky formed his fingers into a closed umbrella shape and kissed them. The crowd cheered.

"The MS *Vulcania* is the best of the Naples line."

"Da best-uh!" Nicky said enthusiastically. "What a line!"

The screen door behind the chief burgess snapped open and his wife emerged.

Rocco turned to Nicky. "This is my wife, the First Lady of Roseto, Pennsylvania. Mrs. Tutolola."

Cha Cha Tutolola was in her mid-fifties and built like a tugboat. She wore a shift dress in broad panels of black, red, and blue, so she was dressed like one too. Her hair was dyed deepest black, her lipstick was rose red, and two bright pink triangles of rouge faked cheekbone hollows. She extended her hand to Nicky. *"Ambasciatore, per favore—"*

"No Italian, Cha Cha," her husband chided her.

"Why not? I practiced for months," Cha Cha whined. "I could give guided tours at the United Nations."

"I learn-uh the English for you." Nicky took Cha Cha's hand in his and held it. *"Bellissima*, signora. *Bellissima."* He kissed it, and the crowd cheered.

"Well, I learned the Italian for you, *Ambasciatore."*

Cha Cha looked into Nicky's blue eyes and then took him in head to toe, drinking in his height, thick hair, handsome face, and bright smile. The sum total of his attributes sent a charge through her that she hadn't felt since she was stuck on the Whip at Dorney Park during a surprise electrical storm, and her metal safety bar was hit with a mild bolt of lightning. "You are much more handsome than your picture."

"And you-uh are-uh more-uh . . . how do you say . . . stunning than the official portrait in the Jubilee book."

"Black-and-white photography doesn't do my coloring justice."

"I can see that."

"I'm a Snow White, you know. It's all about contrast." She lowered her voice and said with a wink, "It's a *brunetta* advantage."

The screen door snapped behind them.

"This is our daughter, Rosalba," Rocco announced. "My only child. Flower of my loins."

A teenage girl slunk down the porch steps without taking her eyes off Nicky. She had the look of a starved fox, her chin pointed down, her brown eyes locked on her next meal. Her full madras skirt was cinched so tightly at the waist that the whole of her rib cage moved up and down when she breathed. The button holes on her white blouse strained over her bust, which was pointed and hoisted high.

Rosalba extended her hand to Nicky.

"I see she gets her beauty from her mother."

"She's shy," her mother whispered.

"Chief Burgess?" Nicky began.

"Please call me Rocco."

"Rocco, *mio figlio*—may I call you *mio figlio*?"

"Of course, of course." Rocco was flattered.

"The-uh United States government generously sent an attaché to accompany me on my travels here. She is-uh from da highest pinochles . . ."

"Do you mean 'pinnacle'?"

"Si, si, *pinnacle* of la government. I would-uh like to introduce her to you now." Nicky opened the sedan door and stuck his head in. The crowd burst into welcoming applause.

Hortense had the expression of an electrified Halloween cat. She whispered, "This better work, or I'll kill you before Al DePino takes a run at you."

"It will work," Nicky whispered back.

Hortense's foot, in a plain black leather pump, landed on the ground outside the car. She stepped out into the light.

As she was revealed, the applause ebbed, replaced with a soft chatter of surprise. An odd sound pealed through the crowd, a sigh of surprise laced with wonder, which turned to a faint grumble, until it was muted entirely. It was so quiet, Hortense swore she could hear the town butcher sawing salami on Garibaldi, a block away.

Nicky broke the impasse. "I would like you to meet Mrs. Hortense Mooney, attaché of Mrs. Eleanor Roosevelt."

The chief burgess and his wife shook Hortense's hand. "Pleased to meet you. Welcome to Roseto."

"I am pleased to meet you both. Mrs. Roosevelt visited Pennsylvania many times. She knew of the Liberty Bell in Philadelphia, and of Ben Franklin's tomb."

"Mrs. Mooney, forgive us, but we weren't expecting you." Cha Cha looked up at her husband anxiously. "We don't have a hotel here. The closest one is many miles away. And the ambassador is staying in our only guest room."

"So you don't have accommodations for me?"

"We don't."

"I'll just return to Philadelphia. It's been nice meeting you. Ambassador, if we leave now, you can drop me at the train station and be back in time for your dinner this evening. Bye-bye, everybody!"

"No, no—surely you have a room to accommodate a very important member of the United States government," Nicky insisted.

"Mrs. Viglione has the apartment over her garage," Rosalba offered. "The men who were staying there moved out."

"How do you know?" Cha Cha asked suspiciously.

"They were from Scranton, Ma. They were here to paint the church. Remember?"

"Those Ukrainians did a good job." Rocco shrugged.

"Oh. Well, I'll call Mrs. Viglione."

"We planned a tour of the Capri blouse mill upon your arrival. Then we thought you could use a rest."

"I could go for that right now," Hortense said under her breath.

"Tonight we have the Cadillac Dinner."

"Very-uh exciting. I much look forward," Nicky said loudly.

"I'll get your bags," Rocco volunteered.

"No, allow me. In Italy, we handle our own bags."

"Why?" Cha Cha wondered.

"Since da war."

"Oh." Cha Cha was enlightened.

Rocco turned to the crowd. "Friends, thank you for coming to welcome our guests. Now, if you would please allow us to get them situated and on with the plans of the day, we'll see you all at the Cadillac Dinner."

The crowd cheered. Nicky and Hortense walked to the car.

"It's not smart to stay in a private home. They'll trip you up," Hortense said under her breath.

"You're safe."

"But you won't be." Hortense looked over at the porch, where Rosalba was perched on the railing like a hungry buzzard eyeballing her prey.

Capri Fashions was one of thirty blouse mills scattered through Roseto, tucked unobtrusively between the houses. The mills' facades were painted the colors of the homes, soft white, pale blue, and coral. The signs on the entrance doors were not industrial but artful; the factories were named after family members—Carol Fashion Company, Kay Ann Sportswear, Yolanda Manufacturing Company, Cascioli Mills, Inc.—or combinations of the owners, names, including Mikro, owned and operated by Michael and Rosemarie Filingo. Still others described the final product: Perfect Shirt.

Nicky stood outside the Capri factory with Rocco. "Your town, it is-uh prosperous."

"Since the war, we've had a boom."

"You have brought *felicita* to Roseto. You must be-uh *populare*."

"I won the popular vote, if that's what you mean. But my victory is conditional. Success has many fathers, but failure has a stench. I've lived through that too. You hold your nose and push through it." Rocco opened the door, and Nicky followed him inside.

The factory was abuzz with the steady drone of fifty sewing machines operating at full speed. Filaments from the fabric floated in a gray haze in the air. Electrical cables as thick as hemp crisscrossed overhead, providing power to the rows of machines separated by a main aisle.

At each sewing machine was a woman, an operator, who swiftly and skillfully sewed pieces of a garment together, performing her particular job on a blouse with urgency. When it was completed, she handed it off to the operator next to her, who added her expertise to the garment until the assembled blouse made it into the bin at the end of each row.

A runner bundled the blouses by the dozen with a ribbon, and wheeled them down the main aisle into finishing, which was in full operation at the far end of the massive room. Clouds of white steam obscured the workers in finishing as they pressed the blouses.

"Anything like this in Italy?"

Nicky shook his head.

"A lot of women in this world, and all of them need clothes," Rocco said practically.

Nicky watched the operators as they focused on their sewing. Their speed was matched by their dexterity.

"The faster they go, the more money they make. If you're determined, you can do pretty well," Rocco said.

It was hard not to be caught up in the excitement of the enterprise and the precision of the operation. The women were beating the clock, working at a furious pace, their ambition laid bare. The process was mesmerizing, and Nicky appreciated a moment to observe instead of working hard to sell his accent. His mind was on the machines until a woman appeared at far end of the factory floor.

She might have been Nicky's age, or a little younger. Her light brown hair grazed her shoulder and was curled under neatly, but it fell out of her barrette and across her face when she turned to check the contents of a bin. She carried a clipboard, which she referred to as she moved. The visitors were far enough away that they couldn't hear what she was saying, but they could see that she acted like a coach, giving a directive to each row of operators at their machines, who would nod in agreement but not look up from their work. As she worked her way down the floor, she stopped to instruct or encourage with the focus of a conductor of a seasoned orchestra.

Nicky watched her walk; the buzz of the machines became music. She was an opera, not a minuet or a ritornello but the bravura of it, the swell of the overture, the transfixing aria, the lively intermezzo, and the emotional finale. She seemed to be coming through a garden, as she wore a dress made of some soft fabric covered in tiny pink roses, belted at her small waist and buttoned nearly from the collar to the hem, skimming her classic curves like the robe on mythic Helena or Nicky's favorite Hollywood beauty, Lana Turner. It was warm in the factory, and a few of the buttons at the collar were undone.

Her face had the look of the women from the rocky shores of the Mediterranean, seaport towns like Santa Margherita and Sestri Levanti, places Nicky's nonna had spoken of when he was a boy. This woman held the colors of the sand in her hair and the sea in her green eyes. The woman's full cheeks and lips were familiar to him. They had never met, but somehow he knew her.

"Who is she?" Nicky asked Rocco, his voice breaking.

"The forelady." Rocco motioned to her to join them. "Mamie Confalone."

Mamie Confalone. Nicky committed her name to memory.

"This is Ambassador Carlo Guardinfante from Roseto, Italy. Can you believe it? He made it."

Mamie extended her hand to Nicky.

"You are-uh in charge of da *factoria*?" Nicky said in his best Italian accent.

"Just the floor."

"Mamie is fluent in Italian. She was going to accompany you around Roseto during your stay. Mamie, you're off the hook. The ambassador wants to speak English."

"Well, too bad, there goes my Italian."

"Maybe you could help me with my English."

"You don't need any help. You speak English in a way I've never heard it before."

"You see, therefore, I need-uh your help. I could always use-uh more, *come se dice*, practice, Miss Confalone."

"*Missus* Confalone," Mamie said with a smile, and went back to work.

"Come, Ambassador. I'll show you the cutting room."

Nicky followed Rocco through the factory, but he had no interest in seeing the cutting room or the finishing department, or watching the shipping crew fold the blouses into cardboard box after cardboard box that would be stacked and loaded onto the truck that would transport the shipment to the garment district in New York City.

Nicky wanted to find a corner to be alone and mourn. He had, at long last, met the only woman in the world who had everything he was looking for; she'd come to him wrapped in roses. But he was too late. *Mrs.* Mamie Confalone was already taken.

"I hope you'll find these accommodations sufficient, Mrs. Mooney," Cha Cha said nervously.

"This is very nice. Thank you," Hortense said, removing her gloves.

The apartment over Mrs. Viglione's garage behind her house on Garibaldi Avenue consisted of one large room, with an alcove in which three single beds were made with white cotton coverlets. A round table and four chairs were set up under a large half-moon window. A door led to a small bathroom tiled in white. The kitchenette had a sink and a toaster oven.

"The kitchenette is tiny, but you'll be taking all your meals outside, so it shouldn't be a problem. Mrs. Viglione lives alone in the front house. Should you need anything, she has a telephone."

"Good to know. Do any Negroes live in Roseto?"

Cha Cha shook her head.

"Not one?"

"Not that I remember. The closest we go outside of Italy are the Greeks, and we only let in one family because they make the candy."

"You have to have candy."

"I'll make sure to bring you some."

"I'm the first colored person you've ever met."

Cha Cha nodded.

"So what do you think?"

"You're very cultivated, Mrs. Mooney. But you do work for Mrs. Roosevelt, and she is a world traveler."

"She didn't pick me up on the continent. I'm from Philadelphia."

"I didn't know where you came from."

"About an hour south of here. Have you been to Philadelphia?"

"To the zoo. Here's the key. We'll be by to pick you up for the dinner around six."

"Thank you. Will I be sitting with my hostess?"

"Mrs. Viglione? No. She never leaves her house."

"Never?"

Cha Cha leaned in. "Not for years. She goes in the garden and sits on the porch, but no further."

"She has a malady?"

"Not of the body," Cha Cha said, and tapped her head.

Hortense hung her good suit on a hanger. She examined her shoes, relieved to see that the black leather was still polished and barely scuffed, and stepped into a simple cotton day dress and a pair of sandals.

She wrote a note to leave on the door. She took the key, left the note outside, and walked through Mrs. Viglione's garden to the house. The small footpath was lined with irregular slabs of slate, in muted shades of blue and purple. She observed that the lady of the house was a serious gardener; she used every inch of earth to grow plants, wasting very little on the walkway or decorative elements.

The garden was not without its charms, however. Hortense walked under a trellis woven from branches of birch wood, which over time had faded to a calico finish of gray, white, and soft pink. The delicate pale green leaves that would eventually shield the summer grapes had twisted through the branches, which gave her an idea for a hat.

Hortense knocked on the back door, which was screen on the top half, wood below, with a solid door behind it. She tapped lightly at first, then put some muscle behind it.

Finally Mrs. Viglione opened the door.

"Mrs. Viglione, I'm staying in your guest apartment over the garage."

"Is there a leak?"

"No, there's no leak. In fact, it's lovely."

"Thank you."

"I wanted to come and introduce myself. I'm Hortense Mooney, with the United States."

"Aren't we all with the United States?"

"Government. I'm with the United States government."

"Cha Cha said you worked with Mrs. Roosevelt."

"Yes."

"I voted for her husband four times."

"I will tell her."

"How is she getting along as a widow?"

"Up and down. You know, up and down."

"I hate it. Being a widow is just terrible. Are you married?"

"Many years."

"Good for you."

"I hope so. Well, I just wanted to say hello and introduce my-self." Hortense turned to go.

"Would you like to come in?"

Hortense smiled. "Thank you. That would be nice."

Minna Viglione opened the door. She was small and thin, her white hair pulled back by two simple braids, attached to a low chignon. She was close to eighty years old, but she had a youthful energy that was obvious in the way she kept her garden and home. Her day dress was simple gray-and-white-checked gingham, zippered up the front, with deep pockets. She wore flat gray leather lace-up work shoes and stockings.

Hortense stepped into her immaculate kitchen. The walls were covered in white marble and the floor pebbled with smooth, soft blue stones. The round kitchen table had an elaborate ceramic top, painted with the artwork of an old map.

"What a lovely kitchen."

"I'm in it most of the day."

"I would be too, if it were mine. Where did you find this table?"

"It was sent from Italy. My husband and I went to visit our families on our honeymoon, and I saw it and had to have it. It's my favorite piece of furniture in the house."

"I can see why." Hortense ran her hand over the smooth tiles.

"Please." Mrs. Viglione invited Hortense to sit. "Are you hungry?"

"I haven't eaten since breakfast."

"It's almost supper time. Are you waiting for the dinner this evening?"

"I won't be attending."

"Don't you have to go with the ambassador?"

"I've done enough for him today."

Mrs. Viglione laughed. "Is he difficult?"

"He has his moments."

"They all do, don't they?"

"He is a man, after all." Hortense chuckled "Are you going to the dinner?"

"No, no. Will you join me for dinner here?"

"That would be lovely."

"You'll miss all the excitement," Minna warned her.

"I think my ticker has had enough of that for one day," Hortense promised her.

Nicky looked at himself in the mirror of his guest room at the Tutololas' house, feeling as though he had landed in a jar of women's cold cream. The four-poster bed was draped with a crocheted canopy. The bedspread was made of ruffled pink organza. There was a white rug, an antique pink dresser, and a lamp whose shade looked like the bottom half of a ballerina. Every surface was covered with a doily.

He folded back the coverlet, careful not to wrinkle the ruffles, and then stepped out of his pants and hung them up in the small closet stuffed with boxes of Christmas ornaments. He was hanging his suit jacket on the same hanger when there was a knock at the door.

He opened the door a crack and peeked out into the hallway.

"I pressed your uniform for the dinner this evening," Cha Cha said from behind his pressed suit, holding it above her head because it was twice as long as she was.

"*Grazie, signora.*" Nicky reached one arm through the door to take it from Cha Cha, but she attempted to push her way into his room with her free hand.

"I am not dressed!"

"Oh my." Cha Cha tried to peek inside. "I wanted to show you the closet."

"I-uh find it. *Grazie.*"

"Is there anything else you need?"

Nicky was close enough to Cha Cha's face through the crack in the door to see that she'd drawn her black eyebrows on over a few sparse white hairs. She felt his stare and patted the left one. "We'll give you a knock when we're ready to leave tonight."

"I will take a rest."

"You do that."

Nicky threaded his costume through the door and closed the gap between him and Cha Cha quickly, knowing that any delay would be a sign of encouragement. The door did not have a lock, but why would it? Who would want to be locked inside this lady lair?

He hung his uniform on the back of the closet door and lay down on the bed, which nearly collapsed under his weight. His feet hung over the edge on one end, as his head sunk through the pillow to the mattress below on the other. Everything was too soft.

Nicky wanted to get up and get a cigarette, but he feared that if he lit a match in this room, he would blow up Truman Street. Instead he put his hands behind his head, closed his eyes, and without moving a muscle, let his mind wander to the exquisite beauty of Mamie Confalone. As she walked down the main aisle of the factory and toward him, he longed for her. As he drifted off to sleep, Mamie Confalone reached him at the end of the aisle and pulled him close and kissed him.

Minna stood at her kitchen window, peering out at the garage apartment.

"Can you see anything?" Hortense whispered from behind the kitchen door.

"Cha Cha is with Eddie Davanzo."

"Who's he?"

"The town cop. Come and look. They can't see you from here."

Hortense peeked out through the kitchen curtains. "He's handsome."

"A bachelor."

"What a waste."

"I don't know what is wrong with the young ladies in this town. But I think he pines for one girl in particular, and he can't have her, so he doesn't settle."

"Unrequited love. One-sided pain for no one's gain." Hortense cackled victoriously. "They're taking my note!"

"What did it say?"

"It got me out of the dinner tonight. I'm just too tired to put up with the staring."

"I understand. They can be cold if you're not one of them."

"They weren't cold this afternoon, but they look at me like they've never seen a colored person. It makes me feel prickly."

"I've felt that way since the day I moved here."

"You're not one of them?"

"I married one of them."

"So you're once removed. You're not Italian?"

"I am, but not from their province, or their town. They like their own. That's it. I'm Venetian, and therefore an outsider."

"Judged by your own kind. That is frosty."

"Do you like all Negroes?"

"Mostly."

"I'm sure you're respected in your community because of your position. How many people can say they work for Eleanor Roosevelt?"

"It's not my job that earns me respect. It's my standing in my church."

"That's important, too. But it's very rare for a woman to have a position like yours. Mrs. Roosevelt saw something in you."

"She's a visionary, only one of her in a million. Franklin and she—well, I can't speak of them without getting emotional. May he rest in peace."

"Best president we ever had."

"I think so. Except perhaps for Abraham Lincoln."

"He was a good one, too."

"For my people he was essential." Hortense put her hand on her heart.

"Do you like to cook?"

"It's my favorite chore."

"Mine too."

"But I do love to garden, too. And you have a lovely garden."

"I enjoy it. I grow my own tomatoes. Lettuce. Cucumbers. How about you?"

"The same. I also raise okra, chicory. We cook with that."

"How do you make your tomatoes?"

"I stew them. Have you ever stewed tomatoes?"

"I haven't."

"My momma taught me. You take about eight big red tomatoes in season," Hortense began. "Slice them in triangles, heat some butter in a skillet, two teaspoons of sugar—slice up an onion—let that get glassy. When it does, throw in the tomatoes and stir them up. Sprinkle about a quarter teaspoon of cloves over the tomatoes as they're cooking. Keep stirring. If you want to make a meal out of it, tear up some bread and throw it in there and stir it all together. You never tasted anything so delicious."

"Tonight I'm going to make macaroni. Is that all right?"

"As long as you serve it with some fruit of the vine." Hortense winked.

"I have a bottle or two."

"Then I am all set. Hallelujah. A little homemade hootch, and I'll forget all my troubles."

"Nothing wrong with that."

"Thank you, Lord!" Hortense went to sit at the counter where Minna prepared the meal. "I always wanted to learn how to make the gravy."

"You must know some Italians. You don't call it sauce."

"The Roosevelts employed some Italians here and there."

"I'll show you how to make gravy Venetian style. In this town, they make it Rosetan style, which is fine, it's tasty." She whispered, "But mine is better."

"I believe you. What's in the Roseto gravy?"

Minna paused for a moment. "It goes like this. Olive oil in the pan, chopped onion, minced garlic, let it get glassy, as you say. Set that aside. Then you prepare the tomatoes. We can them every winter—in summer, we use fresh. One tomato per serving, so a quart of tomatoes serves about four people. When you use the fresh, most of the women like to give the tomatoes a dunk in boiling water and peel them before cooking them into the sauce. Then they strain them into the pan, so no seeds or skin in the gravy—it's just smooth. You'll add parsley, basil, and crushed red pepper. Salt and pepper. You let that simmer. Over the macaroni it goes. Add your freshly grated cheese."

"That's it?"

"That's the Rosetan marinara. Of course, when they make the big pot of gravy, they add the meat. The meatballs, the sausage, pork, chicken, what have you. For the big pot, double the tomatoes. That's the pot the family eats out of all week."

"Right."

"Do you want to help me make the gravy Venetian style?"

"Sure."

Hortense watched as Minna methodically gathered the pots and utensils, including paring knives, colander, wooden spoons, slate cutting board, and a large pot to boil the macaroni. She tied a dishtowel around her waist, washed her hands, and filled the pot with water, placing it on the stove to boil and adding salt to the water. From her icebox, she took one carrot and a bunch of celery. From a bin next to it, she retrieved an onion. From the window, she pinched a bunch of basil from the plant in its pot. From a ceramic dish, she chose three cloves of firm garlic.

Minna lifted her largest skillet from the shelf, placed it on the stove, and poured olive oil into the pan. She handed Hortense a paring knife. "Mince the garlic for me. I'll take care of the onion. I never make company cry."

Minna placed the onion and garlic in the skillet, turning the heat on low. She stirred the onion and garlic, thoroughly covering them with the olive oil. "Peel and slice the carrot in very thin discs for me." As Hortense cut the carrot, Minna pulled the outside stalks of the celery away from the bunch until she got to the heart. She pulled the heart stalks out and chopped them finely on the cutting board.

"Why the hearts of celery?" Hortense asked.

"That's my own choice. The outside stalks make the sauce bitter. Just my opinion." Minna put the carrot discs and chopped celery hearts into the pan and stirred.

"Smells divine," Hortense commented.

Minna stirred the vegetables until they were soft. She climbed up on her stepstool and opened her cupboard, revealing mason jars canned with fresh tomatoes, seeds, skins, and all. She selected a jar and handed it to her guest.

She poured half a quart of the tomatoes into the skillet, blending them with the vegetables. She placed the colander over a stainless steel bowl and poured the mixture from the skillet into the colander. With her wooden spoon, she methodically pressed the vegetable juice and pulp through, leaving behind any skin, seeds, and threads from the vegetables. When she was satisfied that she had pressed all the best pulp and flavors from the mixture, she returned it to the skillet, turned the burner on low, and covered it.

"Now we have a glass of wine."

"Bring it forth, Mrs. Viglione!"

"But before we do, I have to ask you to look away."

"I won't tell anybody you drink, if you won't tell anybody I do."

"It's not that. I have to add the secret ingredient to the sauce."

"You just showed me how to make it."

"I left out one ingredient."

"Why?"

"It's been in my family, and I took an oath."

"You're not going to give me the secret ingredient? But how am I supposed to make the gravy come out like yours?"

"You may have it when I'm dead." Minna shot Hortense a look like she meant it, so Hortense turned away. Hortense heard Minna climb back onto the stepstool. She heard the snap of the cupboard door, the snap of a canister, and the click of a spoon. She heard her hostess lift the lid of the skillet on the stove and return the lid to the skillet. Then she heard her put away the secret ingredient, just as she had retrieved it.

"You can turn around now," Minna said.

"I don't like secrets."

"How can you work for the government?"

"True, it weighs on my Christian conscience. But not as much as a cooking secret weighs on my colored one."

"I promise you'll have the secret when I die."

"I've known you for such a short time, but the thought of that already makes me sad."

"I know. Isn't it funny how that works when you make a friend?"

Minna hoisted the wine jug from under her counter. She poured Hortense a glass, and one for herself.

"To Eleanor Roosevelt." Minna raised her glass.

"To Mrs. Roosevelt." Hortense sipped. The sip of rich, purple homemade wine filled the dispatcher with the pure heat of an Italian sun on a cloudless day. She savored it, closed her eyes, and let go. For the first time in her long and useful life, Hortense Mooney was in the moment.

7

The half-moon over Roseto looked like a broken button through the silver chiffon clouds. A large white tent, the venue for the town's annual Cadillac Dinner, dazzled in the black field as music played by the live orchestra sailed out into the night.

A brand-new dove-gray 1950 Cadillac convertible with a black top was displayed in the field, in a blaze of floodlights. The grand prize of the evening's raffle was decorated with an enormous glittering gold bow, as if an object of such grandeur needed further adornment. Every person in attendance hoped to drive it home.

The dinner guests arrived from all directions, some in cars, others on foot. The quick clicks of the heels of their dress shoes could be heard on the sidewalks as they poured toward the entrance of the tent.

The women were dressed in formal gowns made of satin, lace, and tulle, in spring shades of pink, yellow, and mint green speckled with sequins, crystals, and seed pearls. The ladies looked like a floating garland of blossoms as they lined up to pick up their table cards. The men wore black tie and dress shoes that pinched their feet, and, in a tip of the top hat to the evening's formality, traded their cigarettes for cigars.

The Jubilee Committee had decorated the interior of the tent in the Italian national colors of red, white, and green. Luckily, the colors of Italy's flag were the same as the town Christmas decorations, so the holiday lights that hung across Garibaldi in December pulled double duty inside the tent in June.

The tables were set with red tablecloths and the white church china. The centerpieces were pedestals mounted with cookie trays wrapped in cellophane and festooned with a small bouquet of red carnations attached with ribbons. The women of Roseto had baked biscotti, iced coconut cookies, fig bars, nut drops, jelly centers, pizelles, and chocolate twists by the hundreds for the event. The scent of sugared almonds, anisette, and vanilla filled the tent, competing with the ladies' best perfumes: Tabu, Charles of the Ritz, and Intoxication by D'orsay.

Fifty tables of ten were filled. It was the largest Cadillac Dinner in history, surely because the ambassador of Roseto Valfortore was the guest of honor. In a matter of a few short hours, Carlo Guardinfante had become the most popular man in town. He ingratiated himself to the Rosetani with his excellent English and good humor.

Word spread quickly of the specifics of his Italian lineage (which they shared), his good looks (power and beauty are an excellent combination), his height (a lucky break for any Italian male), and his warm personality (he was one of them). If there were an election the ambassador would beat Rocco for chief burgess handily, and Rocco Tutolola was beloved.

A parquet dance floor had been installed in the center of the tent. The dais, elevated over the crowd where the ambassador and town officials were seated, overlooked it, with the orchestra facing them on the other side. The tables were staggered inside the tent on either side of the dance floor.

Nicky surveyed the bash from his seat on the dais. The place cards had been printed in gold, except the one next to his, which was handwritten: "Mrs. Mooney, Attaché to Mrs. Roosevelt." He rested his arm on the back of Hortense's empty chair.

Nicky checked his watch. Where was Mrs. Mooney? His stomach grumbled. Nothing makes a man hungrier than being nice to people, therefore he was famished. He fished for a coconut cookie through the cellophane as he waited.

Nicky was nibbling on the cookie when Eddie Davanzo handed him an envelope.

> *Dear Ambassador,*
> *I regret I won't make it to the dinner,*
> *but I'd rather kill myself than attend.*
> > *Have fun.*
> > *Mrs. Mooney*

"I hope she's all right," Eddie said. "Mrs. Tutolola and I knocked several times, and she didn't answer the door."

"Mrs. Mooney has the gout. She is probably soaking in a hot bath." Nicky stuffed the note in his jacket pocket as Rocco went off to greet more guests. "Or she got a lift to the bar at the Bangor Hotel, and she's three Pink Squirrels shy of forgetting her name," he mumbled to himself.

Nicky was corralled to appear in a series of group photographs with the important civic organizations and religious clubs in Roseto: the Jubilee Committee, followed by the Our Lady of Mount Carmel Sodality, Columbia Fire Company, American Legion–Martocci Capobianco Post, the Knights of Columbus, the Blue Army, the Roseto Presbyterians (long story), descendants of the town founders: the Rosato, Falcone, and Policelli families, the Pius X High School Chorus, Our Lady of Mount Carmel School science project winners, Columbus School drama club, the Roseto Coronet Band under the direction of Louis Angelini, the officers and membership of the local International Ladies' Garment Workers' Union; and the board of directors and membership of the Marconi Social Club.

By the time the group photographs were taken, every single one of the five hundred guests had appeared in at least one of them. Between set-ups, the guests managed to return to their seats to finish their plates of Beef Wellington served with green beans almondine and tossed salad, and attack the cookie trays as the coffee was served. The band, the Nite-Caps, was ready to swing.

Nicky worked his way back to the dais, his mouth watering at the thought of a hot meal. When he reached his seat, he was too late; his plate had been cleared, and the Tutololas had demolished the cookie tray. All that was left next to his nameplate was a glass of ice water and a lemon wedge. What Nicky would give for one fig cookie! And he didn't even like them.

A dinner roll had been left on absentee Hortense's bread plate. Nicky grabbed the roll, buttered it, and swallowed it whole; it went down like a tennis ball. Being famous meant there was never time to eat. *Give me obscurity*, Nicky thought as he touched his forefinger to the tip of his tongue and gathered the crumbs from the empty cookie tray, savoring a hint of the delicacies that might have been.

Hortense stood by the stove as Minna showed her the final step in preparing her Venetian gravy.

"You see where the sauce has thickened, and most of the liquid has burned off," Minna said as she stirred the thick, fragrant tomato sauce. "Then I'll make a well in the center and add a half a stick of butter, and I'll keep stirring until the butter is mixed into the sauce completely." She handed Hortense the spoon.

Minna drained the macaroni into the colander in the sink. "Never rinse the macaroni," she instructed, gently shaking the noodles and setting them aside. She lifted the pan off the stove and poured some of the gravy into the serving dish. She added the macaroni on top, then ladled the rest of the gravy onto the hot pasta and mixed it together. She grated fresh Parmesan cheese on top. Minna lifted the bowl of macaroni off the counter.

"Bring the tray, please," she said to Hortense. Her guest picked up a tray filled with crusty bread, butter, a salad of dandelion greens, black olives, and sweet onions tossed with olive oil and vinegar, and a carafe of homemade wine.

Hortense followed Minna outside to the table she had set in the garden.

"This is what it must be like in Italy," Hortense marveled.

"Al fresco. Try the macaroni."

Hortense sampled the dish and closed her eyes. "I've never tasted anything so delicious. It must be that secret ingredient."

"It's everything. Do you think you can make the gravy yourself?"

"I'm going to write it all down."

"You should."

"I'd love to make it for my next church supper."

"Do you think they'll like it?"

"I don't know. The only red sauce we ever serve is barbeque, so maybe not."

"If you love to cook, people always love to eat what you prepare."

"That's true. My family loves my cooking," Hortense admitted.

"But you work in an office?"

"Yes. Pays the bills."

"Mrs. Roosevelt must make that work interesting."

"She does. Keeps me hopping. Do you have children, Minna?"

"One son. He lives in Albany, New York."

"All the way up there?"

"His father-in-law has a business."

"Your son didn't want to stay around here?"

"His wife didn't."

"We lose the sons, don't we?"

"Always. Do you have sons?"

"Two daughters. They're grown now. I had a son too. He was born on November 5, 1916. He died the next day. I named him Malachy."

"I'm sorry." Minna placed her hand on Hortense's.

"But I know about boys. I'm around them at work. I mother everyone, I guess you could say."

"We mother the men too. I worked with my husband."

"What did he do?"

"He had a blouse mill. Everybody around here has a blouse mill."

"When did he pass?"

"Six years ago."

"That's difficult."

"I still have a hard time with it. I went to the funeral, and then to the cemetery. I came home and haven't left this house since."

"What do you mean?"

"I don't leave the house. I go as far as the garden and the box-wood hedge out front."

Hortense took a sip of wine. This must have been the mental condition that Cha Cha referred to. "How do you make it?"

"I have good neighbors who shop when I need something, and the priest brings me communion. People look out for me."

"Have you tried to go beyond your house?"

"Can't do it. I try. I bought a ticket to the dinner tonight. When I buy it, I actually believe I'll go. I even planned what I was going to wear. If you go up to my room, you'll find a pale blue chiffon dress hanging on the back of the door. My good shoes are sitting on top of the box, my stockings are on the dresser. But as the time gets closer, I get more anxious. Then tonight you knocked on my door and took the burden off of me. I didn't have to go because you arrived."

"Can I let you in on a secret? I didn't want to go either."

"You must have so many events in public."

"It gets tiresome. If I never have to appear in public again, I will be happy."

"Of course that's up to Mrs. Roosevelt. Hortense, if you could do it all over again, what would you do differently?"

"Everything."

Minna laughed.

"No, I mean it. There was a lot of good in this life. But I would go a different way."

"What do you mean?" Minna poured her guest more wine.

"I'd find my true purpose."

"You don't think you have?"

"I don't."

"That's interesting."

"What's yours, Minna?"

"I'm older than you, a good twenty years, I'd say, so I'm finished searching. My purpose now is to have a peaceful end. That's a purpose too, you know."

"That's why we spend time in church. Just trying to earn our salvation."

"A peaceful end is important, but you have to plan for it. The days and nights leading up to the end have to be filled with thoughts of grace. You can't sit around thinking about what you didn't get in this life, chasing what was owed you, jealous of someone who has what you wished you had gotten, angry at your spouse because he didn't give you what you needed. Believe it or not, there are those people who die that are still angry at their parents for not giving them what they believed they deserved."

"Poor souls." Hortense sipped her wine.

"You can't find grace if you're full of misery."

"If you walked around out there, you'd find plenty of misery," Hortense assured her.

"That's not why I stay inside."

"Have you figured it out?"

"It began after my husband died, and the condition just got worse and worse. I tried to shake it. I tried to get better but the fear has gripped me and won't let me go. A good friend of mine sent a witch over. I burned herbs, soaked in white vinegar, painted a wall peacock blue and stared at it fifteen minutes in the morning and fifteen at night—nothing cured it. They've had masses said, rosaries, novenas. Nothing breaks the hold this has over me. Then I thought it through. And I told myself, just like I fell into this, there will be a day when I walk out the front door and keep walking. It will pass."

"The bad times always do."

"They do. In the meantime, I prepare. I eat from the garden. I grow flowers. And when I'm lucky, I make a new friend."

Nicky was trying to figure out how to leave the dais to steal a cookie tray from a table near the dance floor when he heard a voice from behind him.

"Hey."

He turned to see Mamie Confalone in a cocktail-length dress with a kitchen apron tied over it, handing him a plate full of food. He didn't know what looked more delicious, the food or her. "You're an angel."

"No, I'm in charge of the food service on the dais, and I didn't want your food to get cold."

"I have never been this hungry."

"You almost passed out in the Marconi Club picture. Eat," Ma-

mie ordered, before weaving her way through the crowd and outside to the kitchen station.

As Nicky watched her go, the sway of her hips in the cocktail
dress drove him to distraction, but not enough to stop eating the
food she had brought to him and go after her. He was so hungry,
he forgot she was married. He speared a hunk of potato and meat
and crust from the beef Wellington and had put it in his mouth
when the band started up.

As they played a revelry, Rocco Tutolola walked out onto the
dance floor while two men rolled a large red steel bingo drum out
to the center.

A spotlight hit Nicky as he shoveled in another bite of the Beef
Wellington. He heard the ambassador introduced. He was asked
to come to the dance floor to choose the winning ticket of the
Cadillac. The spotlight followed Nicky until he put his hand into
the drum to pull the ticket.

The crowd shouted:

"SIFT!"

"DIG!"

"DEEPER!"

"They mean don't pick a card off the top," Rocco said quietly.

Nicky put his arm deep inside the drum, as if it were the mouth
of a lion and he were a lion tamer. His arm went so deep it could
have been snapped off if the metal door had accidentally shut. He
pulled a card from the bottom of the drum and handed it to Rocco.

Rocco walked to the bandstand and lifted the microphone off
the soloists' stand. "The winner of the Cadillac is Wayne Rutledge."

"Who? What?" the crowd chattered.

"Wayne Rutledge of Florence, Alabama."

"An *Ameri-gan*?" a guest shouted from a table.

"Where's Alabama?"

"Who cares? It's not Pennsylvania!"

"This is a travesty!"

"Must be a mistake!"

"Yes, it appears an *Ameri-gan* won the Cadillac," Rocco confirmed. "An *Ameri-gan* from Alabama."

"Who sold him a ticket?"

Mike Muzzollo stood up from a table near the dais. "I did. I bought tires for my shop. I asked my regional rep to sell some tickets for me. The guy does tires east of the Mississippi. He has a client in Alabama, and the client sold one to Wayne Rutledge, who does the guy's taxes. And he won."

"An accountant won?" a woman shrieked.

"A tax man? Ugh!" another shouted from a far table.

A local woman stood and shook her fist. "Someone from town should win."

"This stinks!"

"Pick another card!"

"What a bust!" The crowd began to revolt.

"Folks, settle down," said Rocco. "This is a raffle. That means it's a game of chance, which means there's only a chance you'll win. Now you saw the ambassador—he dug in that drum like he was pulling shrapnel from a lung."

"We should've had a Tricky Tray," a woman sniffed.

"The *Ameri-gan* probably would've won that too," a man added as he puffed on his cigar.

Rocco persisted. "We sell tickets wherever we can to whomever we can because it all goes to the betterment of our town. Your generosity raised seventy-five thousand dollars for Roseto. It looks like we'll be able to install a fountain in Borough Park and have plenty left over for beautification. We'll be happy to let Mr. Rutledge know he won the Cadillac. Rosetani are happy for the winner." He placed the microphone back in the stand and urged the band to play.

"A raffle is a raffle," Rocco said to Nicky. "Nobody stole the car out from under anybody else."

"The people are-uh very upset," Nicky said nervously. He felt the black eyes of the men glaring at him.

"They don't like a con."

"How was it a con? It was a raffle, fair and square." Nicky was so exhausted, his accent had left him.

"Pretty good with your English. Fair and square."

"I heard it-uh today-uh at the *factoria*."

"Right. Did you eat?"

"Just a bite."

Rocco checked his watch. He pulled a cookie from a pedestal off a table by the dance floor. "Sorry, Ambassador. The dance is about to begin. You'll need your strength." He handed Nicky a cookie, which Nicky swallowed whole before retrieving another through the cellophane.

Cha Cha approached Nicky. "Ready to rumba?" She swiveled her hips.

"Si, si, La Bamba. I dance with the chief burgess's wife first. My hostess." Nicky thumped his chest to force the dry cookie down.

"Enjoy." Rocco patted Nicky on the back and walked off.

Nicky took the very petite Cha Cha in his arms. Moving on the dance floor with her was a lot like stooping and pushing a wheelbarrow full of sand over a gravel tar pit.

"My husband tells me you enjoyed the tour of the mill today."

"Very much. Mrs. Tutolola, I must-uh ask you, because the resemblance is overwhelming. Is-uh Mamie Confalone your *figlia*?"

Cha Cha stuck her chest out and into Nicky's waist with pride. "You think she could be my sister?"

"Oh, you look-uh so much the same."

"I see what you mean. The tilt of the nose. No, we're not related."

"Who are her people?"

"She's a Mugavero. Prettiest girls in town if you ask me. Good bone structure. That's a lucky break you know. She married Augusto Confalone. Sad story. He died in the war."

"She's a widow?"

"Yes."

"Not remarried?"

"No. In fact, shows no interest. Of course, she has her son. He's five years old, and he's her life. As it should be."

"Yes. Yes." Nicky wanted to pitch Cha Cha out of the tent, find Mamie, and leave town with her, but he must not be rash.

"A woman that has a child doesn't have time for tomfoolery when the child is small. The child has to be raised. That's your first priority as a mother." Cha Cha sniffed with authority.

"Yes, mothers are God's eyes and ears on earth."

"That is lovely."

Cha Cha pressed into Nicky as they danced. The juxtaposition of her chatter about motherhood and her simultaneous grinding into his body with her ample bust and girdled midsection made him dyspeptic, or it could have been the undigested Beef Wellington—he couldn't be sure.

"Once children are raised, that's a different situation. A woman can go back to being girlish. A woman has wiggle room to enjoy herself. She can go out, travel. Dance with ambassadors from foreign countries in uniform."

"You must vee-zeet Roseto Valfortore, Cha Cha."

"Is that an invitation?" Cha Cha ground into Nicky like a drill bit.

"When one invites another to vee-zeet, that is an invitation. No?" Nicky felt the stays of Cha Cha's girdle poke into his upper thigh.

"*Si. Si. Si,*" she purred. Nicky felt a low rumble of desire peal through her body.

"You would love Eee-taly. Your husband would-uh enjoy it. A second honeymoon for two lovers. No?"

"No. Yes. It sounds swell. Rocco doesn't like to travel. He has motion sickness."

"What a shame."

"Doesn't seem to bother him when he takes his friend out on his speedboat on the Delaware."

"You should be happy he has outside interests."

"I'd be happier if it wasn't a girlfriend."

"I am so sorry."

"Politics. You know. Power. Women crave Rocco like chocolate. But I'd like his comare to live with him for a week and see if she'd stick around for the duration. I've had to do things to Rocco a medical doctor wouldn't attempt. I'd like to see his girlfriend go at him with tweezers, a magnifying glass, and ointment and see how long she'd last. Trust me. She wouldn't."

Revolted, Nicky dumped Cha Cha off at the dessert table before sashaying back to the line of ladies waiting for their dance with Carlo.

Rosalba cut the line and grabbed Nicky to dance to a Perry Como medley. She attached herself to his body like a barnacle on the second bar of "Volare."

"You dance like your mother," Nicky said, worried that the wool on his borrowed suit would pill.

"I learned how to dance at the Bee Hive in Bangor."

"Such skill."

"Thanks. How do you like Roseto?" Her hot breath in his ear made it itch.

"A charming *villaggio*."

"How about your room?" She bit his earlobe.

"It's fine." Nicky pulled his head back and glared at her.

"We share a wall."

"I did not know."

"Now you do. It gets hot."

"Where?"

"In the guest room. My mother stuffs it with junk."

"I did not notice."

"Don't open the closet."

"I wouldn't dare." Nicky had dropped his accent, but he didn't care.

"My room has cross breeze. If you get hot."

"I don't get hot."

"Even in this wool uniform?"

"Especially not in this wool uniform."

"How about when you're out of it?"

"I sleep in the uniform in case of an invasion in the middle of the night."

"That could be arranged."

Nicky had had enough. He pulled her off to the side of the dance floor. "How old are you, Rosalba?"

"Eighteen."

"When?"

"A year and a half from next March."

"So you're sixteen."

"I'll be eighteen in no time."

"Do you have a boyfriend?"

"A couple. Well, three, if you count the mechanic I'm stringing along in Pen Argyl."

"Three boyfriends? Isn't that enough for one young lady? Why are you bothering me?"

"I'm bored."

"Get a library card."

"I hate to read."

"You need a hobby."

"I think I found one." Rosalba pulled him close as a Perry Como sound-alike sang "Some Enchanted Evening." Nicky tried to take tiny steps backward. Rosalba mistook his steps as leading and pulled Nicky back onto the dance floor.

"I am a married man!"

"Doesn't count when you're abroad."

"Where do you get these rules? Aren't you a Catholic girl?"

"I do what I want and then I just go to confession."

"That's not the purpose of confession. You confess to sin no more."

"How am I supposed to do that?"

"I have no idea. I'm not your priest!"

Disgruntled, Nicky dropped Rosalba off by the bandstand. He surmised that, with a full orchestra, including woodwind, brass, and string sections, surely she'd find a horn player to amuse her.

Nicky looked at the long line of local ladies lolling along the wall, waiting to Lindy with him. Quickly, he did the math in his head. He estimated the number of women in the queue, the time it would take to do one rotation on the dance floor with each lady, and concluded he could knock out his obligation and flee the tent in forty minutes. He set his mind on his goal like an Olympic athlete.

Nicky plucked the line in order from the front, taking each lady for her revolution, dumping her back at the start, and picking up the next one for her spin. He perspired so heavily, his uniform began to itch, but he did not stop to scratch. He felt like he was in a dance marathon during the Great Depression, except this one came without a cash prize.

Each dance partner had some nugget of gossip to share, and by the end of the dance-floor rondelet, Nicky knew the history of the town, a few of the prominent citizens' peccadilloes, and, most importantly, the story of Mamie Confalone.

Nicky delivered the last lady, his final obligation of the night, into the waiting arms of her husband. He bowed from the waist and headed for the exit, where Eddie Davanzo stood guard in his police uniform.

"Those ladies wore you out. How did you do it?"

"*Che bella*. They were lovely. Fleet-footed. Which one was your mama?"

"The one who smelled like calamine lotion. She worked in her garden all day and got poison ivy."

"I remember her well."

"Your back must ache." Eddie chuckled. "There wasn't one of them over four foot eleven."

"One. The lady from West Bangor was-uh six foot two."

"Statuesque." Eddie grinned.

"It gave my neck a stretch."

"You needed it. Ambassador, if you don't mind me saying it, the only reason you could ever get away with that suit is because you're a foreigner."

"This is the official dress regimentals of my province."

"It looks like the Penn State band uniform."

Nicky blanched. Borelli's accepted donations in the costume shop. He maintained his composure. "I brought this from Eet-taly," he assured Eddie.

"No doubt. It's just funny. One country's ambassador is another's majorette."

Nicky nodded and slipped out of the tent. He inhaled the night air as though he had spent the night underwater in a shark tank, holding his breath, waiting to be eaten alive. It felt good to finally be alone. He pulled up his pants, which were loose from perspiration and gyration. Nicky figured he'd lost ten pounds of water weight on the dance floor, and every ounce of it resided in the wool. He had never been so exhausted, not even when he was in the army and had to walk seventeen miles in the rain in a German war zone in wet boots with a wool sock with a hole in the toe. Nicky was so spent, even the thought of the old mattress in the airless guest room with its lingering scents of stale gardenia, mud plaster, and mothballs was appealing.

Nicky lit a cigarette as he trudged up the hill to Truman Street.

"Ambassador?" a woman called out to him in the dark.

Nicky kept moving.

"You need a key." Cha Cha shook her evening bag in midair like a bell. She jogged to meet him, and then trotted beside him to keep up with his long strides. Soon she began to pant. By the time they reached the house, Cha Cha was heaving. She grabbed the porch railing, trying to catch her breath before climbing the stairs.

"Madame, I wish you a good night." Nicky bowed from the waist, unlocked the door, and once inside, bolted up the staircase, two steps at a time. He was pleased he had figured out a way to ditch Cha Cha—all he had to do was outrun her on an incline.

Nicky went into the guest room and closed the door. He was peeling off the uniform and his drenched undershirt when he heard the bedroom door creak. He slammed his body up against it and waited. After a few moments, he moved away from the door. He cocked his head to listen before he crept back over and peeked out into the hallway. A gray-and-white mixed tabby cat was sniffing at the door. Nicky exhaled, relieved.

He hung the uniform in the closet. A plastic Star of Bethlehem, the Christmas tree topper, fell off the top shelf and almost impaled his skull. He cursed, picked it up, and stuffed it back into its place before lying down on the bed, his lower back and buttocks sinking deeply into the mattress while his legs stuck out straight like cocktail picks where the old mattress was still somewhat firm. He wanted to weep, and he might have, but there was no moisture left in his body; he had left it all on the dance floor at the Cadillac Dinner.

Hortense lay in the center bed in the alcove of the garage apartment. She had opened the windows on the garden side, and the soothing scents of freesia, gardenia, and night-blooming jasmine filled the room. The temperature was just right, cool enough but not cold. The mattress was firm, the pillows were plump, and the bed was made to her liking with cotton shams and fresh sheets.

Eleanor Roosevelt's faux attaché felt divine. The wine Hortense had consumed had a lovely effect on her mood, and the macaroni with the Venetian gravy with the secret ingredient settled on her stomach lightly and without repetition. Hortense was content in a fashion she had not known for years. She drifted off to sleep without a single toss or turn, floating to the land of her dreams like a blue balloon the color of the sky, when it soars high enough and becomes one with the heavens.

Across town, Nicky was overheated, hungry, and restless. He had tried to open the windows in the Tutolola guest room, but they were either painted shut or locked, like a prison's. At this point in the evening, he was so exhausted, he didn't care. He collapsed into the bed and tried turning onto his side, but that produced a muscle stitch that forced him to get up to try and release it. He gave up, climbing back into the bed in the original buttocks-sagging-in-a-hammock position. He was almost asleep when he began to choke.

"Don't say a word," Rosalba whispered.

The chief burgess's daughter was straddling him, one clammy hand over his mouth, the other on his neck.

Nicky couldn't breathe. He pushed Rosalba off his body, but she came back like a cat.

"Get out of my room!" He tried to crawl out from under her and out of the bed, but the pit in the mattress sucked him back into the hole like organza quicksand.

"This won't take long," she said.

"I'll bet." Nicky rallied. He flipped his legs over the side of the bed and catapulted himself into a standing position using the strength of his arms, as if he were launching himself out of the inside of a pickle barrel. He was wearing his undershorts and nothing else in the presence of a young lady, but he didn't care. He'd been in a war and knew when the enemy wanted to nail him. The uniform didn't matter, and neither did the weapon or the ammunition. The only defense was to keep moving.

"I told you this room was hot." Rosalba winked.

"I can't open the windows."

"Because they're glued shut. Daddy did it when he found out I snuck out of the house at night."

"He should have let you go," Nicky said, rubbing his neck.

"That's what I said."

"The poor man." Nicky felt pity for Rocco.

"Some people just need freedom. Let's get out of this sweatbox. It's cool in my room. We'll have some fun." Rosalba flung her hair around. The effect wasn't seductive, but more like a mop when it is flayed around to dust cobwebs off the ceiling.

He opened the door wide. "Get out, or I will call your father."

Rosalba shimmied off the bed and adjusted her nightgown. "You're the worst ambassador that ever came to this town."

Nicky closed the door behind her. He barricaded the door, using his body, which had sunk to the floor. A ceramic commedia dell'arte clown fell off a shelf over the door and clocked him on the head. It did not break, but Nicky wanted to smash it. He reached over and grabbed his cigarettes off the nightstand. If he had to, he'd stand guard behind the bedroom door all night to keep Rosalba out. He pulled a slim volume off the bottom shelf of the nightstand: *The History of Roseto, Pennsylvania*, by Ralph Basso.

Nicky opened the book and began to read. As the story of the town unfolded, he began to understand its people; with history came knowledge. Nicky fell asleep on the floor as the women of Roseto danced through his dreams.

⌒

Frank parked his car in a thicket off Evergreen Way in Haverford, a Main Line enclave whose rolling green hills and horse country had inspired the mural at Borelli's. Now, the lush green fields were lawns, the bridle paths were circular driveways, and the farmhouses were replaced with mansions as opulent as the finest in Europe.

"You sure you can park here?"

"I want to show you something."

Frank took Calla by the hand as they crossed the main boulevard, and led her to a fence line clustered with trees. "This isn't a good spot," he said critically. He led her around the curve of the street to another place along the fence.

"There it is."

Calla's eyes widened as she saw Havercrest, a splendid Elizabethan-style mansion, lit up against the blue night sky. Music sailed over the field and through the trees. They could see the shimmer of the horns of the dance band positioned on the veranda. Elegant cars dropped off guests at the stone entrance, anchored by two fountains that sprayed water like ribbons of diamonds high into the air before they dropped in slate pools.

"Who lives here?" Calla asked.

"The family makes ketchup." Frank leaned on the fence.

"How did you find this place?"

"I built the waterfall at the swimming pool."

"What's that like?"

"Like nothing you've ever seen before. Can you imagine walking out of your house in the morning and jumping into your pool and swimming under your own waterfall?"

"I can't."

"No Italian American has ever lived in this neighborhood."

"Not one?"

"But I will someday," Frank assured her. "I want to be mayor, I want to help people, and I want to live like this."

"I don't know how you do all three of those things, but if anyone can, it's you." Calla kept her eyes on the party as if she were observing a work of art, or a piece of theater. She drank in the way the light played on the scene, and how the people sashayed through the garden party, moving to the music.

"Someday I'll build you a house like this." Frank scooped Calla up off the ground and kissed her.

"I wouldn't stop you." Calla smiled. "Can I have a pool?"

"Whatever you want."

Nicky and Hortense walked through the grounds of the Jubilee carnival, nodding respectfully to the people of Roseto, making their rounds as the guests of honor. The committee had provided each of them with a handmade sash that read "Honored Guest," in case it wasn't obvious.

"I will give this one more revolution through the grounds, and then I'm heading back to Minna's," Hortense said through a clenched smile.

"I wish I had a nice place to stay."

"What's wrong with the chief burgess?"

"He's all right. It's his wife and daughter."

"I bet they serve fresh doughnuts at breakfast."

"I wouldn't know. I don't eat their food. I barely use the water. I take a sponge bath. I brush my teeth like I'm in the Amazon. I don't want to owe them anything because then I might have to reciprocate. The cost is too high. I won't miss Truman Street, I'll tell you that."

"We could leave tonight."

"I have to give the speech tomorrow."

"You know this is all make-believe. You know you're not really the man in the booklet. We can just scram. We can disappear in the bubble of the lie in the dark, right now, like the vapor we are."

"That would be like leaving at intermission."

"People do that."

"Not the players."

"Nicky, this isn't a play, and we're not on a stage. William Shake-speare has been dead so long they named a rest stop after him on the New Jersey turnpike."

Nicky wasn't listening to Hortense. His attention was on the sodality *pizza fritta* stand, nestled between the sausage and pep-per stand and the fresh nuts and torrone stand.

"Hortense, are you hungry?"

"I'm slightly peckish," she admitted.

Nicky walked over to the stand where the ladies of the church sodality were making *pizza fritte,* Roseto's version of a zeppole. The sweet scent of vanilla, the clouds of powdered sugar, and the golden puffs of dough made the *pizza fritte* the most popular treat at the carnival.

Mamie Confalone flipped the dough in the deep fryer under the canopy's strings of twinkling white lights. She gently lifted the fluffy clouds of dough out of the oil and placed them on a rack as another volunteer sprinkled the delicacies with sugar, placed them in paper cones, and handed them to the customers.

Nicky slipped around to the side of the stand.

"Mrs. Confalone."

"Ambassador. Where's your uniform?"

"I had to air it out."

"Too much dancing?"

"If you want to call it that."

"What would you call it?" She tried not to laugh.

"The trot without the fox."

"You showed real stamina."

"The ladies told me all about the people of Roseto."

"I'll bet they did."

"Since I arrived, I haven't seen you out of an apron."

"You should come around when it's not Jubilee."

"Is that an invitation?"

"No." She smiled.

"I'm like a cat. When you put out milk, he keeps coming back. And last night, you brought me dinner. I don't forget a kindness."

"I felt sorry for you."

"Would you let me walk you home tonight?"

"No."

"They told me you're a widow. Maybe you'd like someone to walk you home."

"I have to get home to my boy."

"Ma, look!" A young boy ran up to the stand with a stuffed giraffe. "Grandpop won it for me at the ring toss." Augie Confalone Jr. was around five years old, a sturdily built boy with black hair and brown eyes.

"It's huge," Mamie marveled.

"Can I keep him?"

"Absolutely."

"Mamie, we're going to take him home now."

"Okay, Ma."

"I'm going to sleep in Grandpop and Grandmom's room on the day bed with my giraffe."

Mamie leaned over the stand and kissed her son. "Be good, Augie."

She picked up the tongs and flipped the dough in the fryer. Without looking at Nicky, she said, "Pick me up here in a half hour."

Nicky brought the *pizza fritte* to Hortense. "I'll walk you back to Minna's."

"What's the rush?" Hortense took a bite of the treat. "I like the food in this town. I may sample the sausage and peppers."

"They'll be here tomorrow."

"I might want them tonight. I like a savory after a sweet."

"It will upset your stomach to end the night on a savory. You'll be burping like a backed-up drain. No, eat your *pizza fritte*. End the day with a sweet. It's called dessert."

"You do have a point. Since when have you become a medical expert?"

"Since Mamie Confalone agreed to let me walk her home."

Nicky dropped Hortense at Minna's apartment, turned, and raced back up Garibaldi Avenue to the carnival grounds like a long-distance runner with a hot coal in his pants. He wove through the crowd at a clip to get back to the *pizza fritte* stand. Locals called out to him, shouting *"Ambasciatore!"* He waved, but kept moving. When he made it to the stand, he looked for Mamie. He couldn't find her.

He waited, thinking she might have run out on an errand. A few minutes ticked by, and he began to worry. He followed one of her co-workers into the tent where the ladies kept the dough. He searched the tent for her, but she wasn't there either. It soon became clear that she had given him the bum's rush. Feeling like a sap, he did nothing to pretend he wasn't devastated. He walked out of the supply tent, avoiding the crowds, and slipped behind the stands, away from the lights.

When Nicky reached the end of the field, he looked back at the carnival. The Ferris wheel spun through the air in streaks of pink and purple. He could hear the children as they laughed with glee, whipping around in circles on a ride where the cars were painted as planets. He saw couples lean over the counters as they played the games of chance—a young man intent on winning a prize for his date, and her obvious thrill when he did. The older married couples gathered at the picnic tables, sharing sausage and pepper sandwiches and conversation.

There was a universe of belonging happening before him that

he was not a part of, phony ambassador or not. Whether it was Montrose Street or Garibaldi Avenue, there was no seat at the table for Nicky Castone.

Nicky had always been the extra boy, the pinch hitter, the fill-in when a kid didn't show up, called in sick, or quit. He was the replacement, dutiful, cheery, and reliable. If he was good, he was allowed to stick around. Maybe that's why he was so eager to try on someone else's life for a while, to be Carlo Guardinfante. It hadn't worked out so well to be Nicky Castone.

"Hey, you," a woman's voice whispered. *Good Lord, does Cha Cha Tutolola lie in wait in the bushes every night?* thought Nicky. He didn't want to know, and he didn't want to find out, so he kept moving. He remembered Rosalba was on the prowl. That's when he began to move at a clip.

"Hey, don't make me chase you."

Nicky turned around. Mamie motioned to him before jumping back into the shadows. He ran to her.

"Do you have a car?" she asked.

"Yes. *Si. Si.*"

"Pick me up one block over, behind the rectory."

"*Dove è* the rectory?"

Mamie pointed.

"Behind the church?" Nicky asked. "*Chiesa?*"

Mamie nodded.

"Promise me you will be there?" He was unable to bear the thought of one more goose chase at the end of which he would be nothing but plucked and cooked.

"I promise." Mamie smiled, which intoxicated Nicky with a kind of desire he hadn't felt since he first liked girls.

He broke into a sprint to retrieve the sedan he had parked in the free space in front of the Mugaveros' house on Truman Street. After all he had been through, and all he had run from, at long last he had something to run *to*: Mamie Confalone, waiting for him behind the rectory. She might as well have given Nicky Castone that silver scrap of a moon.

⟋

Mamie settled into the front seat of the sedan. Nicky was so excited, he could barely drive. His fantasy had come true, and he didn't know if he was made of the stuff to handle it.

"Why did you make me pick you up behind the rectory?"

"Because the only person who isn't a gossip in this town is Father Leone."

"Who cares what people think?"

"Obviously you didn't grow up in a small town. Take a left up here."

"Where are we going?" Nicky drove through the black night on a back road.

"Are you hungry?"

"Starving."

"Me too. You can drop the accent."

"This is the way I speak."

"No, it isn't. *L'uomo che si dà fuoco viene bruciato.* What did I just say?"

"Your Italian is terrible. No real *Italiano* could *capisce.*"

Mamie laughed. "You don't speak Italian."

"I speak-uh English when in America."

"Let me translate for you, *Ambasciatore.* The man who sets himself on fire gets burned. Your accent is so bad, you couldn't pass as a waiter in an Italian restaurant and take an order."

"I bet I could!" Nicky dropped the accent.

"There it is."

"All right. Here it is."

"I like this much better."

"You do?"

"The other accent sounds like a continental parlor snake."

"Maybe that's why Cha Cha and Rosalba are barnacled to me."

"Could be. Or maybe they're just barnacles. I knew you weren't the real ambassador when you visited the factory."

"Where did I trip up?"

"No Italian wears Florsheims."

"My shoes!"

"Florsheim shoes are made in Wisconsin."

"Right. I'm in dutch with the costumes. Do you think my regimentals look like the Penn State band uniform?"

Mamie laughed. "A little. Where did you get them?"

"A costume shop. At a theater. But there's a tag in the slacks that says Woodwind."

"It's more than the clothes. You are nothing like the real ambassador."

"How do you know?"

"I translated the letters from him for the town council."

"What's the real ambassador like?"

"He writes in a very somber fashion. The real guy is a real stiff."

"You can tell from his letters?"

"You can tell everything from a letter. The words people choose are the colors they see."

"That's poetic. If you can teach me how to say that in Italian, I'll put it in my speech tomorrow."

"I don't have time to teach you Italian."

"They don't seem to mind that I speak English."

"That's because we love anyone we think is important. And we admire anyone we think is famous. And right now you're the closest we have to either."

"I danced with fifty-two women last night. I have done my penance for the dupe."

"You're going to keep this up?"

"It's over by noon tomorrow."

"Why are you doing this?"

"At first, it was out of pity."

"Why would you feel sorry for this town? The people are close, we have work. There's no crime."

"It's something I felt."

"It's a wonderful place to live."

"That's why you don't like outsiders. You don't want to share."

"It's not that we don't like them, we don't trust them."

"How about you?"

"I'm wary."

"Are you going to tell on me?"

"I'm not a rat."

"I didn't think so."

"What's your name?"

"Nicky Castone."

"Italian boy."

"You're surprised."

"I wasn't sure."

"Mother's side from Abruzzo and father's side from Ercolano."

"What do you do for a living?"

"I'm a cab driver, and I deliver for Western Union. I drove up here from Philadelphia to deliver a telegram. It's in the glove compartment."

Mamie opened the glove compartment and read the telegram by the dashboard light. She folded it carefully and put it back in its envelope. "Why didn't you deliver it?"

"I'm on the lam. The ambassador is in a hospital in New York City and I look like him, and my ex-fiancée's father was on his way over to kill me with his bare hands and probably a weapon or two, so I jumped into the car and came here to hide out. You needed an ambassador, and I needed to be somebody else for the weekend, so here we are."

"What about the colored lady?"

"Mrs. Mooney is a good person."

"How did you get her to take part in your play?"

"I'm glad you see it as a theatrical endeavor. That's how I'm looking at it, to avoid any kind of self-loathing."

"Is Mrs. Mooney an actress?"

"She's the dispatcher at the cab company where I work. There isn't anything she wouldn't do for me."

"Make a right here. This is it."

Nicky pulled in to Perelli's Steaks, a small cinder-block building with a simple delivery window and a sign overhead. An Italian flag flew next to the American flag on the roof.

"You're taking a guy from Philly for a steak sandwich?".

"You're taking me. And these are the best steak sandwiches in the world."

"I'll be the judge."

"Go right ahead. You're the ambassador."

"How do you like your sandwich?"

"Steak, mozzarella, peppers."

"Make that two," Nicky said to the man in the window. "Pick a nice table," he told Mamie. Every table was free.

Nicky brought the sandwiches and two birch beers to the table. "You haven't asked me if I'm married."

"You're not married."

"How can you tell?"

"No married man would dance with fifty-two women in a row wearing a wool suit in a hot tent."

"That's the criterion?"

"And you don't have the look."

"I look like a bachelor?"

"You don't look like a married man on the make."

"You have men figured out."

"What does that mean?"

"You know what they think, what motivates them, what they'll do before they do it."

"Just you."

"I must be easy to read."

"Transparent."

"You're very particular, aren't you?"

"What did you hear about me last night?"

"The music was loud. The women were fresh. When they weren't breathing in my ear, they were stepping on my toes."

"Poor you."

"You want to know everything they said?"

"Everything."

"I know you're a widow. How long?"

"Five years."

"And you have a son named Augie. He's a sweet kid."

"Very. You saw him at the stand tonight."

"I did. He's high-spirited."

"Very."

"I know that you live alone with your son at 45 Garibaldi Avenue in the house that you bought with your husband before he left for the war. One lady thought you paid five thousand dollars for it, way too much, and another said you got it for three thousand, five hundred, and that was a steal. I know that you were the valedictorian of your high school class and that you once told a missionary priest asking for a special collection that he shouldn't ask for money for the poor in Europe when there were poor people in Easton, Pennsylvania. You once belted a boy after mass after he told the boys on the baseball team you had kissed him when you had not. You are a respected forelady in the mill, strong but fair. Another lady said she wouldn't be surprised if you owned your own mill someday. There's a consensus about your heart. A few believe you haven't gotten over the loss of your husband, and there are some ladies in town who think you never will."

"That's a lot of information."

"The real estate information came from Cha Cha Tutolola."

"She's like the *Stella di Roseto*, except you get the story without getting ink on your hands."

"Do you want to know anything about me?"

"It's better if I don't know too many details. That way, if questioned, I can't lie."

"I don't think you're in any danger."

"It's a federal offense not to deliver a telegram."

"Who said I wasn't going to deliver it? On my way out of town tomorrow, I was going to leave it in the Tutololas' mailbox."

"What a scandal."

"That would shake things up."

"At the very least. So tell me about you." She sipped her birch beer.

"My mother died when I was a boy, and my father died soon after the Great War. I don't have any brothers or sisters. I live in my aunt and uncle's basement. They took me in when I was five. They have a cab company—that's their sedan. I work at the Borelli Theater as a second job. Prompter. That's the guy who feeds the actor his lines when he forgets them. I picked up a fare in Ambler, and the man died in my cab. I haven't gotten over it. For seven years I was engaged to Teresa DePino, who is called Peachy. I broke off the engagement recently because I don't think she loved me. And I want to love and be loved."

"Maybe that's why you're posing as an important person."

"I don't care about adulation."

"If you didn't, why not pose as a bricklayer?"

"Because a bricklayer wasn't invited to appear at the Jubilee, and

I wasn't asked to deliver a telegram to the United Bricklayers of Roseto. I am not ashamed of my job, I'm a hack. I'm not a snob."

"Did Peachy know who you really were?"

"No."

"So you can't be angry at her."

"She's angry at me. I think she'd like to have me rubbed out."

Mamie threw her head back and laughed. She hadn't laughed so loud and so heartily since before Augie left for the war. Nicky Castone was so earnest, it hit her funny bone like a tuning fork.

"You're laughing at me."

"No, I'm laughing because you actually think she'd have you killed for leaving her."

"She's thirty-four years old. She's a little desperate. Of course, she admits to twenty-eight, which is her prerogative."

"Absolutely."

"How old are you?" Nicky asked her.

"Twenty-seven. But when you're sad, you're a hundred years old and not a day younger."

Nicky drove Mamie back to her house. They didn't say much on the way back from Perelli's, but it was a comfortable lull.

"This is your house?"

"This is it."

He whistled. "You got a deal at five thousand."

"We paid twenty-five hundred."

"A steal."

"Have to be careful when you listen to gossip."

"Good night, Mamie." Nicky smiled at her. He placed his hand on the car door, to open it, but instead he faced her.

"I was going to try to kiss you. I thought about it on the way back."

"You did?"

"But I don't ever have to kiss you. I never have to hold you. I never have to spend another minute with you because you took a ride with me, and you gave me your time. You laughed at my jokes, and you were kind and beautiful to look at, and you didn't judge me. So, for me, you're a perfect girl, and this has been a perfect night, and now I have a perfect memory."

Nicky got out of the car, opened the door for Mamie, and extended his hand. She placed her hand in his and rose out of the car effortlessly, in the way that a woman will when she's graceful and probably a good dancer and she hears a phrase of music that fills her with a desire to move to it.

Mamie stood looking at Nicky as she decided exactly what she wanted from this wonderful night. Nicky had made it plain what this evening had meant to him, and now she knew. Mamie placed her hands on Nicky's face, pulling him close, and kissed him.

8

Nicky had delivered enough telegrams to enough houses to notice that every home, and therefore every family, has a scent. One house might smell like wet wool, another like creamed corn, and yet another like lemon oil.

Mamie Confalone's home had the scent of anise and vanilla, the plain cookies shaped like half-moons that anchored every holiday cookie tray and appeared on the saucer of espresso like an additional cup handle. Nicky wanted to share this observation with Mamie, but couldn't quite form the words; there was no opportunity to do so, between the urgent kisses exchanged in the dark at the foot of her stairs and the utter lack of thoughts in his head.

She slipped out of her leather shoes, which had a slight heel, a bow, and a strap. Nicky tried to remember what they were called—he knew they weren't Mary Lous, but that it was close. His mind was racing because he couldn't believe Mamie Confalone had invited him inside. His body was keeping up with his emotions, and yet he was in a state of disbelief that his heart's desire had actually manifested into a real-life experience, and that something wonderful was going to happen that he had wished for from the moment he first saw Mamie Confalone.

Mamie took his hand and led him up the stairs. The sway of her skirt was rhythmic as she moved. The skirt was made of a fabric covered with flowers—most of her clothes were—but in this instance there was a sheer overlay of blossoms, leaves, and vines on some kind of material underneath, which might have been satin, since it had a shine, like the inside of the petal of a flower.

When they reached the top of the stairs, a ceiling fan was circulating slowly overhead, not from electricity but from the movement of the night air. He unbuttoned the bodice of Mamie's dress, and it fell away effortlessly, like a veil.

She stepped out of her dress; it cascaded to the floor. Mamie invited him into her bedroom and pulled him toward her and onto her bed.

There was no moon, but the streetlight outside her window helped him see. He had never seen a woman this way before; there was always draping, or an article of clothing, or more, but Mamie was a work of art, her gentle curves sculpted of fine marble and her skin as soft as Trussardi's most delicate silk.

As she removed his shoes, he looked around her room, lovely, simple, and uncluttered. It had a high ceiling, higher, it seemed, than the sky itself. There were windows on three sides, and they were open, the sheers fluttering in the breeze.

The bed was made with a simple cotton coverlet, cool to the touch and soft, like Mamie. She laughed when one of Nicky's socks was stubborn on his foot, and he laughed when she finally removed it, tossing it over her shoulder with such force it went out one of the open windows.

They were old lovers who had just met. There was a history and yet they weren't burdened by one. They made love not in discovery but in familiarity, a knowingness that comes from time, which they had shared so little of but had not wasted either.

Mamie, at long last, was young again.

Nicky held the warmth and tenderness of her so close, he was no longer afraid that he would always be alone. She kissed him, her hair grazing his face, then kissed his neck and his hands before resting on her pillow. Nicky pulled her close.

"Do I have to go back to the Tutololas'?"

"You're a guest. It would be rude."

"They have the worst accommodations in the country."

"That bad?"

"I almost died over there. If suffocation didn't get me, a Christmas star would've sliced my head open, or Rosalba would have pounced and sucked the breath out of me like a cat. Did I mention the Capodimonte? Everything in the room has eyes."

"Tomorrow is the finale of the Jubilee. I think you'll be safe until then."

"I have to give a speech."

"And then home to Philadelphia."

"Or Italy."

"That's imaginary."

"True."

"Have you ever been?"

"I stopped on my way home from the war. I never wanted to leave, except I missed Philadelphia."

"Which branch of the service were you in?"

"The army. Served four years."

"Where were you?"

"France and Germany."

"My husband was in the army too. He was in Poland when he was killed. I try not to be angry at him for dying and leaving me behind. Augie was very stubborn. But that goes hand in hand with loyalty—you can't have one without the other."

"What happened to him?"

"I was told they were liberating a village. They sent my husband and three of his fellow soldiers into a house to let the family know that they were free. The war was over. It was a trap. It was a safe house for German soldiers. My husband went in first, he figured it out, hollered to the other three, they took cover, but my husband was killed. He was coming home the next day. After three years of staying alive, at the very end, they got him."

"He sounds like a great man."

"He had his faults. He wasn't a saint. But he was all mine."

"Did he know his son?"

"I sent him a letter when I found out I was expecting, but it didn't get there in time."

"You named him after your husband."

"Tradition. His boy is just like him. And my son misses him. It's heartbreaking. A son without a father, I can never make up that loss."

"You can't. But he's a good kid."

"I'm trying. Augie knows the story of his father, as much as I'll tell him, but he still plays guns and war like it's a game."

"All boys do."

"I know. When anyone asks him what he wants to be when he grows up, he says he wants to be a soldier like his dad. I'll break him of that."

"I hope you do."

"I won't lose two of them."

"How do you get through it?"

"I don't know. I went back to work, and that helped. Each day I got a little better at focusing on the job. I have to pay attention to details. Every blouse has to be flawless, every stitch has to be straight, every collar has to be even, every placket has to lie flat, every armhole, sleeve, and cuff has to line up with the bodice and the seam in the back, the buttonhole and the button have to be set just so, and the routine of that got me out of my misery. As much as anything can."

"There's more to work than just making a living."

"It can be your salvation. I know it was mine."

Nicky rolled back onto the pillow.

"Perelli's steak sandwich is better than any Philly cheesesteak. That's the final word on that subject," Mamie said.

"You're out of your mind."

Mamie kissed him. "Good night."

She curled up and went to sleep. Nicky had never seen anything like it in a human being. Cats, yes. Dogs too. Even goldfish, who float open-eyed along the surface of the tank in peaceful rest. Only Cousin Gio could nod off this fast, but he was never serene.

He lay in the dark, holding her. He looked at the clock. Hours had passed, but it seemed like minutes, and yet, in other ways, lifetimes. Everything that had transpired between them that night was effortless. He hadn't felt the tug of guilt or the exhaustion that comes from compromise.

The moment Nicky gave Peachy her engagement ring, she offered herself to him, with certain "stipulations"—and she called them that—so her fiancé might pay attention. Peachy had her own code; just as Mrs. Mooney used Morse code, Peachy had invented her own list of rules about what she would and wouldn't do with Nicky physically, concocted from her religious upbringing, her mother's fear-based admonitions, and whatever romantic tips she'd gleaned from *Modern Screen* magazine.

Peachy knew how to relieve Nicky's sexual frustration without having to admit to it in confession, but it wasn't the kind of romantic interlude he dreamed of or imagined. When his former fiancée reached into his trousers to relieve him of his misery, the look on her face was identical to the expression she had when she fished for spare change at the bottom of her purse to pay for the toll on the Pennsylvania Turnpike. She was determined, but her mind was somewhere else. His pleasure was not her joy but a mindless exercise in friction, with Nicky receiving what her gloved hand could provide. She wasn't annoyed by it or stimulated by it. It was executed swiftly, confidently, and without deviation from her skill set. Her clothes stayed on, usually her hat, and always her glove.

Nicky slipped out of Mamie's bed. He covered her gently, dressed in the dark, and went downstairs. In the kitchen, he opened the icebox and found plenty of leftovers. He chose a chicken leg, a bowl of cold mashed potatoes, a heel of bread, and a bottle of beer. He sat at the kitchen table with the gray Formica top and matching chairs. A large red leather button was centered in the back of each chair.

There was a stack of children's books on the seat of the chair next to him. He lifted them up and rifled through them, smiling when he saw *Too Many Mittens*. He had given that to Elsa and Dom when their son was born. He leafed through *Pinocchio*, flipped through *The Sword in the Stone*, and lifted an illustrated volume of *Grimm's Fairy Tales* and placed it on the table.

Something about the artwork in the book of fairytales conjured his past. He wondered if he had read this book before. He'd have to think about it. It was getting harder to recall the details of his childhood.

Nicky finished his snack and placed the dishes in the sink. He washed them and put them in the drying rack. He liked the way Mamie kept her home: neat, clean, and uncluttered. He could think clearly in her house. He couldn't imagine ending up with a wife like Cha Cha, who covered every surface in her home with a saint on a doily.

Nicky went into the living room. He took in the chintz sofa. The background color was tan, and it was covered with pink roses. What was it about Mamie Confalone and flowers?

She had a record player, an RCA Victor with a brown leather flip top and a gold mesh sound panel on the front. It stood on four aluminum legs. He opened the top carefully.

Now he knew who was buying the new .45 records. They were all being sold to the widow on Garibaldi Avenue in Roseto. He shuffled through the stack. "Buttons and Bows" by Dinah Shore, "You're Breaking My Heart" by Vic Damone, "Mona Lisa" by Nat King Cole, several by Rosemary Clooney (something else they had in common), the Mills Brothers, Tony Bennett, Glenn Miller, Perry Como, Frankie Laine, Sammy Kaye, Artie Shaw, and Edith Piaf's hit "La Vie en Rose." That record didn't surprise Nicky—it had a flower in the title.

"Couldn't you sleep?" Mamie asked. She wore a blue nightgown printed with yellow daisies, tied at the neck with a loose satin ribbon. She was barefoot.

"I was restless."

"You should get going."

"I don't want to."

"But you're dressed."

"Right."

"So you must want to go."

"I have to."

"You have your big speech."

"I do."

"Your sock should be in the bushes."

"I'll get it on my way to the car."

Nicky had moved to the door to go when he thought better of it and turned to say good-bye, but Mamie was already there, next to him.

"Everything you own has flowers on it. Why?"

"I like them."

"You like them a lot."

"My name is Rose."

"Why do they call you Mamie?"

"Mary Rose. My birthday is August fifteenth."

"The Feast of the Assumption."

Nicky took Mamie into his arms and kissed her. He had the strange feeling that this kiss would have to last for a while.

"Thank you, Nick," she said.

"Why would you thank me?"

"You'll figure it out."

Nicky walked out of Mamie's house with a bare foot in his left shoe and a sock on his right. He walked down the porch steps and around to the side of the house, where he found the missing sock hanging in the boxwood bush like a flag and stuffed it in his pocket.

When he got into the sedan, he sat still. The whole of his body felt as though it were moving, but he wasn't jittery. This was a new sensation. He closed his eyes and wondered, could a man his age have a heart attack? Is this what it was? Would he be found dead in the Palazzinis' only sedan, in a town where he was posing as a dignitary from another country? Is this how his journey would end?

Nicky found himself fishing in his tip cup in the glove compartment of the car. He found the cup full of dimes. He started the car and cruised down Garibaldi until he found the only phone booth on the Avenue.

"Operator, Bella Vista 8-5746. Thank you."

Calla was in a deep sleep when the phone rang in the foyer, down the stairs from her bedroom. She sat up in bed. She jumped out of it and raced down the stairs, hoping to get to the phone before it woke her father.

"It's Nicky."

"Are you all right?"

"Yeah."

"Why are you calling?"

"I had to talk to someone. To you. I need a friend."

Calla held the receiver up to her ear with one hand and held her head with the other. She sat down on the steps. "What happened?"

"I met a woman."

"Nicky, this could wait."

"No, no, it can't wait. I don't understand what just happened, and I feel badly now, and I need to tell you about it."

Calla heard a creak in the floorboards above her. She looked up and saw her father in his bathrobe. She motioned for him to go back to sleep. "Go on," she said into the phone.

"She is a widow. She has a little boy. And I stayed with her."

Calla stood up and peered around the corner to the clock in the living room. It was close to four. "Stayed?"

"You know."

"Okay."

"I just feel bad about it."

"Because you love Peachy."

"Why do you keep saying that? You're like one of those jack-hammers they use to build railroads."

"I'm hanging up the phone."

"Don't!" Nicky was desperate. "I get impatient because you say it like it's true. But I don't have that. Not from Peachy. Not from any woman. I don't have love."

"Nicky." Calla was impatient now. "You just did."

"It won't stay. Or I'm afraid it won't stay."

"You need to grow up," Calla began. Sam sat down next to her on the steps. "You're running around acting like you can do whatever you want, without any regard for a woman's feelings—whether it's Peachy or this lady. What kind of a man are you?"

"I can't answer that."

"It's about time you decided. Now I have to get off the phone, because I don't want to yell at you."

"I'm sorry, Calla."

"You don't owe me an apology."

"For calling. For waking up your father."

"Oh, right, that. I'll tell him."

Calla hung up the phone.

"Who was that?"

"Crazy Nicky Castone."

"Did they figure out who he was and run him out of town?"

"No. He enchanted a woman."

"The upside of acting on the road."

"That's the only upside."

"Why's he calling here?"

"He needed a friend. That's what he said."

"You're the only one he's got?"

"Maybe this is the only number in South Philly he could remember."

"I doubt that. He's all right. I like him fine."

"You do?"

"He's honest."

"Not at this moment. He's conning an entire town."

"Maybe they need to suspend their disbelief for a moment. Maybe they have their reasons. People need to believe in a man sometimes, even when he is not what was advertised."

"Dad, you don't have to worry about me. I have good judgment. I'm going to marry Frank Arrigo."

"You are?"

"Yeah. What do you think?"

"Do you love him?"

"I wouldn't marry a man I didn't love."

"So there's your answer."

"Am I allowed to have doubts?"

"I wish you didn't."

"I want to be secure. Frank will give me that."

"The thing about security, it's all well and good if the person that makes you feel that way is the person you love. All the money in the world can't make you secure, but all the love in the world can. Funny how that works. Do you want to build a life with him?"

"I want to build a theater with him. He wants to renovate Borelli's and turn it into the showplace it was when you were a boy."

"Good for him. He's young. He has the energy." Sam pulled himself up by the banister and turned to go upstairs. As he climbed, he said,

> *Fear no more the heat o' the sun,*
> *Nor the furious winter's rages;*
> *Thou thy worldly task hast done . . .*
> *Golden lads and girls all must,*
> *As chimney-sweepers, come to dust.*

"Really, Dad? *Cymbeline?*"

"It's all I can remember. You get what you get. Good night, Calla."

"Night, Dad."

Calla crawled into bed. She pulled the blankets and sheets around her and nestled into the pillows. She wished she hadn't told her father she wanted to marry Frank. He didn't seem too keen on it, or maybe he wasn't because it was four o'clock in the morning, and at this hour who could be enthusiastic about anything? Maybe once the blueprints were done, her father would be excited about the possibilities of Frank joining the family.

Minna stood in her living room with Hortense. She looked out the window through the heavy lace curtains.

"I'm so glad you got a sunny day for the finale."

"The ambassador will make his speech, and off we'll go." Hortense turned to face her hostess. "Minna, I never slept as well as I have in the apartment over your garage."

"I'm glad."

"And the food you prepared was so delicious. The macaroni.

The frittata for breakfast. And I don't know what that dessert was in the little ceramic dish—"

"Panna cotta."

"I may have to let this skirt out when I get home." Hortense tugged at the waistband. "I know I will."

"We had so much fun."

"And I'm so grateful for the gravy recipe."

"You make it and think of me."

"Oh, I will."

"Share it with as many people as you can."

"We have a healthy two hundred and seventy-eight members at my church."

"Beyond your church."

"Sometimes we do have an ecumenical gathering. Tri-state. We make a bus trip. I could serve it at the interfaith service. We do a dinner."

"Beyond even that."

"I don't know what you mean, Minna."

"I think you may have found your purpose."

"Chile, I am not opening an Italian restaurant."

"You don't have to."

"Then what are you talking about? If you know my purpose, why won't you tell me?"

"I don't know it. It will come to you. All you will have to do is recognize it." Minna placed a string of turquoise and green and yellow beads around Hortense's neck.

"These are for you."

"You don't have to give me a present."

"I want you to remember our visit. They are magnificent on you."

"They are my colors."

"This is my purpose," Minna admitted.

"You don't say."

"I make jewelry from Venetian glass beads. They came from the island of Murano, close to Venice."

"I'll wear them every day."

"Someday, go to Italy. To Venice. You must see it for yourself. The blue in this glass reminds me of the sky there. And the gold, the architects used on the trim of the palazzos. You see it shimmer in the sun as it reflects off the water in the canals, and you think anything is possible."

"When I'm with you, I know anything is. Minna, will you come with me to the grandstand today?"

"I can't."

"Would you make an exception?"

"If I was going to leave this house, I would do it for you. And of course, in honor of Mrs. Roosevelt."

"I know that."

Hortense picked up her suitcase and hat box and walked out the front door of Minna's house, where Nicky waited for her at the curb in the sedan. He jumped out to help Hortense with her bags.

Hortense turned to wave to Minna one last time, but the front door was closed, the curtains covered the window glass, and she was gone.

Nicky and Hortense sat on the grandstand at the top of Garibaldi Avenue as the Pius X High School Marching Band played "God Bless America." From their perch, the village of Roseto looked like the opening number of a spectacular musical. Colors exploded on flags, banners, and balloons, and in gardens where daisies, roses of Sharon, and peonies burst open in glorious pink and red. The sun dazzled like a spotlight in the clear blue sky against the rooftops made of blue and gray slate that matched the sky no matter its mood, no matter the weather.

The entire town of Roseto had turned out for the finale of the celebration, to witness the ambassador's farewell and the blessing on the town by Father Leone, followed by the Jubilee Parade, the finale of the celebration.

The floats were lined up down Division Street. There was a giant pink crepe paper cake made by the sodality of Saint Rocco in Martins Creek, a gaggle of small children dressed head to toe in red, white, and green who, when in formation, became the Italian flag, and a float of a model of an enormous sewing machine, in honor of the millworkers. People had fussed, but of course they felt obligated, since the ambassador had made a sacrifice to come all the way from Italy to be with them.

Nicky wore his uniform and sash, and Hortense wore her Sunday suit, hat, and a commemorative sash along with her Venetian beads. The dignitaries joined them on the grandstand, along with a contingent of mayors from neighboring towns and the borough council, who also wore official sashes.

Rocco went to the microphone to give his welcome.

"We have been honored to have Ambassador Carlo Guardinfante as our guest for the Jubilee in honor of the incorporation of our town. The ambassador is a resident of Roseto Valfortore, the village in the province of Apulia where our forebears are from, which makes us family. He is married to Elisabetta, and he promises to bring her here the next time he visits our newly incorporated borough, the only incorporated Italian American town in the United States of America. Ladies and gentlemen, our ambassador."

Nicky reached into the pocket of his uniform to retrieve his notes, standing before the microphone. As he was about to read, he tore the speech in half and stuffed it back into his pockets. The crowd was aghast.

Mamie slipped into the crowd to listen.

"I am a very lucky man. *Fortunato!* I came to Roseto, Pennsylvania, how do you say, a nervous wreck-uh. But I have my secret *weapon-i*, Mrs. Mooney, attaché to Mrs. Eleanor Roosevelt, *populare* First Lady."

The crowd applauded politely. Hortense nodded.

"Mrs. Mooney reminded me that I was bringing you something that you needed. I brought you Roseto Valfortore, the place your ancestors called home. I couldn't pack the village in my suitcase, but what I could do was bring you the story. Sometimes when we prosper, we forget the struggle, the sacrifice, and even where we came from. You see, for those too young to remember, and those who have never been, Roseto Valfortore is a village, just like yours, of great beauty. It is situated on a hilltop in Apulia between Roma and Napoli. Our place on the map has put us in a perilous position throughout history. Every army since the Greeks has trudged through our hills. We have been conquered, attacked, ransacked, and pillaged. But we persist. That is the stuff you are made of. That is what you brought to America, and that is why you have found safety, prosperity, and a good life here. You are Rosetani!"

The crowd cheered, blew horns, and whistled.

"Let's move this along," Hortense whispered. "I got a black feeling."

"Sit down, Mrs. Mooney." Emboldened, Nicky waved to the cheering crowd.

A forest-green Studebaker, followed by Car No. 2 from the Palazzini Cab Company, pulled up to the police barricade.

Peachy DePino jumped out of the Studebaker, followed by her nervous mother and her angry father.

"Nicky Castone!" Peachy shouted. "We're going to talk!"

The men in the crowd moaned. The crowd buzzed with the name *Castone.*

Peachy climbed up the steps to the stage. "What is wrong with you? Why are you wearing a Penn State band uniform?"

"I knew it." Eddie Davanzo shook his head.

"Who is he?" Cha Cha was baffled.

"He's Nicky Castone. From Philadelphia," Peachy confirmed.

"What is going on here?" Rocco was perturbed.

"She—she's not what she says either." Peachy pointed at Hortense. "She's the colored dispatcher."

"They can see I'm colored," Hortense grumbled.

"How could you do this to me, Nick? You left my picture behind in your drawer with your mending. Do you think so little of what we meant to each other to leave me stuck in a drawer with your stained and holey underpants?"

"I'm going to kill you with my bare hands." Al DePino, five foot six, lunged for Nicky.

Concetta dabbed her tears. "Nicky, just come home and marry Peachy, and we'll forget this horrible nightmare, this grim incident, this sick situation." She pulled a stray thread off Nicky's lapel. "Remember the love. I beseech you, remember the love."

"I'm gonna kill the son of a—" Al swung for Nicky. Eddie Davanzo grabbed Al by the arms.

"Now the law is involved! Al, you dope!" Concetta yelled.

Dom and Jo rushed the stage. "Don't touch him!" Jo shouted.

"Who are you people?" Rocco asked.

"Family," Dom barked.

"Let's take this discussion off this stage. Out of town," Hortense said softly. "Let's go."

Peachy pointed at Nicky. "I want the whole world to know what he did to me."

"What did he do?" Cha Cha probed.

"He ended our engagement after seven years."

"There was physical contact," Mr. DePino bellowed as he was being handcuffed.

"My daughter is unspoiled," Mrs. DePino insisted to the crowd.

"But there was physical contact?" Cha Cha queried.

"He's a wolf!" Rosalba shouted.

"He did pull me very close when we danced last night," Cha Cha piled on. "There was grinding. But I figured, an Italian from the other side, they get a little fresh. It's in them."

"Please, Cha Cha." Rocco glared at his wife.

"You see what's going on here? This impostor came to town to woo our women and take advantage of them," a man shouted from the crowd.

"Just like he did with my daughter," Al DePino said, egging on the crowd.

"He gave the Cadillac to an *Ameri-gan* from Alabama!" a man hollered. The crowd went wild.

"I don't know anything about the Cadillac car. But, he did not take advantage of me, Pop. Stop it. I don't want you to kill him for that." Peachy dabbed her forehead with her handkerchief.

"How do we know this impostor wasn't here to steal our money? Did you check the take from the sausage and pepper stand?" a woman shouted.

"Where's the money?" A man pointed at Nicky.

The crowd grumbled, and the rancor grew. Individuals stormed the grandstand and demanded action from Rocco.

"Check the kitty! He probably stole the money!"

"He's a brute!" another woman shouted.

"Hold it!" Nicky was furious. "I have never chiseled anyone in my life. I was only trying to help."

"I told you. Put your hand out to help somebody, and when you take it back, all that's left is a stump." Hortense fanned herself. "He who is without sin cast the first stone. *Castone*. Nicky Castone! That's a sign. We need to leave right now."

Nicky frowned at Hortense and turned to Peachy. "And what did you think you would accomplish by coming here? Did you think I'd change my mind?"

"Did you think I'd just let you go? I put in seven years being nice to you! Are you crazy? I'm an Italian girl. Italy isn't shaped like a mattress. I wasn't going to lie down. It's shaped like a boot. I came here to kick you in the . . ."

The women in the crowd cheered.

Rocco turned to Eddie. "Take them in before I have a coup on my hands."

"Arrest them?"

"The two of them."

"For what?"

"Impersonating important people."

"You can't arrest us," Nicky said firmly. "All I did was dance with your women. Frankly, you should give me orthotics and a lifetime supply of Epsom salts."

"When we find out why you did this, and what you stole, you'll be lucky if we don't do worse," said Rocco. "For now, Eddie, his car is parked in an emergency zone. Book them on traffic violation. Take them in. And move it. Before we have an insurrection. The women have mobilized. Be afraid."

Nicky and Hortense left the stage with Eddie Davanzo. The crowd cheered to see the impostors hauled off by the law.

Eddie guided Hortense and Nicky into the squad car.

"We'll call a lawyer," Uncle Dom assured them through the window.

"And we'll get a good one," Jo added. "Not his cousin Flavio, who does everything for cost."

"How did they find us?" Nicky asked his aunt through the squad car window.

Jo gripped her handkerchief. "I'm sorry, Nicky. Peachy blew into the house like a wildcat and went down to the basement and tore through your room. She flipped drawers and even the mattress and she found the flyer for the Jubilee in the wastebasket. She's desperate. And then Al and Connie showed up, and Al said he was going to kill you, and they drove here half-cocked, and we followed them."

Eddie eased the squad car into reverse, to a chorus of boos from

the crowd. He turned the car around and drove down Garibaldi to
the Roseto Police Station.

"I'm sorry, Mrs. Mooney."

"Too late for that. I'm cuffed." Hortense held up her wrists.

"I thought we could pull this off," Nicky said wearily.

"I figured you could too. I figured you could do anything. But
now we know even you have limits."

Eddie Davanzo brought Hortense a Dixie cup filled with water in
the holding room of the police station. Hortense sipped it as she
stood looking out the window as the Jubilee parade went down
Garibaldi Avenue. Nicky sat in the corner, his head in his hands.

"Is there any news?" Hortense asked Eddie. "I need to get home."

"The borough council is meeting. They can go on for a while."

"Can you hear anything?"

"They're squabbling. But that's typical."

"Thank you for not locking us up."

"They haven't determined a crime." Eddie smiled, reassuring
Hortense.

"Because there isn't one," Nicky said quietly.

"You're going to have to let the council decide that." Eddie closed
the door, leaving Hortense and Nicky alone in the room.

"We were seconds away from blowing out of here."

"I'll make it up to you, Mrs. Mooney."

"I want a Lilly Daché hat. The red one with the giant bow." Hortense squinted out the window. "Nicky, come over here."

Nicky joined her at the window to see Ambassador Carlo Guardinfante emerging from a black sedan.

"That must be the real cat." Hortense pointed.

"It must be. He's pretty trim."

"That's all you notice?"

"The medals?"

"No."

"What good does it do us?"

"He's here. They'll want you gone."

"Yeah?"

"You're Italian. He's one of your own. You're going to ask him to cut us loose."

"He might want to kill me too."

"Let him. But first get me sprung."

"I can't. I'm tired." Nicky plopped down in a chair.

"You're tired? You? Nicholas Castone? Sit up. You don't have a right to be weary when all you've done for three days is dance and chase women. Weary is going down in a coal mine. Weary is laying pipe in a city sewer. Weary is cleaning a house top to bottom and washing clothes in a wringer washing machine with bleach and hanging them out in the bitter cold until the skin on your fingers flakes off and then you have to go inside and press all that mess with a slug iron. Weary is pushing out a ten-pound baby after twelve hours of straining. Weary is building railroads."

"I get it. I get it. I'm not sturdy."

"No, you are not. But you'd better buck up. It's one thing to put yourself in dutch, it's another to drag me into a quagmire and leave me to sort it when the scheme goes south. And it went south. So figure this thing out because I need to get home. I have things to do. A life to live." Hortense patted the Venetian beads around her neck. "And I want to see my girls again."

Eddie poked his head in the door. "There are a couple of people here to see you." Eddie opened the door, taking his official position as guard.

Mamie Confalone entered followed by Ambassador Carlo Guardinfante. Augie ran into the room. He looked at Carlo and then at Nicky. "Twins!"

"They look alike, don't they?" Mamie said gently to her son.

"I'm going to take Augie," Eddie told Mamie.

"Can I see the fire truck?" Augie asked him.

"Sure, honey, come on." Eddie held his hand, and led him out, closing the door behind him.

Nicky stood. "Ambassador. Forgive me."

"You don't have to go into the story, I explained the situation. In Italian. The real Italian language that's been spoken since Caesar," Mamie said. "I told him everything."

"*Everything?*"

"The part about you posing as him."

"I want to make reparations to him." Nicky looked at Carlo.

Mamie translated. Carlo nodded. Mamie invited Carlo, Hortense, and Nicky to sit at the conference table.

"I am deeply ashamed," Nicky said to the ambassador as he leaned across the table.

Carlo folded his hands. *"Sono venuto qui per celebrare il Giubileo, si, ma anche per incontrare il mio cugino. Ho un cugino, Alberto Funziani."*

"Funzi," Mamie confirmed. "He has a cousin here. We know him."

"É il presidente della banca," Carlo said proudly.

"No," Mamie said. "He thinks our Funzi is president of the bank."

"No?" Carlo was confused.

"É il bidello presso la banca." Mamie turned to Hortense and Nicky. "Funzi is the *janitor,* not the *president.*"

Carlo put his head in his hands.

"Is everybody in the two Rosetos leading a double life?" Hortense wondered aloud. "Is anybody who they say they are?"

"It doesn't matter, Mrs. Mooney." Nicky turned to Carlo. "What do you need? Maybe I can help," Nicky offered.

The ambassador explained why he had come to Pennsylvania.

"Una strada. Una strada che va dalla cima della collina verso il fondo, una strada di tre miglia per collegare la mia città al resto del paese. In questo momento, siamo abbandonati."

Mamie translated. Hortense shook her head, leaned back, and closed her eyes.

"This is no time to nap," Nicky chided her.

"I'm just resting my eyes," Hortense retorted. "So my head doesn't blow off my body and end up in Albany."

"Mamie, will you please ask Rocco to come in here?"

"They're in session, deciding what to do about you."

"If I can speak to Rocco, I think we can settle the matter," Nicky assured her.

Mamie left them in the holding room for a moment before returning with Eddie and Rocco.

"Rocco, I have a proposition," Nicky began.

"So do I. I'll see you in the county jail. You impostor. You poser. You thief. What kind of a man steals a Penn State band uniform—"

"It's borrowed."

"And thinks he can come to a little factory town and make a fool out of the working people? While you're scheming to make yourself rich and important and use our women for your own perverse pleasure, we're paying for it. You know what that does to the working man? It makes him want to revolt. You've made a fool out of me, out of my position. You made a spectacle of yourself in that ridiculous uniform. I opened my home to you. And you thank me by doing a little shimmy shake on the dance floor with my wife. Cha Cha has her faults, but she's a good woman, and she's stuck by me for more years than you've been shaving. There is no negotiation. There is nothing to talk about."

"I know it may seem like I did this for a selfish reason, and that is partly true. I work at the Borelli Theater in Philadelphia, and I was eager to step into the shoes of someone else. I'm an actor." A bell went off in Nicky's head, a slight ding, not a gong. He admitted a truth he had not fully accepted, not even to himself.

"What's your excuse?" Rocco asked Hortense.

"I'm colored." Hortense closed her eyes again and pulled the brim of her hat over her eyes.

"I want to make it up to you and to Roseto. The ambassador has a specific need, and he came here in the hopes of getting help, and the person that he was planning on asking for that help, a man named Funzi, is not who he thought he was."

"Another one!" Rocco threw up his hands.

"Roseto Valfortore needs a road from the top of the hill, three miles down, to the bottom of the hill. It's the road that your parents traveled when they left to come to America. It's the road that the Rosetani take when they go to Rome to trade or to Naples to work. It's the most important road in the province."

"So?"

"With your help, I think we can build the road. You heard I was to marry Peachy DePino—"

"The skinny one?"

"Skinny as six o'clock," Hortense mumbled.

"I ended our engagement for reasons I had hoped would remain private. I've been saving to buy a home for seven years, and I had put money down on a place which I will no longer be needing, so I'd like to give the funds to the ambassador for his road. He'll need manpower and a builder, and maybe more funds, but I believe he came to the right place. You take care of each other here, and they've had a hard time over there. Will you allow me to make amends? I want to make this right. I will make this right."

A gentle breeze floated through the bars of the window. The room fell silent as Rocco mulled the proposal, until Hortense snored, having fallen asleep in her chair. Before Mamie could reach over to shake her, Hortense let out a loud snort, waking herself up. Startled, she looked around at the faces. "Forgive me. I got a malaise."

Nicky, Rocco, and the ambassador were tucked in a booth at the Marconi Social Club on Garibaldi enjoying a second round of scotch neat like three buddies in a rowboat on a fishing trip that had gotten no bites. It was all about the conversation and the booze.

"Go on, do the accent," Rocco prodded Nicky.

"I-uh bring to you on this vee-zeet."

"*Terribile!*" Carlo laughed.

"We had no idea how lousy he was with the Italian until you showed up." Rocco signed the bill.

"Rocco, do we have a deal?" Nicky asked.

"What deal?"

"You're going to send a crew over to Italy to build the road."

"Oh, that."

"Come on."

"What are you going to do?" Rocco's eyes narrowed. "I should send *you* over there to bust rock."

"I'm making the deal. And I'm impoverishing myself."

"All right. All right," Rocco agreed. "We will come and build your road, Ambassador. And this zsa-drool will pay for it."

Rocco shook the ambassador's hand. Nicky placed his hand on theirs. They had a deal.

Hortense was waiting outside the Marconi Social Club on Garibaldi when the men emerged from the club.

"Can we leave town now? Please?" she begged Rocco.

"You may go."

"Thank you, sir."

Rocco and the ambassador walked up Garibaldi toward Truman Street as Aunt Jo and Uncle Dom rolled up in the cab.

"Let's blow this burg," Dom said.

"Are you all right?" Aunt Jo asked.

"I'm broke," Nicky told her. "But I'm fine."

"You got your life, your limbs, and your mind. Count your blessings." Hortense adjusted her hat.

Nicky heard the familiar clop of Peachy's heels, followed by the click of Connie's dress shoes and Al's wingtips behind him on the sidewalk. The DePino rhythm section.

"They're coming," Hortense said and sighed. "I told you that bar crawl was a bad idea."

Peachy stood before her ex-fiancé with her hands on her hips. "Nicky, I'm going to give you one more chance."

"Peach, I don't need another chance. And when you've prayed about this, you'll be grateful I didn't give you one. You're a good girl. You don't love me. You just want to be married."

"That is love to me, Nicky."

"It isn't to me. It's paperwork."

"It's a holy sacrament."

"With paperwork. I don't want to get married." Nicky turned to the DePinos. "And I don't owe her anything."

"He doesn't, Al," Dom agreed.

Nicky continued, "And I don't owe you anything, Mr. DePino. Or you, Mrs. DePino. I've washed your car every Saturday morning since I returned from the war. I cleaned your gutters every fall. I installed your storm windows, cut the linoleum and laid it in your kitchen, and poured the concrete for your carport. I tried to be a nice fellow to your lovely daughter. She was more than I deserved but she never made me feel that way. I've been respectful and polite. Forgive me for taking so long to realize the truth. And I regret that it took me all this time to make a decision. But that doesn't mean I shouldn't make it. And it doesn't mean I made the wrong one."

Al DePino grunted. "We put down half on the hall."

"I'll reimburse you."

"I don't want your dirty money."

"Then why did you bring it up, Mr. DePino?" Hortense was losing patience. "You either want the down payment back, or you don't. Now which is it?"

"I want him to understand what this cost us."

"Tell you what," Hortense riffed. "You take that hall and throw yourself . . . Mrs. DePino, how long you been married?"

"Thirty-eight years."

"Throw yourself a happily-ever-after party. Show the world how it's done. That's right. And you watch how fast your Peachy finds her own Al DePino. If you lead with gratitude, the world changes its attitude! I won a cross stitch at my church drawing with that saying on it, and it's true. When you're grateful, life opens up and offers you the very thing you dreamed of. Now, my feet hurt. We'll see you all back in South Philly."

Nicky and Hortense walked up Garibaldi Avenue to find the sedan parked by the grandstand where they'd left it. The party was over, the stands abandoned, the streets empty, the carnival lights dark. The air was still, the decorative flags that rippled earlier that day lay flat and uninspired. Even the stage did not look as impressive as it had that morning, filled with important people. The parade floats had taken a beating. The truth was, they all had.

Nicky and Hortense could hear the DePinos and Palazzinis arguing in the distance, but it did not faze them. Nicky held the door for Hortense, and she climbed in. He slipped into the driver's seat, and soon they were headed down Garibaldi. The DePinos and the Palazzinis, still in the heat of their argument, didn't notice when they passed.

"Do you care if I make a stop?" Nicky asked Hortense, looking at her in the rearview mirror.

"Why do you even ask me? You're driving."

"I won't be long. Or, I will be."

Nicky pulled up in front of Mamie Confalone's house. He made it to the screen door and saw Augie in his pajamas at the kitchen table reading a book, while Mamie did the dishes at the sink. He rapped softly on the screen.

Mamie turned, saw Nicky, put aside the dish in the drainer, and came to the door. She looked back at her son and then slipped out onto the porch.

"I wanted to say good-bye. And I wanted to thank you. You saved us back there."

"You would've done it for me." Mamie buried her hands in her apron pockets.

"I'm glad you know that." Nicky smiled.

"Last night . . . ," she began.

He blushed. "What can we say about last night?"

"I don't know that we should ever say a word about it," Mamie said tenderly.

It took Nicky a second to understand what Mamie meant. "You don't want to see me again?"

Mamie smiled. "I live here. And I always will."

"We could," he began to muse, "make a plan. Philly is close. We could meet?"

Mamie shook her head. "We shouldn't."

"Why?"

"Because I was fragile, and so were you. When you fall in love, Nicky, it has to be from a place of strength. It has to be because you want to build something, not because you need to cling to someone to shore you up or save you."

"I can be strong for you," Nicky argued.

"You will be strong, and so will she, when you find her some-day. But I thank you. You were lovely last night. I thought romance was over for me in every way. I was closed off to any possibilities. And I didn't think I'd ever find my way back to anything close to what we shared."

"It meant everything to me too, Mamie."

"I know that it did. So let's take that into whatever we become and treasure it."

Nicky wanted to argue with her, to convince her that they belonged together. He wanted to make a case for them as a couple, but he was beginning to understand what she was saying, what it meant, and why it mattered. It didn't mean he had to accept it. Maybe she needed time. Maybe she just wasn't ready.

Mamie kissed him on the cheek.

"Mama!" Augie called out for his mother.

"I have to go." Mamie touched the cheek she had just kissed and went inside.

Hortense had been observing the scene, but she snapped her neck in the opposite direction as Nicky approached the car.

"Are we finally going back to Philadelphia?" she complained.

"Yes, ma'am."

"Just the two of us?" Hortense asked.

Nicky did not answer. As he pulled out onto the street, he looked in the rearview mirror and caught Eddie Davanzo's police car as it pulled up in front of Mamie's house. For a moment he thought to go back, in case there was a problem, but he thought better of it and kept driving.

"Just keep moving until you see the Hot Shoppe in Germantown. No more pit stops."

"That was important."

"How so?

"You'll see."

"What am I gonna see?"

"Mamie Confalone."

"And who?"

"And me."

Hortense chuckled.

"What's so funny?"

"You gonna move to Roseto?"

"No."

"She's going to move to Philly?"

"She might. You never know."

"You asked her?"

"No."

"You met her kid?"

"No."

"And he was right inside the house, wasn't he?"

"Yes, he was."

"But she didn't introduce you to her kid. Nicky. Face it. You were a meltaway."

"A *what*?"

"A *meltaway*. A delicious candy unwrapped in the moment that lasts exactly as long as it is meant to, which is to say, until it's gone."

"I don't believe you."

"You don't have to. Eventually the truth will make it obvious. Like those plays you love so very much in the theater—when you're in the seat hearing the story, they matter, and in a couple hours it's over. Another meltaway. The truth is, this whole weekend was a meltaway. We are going back to real life—the costume goes back to the shop, this pin goes back in the drawer, your accent dries up, and we go back to work. You can't make pretend real."

"I had something with Mamie. It was real."

"Whatever happened between you and Mamie Confalone was made of spun sugar and air. It was sweet, and you tasted it. When you had it, you had it, but now you don't, and it will never be yours again."

Nicky was relieved when Hortense went off to sleep. It took a few seconds, really. A couple of snorts and she was snoring. What did she know about Mamie? About the two of them? Mrs.

Mooney was old and wizened and didn't understand young love. He wished he had never broached the subject with her. What was he thinking?

As Nicky drove along the silver river with a pink sky overhead, he was driving toward home, and yet the route felt unfamiliar. He was lost, and now he was broken, a penance for the sin of impersonating the Ambassador, or perhaps for taking a chance with a beautiful girl as lovely as Mamie without knowing where it would lead. The thought of Montrose Street and Car No. 4 was history to him now. His life as he knew it before the Jubilee was over. Now who was the impostor?

Calla pushed the front door of her house open with her hip. She carried a bag of fresh peaches in a brown paper bag, her father's favorite fruit.

"Dad?" she called out. "I'm back. Got your peaches. I already ate two." She looked back to the kitchen, where she saw his coffee cup on the table. She went into the kitchen and called out for him again. She touched the coffee cup. It was warm. She looked out the window to the garden.

Calla saw her father lying on the ground. She dropped the peaches, which rolled out of the bag and across the wooden floor. She ran outside, stumbling over a stepstool and the rigging for the awning that went over the walkway off the back porch.

"Dad, what did you do?" She made it to her father's side. He had a cut over his left eye. She checked his pulse. He was barely breathing. She tried to revive him. His face was slowly turning gray. She ran into the house and called an ambulance.

Calla ran back out into the yard to stay with her father until the ambulance arrived. She knelt down in the grass, took off her sweater, and gently placed it under his head. Calla laid her head on his chest to listen for his heartbeat. She had no idea how much time had passed when the paramedics came, but it hadn't been long. It seemed like forever, because she was losing him, and she knew it. Time was seeping away, and she could not control it.

She wanted to hold on to him, to do whatever she could to make him stay, but she knew, even as they placed him on the gurney and lifted him into the ambulance, that he had made his choice. The moment she had dreaded had arrived, and there was nothing she could do. She laced her fingers through her father's and held on as they hoisted him into the ambulance. Then she climbed in beside him, hoping that if she held on, she could pull him back to her.

As the ambulance careened through the streets of South Philly, they sped past the Borelli Theatrical Company.

"Dad, we just passed the theater." When Sam did not stir, Calla's eyes filled with tears. "I remember every play you directed. We can do them all again. We'll do the ones you didn't get to—okay? You never directed *Cymbeline*. I know it's not one of the better plays . . ." She began to cry. "But if anybody could redeem it and put on a first-class production, it's you. Don't leave me, Dad."

The ambulance pulled up to the emergency entrance. Within seconds, the doors flew open, and Sam was lifted out, wheeled into the hospital, past the nurses and the check-in desk, and into a small room that filled with nurses and doctors. Calla watched as they conferred, until she was pulled away by a kind nurse who put her arm around her waist and, taking her hand, led her out into the hallway. The last time Calla saw her father, his hands were open, accepting what was to come.

Nicky stood outside the sedan parked in the alley behind Borelli's and carefully placed the uniform he'd worn as Ambassador Guardinfante on a hanger. He whistled as he climbed the steps to the stage door, and was irritated to find it locked.

Nicky walked around the building and entered through the lobby, carrying the costume. Rosa DeNero was sitting on her perch in the box office, sipping a cup of coffee and reading the newspaper, when Nicky passed by.

"Rosa, how's it going?" He breezed by without waiting for her answer.

She came out of the ticket booth and called after him. "Have you heard?"

"Heard what?"

"Sam Borelli died this morning."

Nicky's voice wavered. "What happened?"

"Calla found him in the yard. He had been trying to put up the summer awning. He must've fell. They think he had a stroke. She went with him to the hospital." Rosa looked around. "This is it for the theater. It's over now. As long as Mr. B was alive, we had a chance. But now, there's no way it will make it."

"Shut up, Rosa."

Nicky pushed through the glass doors of the lobby and went outside. Familiar, old sadness began to move through his body. Grief had its own veins and capillaries, as regret filled his heart. He had meant to visit Sam, spend time with him and seek his counsel. Instead he had been caught up in events that didn't matter. Sam Borelli mattered and now, like all the sages in Nicky's life, he, too, was gone.

When Nicky knocked on Sam Borelli's front door on Ellsworth Street he heard laughter pouring out the open windows through the living room. He peered inside. The house was full to overflowing with members of the theater company as well as mourners he didn't recognize. The folks could not be described as mourners; they were celebrating Sam as they ate, drank, and danced. Nicky had never witnessed such a wake.

Nicky went inside. Tony Coppolella immediately wrapped him in an embrace. "Sam gave me my first job. Cast me in my first show. I was Guildenstern in *Hamlet*."

He patted Tony on the back and gave him a smile of reassurance. Actors mark everything that happens to them, no matter what it might be—falling in love, getting married, death of a loved one, or birth of a child—with whatever role they happened to be playing at the time. They view their lives through the wings, either entering a scene or exiting one. Sam's exit forced Tony to remember his first entrance.

Nicky wove through the crowd. Members of the crew patted him on the back in solidarity, and others expressed their grief with an embrace, but all Nicky wanted to do was get to Calla.

He made it through the kitchen and out to the back porch to the backyard where he found her talking with her sisters and a small cluster of friends. Frank Arrigo was serving drinks and working the crowd.

Nicky tapped Calla on the shoulder. When she turned and saw him, she began to cry. He took her into his arms. "It's going to be all right," he assured her.

"How?"

"It just will. Trust me."

"Okay."

"What can I do for you?"

"Just stay."

"You got it."

Nicky made himself useful. He went into the kitchen and warmed up food, placing it on the table for the guests. Theater folk are always hungry, so as the trays and casseroles poured in, Nicky set them out and the plates filled up. Nicky took a tray and went through the rooms, picking up plates and glasses. He returned to the kitchen, threw a moppeen on his shoulder, and washed dishes to keep up with the volume of guests who came to pay their respects to the family of Sam Borelli.

Frank hauled a bag of ice through the kitchen. "Thanks for helping out."

"Of course."

"You're a good friend to Calla."

"She's very special."

Frank smiled. "I know."

"You better be good to her, Frank."

"I hear that a lot. I've heard it about forty times this afternoon."

"Theater people might wear tights, but they can take you down in a dark alley."

"I'll bet."

Frank lifted the cooler of ice and went out into the backyard. Nicky watched him from the kitchen window. Calla's sisters seemed impressed with him as he freshened their drinks. Nicky wondered if Sam had liked the guy.

"Nicky."

He turned away from the window. Josie Ciletti, wearing a plunging V-neck cashmere sweater, pulled him close to her chest. "I'm a mess."

"Sam thought you had talent, Josie."

"He plucked me from the bowels of Cremon Street by the airport and turned me into an actress. I owe him everything," she sobbed.

Nicky gave her his handkerchief.

"The theater won't last without him."

"Sure it will."

"You know something?" Josie's left eyebrow shot up. "You heard something?"

"No, I just know Calla. She'll keep it going."

"I hope so. I need the stage like macaroni needs gravy."

"What does that say about the cheese, Josie?"

"Nothing. The cheese stands alone."

Around midnight, Frank drove Hambone Mason home because he was so juiced, he couldn't remember where he parked his car. Nicky swept the kitchen floor as the last of the dishes drained on the rack.

"This kitchen has never been so clean." Helen, Sam's eldest daughter, a striking redhead with brown eyes, looked around appreciatively. "We haven't met."

"Nicky Castone."

"He worked at the theater for Dad." Portia, a petite brunette, brought a tray in from the patio. "Right?"

"Yes. I wandered into the theater a few years ago, and he gave me a job."

"That's how Dad did his hiring. He thought if you showed up, you had been led there. He believed a life in the theater was a mystical calling." Helen shook her head.

"It might be if you're good at it," Calla said as she brought a tray of glasses in from the living room. "Sorry, Nick. You don't have to wash these."

"I'd be happy to."

"I'm going to head upstairs. We have a big day tomorrow." Helen looked at her sisters. "Just leave the dishes. I can do them in the morning."

"Go ahead. Don't worry about it. Portia, go get some rest. You must be exhausted. We'll finish up here."

Portia and Helen went upstairs, leaving Nicky and Calla alone in the kitchen. Nicky went to the sink, filled it with hot water and suds, and began washing the glasses. Calla stood beside him with the dishtowel. As he rinsed, she dried, placing the sparkling glasses on the shelf over the window.

"Frank drove Hambone home," she said. "He has a five o'clock call at work in the morning."

"He's not coming back tonight?"

"He'll be at the funeral. You worried I'll be alone?"

"That will never be a problem for you. I was afraid the floor would give, you had so many people here tonight."

"They loved Dad."

"That must be a good feeling, to have had a father that was so beloved by so many. He lived a life that brought joy to people. He entertained them. That's something."

"Is it?"

"Sure it is. What's bigger than making someone feel something? How can you quantify the moment when a person laughs? Or when they cry? When they feel? You can't. It's the human experience. And your father was in the business of illuminating it for people. He showed them that what they were going through was important, and that their lives had meaning. That's a noble undertaking."

Nicky's words went straight to Calla's heart. She sat down at the kitchen table and wept into the dishtowel.

"I'm sorry. I'm talking too much. Can I tell you a funny story?" She nodded.

"I was arrested."

"What?" Calla put down the dishtowel.

"I almost never saw the sky again."

"What happened?"

"We got caught. Mrs. Mooney and me. Evidently without a director, I'm a lousy actor. And your crummy Penn State band uniform didn't help me, either."

Calla laughed. "I forgot to tell you."

"You didn't have to. I heard all about it. There's a lot of Nittany Lion fans in Roseto, Pennsylvania."

"I'm sorry." Calla laughed.

"There you go. Your dad would get a big kick out of my punishment. Let's call it a penance."

"What is it?"

"I'm going to Italy to build a road to the Ambassador's hometown. Playing him in real life cost me everything. My money and my time."

"Do you know how to build a road?"

"I'll learn. I couldn't act until I tried it. So, we'll see." Nicky took the dishtowel from Calla. "Come on, let's get some air."

Nicky put his arm around Calla as they took a walk on Ellsworth. They turned onto Broad. "I know everybody on this street. I wrote a song about it."

"I didn't know you could sing."

"Not the best."

Nicky launched into his aria on the Street of Names. He sang:

> *Farino, Canino,*
> *Schiavone, Marconi,*
> *Terlazzo, Janazzo,*
> *Leone, Francone,*
> *Ciliberti, Monteverdi,*
> *Ruggiero!*

and belting high notes, he sang:

> *Sempre Borelli!*

"Shut up!" A woman of fifty, her wet hair rolled in strips of cloth, hung her Raggedy Ann head out of her second-story window. "You dying moose! Die already!"

"Sorry, lady!"

"You should be!" The woman slammed her window shut.

"No career in the opera for me."

"You needed her to tell you?" Calla teased. "I'm glad Dad gave up the musical theater."

"Don't pile on, sister. I'm being nice to you with all you're going through."

"Yes, you are."

"I'm your best friend."

"You are, aren't you?" Calla nudged him playfully. "My dad never wanted us to get too chummy with the actors."

"Why not?"

"He always worried one of his daughters would wind up with one. Portia married a banker, and Helen's husband is a teacher."

"And you'll best them both with a builder. A contractor who will be king of all this. You will do better than both of your sisters."

"That's not my goal."

"It wasn't for Lear's daughters either."

"I forgot about Lear."

"You shouldn't. Any dilemma a human being might face was dramatized by William Shakespeare. You don't need a priest or a doctor, just read the folios. You'll find all the answers there. I heard your father say that in rehearsal."

Calla stopped and turned away from Nicky, suddenly in tears again. He put his arms around her. "You'll be doing a lot of that. I didn't learn that from Shakespeare."

"I had him at home, you know, to turn to—I could ask my dad anything."

"Therefore, you can handle anything. Your dad saw to it. Nobody can take that away from you—not in your life and not in your work. You're the strongest girl I know, and I would know, because I live in a house crawling with them. You don't need anybody to tell you what to do and how to do it. Not even your big lug of a boyfriend with the rag top knows more than you do."

"I'm not going to tell him you said that."

"Good, because he has about thirty pounds on me."

"Of muscle."

"I'm not hurt by that little dig, because I know you're grieving."

"I've been dreading this day."

"Because you took care of your dad. Do you know how much he appreciated that? More than you'll ever know. You're going to be sad. Plenty sad. You just have to go through it."

Nicky and Calla walked for a long time. They walked through the neighborhood and along Broad Street. If it had been up to Calla, they would have walked all night as she didn't want to return to the house and face the sadness that filled every room. She dreaded the funeral mass and the burial. There would be no comfort in the Latin, the Kyries, the prayers and the hymns. "I'm an orphan now too."

Nicky put his arm around Calla. "You are, aren't you? Well, I'm sorry about that. It ain't great. But stick with me. I'm good with grief. Had a life full of it."

9

A blue jay landed on Hortense Mooney's kitchen windowsill and stared at her. She looked up from the bushel of bright red tomatoes she was coring to boil and looked the bird straight in the eye.

"Lordy, Lordy," she mumbled to herself. "That's a bad sign. Somebody's going to be with Jesus." She looked up. "Safe travels."

Hortense put down her paring knife, closed her eyes, and said a quick prayer. She sat down at her kitchen table, opened her loose-leaf binder, and wrote out Minna's gravy recipe neatly. Again.

Minna Gravy Test #17

For 5 cups of gravy:

6 tablespoons of olive oil
2 cloves of garlic peeled and sliced paper thin
2 small sweet onions, chopped very fine
2 medium carrots, diced
2 hearts of celery, diced (from 2 stalks)

5 pounds of fresh tomatoes (boiled, skinned, and strained like Minna)

5 stems of leafy basil shredded fine by hand, remove the stems

1/2 stick of sweet salted butter

1/2 teaspoon red pepper flakes

salt to taste

Secret ingredient guess #17: 1/4 cup sugar

Hortense closed the binder and went to the stove. She dropped a tomato into the large pot of boiling water, following it with another, and another. She had boiled so many tomatoes since her return from Roseto, she had developed a technique whereby the boiling water engulfed the tomato without so much as a splash.

Louis Mooney entered the kitchen, placed his hat on the hook on the back of the door and a brown bag with a loaf of fresh bread on the table. "You're making that tomato sauce again?"

"Yes, Louis."

"It's a waste of time."

"I don't need your judgment right now," Hortense said patiently, fishing the tomatoes out of the boiling water and placing them in a bowl to peel them. She set the bowl aside before adding more tomatoes to the pot.

"Is this all we're going to eat until we're dead?"

"Until I get it right," she said pleasantly.

"Good to know."

Louis left the kitchen. Hortense dropped a large tomato into the boiling water, but this one splashed. Boiling water ricocheted everywhere, like clear bullets. She jumped back and took a deep breath, pulling her rib cage up and her belly in, before exhaling.

She went to the sink, chose another tomato, and dropped it into the pot. This time, the addition made barely a ripple.

Saint Maria de Pazzi Cemetery was a lovely one, as those places go. The working families who buried their loved ones there were artisans, stonemasons, carpenters, bricklayers, and welders; therefore the headstones, statues, and mausoleums were as ornate and well crafted as any shrine in any cathedral anywhere in the world. The humble were exalted here.

Sam Borelli's fresh grave was covered in black earth, along with the scattered remnants of the flower arrangements from his funeral mass. White carnations, their long stems bent, fronds of yellow gladioli, pink chrysanthemums, and cypress leaves crisscrossed one over the other, a patchwork quilt of grief as Calla stood over her father's grave and wept. She hated every flower in the church, knowing her father would have too. In her hands, she held a bouquet of long-stemmed calla lilies, which had not been represented in any of the arrangements from Falcone Florists. She had stopped and bought these at the flower market herself.

Calla knelt next to her mother's headstone, kissed her fingertips, and touched the stone before rising. She placed the bouquet on her mother's grave.

"I hope I'm not interrupting," Rosa DeNero said from behind her.

"Not at all."

"I couldn't make it to the funeral, but I wanted to pay my respects."

"We appreciate it, Rosa."

"You brought flowers. With all the flowers from the church, you brought more," Rosa commented.

"They weren't the right flowers."

"Falcone does the same thing for every funeral."

Calla shrugged. "My sister went to school with the daughter who runs it now."

"It's all the buddy-buddy system. That's the problem with South Philly. Business goes to who you know. No new blood. So everybody does everything the same." Rosa sighed. "Your dad must have liked calla lilies. He named you after them."

"My mom named me. That wasn't the plan. My father had named my sisters after characters in Shakespeare. I was the last child, so I was going to be Olivia."

"From *Twelfth Night*!"

"Right. But my mother said no. She said we may work for the theater, live for it, and sacrifice everything for it, but Shakespeare will not get the final word on everything we do. So I got named for her favorite flower. It was my mother's only act of rebellion. That I know of."

"She'd probably approve of the theater getting sold."

"What?"

"You're selling the theater."

"Where did you hear that?"

"I must have heard wrong," Rosa said nervously.

"I'd love to know what you've heard."

"The usual gossip. The box office has been weak. Now that your dad is gone, why keep the place going—that sort of thing. Everybody's talking about the future."

"What do you mean?"

"Frank Arrigo had an engineer come to look at the building."

Calla knew Rosa wasn't the sharpest employee at the theater, but surely she knew that Calla and Frank were a couple. "I know about that. Frank brought a city engineer in to make a bid to repair the building. It was my idea. I asked Frank to help."

"He's helping all right. He's booked the wrecking ball."

"What do you mean?"

"Frank Arrigo wants to tear it down and put up an apartment

complex. The engineer said that the building would be too expensive to fix. Frank said it didn't matter anyway. He was taking down the building."

"He said that?"

"I heard it with my own ears. You're going with him. I figured he said it to you too. Everybody says you're going to marry him. Good for you. It's none of my business, but I think you ought to grab him. A tall man is a rarity in South Philly."

Across the cemetery, behind the cross of the risen Lord, stood the Palazzini mausoleum. It was built of Carrara marble and had an elegant open-scrollwork black iron gate over the stone door, which had been welded by patriarch Domenico Michele, one of the two people buried inside. Next to him, in the crypt, were the remains of his grandson, Richard, whom everyone knew as Ricky, Nancy and Mike's son, who'd died in battle during World War II. The mausoleum was large enough to fit eight family members, so admission was a matter of who got there first. The remainder of the Palazzini clan would be buried in the lots behind the mausoleum and, when those were filled, in the field beyond the church parking lot. The arrangements had been made before Dom and Mike's split. They may not speak in this world, but they would reside next to each other in the next one.

Jo Palazzini had cut a large bouquet of flowers from her garden, wrapped them in wet newspaper, and taken a walk over to the cemetery to decorate the mausoleum. Her summer garden was off to a great start. The blue hydrangea had never come in so full and blue, their periwinkle petals like velvet.

As Jo took the stone path up to the grave, she saw Calla Borelli in the distance, which reminded her to send a mass card to the house. She wasn't close to Calla, but she knew that she was a friend of Nicky's, and that meant she was important to Jo.

Jo stopped at the water pump to fill the can. Carrying the large bouquet in one arm like a newborn infant, she held the can with her free hand. As she turned the corner, she saw Nancy Palazzini sitting on the marble bench outside the mausoleum. Her instinct was to turn around, go home, and bring the flowers later, but Jo decided to proceed.

"Good morning, Nancy," Jo said to her sister-in-law.

Nancy turned to face her, dabbing away her tears. "Hello, Jo."

"The flowers are so pretty this year. I listened to Sal Spatuzza and put coffee grounds in the dirt as soon as the snow thawed, and look at this color."

"So blue."

"Like a twilight sky." Jo arranged the flowers in the vase, a metal cone that hung in the center of the iron fence, and poured the water into the cone, all the way to the brim. She took a couple steps back and then moved in and fluffed the blossoms before turning down the path to go.

"Jo? Thank you. Today it's six years since Ricky died."

"Today?"

Nancy nodded. Jo sat down beside her. "I can't imagine."

"Don't."

The years of estrangement settled around them like a low fog. Time didn't fall away, nor did it evaporate into the air. The women felt the weight of their estrangement every day, the ballast coming from guilt.

Nancy and Jo had meant something to each other, beyond their forced sisterhood from marriage to the brothers. They had married around the same time and had babies close together. The jokes were at the ready when they walked down the street with their prams. "What are you girls putting in the gravy over there? The Palazzini men only make boys."

Nancy and Jo were there for one another when the babies had a fever or later when two of the boys were twelve and decided to go joyriding in a spare cab and were picked up by the cops in Queens Village. The women had given much thought to the bond that had broken between them when the brothers separated. Why hadn't they done something? Perhaps they had so much work to do back then, they couldn't take on one more project: making peace. It didn't help that their friendship had been destroyed for the most superficial of reasons: they were different and did things differently, and when their husbands argued, they found reasons to feed the fury instead of stopping it.

Jo had come to the conclusion shortly after the breach that the argument wasn't worth the loss of the family, but she remained silent.

Nancy had not come to the same place until Ricky was killed in the war, and then, only because she wanted everyone that had ever known and loved her son to help her remember every moment they might recall of his life. She would spend the next six years filling in the details like a watercolor, some aspects delicate, a few hazy, others saturated, but all of them together did not create a portrait of Ricky, just a pale version of the original. But she'd take it. Nancy was grateful whenever Ricky was remembered.

"I read your letter all the time," Nancy said.

"I tried to remember everything about him."

"You did."

"I'm no writer."

"You wrote beautifully."

"I'm sorry Dom wasn't there for Mike—"

"Mike wouldn't have gone to Dominic either." Nancy kept her gaze on the flowers.

"It's a shame."

"For everyone. What is a family, Jo?"

"A group of people that love each other and share a common history," Jo said plainly.

"I wish it were true."

"The love is there."

"But not the history. We've lost sixteen years. Nobody on your side shared our grief when Ricky died. Until you wrote to me. That's why your letter meant so much. You took the time. That's love." Nancy nodded.

"That's what a sister does. At least, that's what I believe." Jo stood up and went to the flowers and moved the stems to re- configure the flowers. "But it wasn't enough. I didn't fight hard enough for you. I guess I'm the martyr everybody says I am. I let my husband keep this vendetta going when I should have stopped it. And now my boys will pay for my weak character. I can see the cracks now. When brothers are cruel to one another and cut each other out of each other's lives, it's like a recipe that's handed down. The ingredients don't change, therefore the dish doesn't either. My boys will turn on one another at some point because it's what they know."

"That's too bad."

"Some families inherit money, others flat feet; we got two hard- headed husbands who want to be right more than they want to keep the peace. As if they know what's right." Jo stood to go.

Jo placed her hand on Nancy's as a beam from the afternoon sun lit the bright blue hydrangeas.

"That's the exact blue I painted the boys' room when they were little. Remember? You picked it." Jo pointed.

"I painted our boys' room the same color." Nancy smiled.

"Still the same?" Jo asked.

"Long gone. You?"

"Long gone."

Jo followed Nancy down the long gravel path out of the ceme- tery. When they reached the street, they embraced before parting, one went east, the other west, but somehow that day, they went in the same direction.

Calla stood in the kitchen of her family home. Her sisters, their husbands, and their families had left, and for the first time since their father died, she was in the house alone.

A ceramic lamp, a tiered crystal serving dish, and a small silver clock were arranged neatly on the kitchen table, each item labeled "Helen." On the counter, stacked neatly, was the full set of her mother's formal china, a Rosewood pattern given to her by their grandmother, labeled "Portia." Calla put her hands in her pockets and walked out of the room through packing boxes, walls stained with the shadows of time where there had once been a work of art or a mirror.

This was now her life.

What had once been precious, and in her mind should be pre-served as it was for all time, was now going to be divided, carted away, and disassembled in pieces, which would never be as strong as the whole. Her mother's lamp would never be as lovely as it had been in the front window, where it spilled light out onto the porch, turning the old wood to silver from gray. The clock taken from her father's desk would never again remind him that it was time to go to rehearsal. The tiered crystal plate would never again hold her mother's biscotti, better than any professional baker's in South Philly. The fine china, stacked on the kitchen counter that held the meal that fed them at every holiday and special occasion, washed and dried with such care, would be shipped to her sister's house, where Calla was certain it would be placed in a closet and forgotten, along with their memories.

Calla climbed the steps to her bedroom. She wanted to crawl into her bed and sleep for as many days as it would take to make her feel like herself again. When she reached the top of the stairs, instead of going into her own room, she found herself walking down the hallway to the master bedroom. On her way, she passed her sisters' old bedroom, which had become a guest room for their visits. Calla poked her head inside. Helen, the fastidious one, had stripped the beds; the sheets were in a laundry basket, waiting to be laundered. The tops of their dressers had been cleared of the framed photographs that had been placed there since they were girls. Even though the photographs belonged to Helen and Portia, their absence gave Calla a feeling of abandonment, a signal her sisters had decided never to return home again.

Calla opened the master bedroom door. She stood in the dark and inhaled the scent of the room. Her father had left a window open, as was his habit year round, regardless of the weather. The lilacs that twisted up the drainpipe outside the window were in bloom, filling the room with their sweet scent. She grinned, remembering her father calling them "nun flowers," because his wife would cut bunches of them, wrap them in wet newspaper, and deliver them to the convent, to be laid at the feet of the statue of the Blessed Mother.

Calla flipped the light on. She didn't remember making the bed, but she had. The closet door was open. She went inside, pulled the string of the overhead bulb. The contents were neat, but there was a space where she had removed her father's best suit so he might be buried in it. The wooden shoe trees that had been placed in his dress shoes lay on a shelf. The funeral home had given Calla a list of items they needed, which read exactly like a list of what her father wore to any of his opening nights: pressed shirt, handkerchief, silk tie, dress socks, undergarments, braces for the socks, dress shoes, belt, suit. They asked for his brush and comb, and his shaving supplies. Calla had provided all of it.

In the course of a year, Calla had lost her mother and her father. When she was a girl, her sisters used to talk at night, thinking their baby sister was asleep, but Calla was listening. Helen and Portia would wonder which parent would die first, and what they would do if the worst happened. They gossiped a lot, about boys and school, but Calla remembered how they complained about the things they didn't have. They wanted things that other girls had, things that in their home were impossible to obtain because they cost too much money. Helen and Portia dreamed of a fancy family car, a maroon Duesenberg like the one the Fiorios owned; of faille dresses from the window of Harper's Dress Shop, and red patent leather shoes from Wanamaker's department store.

Calla remembered when Helen and Portia insisted on getting permanent waves in their hair at the beauty salon. Their friend Kitty Martinelli had gotten her hair done, and they wanted to look just like her. The process was expensive, but their mother had figured out a way to get the girls what they wanted. They got the perms and came home in tears: their thick, wavy hair looked like dandelion puffs. Never once did her sisters think that coveting Kitty's lustrous curls was the problem, not the ingredients in the permanent wave.

Calla sat down in her father's reading chair and leaned back. The chair's sage-green velvet, piped in black, was worn at the arms and seat. There was a lace doily on the back of the chair, which had been there since she was a girl. When her father had a wild head of black hair in his youth, he used Macassar oil to slick his hair back, so Calla's mother had placed doilies on all the backs of the chairs in the house to preserve the slipcovers.

The table next to the floor lamp had a few books stacked upon it. Most of Sam's books had already made their way into Calla's room; her father had given them to her as she needed them for her work at the theater. Like a good professor, Sam had introduced Calla to Shakespeare through the sonnets, graduating to the comedies, and eventually the tragedies. Sam's *Riverside Shakespeare* was held together with a wide grosgrain ribbon because the binding threads had dissolved from age and use. Calla didn't have the heart to untie the ribbon, knowing that inside, her father's margin notes would break her heart all over again. She didn't need clues to understand her father, but instead reveled in the layers and depths of his thought process. No matter how many times Sam had read a play, directed it, or seen another company's production, he had found something new in the text. He called reading *an act of discovery*. Calla was too exhausted to discover anything new.

A stack of letters from Sister Jean Klene, with the return address Saint Mary's College, South Bend, Indiana, were bound with a rubber band. Sister Jean was Sam's favorite American Shakespeare scholar and the two had exchanged letters for years. Sam had met the nun when a theater troupe he worked with traveled through Indiana. Sister Jean offered insight on the text and information about productions she had seen around the world.

Calla lifted the book on the top of the pile on his side table. *Life in Shakespeare's England* had been her father's bible. He referred to it a lot, recommended it to his actors, and shared it with Calla. Sam often quoted John Dover Wilson as though he were Shakespeare himself. Calla thumbed through the book, stopping to read what her father had been thinking about in the days and hours before his death.

Sam had an odd habit of marking the places in books he read with matchsticks, strips of newspaper, old bills, even collar stays. Through the years his daughters had given him fancy bookmarks, but they remained unused in the top drawer of his dresser, next to his good cuff links.

John Dover Wilson's book had been read so often, the spine was shot, so the pages lay open flat like a map. Sam often used Italian in his notes, and just as his nickname for his wife had been *Bella*, he added it to each of his daughters' names as a term of endearment. Calla found a note written to her on the front of the monthly electric bill envelope. Her father had drawn a monocle on the cartoon of the mascot, *Reddy Kilowatt*, along with this message:

Calla Bella—page 288

Calla's hand began to tremble as she turned the pages. Her father had drawn an arrow to indicate a passage. He had also doodled small triangle flags around it, like an Elizabethan banner.

Death

The passage was titled aptly, but next to it, Sam had written *"Fine,"* which Calla knew in this instance, did not mean "all right" but rather the Italian word that, translated, meant "The End." She read:

It is therefore Death alone that can suddenly make man to know himself. He tells the proud and insolent that they are but abjects and humbles them at the instant; makes them cry, complain and repent, yea, even to hate their forepassed happiness. He takes the account of the rich and proves him a beggar, a naked beggar, which hath interest in nothing but in the gravel that fills his mouth. He holds a glass before the eyes of the most beautiful and makes them see therein their deformity and rottenness, and they acknowledge it. Oh eloquent, just and mighty Death! Whom none could advise thou hast persuaded, what none hath dared thou hast done, and whom all the world hath flattered thou only hast cast out of the world and despised. Thou hast drawn together all the far-stretched greatness, all the pride, cruelty and ambition of man, and covered it all over with those two narrow words, Hic jacet.[1]

—SIR WALTER RALEIGH,
The Historie of the World, 1614

[1] "Here lies." Raleigh cited in John Dover Wilson, comp., *Life in Shakespeare's England—A Book of Elizabethan Prose* (Cambridge, England: Cambridge University Press, 1911).

Sam added a note to Calla under the passage:

> *Don't be afraid of dying. I am not.*
> *This is scary stuff – but only for those*
> *who live in service to the wrong things.*
> *You won't.*
>
> > > > > *Dad*

Calla closed the old book and held it close. She was grateful to her father for everything. She also felt gratitude toward her mother, who had loved her father so much, she'd sacrificed everything for him and his life's work. Calla was also grateful to Helen and Portia, who valued the things in this world that she did not, and therefore left her with the things she most wanted from her parents' house, which were, luckily for her, of no interest to them.

Calla would keep her father's library and his collection of prompt books, which included the scripts and notes from every production he had directed in his long career. She would also take her mother's sewing basket and her bottle of Trapéze de Corday, with a thimbleful of perfume left at the bottom of the amber flask.

Calla would also remember to take her mother's red-handled paring knife from the kitchen drawer. In her very first memory, Calla was four years old, in the backyard of the house on Ellsworth Street. Her mother, exacting the small knife, quartered a ripe peach for her daughters to eat one summer afternoon. Vincenza Borelli's lovely hands moved with dexterity, the blade of the knife making quick work of the fruit as it fell into golden pink velvet pieces.

Vincenza gave each of her daughters a wedge, pierced the pit with the tip of the blade, and flung it into the garden bed. Calla remembered the pit as it flew through the air and landed in the distance. "Let's see what grows from that," her mother had said. That night Calla dreamed a tree grew in the garden, a stage tree made with papier-mâché, paint, brown velvet branches, gold lamé leaves, and berries made of red glass beads. Everyone thought Sam was the artist in the family, but it was Calla's mother who had given her imagination birth.

Helen would take their mother's silver while Portia wanted the wedding crystal with authentic gold trim. There were lamps made of Italian alabaster topped with silk shades and a set of small Florentine study tables. Her sisters would take those too. It wasn't a teacup or a piece of furniture that Calla needed to remember her parents; she would take tools they had used to build their romantic dreams. Vincenza had created a home and garden that delighted Sam while he created theatrical productions that celebrated love, life, and courage that could only come from the heart of a man who was living it.

Calla wouldn't expect her sisters to understand how she felt. They had left this old house, the theater, and South Philly without looking back. Helen and Portia worried that Calla lived in the past and that, like their father, their kid sister was obsessed with Shakespeare and would remain in his theatrical grip for the rest of her life. Meanwhile, Calla hoped she would; she wanted to be just like Sam, who found purpose in the plays when he was young and wisdom in them at the end of his life.

At least Helen and Portia understood that beauty compelled their parents to create it. And, like the ripe peach the sisters shared on that summer day so long ago, they would taste the sweetness again in memory. Calla would too, and be grateful for it, but because she was an artist she would also take the rest, the parts of the fruit that no one wanted, the soft bruises on the skin, the leaves, and the stem in order to make sense of them. She would also take the pit, from which she would make something grow. There was meaning in all of it and it was an artist's job to find it.

Garibaldi Avenue looked like a red satin ribbon as geraniums spilled out of hanging baskets and rosebushes burst with plump blossoms of burgundy and fuchsia. The summer heat had turned Roseto's main street into a hothouse garden in full bloom. The banners welcoming the ambassador had been taken down, the streamers yanked from their poles, the flags from their wires, and the scandal was almost forgotten, replaced by a new one: the deacon having run off with his secretary and the collection basket from Saint Rocco's in Martins Creek.

Mamie Confalone carried two brown grocery bags up the walkway to Minna Viglione's front door. She rang the bell and waited. Soon, Minna appeared.

"Two bags?"

"I'm going to the shore this week. So I shopped double for you."

"Right. It's vacation week at the mill."

"I live for it." Mamie followed Minna into the house and back to her kitchen.

"Where are you going?"

"Ocean City."

Minna clapped her hands together. "The beach."

"My folks rented a little shack down the shore. And I can't wait."

"I used to love to go to the ocean."

"You're welcome to come. It's not far. We could take you. We have room."

"Maybe next year. I want to see the ocean again." Minna smiled as Mamie began to unload the groceries from the bag. "You don't have to do that. I can do it."

"I'm a full-service delivery operation. From Ruggiero's Market to your cupboard." Mamie looked out the window. "Your garden is gorgeous. Who rigged the muslin?" Minna's garden was draped in a canopy of white fabric to protect the plants from the hot sun, and to discourage the birds from eating the grapes.

"Eddie Davanzo."

"That was nice of him."

"He's handy. He's kind, and he's handsome."

"And you have a crush on him."

"I'm too old for him. But you're not."

"You like him for me?" Mamie folded her arms and leaned against the counter.

"He's a man like they used to make them. Solid."

"He *is* a policeman."

"I am not talking about his job."

"I know, Minna. But I haven't thought about him in that way."

"Maybe you should."

"I wasn't ready for romance for the longest time. Five years. More. And then, one night, a storm came through and blew the windows out of my house. And I could breathe again. The despair lifted. The grief wasn't gone entirely, but it felt different. I could put it in its place. Manage it. It wasn't my life anymore, it was just a part of it. Sadness wasn't the only thing I felt. I could feel other things too."

"I'm happy for you."

Mamie looked off. "It's a start."

"You give me hope," Minna admitted.

"Do you think you'll ever leave this house?"

"Every morning I think, this is the day, and I get up, I've got gumption. So, I tend the garden, do the wash, make the gravy, do all those things someone does when they take care of a home. And soon it's late afternoon, and by then I'm tired and I've lost the courage to try. And I tell myself, tomorrow will be the day."

Mamie understood the inertia. It had been the same for her—except she had a goal: she vowed that she would get Augie raised, and afterwards would live again. "But we don't know about tomorrow, Minna. With all the choices we make, we don't really make the important ones, those are made for us. Think about the shore, will you?"

"I will."

Mamie gave Minna a quick kiss on the cheek before leaving.

Minna heard the front door close. She thought about baking a pie, but decided she'd put it off until the next day. She took off her apron and walked to the living room. She peered out the curtains. She stood at the front door, opened it, and went out on to the porch. She felt the warm air envelop her like a cashmere shawl.

Minna went down the front walk on her way to the street but stopped short of the sidewalk. The last inlay of blue slate on the walkway was the boundary that separated Minna from the rest of the world. She could stand on that stone and greet a neighbor, collect the mail, or welcome a guest inside. But this morning, instead of remaining behind the boxwood hedge that hemmed the small patches of green grass, she closed her eyes and stepped out onto the sidewalk for the first time in seven years. She placed one foot on the cement square, and then the other. Her mind flashed with an image of mud, her sandaled foot pulled into muck. She shook her head to rid herself of the picture. Instead of living inside the fear, she opened her eyes and looked down at her feet. She confirmed she was safe, but stood there, unsure, her hands formed into tight fists, as she fought her deepest anxiety.

Minna stood on that spot for as long as she could bear it, a matter of seconds. She inhaled, exhaled, and tried to control the waves of panic. She heard a cacophony of sound, the voices of every person who had ever spoken to her since the day she was born, living or dead, in a loud chorus. Her brain filled with the goo of their conversation, and she was afraid as they talked over one another, loudly admonishing her to *turn back, go back, get inside.* She shook her head, again certain their voices were imagined, not real, and therefore didn't matter.

Minna had taken the first step out of her prison. Instead of collapsing, she stood tall. Tomorrow she vowed she would take another. And the day after that, yet another until she reached Mary Farino's, then Constance Stampone's, then the post office, then the coffee shop, until she reached her goal. Minna had a mission, and more important than making the effort, she believed she could achieve it. Someday soon she would walk to the top of Garibaldi Avenue into Our Lady of Mount Carmel Church where she would sit in a pew surrounded by the saints and inhale the scent of the beeswax candles and incense and kneeling at long last at the altar of the Blessed Mother, she would pray and be healed. As Minna walked back into her house, she envisioned herself sitting in the pew and she could see it clearly. Tomorrow she would take another step forward.

Calla had been directed by Ed Shaughnessy's office to the Fountain of the Sea Horses, where after months of repairs, he was scheduled to turn on the waterworks.

Calla wore the prettiest sundress she owned that day, a hand-me-down from her sister Portia. It was an ice-blue cotton number, with a full skirt and bows tied at the shoulders. She wore flat sandals and brushed her hair until it was as shiny as her mother's gold bangle bracelet from Sorrento, which dangled from her wrist. She had learned the importance of choosing the right costume when putting on a show.

"Mr. Shaughnessy!" Calla waved from the footpath behind the fountain. "It's me, Calla Borelli, from the theater."

Ed wouldn't have connected the woman in paint-splattered coveralls at Borelli's theater to the one in the dress. This fetching girl was a dish.

"You got the old Bernini going." Calla splashed her hand in the cool water.

"What's Philly without the fountain?"

"Dry," Calla joked. "My dad always wanted to put a small park and fountain next to the theater. I guess that will stay a dream for now anyway. Frank just told me all about his plan for the theater. What do you think?"

"I hate to see history die in a neighborhood."

"Ed, how relevant is that old barn to the audiences of today?"

"I don't know. That's not for me to decide. You're a theatrical person, I work for the city."

"It's too expensive to renovate, don't you think?" Calla was coy.

"It can be done. If you want to renovate that building, you could do it. It would be expensive. Getting it up to code would mean gut work from the inside out."

"That's what Frank says."

"He knows what he's doing."

"Thank goodness. I don't know what I'd do without him. He doesn't like to burden me with the big decisions."

"That's what he told me."

"I need my mind clear for the creative aspects of my job."

"Makes sense."

"What do you think about his plans for the lot?"

Ed shrugged. "He thinks there's a market for apartments on Broad."

Calla swallowed hard. "Do you?"

"South Philly needs housing. It's lucrative. Frank knows how to take an opportunity and make something out of it." Ed turned on the water that filled the dishes in the fountain. The water rippled in the sun, sparkling like sapphires. "But, I'd hate to see a building of the Belle Epoque era brought down for an ordinary apartment complex. I like the historical stuff," Ed admitted.

"There's no way to save the building and put up apartments?" Calla asked.

"I don't see how. Frank says it can't be done."

Calla's worst fears were confirmed. She felt faint. "Thank you for your time, Mr. Shaughnessy."

Ed Shaughnessy jumped into his truck and drove off as Calla sat on a bench by the fountain.

Bernini's sculpture was resplendent in the sun as waves of water cascaded over the tiers of marble in bright blue sheets into the wide pools of stone, held high by the carved sea horses. It was then she saw the future. Calla imagined the fountain toppled to rubble; in a hundred years or less, it would be gone. Sooner than later every available space in the city would be filled with a high rise, streets jammed with cars and sidewalks cluttered with people who were strangers to one another. Borelli's Theater had no place in such a world, unless someone saw the merit in its existence. Calla surprised herself, as she smiled instead of giving in to the futility of her situation. It was the splendor of Bernini's creation that changed her mind. The art was worth the fight. If Borelli's Theater was to survive, then a Borelli had to save it.

The members of the Borelli Theatrical Company were gathered on the stage of the theater, under the work lights. A few of the actors sat on folding chairs, others on the stage floor, while the crew stood, but all were waiting for their director.

Calla sprinted down the aisle and leapt up the steps to the stage.

"Thank you for coming today. I want to thank you for being such wonderful friends after the passing of my father. He loved you all and thought the world of you. He was a great teacher. You know there was no better director and producer. He never told you anything that wasn't true, and I'm going to keep my word to you too. I hope to honor his long legacy in the theater, especially his artistry, which was something to behold. I'm not saying I can ever be as good, but I am saying I will try. There are a lot of rumors flying around, and they're just gossip. I am determined to keep this theater open. We're going to do Shakespeare until we're all too old to play Lear. So, with that in mind, I want you to keep your hopes up, and trust that I've got all this under control. I plan to post the next production on the board in six weeks and I hope you'll all be part of it."

The company erupted in applause, underscored by a spirited stomping on the stage floor. Calla embraced members of the company and crew one by one. She thanked them for their service. As she reached the end of the line, she saw Frank Arrigo out of the corner of her eye, standing in the wings. She joined him.

"Hey, babe, I made reservations at Palumbo's."

"I can't go to dinner, Frank."

"You're busy?"

"No. We're through."

"What do you mean?" He was stunned.

"I know all about your scheme. It's not my charms that reeled you in—it's this half-acre lot on Broad with the unlimited air space that enchanted you." The members of the company gathered behind the scrim and listened.

"I don't know what you are talking about," Frank said defiantly.

"Your plan to buy the building and put up apartments."

"Honey, I say that about every old building in the city."

"Well, not this one. Not anymore."

"Okay. Fine. Keep the theater. Whatever you want." Frank took her hand in his. "You should know what I want. I'm serious about you. The building is just a pile of bricks. Nails and wood. I don't care about it. It doesn't mean anything to me. You mean everything to me."

"If that's true, then you'd understand what this theater means to me. It's not just a pile of bricks."

"You know what I'm saying. Look, you've been through a lot, you're grieving for your father."

"That's true. But I'm not inventing scenarios. Just tell me the truth. You wanted to buy this building."

"Okay. Sure."

"If I were selling."

"Right."

"And you wanted me *and* the building?"

"Why not? You're my girl. And I can build you a theater any-where in Philly. A new one. With state-of-the-art lighting. Sound. Seating. A lobby. Everything you'd ever want. And better parking."

"Everything except history."

"You need a new building. A modern facility. Something new and exciting to bring the people in. Give me a chance to give you everything you want."

"I have it already. Every time I walk through the stage door, I see my dad. When I look out into the house, I see my mom, sit-ting quietly during rehearsal sewing the hem on a costume. And I look up to the mezzanine, and see my sisters, little girls, running back and forth across the aisles. I remember every production— the hits, the flops—was equally spectacular to me. My childhood is in this theater and now it's my life. And it would have been nice to share it with you."

"We can share it. We will."

"But I don't want you anymore, Frank," Calla said calmly. "You failed the audition. Your performance wasn't truthful."

Frank took a moment to think. "You mean it?"

"I do," she said. Her voice broke. Calla was sad, but resolute.

"You're making a mistake."

"Could be."

"You'll never survive here without me."

"Do you think that's what I've been doing here?"

"You're not making it, Calla."

"Maybe not on your terms. But I get up every day and come to work and do a job I love. I pay seventeen artists a week, and that goes up to forty artists on the payroll during a large scale produc-tion. I think I'm doing all right."

Frank Arrigo walked out of the theater. It seemed of late as though every man that Calla Borelli loved left her. This time, however, was different. She was the one showing the gentleman the door.

Calla walked backstage to find the entire company waiting for her. From the looks on their faces, she knew they had heard the conversation. Like children overhearing their parents argue through bedroom walls, there was no hiding the truth. Calla was producer, director, and mother to this troupe of talented semi-professionals who loved Borelli's as much as she did. She knew their secrets and they knew hers. In this moment they needed her reassurance.

By day, an actor might drive a soda truck, a costume assistant might work the steam presser in the blouse factory, an actress might wrangle six kids and work a shift in a doughnut shop— but at night when they came to Borelli's, they put on their costumes and makeup, they became a company of players who stood in beams of candy-colored light and acted in the plays of William Shakespeare. They lived for the life behind the velvet curtain, where they slipped out of the present and away to another place and time, to make some sense of words written by a man long gone but who somehow understood everything. This wasn't just a theater, and the process wasn't simply show business or entertainment to them, it was their chance to be part of the poetry.

Interlude

OCTOBER 29, 1949
ROSETO VALFORTORE, ITALY

The silk curtains blew into the bedroom of the palazzo like the billowing skirt of a woman's ball gown mid dance. Nicky laced his work boot, looping it across at the top and tying it snugly with a double knot. He stood up and marched in place. The boots felt secure, not too tight, one more trick he had learned in the army that had held him in good stead ever since.

He walked over to the curtains, securing them behind a hook. He opened the French doors out onto the balcony and went outside. The sun was cresting over the mountain to the east. He imagined the cobalt blue waters of the Adriatic beyond the mountain and smiled. How different this journey had been from his visit after the war. Peacetime had an elegance, a courtly manner that only a soldier who had been in a brutal war could appreciate. A teaspoon of honey on hot bread might as well be gold. Icy water from a stream unpolluted by sulfur and shrapnel was an elixir. Air, in its purest form, where wind made the sound of silk as it grazed a woman's skin, was a delight.

Italy had changed Nicky Castone for the better.

He stretched his arms over his head and inhaled deeply. The war had built the muscles in his legs; laying stone in Roseto Valfortore had built his arms. His penance had empowered him, as true contrition might. The sinner sheds his selfish intent, and when he does, his true purpose reveals itself.

Nicky leaned against the iron grid of the scrollwork fence of the terrace. His biceps now possessed the chiseled grooves of a Michelangelo sculpture. His back had broadened, his waist had whittled, and his mind had been cleared. With the road near completion, it would soon be time to return home. He wasn't anxious to leave Italy, but he was determined to take what he had learned here and change his life.

The annual fig harvest on the hillsides of Roseto Valfortore was nearing its end. Autumn in Apulia was a race to prepare for the winter, as the Rosetani cured meat and made hard cheese that would last through the long months of barren cold. Folks had gathered their baskets and were scattered across the hills that morning, plucking the trees clean of what remained of the figs. Some would be sliced and eaten now; Nicky savored them, tossed in fresh greens with a bit of lemon juice and salt. A few bushels would be made into jam for each household, and the rest would be dried, cut into small wheels, and saved in cheesecloth bags, to be baked into pastry or layered with cured meat for a meal when the skies turned to snow.

There was a soft rap at the door. Nicky called out.

"*Finalmente.*" The ambassador stood in the doorway of Nicky's room, with a look that was both happy and sad, if there were such a thing.

"Will you walk the road today?" Nicky asked him, partly in words, partly in mime. *"Andiamo Spadone!"*

"Si." Carlo marched in place: *Every step*, he indicated.

Carlo Guardinfante and Nicky Castone had been thrown together under the strangest of circumstances, but they had an affinity for one another that neither of them could explain. Perhaps both men had secretly longed for a brother and when they met, they recognized one another. Whatever the case, their affection for one another had grown over these months, surprising them.

The Rosetani in Italy thought that their connection was mystical. *Gemelli!*—long-lost twins, reunited over a vast ocean. For the Italians it was a spiritual manifestation of God's hand on earth. On the American side, it was a con. Nicky had played a part, a vaudevillian type, and when the real guy showed up, so did the cops. It was hilarious until it wasn't. It's only a great story if you can get away with it, blow town before you're discovered. That's the American way.

To the two men, it was something more. Nicky's Italian hadn't improved, nor had Carlo's English, so they communicated as children do, mirroring behavior, checking for cues, and making each other laugh. They developed an empathy for one another that became their language. There was an undeniable solidarity when they walked together during *la passeggiata*; the Rosetani observed their bond with admiration. Loyalty, the deep river of sympathy whose currents flow on the understanding that one brother would give his life for the other, was the center of every Italian family. In that sense, Carlo and Nicky were brothers.

The ambassador was dressed for the trek to the bottom of the new road in work boots, a chamois shirt, and wool pants. Nicky grabbed the straw palmetto hat with the bandanna on the brim off the finial of the chair, motioning that he would follow Carlo out.

Below the piazza, down the mountain, at the entrance of the road to Roseto Valfortore, the band of American workers from Roseto, Pennsylvania, hurried to finish the job. They had worked side by side with the local men to build the road, and as they were in America, they were in Italy. Their skills and stations crossed the Atlantic. Therefore, Rocco Tutolola was the leader.

Rocco had been elected chief burgess in a landslide, and there was good reason. He had a natural way with his people, knowing what they needed (plumbing, parking, and roads), devising a plan, executing the work while encouraging them to use their talents to achieve the goal. He was a good man, but he had a wanderlust that could only be satisfied off hours by the attention of women at the Stone Crab Bar in East Stroudsburg, Pennsylvania. But after months away from Cha Cha, working in the sun, his hands in the dirt, laying stone, he made the decision to reinvigorate his commitment to his wife, which unleashed a passion in letters that he wrote and sent, which she read week after week as she hiked the steep hill of Garibaldi Avenue in tears. Up and down she went, working through her feelings while reading her husband's thoughts, described ardently in navy-blue ink on onionskin paper.

Rocco would return home to the sweet girl he married. Cha Cha's figure had returned to its former glory, along with her attitude, but now she had the benefit of experience under her tightened grommets, which gave her an edge. She knew how to make Rocco happy. His letters assured her that he was ready to do the same for her.

"Hey, Funzi!" Rocco hollered as he headed down to the bottom of the road. He had checked the gutters on either side of the road from the top to the bottom, installed to handle any flooding of the Fortore River in the future. These drainage channels had been time-consuming to put in, adding two months to their stay, but the Americans would leave knowing the road was secure.

Funzi stood up, wiped his hands on the bandanna in his pocket, and looked down at his handiwork. He motioned for Rocco to join him and showed his boss the flat curbing of the road. "What do you think? Not bad for a janitor."

Rocco looked down and smiled. "What do you think the ambassador will say?"

"What can he say? It's done."

Funzi had laid the stone at the entrance of the road and selected stones with hand-carved letters, set among the native fieldstone. R O S E T O P A was spelled out across the expanse of the entrance.

Rocco whistled up the hill for the remaining crew of eight Americans, who hiked down the new road to join them. The men looked up and saw Nicky and the ambassador approaching in the middle distance. Rocco grinned, happy at the completion of the mission, and pleased with the quality of work they had done. It was the Roseto way in Italy and America, one shared philosophy: Everybody gives a little, what they can—a little cash from Nicky Castone, some more from the proceeds of the Cadillac Dinner, the Italians pitch in their lire—and everyone lifts the stone, whatever weight they can carry, and soon the road is built.

"Good work, boys," Rocco marveled.

"Sometimes you got to roll up your sleeves." Funzi stood back and surveyed the road, which hugged the hillsides and laced through the curves and corners of the terrain like corset strings.

"You homesick?"

"I guess I am," Funzi admitted.

"But this is home, you know. This is where it all started," Rocco reminded him.

"It did, for my mother and father. And I imagine wherever they were when I was a boy was home to me, too. But give me Roseto, Pennsylvania, and my front porch on Chestnut Street. I miss my card game at the Marconi Social Club on Saturday nights. I like knowing my kids are in school getting smacked by the nuns and can walk home for lunch. I like Harry Truman and the Dodgers. We got the Jersey shore in the summers and the Poconos in the winter. What more can a man ask for?"

Italy, the motherland, was now a dreamscape for the men. Home was America now, but it was unlikely that the Rosetanis would forget the dream.

Nicky and Carlo joined them at the base of the mountain. They turned and looked up in awe, surveying the magnificence of the new road, a purple carpet of native stone that curved from the base of the mountain to the top like the royal sash of a king.

Instinctively Nicky removed his hat, and the ambassador removed his too, as though they were in church, as reverence was required.

The Americans had done everything they promised, making the road wider at the curves, leveling the base with alternating layers of gravel and sand so water might flow through when it rained, and capping the edges with modern gutters so the new road would not wash away should the Fortore River ever rage again.

But for Carlo, it was the artful diagonal pattern of the purple stones that thrilled him. What an entrance to the piazza! The beauty was Italian, the craftsmanship was American, and the combination would last until the end of time.

"What's the date today?" Nicky asked.

"October twenty-ninth."

"My wedding day."

"Congratulations," the men mumbled.

"*Dove è la tua bella sposa?*" Carlo asked.

"In Philly," Nicky told him.

"Why don't you go home and make nice. Beg her forgiveness," Rocco suggested.

"Or stay in Italy, remain a bachelor, and add twenty years to your life," Funzi cracked.

"It's going to be neither, boys," Nicky promised them.

Carlo's houseman drove a rustic flatbed truck down the new road.

"Climb aboard. We're going to eat and drink and celebrate," Nicky told the crew as they hoisted themselves onto the flatbed. "And then we're going home."

Carlo took a seat in the front cab with the driver. The Americans sat behind them, their legs dangling over the lip of the back of the flatbed, as the houseman made the turn to drive the truck up the mountain.

"Smooth ride," Funzi commented.

Nicky leaned back on his hands as the road under them became a long ribbon as they drove higher up the mountain. Every stone in the road, placed with the labor of their hands, had brought Nicky closer to his truth. He didn't belong in Italy, though he had an affinity for the people and the countryside. He didn't belong in Roseto, Pennsylvania, where he would be reminded of his folly, contrition, and penance, though without them, he would not be present in this moment. He couldn't return to the streets of South Philly, driving Car No. 4 and living on Montrose Street in the basement, as though all of this hadn't happened. He'd outgrown his boots. His old life belonged to the guy who wore Florsheims.

Nicky had decided that he was going to New York City to fulfill his dream of being an actor. He would live there and act on the stage, the only thing he had ever done that filled him up, thrilled him, challenged him, and scared him, which made him feel alive. Nicky had left all his regrets in the road to Roseto Valfortore; he had paid for his sins, as he hauled the sand, raked the gravel, and set the stone. Now he was ready to build a new road, the one that would lead to his new life.

Nicky stood in the basement kitchen of 810 Montrose Street, inhaling the scent of the fresh strands of vermicelli that hung like ropes as they dried on the wooden dowels. He would miss listening to the women of the house as they made the macaroni, and gossiped and laughed as they worked.

He would miss Aunt Jo as she sang along to the music on the *Philly in the Air* radio show. He hoped he would never forget the worktable where the fresh macaroni was made, and how Aunt Jo knew exactly how many handfuls of flour it took to make a small volcano, which Nicky would topple with a spoon. Once there was a well in the center of the flour, Aunt Jo would crack eggs into it and allow Nicky to mix the yolks and flour together until it created the paste that would become the dough that she would knead with her hands.

Under the window his mother remained in the past, in the light. There would be an aspect of her that glittered, a gold hoop earring, a pin on her dress, the shiny side of a barrette or a dime she gave him to put in his piggy bank. Nicky would be sad to leave this room behind because it was a sanctuary of memories. He closed the wooden door between the kitchen and his bedroom.

Nicky placed the last of his clothes in the suitcase. He hung his Western Union uniform and cap in the closet, in case his replacement needed it.

"Do you know where you're going?" Elsa asked.

"I got a place," Nicky lied.

"You're really going to leave us?" She sighed and sat on the edge of his bed.

Nicky would miss Elsa's soft voice and graceful movements. He had a favorite cousin-in-law. He knew it, and so did she.

"Elsa, I think it's time. The family needs the space, and I need to move on."

Mabel and Lena entered the room together.

"What's this about you moving out?" Lena asked.

"I was just teasing you about the room," Mabel said. "We have plenty of space upstairs."

"It's time for me to grow up and find my way on my own. I want to be an actor and audition for all kinds of plays, so I have to go to New York."

"You never have to leave this house." Aunt Jo brought Nicky a stack of pressed handkerchiefs and put them in his suitcase.

"I know, Aunt Jo, and I appreciate that. If I could pack you all up and take you with me, I would."

"My brother lived with my mother until the day he died," Aunt Jo said, twisting the hem of her apron.

"Ma, that's a bad example." Dominic came in the room carrying his son, who he handed to Elsa. He took a seat in the rocking chair. "Uncle Jimmy fell off the roof and landed on his head when he was fifteen. He was never right after that. He *couldn't* leave the house. You can't compare him and Nicky."

"It was an example of someone who never left, that's all I was saying," Aunt Jo retorted.

"No offense taken," Nicky assured her. "To me or Uncle Jimmy."

Gio edged into the crowded room. "When you come back to us, and you will, don't bring home a fancy New York girl."

"Please don't!" Mabel pined. "They're fast."

"Why would I do that? Only Philly girls, Jersey girls, or Polish girls," Nicky promised. "Let us not forget the Irish. Nothing like an Irish lass."

"Nothing wrong with a New York girl. I have cousins in Brooklyn," Lena said defensively.

"Don't get your feelings hurt—they don't mean your particular cousins." Nino sat next to his wife on the bed. "Your family is a gallery of saints."

"I couldn't figure out where the hell everybody went," Uncle Dom said, ambling into Nicky's room, his bad knee crackling softly. Dominic Jr. got up from the rocking chair and offered it to his father, who took a seat.

"That's because you never come down to the basement. This is where we make the homemades, Pop. And can the tomatoes. And ferment the peaches in wine." Mabel sniffed.

"I know where the work is done in this house."

"Do you know who does it?" Aunt Jo joked.

"Yes, Joanna, as matter of fact, I do."

"You could show your appreciation once in a while."

"What do you want? I bust my coolie for you."

"Here we go," Gio said under his breath.

"You have the best equipment. The best appliances." Dom flailed his arms.

"They don't do the work, Dominic."

"I run a good business to keep your sons and their families close."

"True."

"I put the Western Union in for you."

"What kind of a present is that?"

"I'd rather have jewelry," Mabel barked. The girls laughed.

"No, it was the best gift my husband ever gave me. I never wanted that man to walk up to the front door and tell me I had lost a son in the war. Western Union went in, and it was good luck. You all came home." Jo kissed Dom on his head.

"We did." Gio thought about the odds.

"I live for you, Jo. Look at me. A prize. A joy to live with. I make love to you like we're on our honeymoon."

Their sons moaned in disgust. Mabel looked off into the distance, repulsed; Lena looked at her nails, while Elsa shook her head.

"That, too, is true," Aunt Jo admitted.

"I'm happy for you, Uncle Dom, and Aunt Jo, my deepest sympathy." Nicky placed his wallet in his pocket.

"But with all you've done for me, you couldn't keep Nicky here."

"I tried," Dom said.

"He did. Offered me all the airport runs I could do. Very tempting." Nicky snapped his suitcase shut.

"How can you leave us, Nick?" Nino said. "We have such a good time."

"I'll visit. New York is close. When I get my first play, I hope you'll come and see it."

"You let me know date, time, place, I'll alert the AFL-CIO in the city, and we'll pack the house."

"Thanks, Uncle Dom."

"If there's ever anything we can do for you, will you let us know?" Elsa's voice broke. From the moment she arrived at 810 Montrose, Nicky had made her feel a part of things. Elsa would miss him most of all.

"There is something you can do for me."

"Of course," Elsa agreed.

"You're such a good sport. You go to mass every Sunday, and you hand out the doughnuts afterward. You press the altar linens for the church and the vestments for the priest and make the crowns for the May Day celebration."

"She does a lovely job with the altar flowers," Aunt Jo said appreciatively.

"People probably think you're Catholic," Nicky said.

Elsa blushed.

"But what about you and your traditions and the things you did growing up?"

"Elsa enjoys our holidays. Don't you?" Mabel asked.

Elsa nodded.

"What's your point, Nick?" Dominic asked impatiently.

"Elsa, I guess what I'm saying is, everything you are, and everything that you come from, is just as important as who we are and what we come from. It matters just as much. I lost my parents, and Uncle Dom and Aunt Jo took me in. My cousins are like brothers. And whatever I wanted to do, I didn't do because I wanted to do it, but because I needed to fit in and please the good people who were kind enough to let me stay. I was so grateful to them for taking me in that I didn't think about what I wanted. And I was so in awe of Dominic and Gio and Nino that I wanted to be just like them, so I buried my true heart. But it turns out that even when you try to hide what you are, it finds a way out. And that gets tricky, because when you've buried the truth, when it's revealed it can hurt some people you care about. So forgive me for that. But not for admitting it. I've realized there's no reason to hide; it makes you what you are, and that's what we love about you. You can be yourself here. That's what it means to be in a family. You're safe. So before I go, I just want to say, let everyone know who you are. You deserve that. Be a Jew."

"Elsa *is* a Jew. Dominic brought her from the camp," Aunt Jo said softly.

"Don't say camp, Aunt Jo," Nicky corrected her. "Can't you see it hurts her?"

Aunt Jo turned to Elsa. "It hurts you?"

"When you say it as though it is the place that I come from, yes, it hurts me. I am not from the camp. I am from Lanckorona in the south of Poland, south of Kraków."

"The big city," Mabel commented.

"Our town was small. My father was a teacher. His name was Ben. We lived at Fifteen Gris Street in a house the color of gingerbread, with pale green trim. We had a stream in our front yard and four pear trees."

"It sounds like a picture in a book," Lena said.

"It was. I had two sisters, Ada and Edith. Ada was the beauty, and Edith was funny. My mother's name was Anna. She taught violin. I never tried it because a poor student will make you hate the sound of it. I had a life of privilege, and it changed over time, slowly, like a leak in the roof that goes unattended—soon it destroys one room, and in time, the entire house. Small changes, little shifts, so insignificant as not to cause alarm, happen, and you ignore them because they don't seem important. There were very few of us in Lanckorona—we went to Brody for holy days, because the synagogue was there. At home, we kept Shabbat and our prayers and our traditions. My father would receive letters from the state, and he would abide by whatever he was asked to do— again, no urgency. He continued to teach, and he didn't notice anything odd at the school until one day he was dismissed from his position of twenty-seven years without any cause. Suddenly we didn't receive our mail, we had to go to the post to collect it. My mother had ordered certain foods for our holiday table, and one day the butcher wouldn't sell her the meat and the baker refused to make our bread. We believed we had done something wrong, or offended our friends. We didn't know it was happening every-where. Or maybe we suspected it, but we couldn't believe it."

Mabel reached out to her. "What happened to your family?"

"We were separated in Dachau. My only prayer was that they stay together. Dominic found out what happened to them."

"They were together," Dominic said quietly.

"Dominic found me in the work camp."

"Elsa was the only person in her family that was spared."

"I feel sorry for you," Elsa said to her husband.

"Why?"

"You should have married a nice American girl. A nice Philly girl. You found a hopeless girl when you deserve a happy one."

"I didn't want a girl from the neighborhood. I wanted you. What difference would it have made if we met in Atlantic City on the boardwalk or if I found you holding a dance card wearing a flower in your hair at the Knights of Columbus dance?"

"Highly unlikely. No Jewish girls go to that dance," Uncle Dom said.

"Okay, wherever it would have been, under whatever circum-stances, I would have fallen in love with you. You're my wife. You're the mother of my son."

"I want to go to temple," Elsa said quietly.

The room was quiet, and now it was also hot. Nino reached up to open the levered windows.

"All right. I'll go with you. And we'll bring the baby," Dominic promised.

The room was silent except for the sound of the creak of the rocking chair as Uncle Dom rocked to and fro. After a while Aunt Jo spoke.

"What about Christmas?"

"What about it, Ma?"

"It means family."

"So do Elsa's holidays, Aunt Jo."

"You can't be both things. You can't be a Catholic and a Jew. You have to pick, and you can't confuse the boy." Uncle Dom hit the arm of the rocker for emphasis.

"Aunt Jo is devout. Uncle Dom, you never go to church. Your boys didn't have to pick between being Catholic and whatever it is you are. Why should your grandson?" Nicky asked.

"Why can't he be both?" Lena proposed.

"When Catholics marry outside the church, they are banished. I have a cousin in Rochester who married a divorced Presbyterian, and she might as well be on a chain gang," Mabel said, worried.

"After what Elsa has been through, I think she has a choice," Nicky said.

"It'll be a year-long extravaganza of holidays over here," Uncle Dom groused.

"So what? Now you have the extra room to roll the kreplach." Nicky smiled. "This one."

"What will Father Mariani say?" Mabel wondered. "He can be a stickler and a pill. He wouldn't let my cousin Noogie Finelli get married in a sheer sleeve, said it was too revealing. Said it would offend Jesus. What's he going to say about two religions in one house?"

"Dom and I will pay him a visit with the grappa. And we'll explain the situation. He'll agree to our . . . situation—"

"New tradition," Nicky interjected.

"And if he doesn't, Daddy will build him a new rectory. Right, Dom?"

"It all comes down to the plate. Never forget it. It all comes down to the plate. You give to Mother Rome, and she sticks it to you," Uncle Dom assured them.

"Now that you've made it clear how we earn our eternal salvation, I think I'll sign up for novena," Mabel said.

"You do that. And pray for me. Because I pray for you. I may not go to church, but it's in here." Dom thumped his chest.

"I should get going, so you can fight over who gets my room. And besides, if I don't get out of here, somebody will have another baby, and there will be no end to the good-byes." Nicky embraced each of his cousins. Mabel, who everyone believed was made of something stronger than Bethlehem steel, found herself weeping uncontrollably. Gio held his wife.

"Thank you," Elsa whispered in Nicky's ear.

"They took it well."

"How did you know?"

"You had the key all along."

"I did?" Elsa's eyes widened.

Nicky looked at his Uncle Dom, holding his first grandson, baby Dom, as Dominic fussed over him. "A little Italian tip for the Polish girl. The mother of the prince is always a queen."

Nicky embraced Elsa. He picked up his suitcase.

Aunt Jo called out, "Wait. We have a present for you."

Gio emerged from the basement kitchen, holding a large box with a bow on it. Nicky's cousins burst into applause as he opened the gift. Nicky lifted the lid off a box of a full set of dishes, service for twelve, white ceramic with a daisy-chain pattern on the edge.

"You were supposed to get them at your wedding shower," Mabel blurted. "But that went south."

"Thank you, Aunt Jo."

"Don't thank her. Thank the First National Bank of Philadelphia."

Nicky climbed the stairs with his dishes and his suitcase. The cousins followed behind him, single file, until they made it upstairs to the kitchen and into the light.

"You know? His room ain't half bad," Uncle Dom said to Aunt Jo on the stairs. "We could rent it out."

"Don't get any ideas."

"It could be a honeymoon suite." Dom pinched his wife's behind.

"On the other hand, we could rent it out," Jo decided.

The family followed Nicky through the dining room on his way to the front door. Nicky knelt next to Nonna's chair in the dining room. She was napping under the afghan. "Nonna? It's Nicky."

Nonna opened her eyes.

"I'm moving out. I'm going to start a new life. I'm going to New York City to be an actor."

"Be good and don't take any shit off of anybody," Nonna said, then went back to sleep.

"The wisdom of the ages," Uncle Dom said, "that goes for all of you."

Nicky carried the box of dishes on his right shoulder and the suitcase on his left, balancing the load, as he descended the porch steps onto Montrose Street, where Hortense was waiting for him on the sidewalk.

"I see. You were going to sneak off."

"No, I was going to stop by."

"No, you weren't. You left your keys on the hook in the office."

"I was going to sneak off," Nicky said sheepishly.

"You don't like me to get upset. Guess what. Neither do I."

"I don't know where I'm going, and I couldn't face a round of questions."

"You're going to go to New York City, you're going to make friends, and you're going to find something to do that makes you happy."

"That would be nice."

"You have to."

"I do?"

"Because you blew up everything in Philly, and we had to leave Roseto in a bail jump, and you're running out of options. There's only so much of the East Coast left for you to torch, so you have to make something of yourself in New York City."

"I feel worse."

"Don't. I believe in you, Mr. Castone. I know you are capable of great things."

"I bet you say that to all the hacks that leave the garage."

"No one's ever left before."

"Must be a good company."

"It was. There was a time when it was the best. Now, like everything else that ever once was new, it's on its way out. That's just life. That's just the world. That's just the way it goes."

"Come see me in Manhattan."

"Oh yes."

"I mean it."

"I know you do."

Nino pulled up in Car No. 3. "Let's go, cousin."

Nicky put the box and his suitcase in the trunk of the cab. He got into the front seat next to Nino.

"Be careful," Hortense said to both of them. "The traffic around the train station is always a little squirrely."

"I know, Mrs. Mooney." Nino pulled out into the street.

Nicky looked back at Hortense. She was still standing on the sidewalk, watching them drive away, when Nino made the turn onto Ninth Street.

⁓

"Nino, can we swing by Broad Street? I need to make a quick stop at Borelli's."

"Sure."

"Take that turn there in the alley." Nicky got out of the cab, the russet leaves crunching under his feet. He climbed the steps to the stage door. The bare lilac branches twisted over the door, as gray as the drainpipe. Nicky thought the place looked shabby, and it made him sad.

Inside, the set crew was painting a series of flats lined up on the stage wall. Nicky looked around until he found Calla, sitting cross-legged on the prop table, looking at her prompt book. A pang of regret pierced his heart when he saw her.

"I'm sorry I haven't been over since I got back from Italy."

Calla looked up from her work. At first she was happy to see him, but then her mood changed. "I know you're busy. We're all busy. I hear you're moving to New York City."

"Yeah."

"When?"

He looked at his watch. "The four-ten train."

"You're a piece of work, Nicky Castone. Were you going to tell me?"

"This is it. I've stopped in to say good-bye."

"Good-bye, Nicky." She looked down at her reading.

"Give my best to Frank," he said.

Calla put the prompt book down and looked at him. "You're on your own with that."

"What do you mean?"

"I broke up with him months ago. When you were in Italy."

"You were going to marry him."

"He tried to sell the theater out from under me. He wanted to tear it down and build apartments."

"I'm sorry." Nicky suddenly felt helpless. And trapped. And oddly responsible.

Calla could read his feelings in his body language. "I got through it."

"Why would he do that?"

"Why would anyone do anything unkind to someone they supposedly cared about?"

"I don't know."

"If you find the answer to that one, please let me know. I can't find it in any of the Shakespeare folios. And I've looked."

Nicky felt terrible. "Calla, I—" His voice broke.

Calla could hear the wind-up of excuses about to roll, so she put her hand up in the air to stop him before he humiliated himself and infuriated her.

"This is the worst audition for loyal friend that I've ever seen. Save it for the New York casting directors. They're more likely to buy your line of bull." Calla put her head down and went back to her reading.

Nicky was incensed. He was probably going to miss his train after doing the right thing and stopping to say good-bye to an old friend. He crossed the stage to walk out the door. He heard Nino tapping on the car horn outside. He looked at his watch. He was late. But he was more furious than he was anxious about missing his train. Now he didn't care if he missed the train and had to walk to New York City with those dishes on his back. How dare she? He turned around, went back to the prop table, took Calla's prompt book out of her hands, and threw it on the floor. He was going to tell her off for good, but he looked at her, and her eyes were glassy, probably from autumn pollen, who knew? But her mouth was set like an empress about to call out the executioner. He was angry that she was the best girl he'd known and had the nerve to hold him accountable for his behavior. He swept her up off the table, into his arms, and kissed her.

Calla's feet were off the ground; she was flying in his arms. But when he gently placed her back on earth, she came back to her senses. The kiss was delicious, but she hated him. He hadn't written her a single letter, sent a postcard or a telegram, or called her since he returned from Italy. He'd pulled a disappearing act, like the rabbit in the black felt hat in the magician's kit she played with as a child. He had toyed with her. All the hurt she carried and stuffed down rose within her, and the abandonment she felt pained her anew.

Nicky could see the hurt he caused, but he justified it. He hadn't known Calla's situation with big Frank, and since when was he responsible for her? Maybe there wasn't an excuse—certainly not one that could make up for being a lousy friend to someone who had been a good one to him. The only thing he could think of was that he couldn't let her or anyone stand in the way of the life that lay ahead. She seemed like a walking conundrum, with her struggling theater and her box of grief that she carried around, reminding him of his own. He didn't want to be reminded of the pain anymore. He wanted everything in his life to be easy! New! Uncomplicated for a change. He wanted to start over fresh, to reimagine his dreams and create a new life. That was his right. He didn't want to be anchored to a girl who hung on to an old building and scrubbed the toilets because she couldn't afford the janitor. He wanted more for himself than *that* struggle. The decision he had made was not an easy one. It took guts to leave Montrose Street, but instead of giving him credit for being courageous, she whined about some letters she had been sitting around waiting for. Calla Borelli was small-time. Nicky Castone turned and walked out the stage door, vowing to never look back.

Calla watched him go, her pride freezing her in place. She didn't call or run after him; she watched him go out the stage door and let him, knowing she deserved better than a hack who thought he'd move to New York, and the world of theater would bow down and take him, as though his talent would save them from film and television and whatever else the mad inventors threw in the path of quality. Even the thought of never seeing him again couldn't make her run after him. Nicky Castone was cleaning out and clearing out—but what he couldn't know was that Calla had beaten him to the punch.

Hortense climbed the steps up to the office. She sat down at her desk and looked out the window into the garage. Car No. 4 sitting empty in its parking spot was a sad sight.

The board on her desk lit up. She picked up the phone.

"Palazzini Cab Company. May I be of service?" she said in her honeyed tone.

"This is Father Leone of Our Lady of Mount Carmel in Roseto, Pennsylvania. I am looking for Mrs. Hortense Mooney."

"This is she. What can I do for you, Father?"

"I'm calling with sad news."

"Don't say it, Father."

"I'm sorry, Mrs. Mooney. Mrs. Viglione has died."

"Oh no. Poor Minna."

"Very peacefully, though. In her own bed. I was called over to give last rites yesterday afternoon, and she was ready."

"Thank you Jesus."

"Yes, thank God. Minna asked me to call you."

"She did?" Hortense reached into her pocket for her handkerchief, which wasn't there, so she wiped her tears away with her hand.

"Yes, and she said that you would understand this message."

"Yes, Father?"

"The message is: one half a teaspoon of nutmeg."

"Nutmeg?"

"Nutmeg. One half a teaspoon."

"Are you certain, Father?"

"Absolutely. Minna made me repeat it, and she made me write it down."

"Well, then, that's what she means."

Hortense hung up the phone. She straightened the string of Venetian beads around her neck. She had made a habit of wearing Minna's gift to her to work every day. The beads were cool to the touch, shaped like pulled taffy candy, in colors that suited Hortense, strung in a length that didn't interfere with the telegraph machine. The beads served a purpose besides adornment; they were like a string tied on her finger to remind her to push harder and stay focused on the dream. With Minna gone, it would be up to Hortense to define the terms of that dream and reach for it.

A ray of light in the corner of Hortense's soul dimmed at the loss of Minna. Hortense's friend would not be here to encourage her on the journey. Hortense was alone now. She had to make her way as best she could on the merit of her own skills, without her mentor. It felt an awful lot like her first day at Cheyney College. This time, Hortense vowed the process wouldn't take her five years. This go-round, she no longer had the luxury of time, the innocence of youth, and the energy to suffer fools and their silly obstructions to her goal. This time around, Hortense had her wits and the gift that comes with age: patience. She figured a lifetime of experience was as good an ingredient to add to the gravy as Minna's secret nutmeg, though that, too, going forward, would make it into every pot.

Mamie Confalone led the ladies from the Our Lady of Mount Carmel sodality down Garibaldi Avenue to Minna Viglione's house to provide the sympathy dinner for the grieving family.

Mamie had a white damask tablecloth tied around her waist in a giant bow. Inside the pouch of the cloth she carried the dishes and cutlery. Following behind, the ladies carried the components of the meal, in various pots, pans, and covered ceramic dishes. As they turned onto Minna's sidewalk, they were met by her son and daughter-in-law.

"Thank you, Mrs. Confalone."

"It's our honor to make dinner for you, Mr. Viglione, and for your family."

Minna's daughter-in-law thanked Mamie and the ladies and offered her help, which they refused. The ladies followed Mamie into the house and back to the kitchen, where they fanned out and took over every surface to serve the meal. Mamie went into the dining room, untied the bow around her waist, and placed the dishes and utensils on the server. She laid the tablecloth neatly on the dining room table and began to set the table for twelve.

"Need a hand?" Eddie Davanzo came into the room with a small arrangement of red roses for the center of the table. "Marie Poidomani said to place this vase dead center."

"Always follow Marie's instructions."

Eddie placed the flowers on the table. "I wanted to ask you a favor."

"Sure."

"Could you teach me to speak Italian?"

"There's a class at Northampton Community College."

"I didn't do too well in school. I'm better one-on-one."

Eddie's flirtation caused Mamie to put the soup spoon in the wrong spot on the place setting. Eddie reached over and put it in the correct spot. "What do you say?"

"I'll think about it." Mamie turned away so Eddie wouldn't see her blush, but he caught her reflection in the dining room mirror over the server. When she looked up, her eyes met his. "Don't you have a beat to walk?"

"I'm on my break."

"How lucky for me."

"I'd say so."

Marie Cascario, a lean blonde, stood in the doorway with a tray of glassware observing the pair. "Am I interrupting something?"

"No, no," Eddie and Mamie chimed in unison.

"It sure looks like it. And it's about time."

"I'll take those." Eddie took the tray from her.

"Good. Because I'm boiling penne in there." Marie turned to go, but not without taking one last look at Mamie and Eddie, and shaking her head.

"Minna thought you'd be a nice boyfriend for me," Mamie said as she placed the napkins.

"What do you think?"

"I like the idea of a man who can fix a furnace. I almost blew up Chestnut Street last winter when I lit the pilot light."

"So, you need a man around to fix things?"

"Doesn't everyone?"

"I can give you the number for the plumber."

"Thanks."

"Do you ever think about me?" Eddie asked as he set the wine glasses on the table.

"As much as you think about me."

"Then you're giving me some serious thought, Mamie. I'd like to take you and Augie to the Saint Rocco Feast."

"We'd like that."

The ladies of the sodality gathered in the doorway. "We're ready to serve the meal, you know that's why we came here." Marie Cascario stood with her arms folded. "The girls have everything ready."

"Great. Call the family in."

"Are we doing this with a butler this time?" Marie crooked her head to indicate Eddie.

"No, I'm on my way, ladies." Eddie waved on his way out.

"Just checking," Marie said, annoyed.

Eddie left the dining room and went out the kitchen door through the garden.

"I think he's the most handsome man I ever saw," Grace Delgrosso said longingly. She was seventy-seven years old and still had the muscle tone in her thighs to pump the pipe organ at Our Lady of Mount Carmel. "If I was twenty-five again, I'd set my cap for him."

"You would?" Mamie smiled.

"I'd take him on a hayride that would never end."

As the Viglione family filed into the dining room, the ladies served them their sympathy dinner. The tradition of the sympathy dinner, which their mothers had brought from Roseto Valfortore, was one that made them feel useful in times of loss. They remained in the kitchen as the family ate their meal, taking turns serving the guests. After dessert and coffee, the women lined up in the kitchen, as the family came through to thank them for preparing the feast.

Then, without fanfare, the ladies packed up the pots, pans, and ceramic dishes to take them home. The glasses were placed back in the basket unwashed. The dishes at the table were stacked, the silverware rolled inside a cloth napkin. Mamie set the centerpiece of roses aside and took the damask tablecloth, tied it around her waist, and knotted it with a large white bow. The ladies helped her load the pouch with the dishes and cutlery.

Marie Cascario placed the fresh roses in the center of the empty dining room table and turned off the chandelier.

They picked up their empty pans and formed a line, as they had when they entered the house. Led by Mamie, they left Minna's home and, faithful to their tradition, did not disturb the household by washing the dishes before leaving; they carried them away so the family might rest before the funeral the next morning. There was not a crumb, a splash of gravy, or a lone olive on the kitchen counter. They left the house as they had found it: tidy and clean. They left it as Minna would have liked, in honor of her, in her memory.

ACT III

Can we outrun the heavens?

—*Henry VI, Part 2*

10

There wasn't a star to be seen over Queens as night fell. The sky was peppered with charcoal-colored clouds as Nicky Castone drove his cab onto the lot of the Woodside Taxi Company to park after his shift. The air had the scent of an oncoming snowfall. Nicky flicked his cigarette out the open window before rolling it up. He grabbed the fare envelope filled with cash and got out of the car.

Strands of red, green, and navy-blue Roma Christmas lights swung haphazardly over the fleet of bright yellow cabs as he dropped the keys into the can outside the dispatcher's hut. He slipped the envelope of cash through the deposit slot of the entrance door, which was crisscrossed with silver tinsel. Nobody ever accused hacks and grease jockeys of having an eye for holiday decorating, and if they saw the hut, they still wouldn't.

Nicky waved to the attendant inside on his way off the lot. He pulled on his gloves as he passed the familiar storefronts on his way to the train station. The shop windows were fogged from a combination of steam heat and holiday crowds clustered inside at the cash registers. Bells jingled on the doors as customers exited with their packages. Christmas music poured out of speakers attached to the roof of the toy store. Only the rumble of the subway train on the elevated tracks overhead, its wheels heavy with a cargo of standing-room-only passengers, interrupted the Christmas din.

A flurry of snowflakes began to swirl around Nicky as he trudged up the steps to catch the train back into Manhattan. He groaned at the possibility of a white Christmas. The Woodside mechanics had already installed chains on the cab tires, so no matter what happened weatherwise, he was set.

Nicky squeezed on to the hot, crowded train car and grabbed the pole as it pulled out of the Woodside station and jerked onto the tracks over the expressway. He looked out the window and took in Manhattan's skyline, which looked like a stack of blue velvet jewelry boxes sprinkled with pearl dust. Snow or not, the twinkling city at nightfall always gave him a lift and filled him with a sense of his own potential, even though his big dreams had not panned out as he had hoped.

When Nicky got off the train, he was in no hurry, so he stepped aside and allowed the rush-hour throng to flow past him like the rushing waters of a mighty river. He imagined their lives, husbands on their way home from work, stopping for milk before dashing home to their wives and apartments filled with children. The guys at the cab company reminded him he was lucky to be free, but Nicky knew luck had nothing to do with it.

Nicky stopped at the deli on the corner of Thirty-Fourth Street and Third Avenue and bought a turkey sandwich on a roll with two dill pickles on the side, one serving of rice pudding, and a cup of hot coffee. As he walked home, the pockets of his trousers were heavy with quarters, his own version of Christmas jingle. Holiday shoppers were always good for tips. There was probably fifteen bucks' worth of coins that day, two shifts straight on the streets of Manhattan. He had earned every dime; this hack was beat.

Nicky went down the steps to his building and pushed through the common door. He stopped at his mailbox and flipped the brass plate. Finding his box full of envelopes, he stuffed the mail into his coat pocket before heading downstairs to his basement apartment.

"Surprise!" His neighbors, the Silverbergs, a young married couple who lived on the second floor, and the bachelor Ralph Stampone, a handsome bon vivant who lived on the first, stood next to Nicky's dining table, decorated with a birthday cake and a bottle of wine alongside paper cups, plates, and napkins printed with balloons and stars.

"What would I do without my neighbors?" Nicky gave Mary Silverberg a kiss on the cheek and shook Mark's hand and then Ralph's. "I'd be a forgotten man."

Nicky placed the sack from the deli in the refrigerator. The studio apartment was painted almond white, the same color used in the garbage room of the building, but a shade warmer than the odd pale green used on the walls in the hallways. There was a table with four chairs near the efficiency kitchen. A twin bed was made neatly under the only window in the apartment, which had a view of the sidewalk. As he lay in bed, Nicky could see people's feet as they walked by. He had almost become an expert in guessing the whole of passersby based upon their footwear and gait. All the art was outside the window, as there were no paintings or photographs on display in the apartment, no hi-fi or record collection either. However, there were books from the Twenty-Eighth Street branch of the New York Public Library. Lots of them.

Nicky flipped on the radio to underscore the surprise party. "I'm glad you let yourselves in, and made yourselves at home."

"You really should lock your door," Ralph said, looking around, "though there's nothing in here to steal."

"This is a bachelor apartment," Mary reminded him. "Very few frills."

"It's a prison cell. I'm a bachelor, and I have furniture. A sofa. Sconces. And lamps with shades." Ralph eyed the studio, imagining what he could do to make it presentable. "It doesn't take much to make a cinder-block room a home."

"I'll get to it someday," Nicky promised. "Or you will."

"That's right. You're a decorator," Mark reminded Ralph, not that he had to. "To you, every room is a blank canvas. Including a prison cell."

"Hey, hey, hey," Nicky teased Mark defensively.

"You know what I meant." Mark chuckled.

"In the world there are those who make beauty and those who appreciate it. You see a lowly medicine cabinet, and I see the hall of mirrors at Versailles. It's all about the imagination," Ralph mused.

Nicky clapped his hands. "Let's have cake."

"Have you had dinner?" Ralph felt badly he hadn't made a dip and brought crackers. He looked at Mary, who made a face.

"I've got a sandwich."

"How were the streets today?" Mark uncorked the wine.

Nicky emptied his pockets into his can of change. "Passengers were generous. Stop lights were long. Green lights were brief. And I squeezed my share of lemons."

"There's a color scheme for you."

"Those are the last three colors I want to see when I come home," Nicky assured Mark.

"Why don't you get another job?" Ralph suggested. "You're a capable person."

"I know how to drive."

"So do I, but I don't do it for money."

"Maybe he likes to drive," Mary defended Nicky gently.

"It's a terrible job," Ralph insisted. "Surly people. Crowds. Traffic jams. I don't know how you don't go crazy."

"My mind is elsewhere."

"Daydreaming." Mary cut the cake.

"A great philosopher, I don't know who, or maybe it was a playwright, I don't know who he was either—"

"Mark, this may be the worst windup to a birthday toast I have ever heard."

"Sorry, honey, I can't remember—anyway, whoever it was, he said that in your daydreams you will find your purpose." Mark poured wine into paper cups.

"If that's true, I should be in a hut in Honolulu, sipping a Singapore Sling and eating wild boar off the bone roasted on a spit on the beach," Ralph joked.

Tropical drinks made Nicky think of Peachy DePino, which managed to make him feel even worse on his birthday.

"How old are you, Nick?" Mary handed him a piece of cake.

Ralph took a bite of his slice. "Must we go into the gory details?"

"I didn't ask you, I asked him."

"I am thirty-two years old."

"You've still got lots of time," Mary assured him.

"For what?" Nicky wanted to know.

"To hit it big." Mary toasted him.

"Oh yeah. That's why I'm here." Nicky toasted his friends. "And that's why you're here: to remind me why I'm here." The tap of the paper cups sounded as hollow as his birthday wish, so this year, Nicky wouldn't make one.

Nicky lay in bed, smoking a cigarette. Across the room, on the kitchen table, his birthday cake had been reduced to pink rubble on the gold cardboard doily. The scrape of the snow shovel on the sidewalk outside was getting on his nerves as the super pushed it back and forth in front of his window. Nicky could see Mr. Guarnieri's pajama pants peeking out over his galoshes where his coveralls fell short of the top of the boots. It gave Nicky no comfort that somebody in the world actually had a worse job than he did.

Nicky figured he was destined to live underground for the rest of his life. He had lived in the basement on Montrose Street, and here he was again, subterranean, like a rusty pipe. The same was true of his career as a hack. Evidently he had a hard time breaking with tradition. He knew the streets of Manhattan and its five boroughs as well as he knew the grid of Philadelphia. Nicky Castone's map of the world was anyplace he could take a fare on a meter.

Nicky had propped his birthday cards on the windowsill, just as he had done in his room in South Philly. He reached up and pulled the two cards off the ledge. A large one, with a felt yellow, black, and white bumblebee on the front, read *Cousin, You are the Bee's Knees* and opened to say *Have the sweetest birthday!* It was signed by every member of the family residing at 810 Montrose, including Dominic III, who had written *Hi* in black crayon. Nicky set it aside and picked up the other card, which had a foil cake on the front with a message in blue glitter: *You Are Special.* Inside, the poem read:

> *You are special*
> *Don't forget it*
> *Here's your cake*
> *Come and get it!*

It was signed: *Happy Birthday, Nicky. We miss you around here. Mrs. Mooney.*

Nicky didn't pine for his old life, because after three years in New York, he was living the same life he had been living in South Philly, except in this incarnation, he was isolated, without a family, a fiancée, a night job at Borelli's, or his old friendships to sustain him. When he was brutally honest with himself, he admitted that he had only lost ground in his move to New York City.

What Nicky *did* have was a routine. He went to work, drove a cab, returned home, and counted his tips. If he saw a pretty girl on the street, he might smile at her, but wouldn't pursue it beyond the pleasantry. He couldn't remember the last time a woman had turned his head. He thought about calling Mamie Confalone, but he had nothing to offer her. When he went deep blue in his mood, and loneliness gnawed at him with a toothless hunger, he considered moving to another place entirely or even returning to South Philly. He imagined what it would be like to get an apartment near Montrose Street and look into the windows of 810 instead of out of them. That didn't sit well with him either, so he stayed put.

Tomorrow, he'd make a change. Nicky wouldn't wait for the new year (1953!) to start over, like every other crumb bum in the world— no, he would beat the crowd and start over fresh in the morning, resolute to crawl out of this hole and find the light. With a glimmer of hope, he put out the cigarette, threw his legs over the side of the bed, and went to the bathroom to brush his teeth. He leaned over the sink, looked in the mirror, and thought, *Everything must change.*

Calla sat in the costume shop, trying to decide if she should call Nicky Castone on his birthday. It had been ages since he'd left in a huff after kissing her good-bye without asking for her permission. She hadn't seen him since. But she had seen Jo Palazzini at novena, and Jo had told her that Nicky was going through a rough time, which made Calla think about her old friend. If Calla Borelli was anything, she was loyal.

In between the arduous tasks of sewing beads onto the bodice of Norma's gown and stitching the hem, she would stick the needle into the tomato pincushion, pick up the phone, place it on the worktable, and spin the dial without picking up the receiver to make the call. Buying time, she poked her finger into the hole of number 1 and spun it, and then 2, worked her way down to 0, which purred around the entire dial until it clicked to a stop. After an evening of vacillating, it was time to go home. Calla picked up the telephone to return it to the desk, looked at the clock, and realized very little time was left of Nicky's birthday. If she was going to call him, the moment was now. She closed her eyes and imagined him out on the town, in a crowded bar, surrounded by fellow actors, the air filled with smoke and music. Nicky was being toasted and celebrated. The realization that Nicky wouldn't be home to pick up the phone made her dial the number. Her Catholic conscience would be assuaged in the morning knowing she had made the effort. Calla dialed Nicky's number, which Jo Palazzini had scrawled on the back of the church bulletin.

The phone rang in Nicky's apartment. She was stunned when he answered.

"Happy birthday, Nick."

"Who is this?"

Calla's heart sank: he hadn't recognized her voice. So, she spoke deliberately and loudly. "It's Calla. Calla Borelli from South Philly."

Nicky sat down at his kitchen table. "You're kidding."

"Nope. It's me."

"You remembered?"

"I ran into your aunt. She gave me your number. I hope that's okay." Calla's face flushed. Maybe he wasn't alone. This call was a colossal mistake.

"Sure, sure." Nicky pressed the receiver to his ear so he wouldn't miss anything she said. "How are you?"

"I'm doing just fine. Is this a bad time?"

"No."

"Good. Well, I won't keep you," she said.

"I've got some time. How's the theater?"

"Very busy."

"What play are you doing?"

"*A Winter's Tale.*"

"Good one."

"For this time of year. I'm putting snowflake-shaped sequins on Norma's gown."

"She'll sparkle."

"Always does. How about you? How are you doing?"

"I love this city." Nicky picked up a plastic party knife, lifted a section of the frosting border off what was left of his birthday cake, and spackled it to the cardboard plate. "So much to do. I'm hardly home."

"Do you see a lot of plays?"

"I try. On my end, I'm still trying to break in. So much acting work here. Union work. It's all good, all promising."

"Do you get back to Philly much?" Calla hadn't asked Jo Palazzini about Nicky's visits. She didn't want to know. He hadn't been back to the theater to see his old friends or take in one of their productions. She assumed he had outgrown Borelli's and his old friends, especially her. "I know you're busy."

"I haven't been home." Nicky hadn't been back to Philadelphia to visit since he moved to New York City. He'd vowed he wouldn't return until he had gotten a part in a play. "My cousins came up here to see me. That was nice. We went to Lüchow's."

"I've heard of it," Calla said.

"It's an institution. I don't have time to leave the city, really. Got my eye on a couple of agents."

"That's terrific." Calla remembered when her father signed with an agent. Nothing much had come of it, but Sam had high hopes at the time. "You need a representative."

"Yeah. And I try to pick up extra shifts when I can. It gives me free days to go to open calls."

"Shifts?"

"Yeah. I drive a cab to pay the rent."

"Well, you're good at it. And you have the livery license. Might as well use it."

"I meet some characters. Sometimes I hit the jackpot. A couple weeks ago, Kitty Kallen got in the cab. The best girl singer around, I think."

"I agree. She's very special."

"And a looker, too. Black hair. Like yours. And she wears English Lavender, like my cousin Elsa."

"Maybe you'll come home for Christmas?"

"Can't make it this year." Nicky winced as soon as he said it. The idea of being home with his family was a tonic to him, but he couldn't do it. He couldn't face the Palazzinis, their hopes for him higher than his own for himself. If he went, they'd try to lure him back to Montrose Street. They had spent most of the dinner at Lüchow's begging him to come back to South Philly, but Nicky wasn't about to give up. He was as stubborn as he was talented.

"That's too bad. We're having a big cast party on December twenty-third. Everybody asks about you."

"They do?"

"The acting company holds you up as the gold standard. You broke out of Philly and made it to Broadway."

"I only drive on a street marked Broadway. I haven't acted on Broadway yet."

"You're close."

"I'll get there."

"I know you will. It just takes the right director to cast you in the right role."

"Thanks for the encouragement, Calla."

"Everybody can use a little of that."

"Ain't that the truth?" Nicky laughed.

"I'd better get going. I have to finish my work."

"But it's late."

"I don't mind the hours."

Calla hung up the phone after saying good-bye. She would

sleep that night, soundly and deeply, having heard Nicky's voice and knowing he was all right.

Nicky would not have restful slumber on the night of his thirty-second birthday. He would hear every footstep on the sidewalk as it crunched overhead on the snow and ice. He'd hear every siren and car horn and the clank of every dumpster on every garbage truck, blaming the city for his insomnia. The birthday cake hadn't sat well on his stomach. The red wine had given him a slight head-ache. Nicky would blame everything but the truth for his inability to surrender to a peaceful night's sleep: he needed a friend. He had not kept the close counsel of a trusted confidante since he left Philly. Sure he had made friends, but in the process he had revealed very little of himself to them. Like so many young men and career girls who moved to the city, he was struggling to sur-vive and pursue the work he had relocated to do with equal focus. Time was passing and he wasn't moving forward. It pained Nicky to look into the future. Nicky had so much more to say to Calla Borelli. He would have liked to ask her advice, but he was ashamed he hadn't *made it*, landed *that role*, or *hit the boards*. Instead, he had done everything he could to avoid telling her what his life was really like in the most important city in the world, where he felt like the least significant person in it.

Calla sat in front of Mr. Collier's desk at the Third Federal Savings and Loan of Philadelphia wearing her best blue velvet hat, black wool coat, and kid gloves. She knew to wear her Sunday best to any meetings at the bank. Sam Borelli hadn't cared for institu-tions much; when he stood on line to make a deposit to meet payroll, he would grumble about the grandeur, the granite floors, marble counters, and gargantuan mother-of-pearl-faced clock, re-minding his daughter that it was the customers who paid for this opulence. He called the intimidating decor "the splendor of the lender.".

A row of fine mahogany desks were lined up across the room, the contents of their polished surfaces identical down to the leather pencil cups. The men that sat behind them looked alike, as though they had been ordered from a catalogue that sold bankers like farm equipment or trousers. *Buy your financial expert here!* the advertisement might have read: choose a gray, myopic, balding middle-aged man with roots in England to handle your money. He knows something you don't. No wonder most of the *paisans* in South Philly kept their money under their mattresses.

Elwood Collier, the jovial bank manager caring for Calla's interests, looked like the rest, but at least he was pleasant. He returned to his desk with three envelopes for her.

"Here you are, Miss Borelli." Mr. Collier handed her the bundle of envelopes and took a seat. He looked at Calla's face and reassured her. "Don't question your decision. Since the war, houses are going for fair prices. You did well."

"You know, I always wondered," she said softly.

"What's that?" He pushed the cancellation of Sam Borelli's mortgage across the desk for Calla to sign.

"If having money makes you feel better."

Mr. Collier smiled. "I think it helps."

"I don't think it does." Calla picked up the fountain pen and signed the document.

Collier stamped the contract PAID IN FULL and placed the receipt in the file. He folded his hands on the desk and leaned forward. "This happens in every family. It happened in mine. The parents pass away, and the children are left behind and have to make a decision about the family home. Your sisters don't live in the city any longer. They're married, with their own families. Someday you'll marry and have a family and you'll look back on this and know that you made the right decision. A house is nothing more than wood and stone."

"A pile of bricks?" Calla added.

"That's right."

"Not to me."

"I didn't mean to sound insensitive. But it isn't the house itself that matters, it's the people in it that make a home."

"I don't know. Places are important, Mr. Collier. At the theater, sometimes we think to do the play without a set, just lights and black walls. We call it minimalism. And pretty soon we're in rehearsal, and we realize that the actors need things to fill out the world. They need places to sit. Doors to move through. Rooms to make memories in, to live inside. A place to hold their stories. A context to *be*. Familiar places that we return to, where we remember the scent of the kitchen when our mother's baked or the wallpaper of roses in the stairwell or the old porch with the bum step; they aren't nothing. They are part of what makes us human. We're defined by where we dwell and how we take up space in this life and what we choose to put in it. I'll always mourn the sale of my father's house, my mother's garden, and the kitchen table where I ate every meal of my life. Why wouldn't I? I don't know how you sell off every memory you ever made and feel good about it."

"I can't answer that for you. But I do know, when it's time for you to buy a new home, you come and see me." Mr. Collier handed her his business card. "And this bank will be happy to help you with your first mortgage."

Calla stood. She exhaled slowly from her mouth, and the sound she made came out like a whistle. The bankers looked up from their desks to see where the whistle came from as Mr. Collier rose to shake her hand.

She placed the envelopes in her purse, the individual checks cut for the proceeds of the sale of the family homestead on Ellsworth

Street. There was a check for Helen and one for Portia, and the final one belonged to her.

As Calla walked out of the bank, she wished for the first time that she were wealthy—*Really rich!,* as the cartoon character Little Mary Mix-Up had shouted that morning on the funny pages—because if Calla were loaded, it would have never come to this. She would have bought the house from her sisters and lived in those rooms all the days of her life. She needed those walls, for reasons she could name and for others that she couldn't. Calla believed there was something terribly wrong about selling the house, but she couldn't convince her sisters to hold on to it any longer. They had reached the limit after three years of Calla buying time with nothing but empty promises and hopes of a hit at the theater to provide extra cash. Surely her brothers-in-law had put pressure on their wives, and they had issued an ultimatum. Calla was not their responsibility, they were raising families of their own, running businesses. She accepted that, so Calla sold the house. Everything her parents lived, worked, and struggled for was gone, divided into three parts, never to be whole again.

The Drama Bookshop was on the second story of a building on Forty-Second Street whose street-level store sold musical instruments. Nicky climbed the stairwell off the street and entered the shop, filled with books and light that poured in through the storefront windows. The shop had a clear view of Times Square, the sidewalks were packed with people while the streets cluttered with cars and trucks. The last of the gray snow had melted along the gutters of Midtown, turning into black streams before disappearing into the grates on the street corners. Nicky was happy to have a day off, out of the traffic, noise, and cold.

The dark walnut floors of the bookstore were buckled from age. The warped shelves were filled with books about the history of theater, biographies of the players, plays, and academic volumes on directing, acting, and producing. A felt-covered game table was filled with a display of coffee table books with elaborate illustrations of costume design, rendering of sets, and photographs of evocative stage lighting.

Nicky wandered to an open area, where a large, polished table was stacked with books about Shakespeare, surrounded by individual copies of his plays for purchase. Nicky picked up *A Midsummer Night's Dream*. As he leafed through it, it brought back good memories of the Borellis.

Nicky took his time going through the stacks. He had a giddy sense of anticipation at all there was to learn, but he also wondered: At his age, why should he try? Was it too late for him? What would he do with the knowledge once he had acquired it? Nicky was desperate to act professionally onstage in New York. He had come close at several auditions, only to lose out to actors with more experience. Coming close kept Nicky in the game; it also led him to the shop, to look for a manual to help him do better at auditions.

Nicky did not have the benefits of an education; everything he learned was from observation and the practical knowledge he had gleaned from his work at Borelli's. He was an eager student, though, and in Nicky's favor, he had a natural acumen for Shakespeare, the language came easily to him. Sam Borelli said some people were like that; they read the verse, understood the intent, and it made sense to them.

Nicky discovered a low shelf behind the new releases:

USED BOOKS FOR YOUNG THESPIANS

He sat down on the floor and looked through the children's books, thinking he might find something for the Palazzini kids, who were multiplying at a rate that rivaled the tomatoes on the roof of the Montrose Street house. There had been some changes, but the family remained close. Mabel and Gio still lived with Jo and Dom. They had a daughter, Giovanna, who was probably walking by now. Elsa and Dom's son had started school, and they had a second baby, Joseph, who had just begun to crawl. Elsa sent a photograph of their new home two blocks down on Montrose. Lena and Nino still lived in the homestead, and were expecting their first baby.

Nicky was sorting through the spines of the children's books when he recognized a title. He pulled the hardcover book from the shelf. The size and weight of the book were also familiar, as was the jacket art.

"You need help there?" the salesman asked.

"I don't think so."

"Good book," the man said as he passed.

Nicky's heart began to beat faster as he turned the pages of the book. Of late, when his heart raced, it was a result of anxiety, but not today. He remembered this book, and it brought him back to the beginning. The illustrations had not been forgotten but had simply been layered upon by time. They were there in his mind's eye as clearly as the moment he first saw them. He had been told, as a young boy, that the pictures in this book were called *plates*. Between the plates were translucent sheets of sheer paper etched in gold to protect the artwork. He even remembered the flimsy paper!

At five years old, Nicky had been confused by the use of the word *plates*, knowing that was where food was placed, not art. He recalled being afraid of a character on the jacket art, which showed Elizabethan actors in a theatrical parade. All these years later, the face of the sinister court jester holding hands with a young man clutching a balloon still gave Nicky pause. How Nicky had wished he could jump into the picture and warn the boy about the jester with the face of the devil.

Nicky ran his hands through his hair, trying to remember more.

Tales from Shakespeare

Charles & Mary Lamb

COLOUR PLATES BY A. E. JACKSON

The touch of the sleek jacket paper, embossed in black, and silk-screened with velvet-rich tones of sapphire blue, ruby red, and harvest gold, sent him back in time. The endpapers were deepest maroon, and made Nicky feel that way, lost, yearning, marooned and longing for a time that had defined him.

This was the book his mother had read aloud to him night after night, before he went to sleep. She would curl her body around him as he lay in his bed, resting on his pillow. Nicola would hold this book open with both hands while her son, cradled in her arms, tucked under the blankets, followed the pictures as she read aloud. The renditions of Shakespeare's plays were presented as simply as nursery rhymes and as dramatically as fairy tales. Shakespeare's tales were the smooth stones that built the mosaic that became Nicky's imagination as a man.

Nicky was bereft when he recalled the night his mother stopped reading aloud to him. So ill, she lost her voice and could no longer speak. The loss of that ritual from his life was as central to his present loneliness as was the loss of her. These stories, typeset in black ink, letter by letter, were imprinted on his heart. The plain font, offset by the scrolling of the Elizabethan calligraphy, with its arcs and swirls placed by hand on paper—they had not disappeared from his memory either.

The illustrations had shaped his romantic view of women. Every girl he ever lusted after looked like the drawing of Beatrice in the garden. She was painted as a mischievous brunette wearing a yellow taffeta gown and a knowing expression. He was compelled to Beatrice when he was a boy, and she struck his fancy now, echoes of her in the real women he had loved.

Nicky closed the book and held it, as though he had been reunited with his oldest friend on his darkest day. His knowledge of Shakespeare hadn't come from his keen ability to decipher the text, it had come from his mother.

"This is an old one," the cashier said over his reading glasses. "From England."

"I read it as a boy."

"You're lucky," the cashier said as he rang up the book.

Nicky nodded, but he disagreed with the fellow. How was Nicky Castone lucky? Nothing had panned out for him—at least none of the things he had set his heart upon. *People just say things to fill the air*, he thought.

"There are no reprints of this book that I know of," the cashier offered. "Last copy I've seen in a while. Maybe they have it at the library."

"Good to know." Nicky pulled out his wallet to pay for the book.

"You shopped here before?"

"No. I've heard about it from other actors."

"You're an actor? I was too. A hundred years ago." He grinned.

"That's when they lit the stage with smudge pots."

The cashier laughed. "That's right."

Nicky looked at the man. The city was filled with second-story shops tended by former actors, dancers, and singers who had moved to Manhattan for the same reasons he had with the same goals in mind. He felt a kinship with the man and the bookstore, so he asked, "Are you looking to hire anyone here?"

"You looking for work?"

"Something part-time. Something in the theater."

"I don't have anything right now. But there's a board in the back with job listings."

Nicky thanked him, tucked the bag under his arm, and headed to check out the job board. He took down names of theaters, a prop house, and an electrical supply company, and the telephone number of a well-known actress who needed her dog walked on matinee days. He was delighted to read the listings; they reminded him of his old second job at Borelli's. Nicky moved closer to the board when he saw this advertisement:

Monthly productions! A three-hundred-seat theater! Weekly seminars! Nicky could picture the building on Riverside Drive; he drove on that street daily picking up fares, dropping them off. Surely it was fate that he'd found this post, but more so, the five words in the ad that would make it all possible: Accredited by the Veterans Administration. Not only would Nicky be able to study theater, it would be paid for on the GI Bill. If they wanted him. If he could get in. The sacrifices he had made during the war might give him what he most yearned for: a second act.

Hortense hid in the Palazzinis' mud room as Jo ladled Minna's Venetian gravy onto the fresh penne at the stove in the kitchen. Dom was home for lunch, and Jo had agreed to be part of the dispatcher's secret experiment. Hortense stood behind a fig tree that was ready to be planted out in the garden. The Spatuzzas had made their annual spring drop-off, and one tree at a time, Jo was planting the bounty.

"Is this how you want it to look?" Jo whispered, showing the dish to Hortense on her way to the dining room.

Hortense nodded.

"Here goes." Jo went into the dining room with the plate of macaroni and placed it in front of her husband. She scooted the bowl of grated cheese and the red pepper grinder in front of her husband. "What's new, Dominic?" she asked casually.

"I need a new lift at the shop."

"Are they expensive?"

"What do you think? Hydraulic. It's not like the old days. Everything costs."

Dom placed his napkin over his shirt. He picked up his fork and pierced the penne. He tasted the pasta and chewed.

"How is it?" Jo asked.

"You got more gravy?"

Jo went into the kitchen. Hortense watched as Jo ladled gravy into a small ceramic boat. "He wants more!"

Hortense raised her hands in a silent *Praise be!* as Jo brought the gravy boat into the dining room. Dom doused his pasta with the gravy. He sprinkled fresh grated cheese on the gravy before spearing several flutes of penne and putting them into his mouth.

"What do you think of the gravy?"

"What do you mean, what do I think?"

"Do you like it?"

"It's good."

"It's different, Dom."

"You tried something new?"

"Yeah."

"What did you do?"

"Nothing important."

"I like it."

"That's all that matters," Jo assured him.

"If that was all that mattered, you wouldn't change the food around here. I like what I like."

"If I can improve things, why wouldn't I?"

"You have a point."

"Thanks, honey." Jo gave her husband a quick kiss on the cheek before returning to the kitchen. She joined Hortense in the mud room. "He likes it."

"Does he know it came from a jar?"

"If I told him, he'd spit it out."

"Even if it's delicious?"

"It wouldn't matter to him. He's off the boat. They're impossible. If he could have me pounding cornmeal on a rock in Calabria in the hot sun to make his polenta, he'd be happy. Gravy is supposed to be from scratch. He has to know that I have stood there for hours pressing tomatoes through a sieve. Somehow, in his mind, my efforts translate to love."

"I understand."

"I knew you would."

"I've been working for him for over thirty years. He is a man who sets parameters." Hortense turned to go back to the office.

"I can test it out on the whole family tonight if you want," Jo offered.

"Would you do that for me?"

Hortense climbed the steps to the dispatch office. She placed her straw hat on the file cabinet before fishing out the ring of keys from her purse. She sorted through them and unlocked her private drawer in the filing cabinet, pulling out a large black ledger marked TESTING. She opened it and made a series of quick notes under the column header Batch 77. She closed it, slipped it back into the cabinet, and looked up to heaven. "Come on, Minna. Give me a sign."

Riverside Drive curled along the cliffs above the Hudson River like a garland. The Beaux Arts buildings along the wide, tree-lined boulevard of Manhattan's Upper West Side, built of white sandstone, cream-colored granite, and gray fieldstone with bold architectural flourishes, including copper-tipped cupolas and shingled turrets, reminded Nicky a lot of Paris. Over the drive the steep hillside sloped down into Riverside Park, which, at twilight, was filled with children as they finished playing before supper.

Nicky stood on the steps of The Master at 310 Riverside Drive, the tallest building on the street, at twenty-seven floors. He was already nervous about meeting the possible players in his bright future and auditioning for them, and the imposing building, built with bricks in shades of every color from purple to rose to indigo, somehow made his anxiety worse.

A white-gloved doorman opened the brass-plated door, nodding at Nicky. He entered the lobby, an Art Deco masterpiece, elegantly polished in black and silver. Nicky came prepared; he'd completed his paperwork at home, including a résumé for the directors of the theater, a copy of his honorable discharge, his approved application for education entitlement under the GI Bill, his birth certificate, and a document stating that he had not exercised his education option prior to the Abbe Theater course work. Most importantly, he had revisited *Twelfth Night*, and prepared a monologue.

The doorman directed Nicky to the theater off the main lobby. Nicky poked his head inside, and immediately fell in love with the

midnight blue jewel box. The stage floor was painted in black lacquer, reflecting a gold velvet stage curtain. The three-hundred-seat
house was modern, and if Nicky had to describe it, he would have
called it a Broadway house, north of the grid. He was itching to
get on that stage. He could see himself there, feel the floorboards
beneath his feet, and the beam of the follow spot on his face.

He checked his watch, on time for his appointment, went up the
stairs to the second floor, and rang the bell marked Abbe Theater
School. Removing the wool cap he wore when he drove the cab, he
folded it in half like a slice of pizza. He took a seat in the hallway on
the bench.

Soon a young woman in dungarees and a white blouse emerged
from the door of the studio. "Are you Nick Castone?"

"I am."

"Mr. O'Byrne will see you now."

Robert F. O'Byrne had been in the movies in Hollywood. Nicky
was nervous about meeting him, but he pulled himself together,
knowing confidence was at least thirty percent of any performance.
Perhaps he was off on the percentage. Hadn't Sam Borelli taught
him about confidence? Suddenly he had no memory; Nicky's anxiety took over.

When the lanky, bespectacled man in his mid-thirties opened
the door to pick up a file from the secretary's desk, he smiled and
looked at Nicky. "Are you an actor?"

"Does one run of *Twelfth Night* count?"

"Depends on the scene. Depends on you. Come in."

Nicky followed Robert into a room with a table and chair at one
end. Robert grabbed a folding chair from a small utility closet and
handed it to Nicky.

"I saw you in the movies, sir," Nicky offered.

Robert smiled. "You did?"

"My cousin Rick took me." Nicky didn't know why or where
they came from, but his eyes filled with tears. "He got killed in

the war. He's the only one in my family that did. We all went too. There were seven of us altogether, seven boys. Three brothers in my Uncle Dom's family. Three in my Uncle Mike's. I'm an only child. Orphan actually. Uncle Dom and Aunt Jo took me in. Ricky was the one who loved the show. Every Saturday, cartoon, newsreel, double feature. He sat through it twice. I know he'd be happy that I was here. That I was going to be an actor."

Robert sat down at the table and indicated that Nicky should sit across from him.

Nicky pulled all his paperwork out of his pockets and put it on the table. "I would have been here sooner, but I had to wait for your spring semester to commence."

Robert looked down at the pile. "You can give this to Miss Fletcher when we're done," he said kindly. "She handles the paperwork."

Miss Fletcher closed the shades on the windows of the outer office. She knocked on the studio door, pushing it open enough to peek in. "Mrs. O'Byrne said to remind you you have theater tickets tonight."

"That's right. Thanks, Kathy. Here's what we've got." Robert turned to Nicky. "You can enroll in our first-year classes."

"I'm in?"

"You're in." Robert grinned.

Nicky exhaled, realizing he had been holding his breath the entire time that night, but perhaps even longer, since the day he found the posting at the Drama Book Shop. "Thank you."

"You show a lot of promise, Nick."

"Thank you. I won't let you down."

"We need an actor to read during auditions. You would sit in and read lines with the actor up for the part. Would you like to do that?"

"Sure. Absolutely."

"We can't pay a lot."

"I drive a cab."

"How many hours a week?"

"As many as sixty."

"You have to drive those hours to make ends meet, don't you?"

Nicky nodded. "More and more all the time, sir."

"What else can you do?"

"Anything."

"It's important for you to be around here as many hours of the day as possible. We encourage the students to sit in on scene classes, as many as you can, in addition to your own course work. We're open six days a week."

"I'd be here seven if I could."

Robert leaned back in his chair. "We just lost our janitor in the building."

"I could clean up around here for you."

"I'll talk to the owner. He asked me if I knew anyone. Unless you love driving a cab."

"I can take it or leave it."

"Call me tomorrow, and I'll have an answer for you. And it would be great if you could come in on Wednesday. We're holding auditions. You'll meet my wife, Gloria. She's the director of the play. And the truth is, in our partnership, she's the one with the talent."

Nicky shook Robert's hand. "I can't thank you enough."

"You did a fine job, Nick. Thank you."

Nicky turned to leave the office. "Mr. O'Byrne?"

"Please call me Robert."

"I don't know what happened to me before. You know, when I came in. I haven't thought about my cousin in the longest time."

"Maybe you needed him, and he entered your consciousness at the right moment."

Nicky left the office and went down the stairs and out into the night. His pockets were lighter, now that he'd left all the docu-

ments on the secretary's desk, or maybe he was just lighter because he was sailing.

It was a cold April evening that had poured rain while Nicky
was inside. All that was left of it was the glassy hue on the sidewalks and the cold wind that follows a spring storm. He put on his
cap and pulled up his collar as he walked to the subway station.
He was filled to the brim with the possibilities of his own potential. He didn't know why he had been led to the Abbe Theater
School, but he had never felt such a warmth and connection to a
place in his life—well, not since Borelli's. Nicky knew he wasn't
going to do anything less than his best as long as they'd have him.
He would not squander this magnificent piece of luck.

The water in the pan on the hot plate boiled, making bubbles of
white foam. Nicky added spaghetti to the water, careful to stir it
thoroughly so the noodles wouldn't clump. On the other burner,
he placed a small pan. He drizzled olive oil until it danced in drops
in the heat. He added garlic, picking up the pan and shaking it to
cover the cloves in the oil. He drained the spaghetti, threw it in
a bowl, and put a pat of butter on the hot strands. He cracked a
fresh egg into the olive oil and garlic, cooked it sunny side up, and
then threw the egg onto the spaghetti, tossing it thoroughly, until the strands were glazed golden yellow. After sprinkling cheese
on the spaghetti, he poured himself a glass of homemade wine
from Uncle Dom's basement vintage and sat down at his table in
his apartment to read the paper.

When he'd finished his meal, he felt satisfied. He lay on his bed
and picked his leather address book off the nightstand. He had to
share the news of the Abbe Theater School with someone who
would understand the importance of it. It's not every day a man's
life changes for the better. He flipped to the B's and found Calla
Borelli's phone number.

He dialed her house, picturing the old gray clapboard on Ellsworth. He wondered if she had fixed the warped planks on the front porch or had the concrete repoured on the front walk. Probably not; Calla wasn't a homebody. Nicky dialed the number. He took another sip of Uncle Dom's wine.

An operator came on the line. "I'm sorry, that line is no longer in service."

"What do you mean?"

"It's been disconnected."

"For how long?"

"The phone company does not release private information."

"Can you give me a hint?"

"No, sir. I cannot."

"Thank you." Now it was Nicky who felt disconnected. He flipped through the book and called the theater box office.

"Borelli's." From the flat greeting, Nicky knew it was Rosa De-Nero on the line.

"Rosa, it's Nicky. Nicky Castone."

"Who?"

"Nicky Castone. I used to work at the theater."

"Oh yeah."

"A couple years ago?"

"Yeah, I remember you. The actor that went to New York to make it. You were always busting my chops."

"That's me. Is Calla Borelli there?"

"I think she's down in the dressing room."

"Could you ask her to come to the phone?"

"I have to leave the booth."

"It's important.

Rosa sighed, and for the next three minutes, Nicky had enough time to beat himself up for being a bad friend. He wondered if Calla would even take his call.

"Hi, Nicky," Calla said breathlessly into the phone.

Nicky couldn't tell from the tone of her voice if she was happy to hear from him. "How are you?" He sat up straight and held the receiver close to his ear.

"I'm doing well. How are you?"

"I'm still in New York."

"Your aunt Jo keeps me informed, when I see her. I haven't seen her in a while."

"Well, this time you'll have to give her the news."

"Okay."

"I've been accepted at the Abbe Theater School. I'm going to study there and read with the actors when they audition."

"That's wonderful."

"Thanks. I knew you'd approve. Hey, I called your house. Your phone was disconnected."

"We sold it."

"You loved that house."

"It was too much to keep up with."

"I understand. You're talking to a guy who lives in one room. Besides, you're a career girl. Do you really need a big house?"

"Even if I did, it wouldn't matter. It's gone."

"How's it going at the theater?"

"We're working hard. Doing *A Midsummer Night's Dream* right now."

"Great play."

"You know, my dad always said to direct what you're feeling, and I'm feeling like I'm living in a very strange world."

"Why's that?"

"Frank Arrigo got married."

Nicky sat up. "To you?"

"Nope."

"His loss."

"You'll never guess who he married."

"I don't know. Faye Emerson from the television show."

"She's already married."

"Forgive me. I don't have a television set yet. I don't know who is married and who isn't."

"You only know pretty ladies who you don't watch on television."

"Right."

"Frank married Peachy DePino."

"My Peachy?" Nicky was stunned.

"She's not yours anymore."

"I guess not."

"Big wedding at Palumbo's. Somebody said Mario Lanza sang 'Be My Love.'"

"Pure corn. I hate that song."

"Me too." Calla chuckled.

"She got Mario Lanza?" Nicky was mystified.

"Frank got Mario Lanza. Frank thinks big. He's built her a big mansion in Ambler."

"Is that all?" Nicky felt peevish. Frank had even stolen the site of his personal epiphany as the place to reside with his former fiancée.

"There will be more. Much more," Calla assured him.

"All of it could have been yours," Nicky teased her.

"The marker was too high."

"You'd have gotten used to it. You would have adjusted to the altitude."

"I doubt it. Hey. Maybe you should come home sometime and see the circus for yourself."

When Calla hung up the phone, she knew Nicky wouldn't come home anytime soon—not for a visit, not to see the play, even if it was his favorite. He hadn't come to any of the others since he moved away; why would this one be any different? Whatever he was doing in New York was so much more compelling than any production at Borelli's—or at least, that's how he made her feel.

She wanted to tell Nicky that Peachy DePino had met Frank at the theater around the time Frank was trying to sell the building out from under her. But that might have hurt him, and she wouldn't do that.

Calla had kept the biggest news to herself. The theater was closing. She had run through the money that she had inherited when the house was sold, and the current slate of productions had not done better than break even for the company, despite their best efforts to promote them. Calla wasn't sleeping, haunted by her own regrets.

Nicky hung up the phone in New York. He felt odd. Calla seemed happy to hear from him, pleased about his news, but distant. Maybe she was upset about losing Frank. He couldn't figure out why. Arrigo was nothing more than a big hunk of cheese, and everyone knows cheese is only an accompaniment, not the meal. He was surprised that Peachy had married him, but on the surface of things, they did seem an awful lot alike. Nicky was happy for her. After all, the acquisition of Peachy DePino's long-term security by way of a proper marriage was another indulgence paid on the road to Nicky's salvation—or, as they say at the Steinway & Sons factory, another piano off his back.

11

At twilight the blossoms on the trees along Riverside Drive swayed like marabou feathers in the breeze. The windows of the Abbe Theater studio were propped open, as Nicky had just washed them. He could hear the muffled cheers and whistles from the fans watching a softball game in Riverside Park. The field lights pulled on and glowed in the trees like white moons as he dusted the window seats. When he was finished with that task, he collected the sides left behind by the actors who had come through to audition for the summer production, *Of Mice and Men*.

The last student had signed out of the studio, leaving Nicky free to give the large studio, waiting area, and office a good mopping and dusting. He'd assembled the buckets, mops, and rags when his boss, Gloria Monty, came out of the studio, stuffing her purse with a script and her notes, which spilled out of a folder in bits and pieces like confetti.

Gloria was a high-energy dynamo, slim, sleek, and small, built like a cigarette. She cursed and crammed the bits of paper inside before snapping the handbag shut. "Sorry you had to hear that." She laughed.

Her dark brown eyes were expressive; her matching hair was

chopped into a bob. She had college-girl style, preferring trim pencil skirts, sweaters, and low-heeled shoes to day dresses. Though she wore simple wool swing coats, her hats were works of art. Gloria would use typewriter ribbon on the crown, or line the brim with a row of cocktail picks. There was a swizzle stick twist of the avant-garde Elsa Schiaparelli in her otherwise traditional style.

Nicky noticed that the best directors, including Gloria, had a distinctive style. Sam Borelli wore the same tweed jacket with a tan-and-black weave to every rehearsal, but his neckties expressed a flair. Sewn by hand by Vincenza, they were made of bright silks in shades of turquoise, magenta, and purple. Calla certainly had a knack for fashion. The directors who taught at the Abbe School were original too. The professor who taught character study wore silk tunics and Nehru jackets.

Nicky pumped the mop into the fresh soapy water.

"Now the prince turns into Cinderella," Gloria joked.

"As long as I'm the prince once in a while, I'm fine with being Cinderella, or even her understudy." Nick grinned.

"You're not the only person around here pulling two shifts. I have to go home and make Robert dinner."

"You're a good wife."

"I'm a better director."

Gloria sat down on the top of the receptionist desk in her hat and coat and lifted her feet off the floor so Nicky could mop under them. "How long have you been an actor?"

"I worked at a theater in Philadelphia before I moved here. I did a little of everything."

"That's why you do anything we ask around here."

"I consider this church. I'm here to serve."

"You're very generous. And you're a natural.

"I can't take any credit. I learned everything at that Shakespeare company."

"Oh. That's why you know how to read with actors. And that's how you know the classics."

"I appreciate when you let me sit in during auditions."

"You're the first person to ever thank me for that job. Most actors hate doing it. It's a chore."

"Not to me. The words change colors every time a different actor interprets them."

"You're nimble with a love scene. A lot of practice?"

"Just enough to be grateful."

"You don't have a nice girl?"

"I was engaged for seven years."

"What happened?"

"I didn't love her enough." Nicky wrung out the mop and pushed the pail off to the side.

"And then you heard the siren's call of the American theater."

"I always leave that part out," Nicky admitted.

"I'm working on something I think you'd be right for."

"A play?"

"Not exactly. It's a teleplay."

"Television?"

"I'm directing something new in Midtown. It's a saga. We film it every day. They're very popular. We tape them, like a movie, but they go on the air live like the theater."

"I've never done anything like that."

"I think you could. My husband does too."

"If you think I can do it."

"It's not a big part. But I call it glue. You'll play a cabbie. A hack. Who moves the characters through the action by driving them around off camera. It's a notion I had that I think might work."

"I know how to play a hack. I've been one long enough."

"The show is called *Love of Life*." Gloria fished in her purse for a subway token. "You'll have to change your name."

"Why?"

"More people will see you on television in a week than all the audiences that saw all of Shakespeare in his lifetime and ever since."

"That can't be true."

"It is. You need a name that they can spell and that you can give away without missing it. Keep Nicky Castone for you. You'll be glad you did."

"But I'm proud of my name."

"I understand. I'm Italian too. Montemuro is my name."

"That means *someone who climbs mountains.*"

"It does. But that wouldn't be enough for me. I had to change it. See, Gloria Monty wants to rule the world."

"*Mondo-muro,*" Nicky offered.

"Right. Perfect, but not as a surname. Just as a philosophy." Gloria swung her legs off the desk and grabbed her purse. "Lock up. And see you tomorrow. And don't cut that mug shaving. The television camera is unforgiving."

As Nicky buffed the floor, he began to whistle. Television. The thought of it made him nervous, but he'd follow Gloria and Robert anywhere. As he concentrated on buffing the floor, a pang of guilt pealed through him. He remembered giving Calla Borelli the business for cleaning the theater, thinking it beneath her, and here he was, doing the same job. It was almost like a penance for having judged her.

The monthly potluck dinner in the Philadelphia Freewill Baptist Church Fellowship Hall was full to capacity for the last supper before it was suspended for the summer. The Ladies' Guild had set the tables with bright centerpieces of white lilies, daisies, and black-eyed Susans, crisp white tablecloths, and the church's good china. The basement was hot; the windows were propped open, and fans whirled to move the air through.

Hortense, who chaired the food committee, stood behind the buffet table. She kept an eye on her contribution to the meal: a large chafing dish filled with cavatelli dressed with Minna's Venetian gravy. As chairwoman, she had control of placement, so the cavatelli had a prime spot next to the macaroni and cheese, which was served in order next to the fried chicken, stewed tomatoes, cornbread stuffing, fried okra, and collard greens.

Hortense knew that the folks of her church held certain expectations regarding the menu. There had to be coconut cake for dessert, with an option of banana pudding, sweet tea, and hot coffee. The entrée was always fried chicken. The side dishes had been consistent since the ground was broken for the church in 1897, not a single change. Cavatelli with red sauce had never been served. Hortense figured God-fearing Baptists would give her an honest opinion about her product. She figured if they liked it, she had something special.

When the ninth person in line passed over her cavatelli and went straight for the macaroni and cheese with the buttery breadcrumb topping instead, Hortense picked up a serving spoon and got to work.

"Sister, do try my dish," she said sweetly, ladling a sample onto a churchgoer's plate. She placed the spoon back in the chafing dish, as a potluck was self-serve, but gently insisted her fellow Baptists try her dish by offering the handle of the cavatelli serving spoon to them. As they processed through the line, some took a small sampling to be polite, but the chafing dish remained full.

"Hortense, you're trying too hard. You're being pushy," Louis whispered as he stood in the line with his plate.

"As deacon of the congregation, you could help. You could make an announcement about my cavatelli."

"I'm not going to do that."

"I didn't ask you to cook it. I asked you to tell the folks it's available to taste. As a favor to me."

"Nobody likes that kind of food here."

"They would if they tried it."

"Well, give me some, and I'll talk it up at the men's table."

"Thank you." Hortense ladled the cavatelli onto her husband's plate.

When the last of the congregation had gone through the line, Hortense fixed herself a plate. Her friend Willa Turnbough waved to her from the corner table where she had saved Hortense a seat.

"Does anybody like my dish?" Hortense asked as she sat down.

"The red sauce?" Willa asked. "I think it's tasty. Ladies, what do you think?"

The ladies nodded politely.

"The membership seems to be enjoying it," Willa lied.

"Willa, are you at the same covered dish as me? Look over at that serving table. I still have a chafing dish full of my macaroni. It's like the loaves and fishes. Every time I serve a spoonful of cavatelli, it seems to multiply in the dish."

"Why are you so determined for everyone to eat it?" Willa wondered.

"I'd like to sell it."

"Nobody pays at a potluck."

Hortense lowered her voice. "I mean to the public."

"You opening a restaurant?"

"No. I want to sell the sauce. I want to put it up in jars and put it in stores. I just don't know how."

"Did you pray about this?"

"Yeah. Yeah. I've been praying about it. I'm not getting the sense our dear Lord is a red gravy fan either."

"I'm about to retire from the employ of Edna Oldfield," Willa said proudly. "Thirty-two years of service for the one family. Her husband died years ago and left her the family business. The family *food* business. They are the Oldfield Food Company."

"The soup people?"

"Soup. Sauce. Canned vegetables. You name it," Willa assured her. "They do it all."

"Can you get me a card?"

"What are you going to do with a card? You need to get over there and see the missus. She owns the joint. But you need to hurry."

"I can be there. Name the day."

"You have to take the bus. It's far. Main Line. You have to change buses. There's a wait."

"I can do it."

"There's rumblings she is going to hand the entire operation over to her son very soon. You could say my boss and I are retiring together."

Hortense's mind raced with the possibilities of a meeting. She had a lot of work to do before she took the bus to meet Mrs. Oldfield. Hortense didn't even have to pray about it; this opportunity felt right. As the membership split into groups to play Torch Bearers and Bell Ringers, led by Louis, Hortense stayed in her seat. She couldn't participate in any games, her mind was on a much greater prize.

Hortense climbed into bed next to her husband, who was asleep with his back to her. She adjusted the collar on her flannel nightgown and lay back on the pillow.

"Hortense?"

"Yes, Louis?"

He rolled over to face her.

"I thought you were asleep," she said softly.

"I can't sleep. You made a fool out of yourself today at the covered dish."

"Did I say something wrong?"

"No. You pushed that macaroni. Nobody wanted to eat it."

"I wanted folks to try it. That's all."

"Hortense, you need to stop. You're not going to sell that sauce."

"Louis, I know I can sell it. It's special. It's delicious. It's easy to prepare."

"What makes you think you can sell anything?"

"I've been in the work world for almost forty years of my life."

"Selling what? Doing what? Working for somebody else."

"I run the office. I handle all the money. I do the books. I learned Morse code."

"And I don't need to hear that every time you talk about work. I know all about you and Morse code."

"It's a skill, Louis."

"What's your point?"

"You should give me some credit from time to time. It wouldn't kill you, and it would do me some good."

"That's your problem. You need praise all the time. You think the world is all about Hortense Mooney. Well, you need to look inward and be more Christ-like. You think about yourself and your earthly needs too much. You got to look up for your purpose."

"God doesn't want me to fail."

"He wants you to work hard and do the job you know how to do. He wants you to take care of your family. That's it. You don't need to do anything else."

"I want to do more."

"You don't have it in you, Hortense. You got no follow-through. You never have. Not since the day I met you. You start all kinds of projects around here that you never finish. I had to finish the tile in the bathroom. I had to paint the steps when you ran out of steam."

"Poor Louis."

"Yes, poor me. Without me, what are you? You need to think about somebody besides yourself around here. "

Louis rolled over. At first, Hortense was so furious, she couldn't move. But she thought about the words he'd said to her, and she was more wounded than angry. She turned away from him, tucked the pillow under her chin, and wept without making a sound.

Mabel Palazzini moved through the grocery store like a shot, grabbing ingredients to make her daughter's birthday cake. She turned into the dairy aisle and ran into Peachy Arrigo.

"Hey, Mabel." Peachy looked at Mabel, her enormous brown eyes narrowed into ovals like black jelly beans.

"Peachy?" Mabel was taken aback. Peachy was very pregnant, and about sixty pounds heavier than she'd been when Mabel last saw her, years ago, bent over Nicky's chest of drawers in his basement bedroom searching for clues as to his whereabouts before he blew town to pose as an Italian ambassador.

"It's me." Peachy circled her face with her hand, framing it. "I'm in here somewhere."

"You look good," Mabel lied.

"How can you say that? I have arms like canned hams. I'm fat all over. Like a globe. If I started spinning, I'd knock this one off its axis."

"But it's good fat—I mean, weight. You're having a baby," Mabel said supportively.

Peachy looked Mabel up and down enviously. "You slimmed down."

"Giovanna is four years old today."

"Dear Mother of God, has it been that long since Nicky dropped me?"

"I'm afraid so."

"Tell me he's miserable."

"Not exactly. He's on television."

"What?"

"Television."

"I know all about the television. We have a Philco. "

"He's on that daytime serial *Love of Life*."

"I don't watch during the day. I like Milton Berle."

"Me too. But I watch Nicky when I do the ironing. He changed his name to Nick Carl."

"That's a stupid name," Peachy blurted.

"He had to. They didn't like Castone."

"I didn't either, to tell you the truth. Peachy Castone sounded like a pit got stuck in somebody's gut."

"I like Castone. It's a fine Italian name, if not simple. Try spelling Palazzini when you're talking to the phone company."

"Arrigo isn't easy either." Peachy sighed.

"Is it true you're putting in a pool?"

"It's in."

"Diving board?" Mabel queried.

"Yeah. Slide for the kid when he gets here. A fieldstone fountain that drips fresh water into the deep end and lights up at night. Frank is very particular about the accoutrement. It looks like a crypt in Sorrento."

"We go to the public pool on Broad." Mabel put her hand on her heart. "You are so lucky."

"Lucky is if I can fit in a swimsuit to enjoy the water next summer."

"You will. You'll go right back to your skinny self."

"You think so?"

"It's called body memory. Tucked inside all that fat and fluid is slim-sational Peachy. And even if that weren't true, look at me. It falls off when you're chasing children around. And if you cut out bread, replace it with melba toast, and eat cottage cheese until you think you're going to turn into a curd, you'll be slim in no time."

"If you say so." Peachy remained unconvinced.

"Peachy, you don't sound happy."

"I get in moods with this pregnancy. I imagine killing people with my bare hands, and then a minute later I'm weeping for the poor pagans around the world. I never had these mood swings when I was working at Wanamaker's. Sometimes I wonder if I'm cut out to be a housewife."

"Who is? Your moods will settle down."

"My husband is praying they will. Poor honey."

"Well, come and see us sometime, will ya?" Mabel offered.

"That would be awkward."

"No, it wouldn't. It really wouldn't."

"And inappropriate, too. I don't ever want to set foot in 810 Montrose again. It's like quicksand for me. I'm sucked down to the bowels of my deepest shame every time I think of Nicky Castone. I actually churn within myself with regret."

"Then we'll meet somewhere for a cannoli. Sound good?" Mabel said brightly.

Mabel pushed her cart to the checkout, in a rush to get home and make her daughter's cake. She looked back at Peachy, who stood in the harsh light of the dairy case, shaped like the volcano in tintype on the brochure for the trip to Honolulu the Knights of Columbus were offering in their fall circular. Poor Peachy. But not really. Mabel couldn't feel too sorry for her—she had a swimming pool.

Hortense got off the bus at the Philadelphia Museum. She walked through the sculpture garden, past the fountain, which misted her face, carried by the summer breeze.

Once inside, she showed her alumni card from Cheyney College, which gained her admittance, picked up a map, and moved into the atrium. The marble room was filled with pale blue natural light that poured in overhead from a skylight. As she moved through to the galleries, where the immaculate white walls were the backdrop for paintings by Caravaggio, she became enthralled by the colors: skies of turquoise, gold clouds with gleaming silver hems, a burgundy landscape speckled with lavender foliage. The characters in the paintings fascinated Hortense; their features reminded her of the colorful Palazzini clan, who showed emotion in matters great and small with the same intensity.

Hortense did not wander through the galleries, or join a walking tour: she had a specific mission. A traveling show of ancient maps was making its way across America through the museum system and was on view.

Hortense pulled a newspaper article out of her purse. The *Philadelphia Bulletin* explained that maps of Italy, dating back to 1350, including those of the Veneto region, would be on display, under glass, because they were very rare, and in delicate condition. The Carole Weinstein exhibit would only be on display for a month. Minna had wanted Hortense to visit Venice someday, but since that was unlikely, the maps would show what she was missing.

Hortense skimmed past the bright murals, pastel paintings, and sculptures and found the maps. She waited her turn as a group of students huddled around them, stepping aside when a professor and his class from Temple University studied one.

When the students had moved away from the display case at last, she took out pencil and paper, making a list of the names of the villages of the Veneto. She also wrote down the names of various streets, bridges, and palazzos in the city of Venice before she moved to a diorama depicting Treviso and the farms that crowned the hills at the foot of the Dolomites.

Her eye fell on a particular palazzo outside a town called Godega di Sant Urbano. Villa Hortensia, owned by the Borda family, had once been visited by Michelangelo.

"Well, I'll be," Hortense mumbled to herself. She walked over to the window and wrote *Villa Hortensia Fine Italian Tomato Sauce*.

Her dream now had a name.

Hortense got on the bus for the return trip to Charlotte Street, disembarked, and changed to the crosstown. She bounced slightly up and down on her heels as she waited at the bus stop. She had pep, enough to go around and enough to spare. She climbed aboard the crosstown bus, taking a seat by the window. As it turned in to her neighborhood, it stopped at a light. She was looking out the window when she saw her husband on the corner of McDowell, standing alone and checking his watch. Hortense reached up to try to open the window to holler a quick hello, but the latch was stuck. She gave up and sat back down.

A woman joined Louis. Hortense recognized her from church. It was the new lady—a widow, if she recalled. Hortense's stomach dropped inside her as she witnessed her husband lean down and lightly kiss the new member of their church on the lips. She rose up out of the bus seat as Louis kissed the woman again.

Louis Mooney offered the woman his arm, and she took it as naturally as the bus driver had taken Hortense's fare. Louis had not offered his arm to Hortense in that manner in years. She watched as her husband behaved splendidly, like a duke. It was as if she were observing a man she had never met, displaying manners she had not seen since she was a girl, when her father deferred with similar respect to her own mother.

Hortense broke out in an anxious sweat. The bus couldn't move, locked in a traffic jam, as her life flew by. Every mysterious thing about Louis Mooney that had confounded her over the years came into focus. The bus lurched forward back into traffic, careening past the next stop and the next as Hortense's mind reeled. The litany of excuses Louis had rendered regarding his whereabouts so poorly over the years began to line up in her mind like file folders, one after the other. Because she was a faithful woman, it took her eyes to convince her of the truth. She reached up and yanked the rope to stop the bus, then gripped the handle on the back exit bar tightly, fearing her legs wouldn't hold her. She could not breathe.

As soon as the door opened and fresh air hit her face, she began to cry. She had convinced herself long ago that the love that had brought them together in the first place could be salvaged if they prayed together and committed to saving their marriage. She had intended to pay attention to Louis again, to give him what he needed, but time, work, and other obligations had created too much distance. It made it harder for her to reach Louis across the divide, when it should have been easier.

Her mother, long passed, had taught her that a man only treats a woman poorly when he's behaving poorly behind her back. Hortense knew that Louis had struggled, and it was all right if he needed to take out his disappointment on her. After all, she was his wife. She could keep the ugliness hidden, and she had, for many years. It didn't hurt any less to understand it, or to see it. And now, Hortense didn't care if anyone saw her misery either.

A stranger, a young woman of twenty, placed her hand on Hortense's arm before reaching into her purse. Her white-gloved hand shuffled through its contents until she found a starched white cotton handkerchief, which she gave to Hortense. The girl's skin, the color of rich coffee, was unlined and clear. "You all right, ma'am?"

Hortense took the handkerchief and dried her tears.

"You keep it." The young woman patted Hortense on the arm before joining the crowd on the sidewalk.

Hortense stood under the awning, holding the handkerchief. She wasn't weeping for her marriage, or for the loss of her husband, or even for having her high hopes dashed. She wept for the time she had lost. There was no getting it back. She stepped out from under the shadows of the awning and into the sunlight. If there was one thing Hortense Mooney knew how to do, it was walk in the light.

The CBS Television studios occupied a full city block near the Hudson River in New York City. Inside the open main floor, the sets for the network of television shows, including news, serials, and musical variety were pushed, rolled, wheeled, and shoved into position on islands mounted on wheels. From the fly space overhead, electric cables that provided power were looped and draped from an overhead grid to accommodate the camera's movement. Lighting equipment dropped, and flats flew in, to segregate space as a living room turned into a kitchen, only to become a hospital room flipping to a department store, to a news desk anchored by world maps, all within moments.

In the center of the circus was Gloria Monty, the methodical, calm director of theater who took the scripts the writers created and staged the scenes for the cameras. Television wasn't cinema or Broadway, so Gloria was free to invent her own approach to a new dramatic form that showed no signs of lasting beyond the initial novelty. She did her job by doing what she did best: casting an interesting group of actors, providing them with dramatic scripts, and creating a family atmosphere of support whereby the actor could be daring and experiment. The daytime serial moved so fast that if one scene failed, the next might work. The mission was to keep the story moving and the tension high, which meant the well-drawn character carried the weight of the serial. The woman watching at home began to watch *her stories* on television just as she had listened to serialized radio plays and read serial stories in her favorite magazines.

For Gloria Monty and other serious theater artists, television was not yet an art form; it was too new to categorize, but it quickly became something the stage was not: a lucrative way to make a living.

"There he is! There's Nicky!" Mabel pointed through the viewing window of the audience room.

"Can we hear what he's saying?" Uncle Dom asked. "Why can't we hear anything?"

"Pop, they said we won't be able to hear anything, we only watch."

"This isn't modern. It's like a silent movie. Why did we come? We could stay home and hear it."

"He looks so handsome. He's the most handsome of all," Aunt Jo raved.

"I didn't know he had it in him." Uncle Dom watched as Nicky argued with another character. "I never saw Nicky blow. He lived with us how many years, Jo?"

"Twenty-five."

"Look at him. He looks like his head is going to pop like a cork."

"It's just acting, Pop," Lena said, and sat down on one of the benches. She was swollen in the last weeks of pregnancy. "It's all pretend."

"I bet I could do it," Gio said.

"You can't act," Mabel retorted. "You're the worst liar there is."

Gio sniffed. "It doesn't look that hard to me."

"It's very difficult," Elsa told them. "Nicky has been studying with Miss Monty. He doesn't come by this naturally."

"But it sure looks it," Dominic said, impressed.

"Who's that tomato he's with, in the pink suit?" Dom wondered.

"That's the star of the show," Lena told him.

"I can see why. She's got what it takes."

"How much longer?" Lena whispered to Nino.

"A couple minutes. Don't you feel well?"

"I'm okay. Just puffy."

"I keep waving to Nicky. Can he see us?" Aunt Jo wondered.

"No, Ma. They have that special film on the window so we can see out but he can't see in."

"What's happening?"

The set was disassembled in pieces, the lights flew up on the grid, the cameras rolled away, and the island sets rolled off to the side.

"That's it," Dominic said.

"That's the show?" Mabel stood up.

"See the red light? They're clearing the sets." Gio pointed.

Nicky navigated through crew on the stage until he made it to the audience viewing room.

The family greeted Nicky with an enthusiastic ovation. "We couldn't hear a word in this can. But you looked good," Uncle Dom said proudly.

"You are the best actor on the show," Aunt Jo raved.

"She says that but if she's honest, she has a thing for that Joe O'Brien," Dom groused.

"I do too! He's from Scranton, you know!" Lena swooned.

"He's a nice guy," Nicky said. "How are the babies?" Nicky embraced his cousins.

"Giovanna is sleeping through the night," Mabel bragged.

"Dominic the third is learning the alphabet," his father bragged. "Joseph is good with numbers already."

"Uh oh," Nicky warned.

"Don't worry. Uncle Gio hasn't taught him blackjack."

"Yet." Gio laughed.

"Lena, you have a lot to live up to."

Lena burst into tears. "I know."

"I'm sorry."

"It's not you, Nicky. I'm crazy, I laugh, I cry. I don't know what's wrong with me."

"You're having a baby—nothing wrong with you. You need to put your feet up. Can you all come over to my place?"

"We would love it," Aunt Jo said.

"The pictures were gorgeous. You have a rooftop garden."

"Thanks to the Lucky Strike commercial."

"They should pay you double—you've been smoking them since you were thirteen," Gio teased.

Gloria entered wearing a chic dress of emerald-green and black brocade. The only indication that she was a director was the headset draped over the pearls around her neck. "So this is your family! I feel like I know you all."

"Everybody, this is Gloria Monty, the director of the show," Nicky introduced her.

"Such a wisp," Uncle Dom commented. "You're pretty too."

"She just needs her brain to do her job, Dom," Aunt Jo chided him.

The Palazzinis surrounded Gloria. They had an instant rapport; she was a New Jersey Italian who understood the South Philly ways. And, of course, she had hired one of their own, which made her one of them too. Nicky fished in his pocket for his pack of cigarettes. He stood back and watched his current life and his old one blend, like whiskey and ice.

"Your family is so Italian, Nick."

"Is that a compliment?" Dom challenged her.

"It better be. I'm Italian too."

"We're running the world," Dom said proudly.

"Don't forget the Irish!" Mabel hollered.

"I couldn't! I married one." Gloria laughed.

It was only after Nicky moved out of 810 Montrose that he knew for certain how much he was loved. All those years, he believed he was a burden, a bother, an extra mouth to feed, a charity case who went from the trundle bed in Nino's room to the cot in Gio's to the room in the basement, where he stayed until the day he left for New York City. All that time, Nicky figured he was the poor relation with a different surname, whose parents had died and left him to rely on the only relatives that would take him in. But Nicky had it all wrong.

Nicky Castone had been a balm to his aunt, a loyal friend to his cousins, a helper to their wives, and a hardworking nephew in his uncle's business. But out of his own insecurity, and his own need to fit in, to wear the Palazzini uniform and hope that it looked like it fit, he had not claimed his life as his own. All that time, he had never really unpacked but lived out of a suitcase, which in his mind must always be at the ready in case he was asked to leave. Now he knew they had wanted him to stay.

Why had it taken leaving them to see who they were? Why hadn't Nicky seen them clearly when he sat at their table every night? He wanted them to love him, and they had, they did, and they always would. Why had it taken Nicky so long to believe it? Nicky Castone had been raised by the Palazzinis, and he'd become one.

Grief and its tangled vines of regret, hopelessness, and fear had grown wild around his heart since the day his mother died. The only way to crush the vines was to kill them at their root, to cut off the source of their growth, the guilt that fed them. Nicky could, at long last, let go of the wish that his life had been different. He let go of the self-recrimination that had haunted him as he blamed himself for his mother's death.

For years, he'd believed that he wasn't worthy of a home and a family to call his own. He had been abandoned; the circumstances were unimportant compared to the displacement he lived with because of it. Nicky had learned that the security that comes from knowing where your parents are when you lie down to sleep at night isn't a given, but a gift. He realized now, as a man, that he had missed out on very little as a boy, because he was loved, and yet even with all the attention and reassurance nothing could replace his mother. Yet in her youthful wisdom his mother had made sure he had what he needed. His mother had chosen her replacement wisely. There was nothing in his heart but gratitude for Aunt Jo, the woman who raised him, and for her husband, who stepped in to father him, and for his cousins, who had been brothers all along.

"You're famous, Nicky. My sister would be so proud."

"Are you?" Nicky asked Jo, knowing that her high opinion mattered to him as much.

"More than I can say," Jo assured him.

Nicky embraced his aunt before turning to the group. "Who's hungry?"

The Palazzinis began to talk over one another, weighing in where to go, what to eat, and how hungry they were. Nicky ignored the cacophony, the music that had underscored his life growing up in South Philly. He led them out of the studio to the restaurant next door and the reservation he had made for his family. No longer the guest, Nicky was, at long last, the host.

The purple leaves on the red maple tree flew off their branches, cascading slowly to the ground outside Mamie's kitchen window that afternoon. Autumn had come early in Roseto. Mamie snapped the kitchen window shut and opened the valve on the radiator beneath it, releasing a whoosh of warm steam. She placed her hands on the cold metal as her husband, Eddie Davanzo, pushed the door open, handed his wife a loaf of fresh bread from LeDonne's Bakery, and kissed her on the cheek before hanging up his policeman's cap.

"I'm warming up the soup."

"Augie's staying at school."

"Is he in trouble?"

"The nuns asked a few of the boys to move some boxes for them. Sister Ercolina said she'd feed them." Eddie removed his gun and holster and placed it on top of the refrigerator.

Mamie smiled and ladled the soup into a bowl.

"When Augie's happy, you're happy," Eddie remarked.

"You'll be the same when the baby's born." Mamie placed the bowl of tomato and rice soup in front of Eddie. She handed him a cloth napkin before slicing the fresh bread. Eddie slathered the slice with butter and dipped it into his soup. Mamie poured her husband a small glass of red wine. She examined the apples in a wooden bowl in the kitchen window, and chose a ripe red one. She sat down next to her husband and sliced it into sections for him.

"I can't wait to go back to work," Mamie admitted.

"When the baby's born, you won't miss your job."

"I think I will."

"You're the only woman I ever knew that didn't complain about working at the mill."

"I feel like I accomplish something there. How many times can I wax the floor? It's like an ice rink in here."

Mamie got up and went into the living room. She turned on the television set. The Philco hummed warming up before the picture appeared. Mamie returned to the kitchen and picked up the cruet of olive oil from the set on the table.

"Is your skin dry?" Eddie asked her.

"A little." Mamie went back into the living room with the olive oil. The picture on the television was now clear, in shades of gray, black, and white. Jinx Falkenburg was selling a Buick Skylark. Mamie liked her hat. It had a leopard band and a snap brim of black velvet. She leaned in closely, figuring the hat was an original by Helen Rosenberg. When she went back to work, Mamie would buy herself one.

Mamie placed a few drops of olive oil in her palm and rubbed her hands together to warm it. She reached under her maternity blouse and was massaging her stomach gently when a male voice announced, "And now our story."

The screen filled with the main title *Love of Life*.

"Eddie, get in here! The show is on!"

"I have to get back to work."

"You can watch for a minute."

Eddie stood in the doorway. There was nothing he wouldn't do for Mamie, so he joined her on the couch.

"This is not for me," he said.

"You like *The Lone Ranger*."

"That's got adventure. This is like going over to my mother's and we sit at the kitchen table and listen to her and her sisters gossip."

"It's a little like that." Mamie squinted at the set. "There he is!"

"Yep, that's him," Eddie confirmed.

"He got thin."

"Starving artist."

"Professional actor."

"You think so?"

"He's on every day. He's doing fine."

"How many people watch this show? Can't be that many."

Mamie watched Nicky intently as he played his scene. He had a specific talent, a way of being, that transcended the muddle of the charcoal images. Nicky emerged sharper, more clear somehow; the light hit him, and his face lit up like the moon in full on a black night.

"You miss him?" Eddie asked offhandedly.

"Oh God, no." Mamie turned to look at her husband and patted his thigh. It had been a few years since the Jubilee, but the memory of the two Carlos remained.

"Why do you watch, then?"

"I don't know. Maybe because he's the only famous person I ever met."

"But he was an impostor."

"That sounds criminal."

"He pretended to be somebody he wasn't."

"But he had good reason." A smile curled Mamie's lips, as she remembered the moment she first heard Nicky's funny accent, and the moment he dropped it in private just for her.

"I don't know what spell he cast over the women around here," Eddie complained.

"Eddie."

"I'm curious. I'd really like to know. It's like he raised women from the dead. A pack of Lazarus ladies in half slips."

Mamie motioned to Eddie to be quiet as she watched the show. Eddie took the olive oil, warmed a few drops in his hands, and rubbed it onto Mamie's stomach. She closed her eyes and felt the warmth of his touch, and the smooth heat of the oil as it penetrated her skin.

"I can feel him kicking," Eddie said proudly. "Muscle tone."

"He never stops, this baby."

"I wonder what he's thinking in there."

"He's thinking he's safe," Mamie said, lifting her husband's hands to kiss them.

"Well, he is. His father is a cop."

"And he lives in Roseto, where no harm will come to him."

"Because we take care of our own."

"That's what Nicky said."

"The impostor."

"The *actor*. Who played the ambassador. Anyway, he admired that about us. About Roseto. He liked that we were just like his family in South Philly. That we looked out for one another—that we watched out for each other's kids and shared the harvest of our gardens and took care of our old people, and when we did the little things, like bake a cake, we'd bake two, one for home and one for the neighbor. He was one of us."

"That's how he conned us." Eddie nodded. "We believed him because he was like us."

"A stranger can show up and be part of the family."

Nicky came back on the screen, and Mamie motioned for Eddie to hush. Onscreen, Nicky lit a cigarette and leaned against the bar in the background while a couple had an argument in the foreground. Nicky, however, didn't take his eyes off the fight, which forced the audience at home to focus on it too.

"You never answered my question, hon."

"What's that?" Mamie kept her eyes on the screen.

"Why did every woman in town go for him?"

"Eddie, it's not important now. It's yesterday's news. Irrelevant."

"I want to know."

Mamie sighed. "All right." She straightened her maternity blouse over her stomach and looked up at her husband. "He listened."

The Oldfield estate in Radnor was a splendid Tudor mansion which sat high on a hill before a clear blue lake so large it reflected the timbers on the facade. The footpaths leading to the house from the circular driveway were carpeted in thick emerald green moss. Hortense could not hear the sound of her own footsteps as she approached the front door. She observed that rich people lived in quietude; a perk of wealth was tranquility. Hortense stood back from the doorbell and took several deep breaths before pressing the gold button.

A butler answered the door. "May I help you?" he asked in a polished British accent.

"I am Mrs. Mooney. Mrs. Turnbough made arrangements for me to meet with Mrs. Oldfield."

The butler invited Hortense into the house. She stood in the entry hall, which gleamed under the lights of a chandelier dripping with onyx daggers and glass medallions. Hortense had never seen a chandelier made with black crystals, but she liked it.

The butler led Hortense to the library. The circular room was filled ceiling to floor with bookshelves. The walls were covered in red damask fabric. A suite of chairs and a sofa in forest green leather were arranged before a formal fireplace.

Edna Oldfield stood at her writing desk. Slim and tall, her white hair matched her pearls. Her plain suit was made of navy blue silk wool, the Main Line standard.

"Thank you for agreeing to see me today," Hortense said as she and Mrs. Oldfield sat across from one another in front of the fireplace.

"Mrs. Turnbough tells me you've been busy."

"Yes, I have. I have a passion and I've created something, I believe, is special and essential." Hortense sat up straight in the chair.

"Mrs. Mooney, tell me your story."

"I met an Italian woman whose people were from Venice. And she shared her very delicious tomato sauce with me. She passed away and left me the recipe and its secret ingredient. I have tested it for two years, done my own canning, and now I'm ready to sell it to the public."

Edna leaned back in the chair. "Let's say you have the best sauce in the history of sauce."

"I do."

"Why should I invest my money in you?" She squinted at Hortense.

"Because you'll make more money. A lot more money." Hortense squinted back.

"Why shouldn't I invest my money in you?"

"Because I'm colored?"

"You bring up a good point. Why would anyone buy Italian sauce from a colored lady?"

"Because the only color they will see is red. Marinara. The recipe is Italian, from a woman of pure Venetian descent. Though I do know, from studying history, that the spice market thrived in Venice as far back as the thirteenth century. I imagine some of my African relatives made their way to Italy with cardamom and cinnamon and anise. So you might say my people have a long history with the Venetians."

"That's a lovely story."

"I can't change my color, Mrs. Oldfield. And once you taste this sauce, you will not want to alter one ingredient. No one ever rejected Madame Curie's radium because she was French."

"True."

"Villa Hortensia is not about a face on a label, it's about the flavor in the jar. And I'm ready to work to bottle this product just right, put it in stores, and sell it all over the country."

"You are not young, Mrs. Mooney."

"There's not much I can do about that either. It took me a lifetime to get here. I can't apologize for that, and I shouldn't be penalized for taking the long road to success. There's no sell-by date on the American dream. Well, not on mine anyway. But if you're concerned about my age, why don't we rely on the wisdom of your husband? He left the company to you."

"He trusted me."

"He'd have to do more than trust you. He must have thought you had a brain and the skills to run a corporation."

"He did."

"And you weren't young when you took over, were you?"

"Hardly."

"So let's put my wisdom in the plus column, shall we?"

"We could, Mrs. Mooney."

"Have you had lunch, Mrs. Oldfield?"

"I haven't."

"May I make you lunch?"

"Perhaps another day." Edna forced a smile. "I have an important meeting at the office this afternoon. I am handing the reins of the company over to my son, and there is a lot of work to be done before that can happen."

"I just need enough time for water to boil."

"It's not a good day." Edna Oldfield stood. The butler opened the doors to the library to see Hortense to the door.

Hortense stood. "Mrs. Oldfield, I took three buses to get here today. And I don't want to tell you about the road to get to those three buses. You were kind to see me and you owe me nothing. However, if I were in your position, I would taste the sauce, if only to stay current. You want to look good to your son when you hand him the company. You want him in the best possible position when the news breaks and that stock market reacts."

"What do you mean?"

"Well, I have three more meetings scheduled, the next one at the Campbell Soup Company. That's right. You've heard of them. The Dorrance family. They live right over the hill due west. One stop on the bus. And they want to get into the Italian food business because they like the numbers they see coming off Chef Boyardee. I'm sure you've seen the profit margins yourself. Now, those numbers could be yours with Villa Hortensia. I'm not asking for much, Mrs. Oldfield—just twenty minutes to convince you, taste it for yourself before it's too late. Once you sample my sauce, I guarantee you will want to get into business with the person that will take you into that market share, Italian style. Now, may I fix you a dish of macaroni?"

Edna exhaled. "All right, Mrs. Mooney."

"Thank you kindly." Hortense turned to the butler. "Now, which way to the kitchen?"

Lena Palazzini modeled the latest Dachette hat for Mabel, a pink silk number with a large turquoise button on the crown.

Da Ponte's had just received a new shipment from New York, which meant the women of South Philly swarmed the swanky shop for the latest hats. The shop was painted ballerina pink and the glass cabinets that lined the wall were filled with hats positioned on mesh wire displays. A wall of mirrors, reflecting all angles of the customer, made trying on the latest Lilly Daché, Mr. John, Nettie Rosenstein, or Luray hat out of Paris, a pleasure.

"You look good in the cloche, Lena," Mabel remarked. "You have a small head. I need a brim."

"They have a knock-out Venetian gondolier hat." Lena handed her the big hat.

"If I buy that hat, my husband will have me working on a canoe on the Delaware," Mabel complained. "I don't want to give him any ideas."

The entrance door pushed open to the jingle of bells. Freda, the shop girl, poked her head out from the back room. Lena looked up and saw June and Diane, the wives of her husband's cousins, Micky and Tricky, the Palazzinis of Fitzwater Street. The ladies were a matched set, sleek and polished. June was a slim brunette shaped like a bottle of Coca-Cola, while Diane was a curvy blonde, strictly 7-Up.

"Hi girls," Mabel said from her seat on the bench. "I mean, cousins."

"Hi," June and Diane chimed together. The cousins stayed in the front of the store, avoiding Mabel and Lena until Mabel placed the gondolier hat on her head.

"You know, we can be friends," Mabel said loudly.

Diane and June looked at one another. After a moment, Diane summoned the courage. "You think so?"

"Why not? We didn't start this malarkey. I find plenty wrong with the Palazzinis, if you want to know the truth. Now, not enough to get in a vendetta over it. But they're not so perfect, are they?"

"Mabel," Lena chided her.

"I just think we should be friends with these girls because we probably have a lot in common. Right?"

"I think we do." Diane looked at Lena. "I was coming in here to buy that hat."

"See? Progress." Mabel modeled the gondolier hat. "What do you think of this?"

"I don't like it on you," June said.

"We will be very close," Mabel assured her. "You're honest." Mabel took the hat off and gave it to June.

"A snap brim would suit you better. It would show off your eyes." June handed Mabel a lovely periwinkle straw number with an orchid bow.

Mabel put the hat on. It lit her face romantically like blue moonlight.

Lena was amazed. "She's right."

"I won't say a word to our father-in-law," Mabel said.

"And I won't say a word to ours," June promised.

Weeks had passed since Hortense Mooney had made Edna Oldfield a dish of macaroni. The old lady had enjoyed it, and said as much. Hortense made sure Edna had brought extra to the office for her son to sample. She had even left the kitchen as spotless as she had found it. She didn't know what else she could do to convince Edna to take the sauce into her company fold.

Since she hadn't heard from Mrs. Oldfield, Hortense decided to spend some time at the Free Library and conduct some marketing research. She had spun a convincing fable about competition in the food business; now the facts were needed to back it up. There must be more companies in the country that would be interested in canning and selling Italian tomato sauce. Hortense simply had to find them.

Hortense was putting on her hat just so when the telegraph machine began to tick. She sighed and sat down at her desk. She lowered her head and placed her thumb on the lever as the message came through.

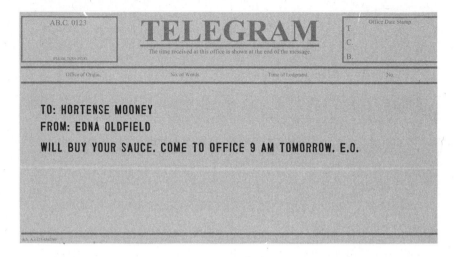

TELEGRAM

AB.C. 0123

The time received at this office is shown at the end of the message.

Office Date Stamp

Office of Origin.   No. of Words.   Time of Lodgment.   No.

TO: HORTENSE MOONEY
FROM: EDNA OLDFIELD
WILL BUY YOUR SAUCE. COME TO OFFICE 9 AM TOMORROW. E.O.

Hortense's hand began to shake. She checked her work. Twice. Three times. She typed out the message, glued it to her favorite telegram letterhead, filigree angels on hearts, and typed the envelope with her home address. She placed the telegram in her purse.

Hortense went to the file cabinet and unlocked the bottom drawer, where she kept her private stash: a bag of chocolate-covered raisins, a jar of Sanka, and the sheaf of her private correspondence. She shuffled through the folders until she found one marked, in her own handwriting:

FREEDOM

She lifted out the unsealed envelope, which had a typewritten letter folded inside. She took out the undated letter she had typed nearly thirty years earlier and read it.

Dear Mr. and Mrs. Palazzini,
I am grateful for the steady employment provided by your
company. The time has come for me to move on, and this
letter is to respectfully tender my resignation. I wish you
nothing but the best. Thank you.

Very truly yours,
Hortense Mooney

Hortense slid the letter into the carriage of the typewriter and typed in the date.

She picked up the fountain pen, shook it, and signed her name with a flourish. The ink dried while she put on her hat.

She left the letter on her desk and placed the bag of chocolate-covered raisins and the jar of Sanka in her purse before snapping it shut.

Hortense didn't take the bus home that night. She walked.

She walked through two Italian neighborhoods, one Irish, one Jewish section, and one other colored neighborhood before reaching her own—four miles in all, but she didn't feel it, not a single step, not in her knees or her hip, because the concrete beneath her feet had become air. She floated home over the streets in a bubble, under a cloudless sky that looked like a bolt of silver moiré.

Hortense had found, when she wasn't looking for it, when she had not made a plan, her divine purpose. She had waited for this moment all of her long life. She had been so eager for it to arrive, sometimes she'd mistaken lesser opportunities for it. When she learned how to type, or when she graduated first in her class from Bland High School, or when her great-aunt left her an acre of land in Metuchen, New Jersey, or when she graduated from Cheyney, or learned Morse code, she'd figured those were skills, breaks, or accomplishments that would reveal her path and lead her to the revelation of her destiny. But they had not. Yes, they were all points of growth, arrows in the right direction, but none were her purpose.

Villa Hortensia was her purpose.

Hortense Mooney used her sense of taste, her talent for cooking, her affinity for the Italian people, and her love of tomatoes to create a product people would buy. Tomatoes were life. They were delicious, and they grew in abundance. They were equally the fruit of kings and peasants. They were lovely to look at, rich in color, and round in form. Hortense learned to appreciate every aspect of the simple tomato: its firm skin, meaty pulp, and even the element she would discard, the translucent seeds in the grooves of the pith, which reminded her of precious pearls.

The new entrepreneur took advice. She had listened to Minna, trusted her, and that cleared the path for her to trust her own instincts. Never once did Hortense look back and question how long it had taken her to reach her goal, or second-guess her competence, or count herself out because of her age or her color or her bank account when her purpose was finally revealed. She believed in the excellence of her product, and that made her believe in herself. She could not fail.

Hortense hadn't dreamed of making spaghetti sauce all her life, but she accepted that Americans had a need for it now. Destiny reveals itself when need and desire merge in the moment. The world had changed since the war; when the boys returned home from Europe, they were all a little Italian, it seemed. Women were cutting their hair short: the Italian cut was all the rage in the women's magazines. The airwaves were full of the music of Vic Damone, Perry Como, Tony Bennett, Frank Sinatra, and Louis Prima. Fellini, Visconti, and Rossellini were making movies, the Agnellis made cars, the Ferragamos shoes—and all were popular with Americans. Franco Scalamandré was decorating the White House with his handwoven silk fabrics, and the Italian pope, the head of the Holy Roman Church, was planning his first visit to America. Hortense had spotted a trend, before it became one, and she would have the macaroni and gravy ready *per tutti*.

Bottled Italian tomato sauce.

Authentic recipe in the Venetian style!

Villa Hortensia would be on shelves long after she was gone, she believed, and like a good book, it would find a new and hungry audience as the years rolled on—those who appreciated the ripened tomatoes made sweet by slow simmering with garlic, hearts of celery, one carrot, onions, a touch of butter, olive oil, and the secret ingredient. The sauce would save women time and bring immediate joy to the family table. Easing a woman's burden was as important to Hortense as making a top-shelf item. A profitable business venture needed to have a touch of goodness to it, or so Hortense believed. Making a housewife's meal preparation a breeze was Hortense's idea of God's work.

The telegram from Edna Oldfield that arrived that day would be framed, and when the time came, it would be buried with Hortense Mooney.

Hortense took off her hat and gloves, placing them on the bench in the foyer of 34 Charlotte Street, where she had lived with her husband and daughters for almost forty years. She took a deep breath and looked around the dark house before opening her purse and removing the telegram in its envelope.

The wallpaper she had hung herself looked outdated; the yellow roses climbing up the gray trellis seemed from another era. Hortense thought she would have to do something about that, now that everything in her life was about to change for the better. She flipped on the lamp in the living room on her way to the kitchen. There was already a light on in the kitchen, so she knew Louis was home.

"I'm making eggs. You want some?" Louis asked her as he stood at the stove.

"I had half a sandwich at three."

"All right." Louis flipped his eggs in the pan, and his toast popped up in the electric toaster. Hortense moved to help. "I got it," he said.

Louis prepared his plate and placed it on the table. "There wasn't anything in the icebox for me. So I went ahead and made myself something." He sat down.

"I've been busy with the sauce."

"It's your life and your lover. Takes all your time."

"I know. You've been so patient." She sat down across from her husband at the kitchen table. "I got news today."

"Palazzini gave you a raise?"

"No. I quit."

"Why'd you do that?"

Hortense unfolded the telegram and handed it to Louis. He wiped his hands on the napkin before taking it from her.

"You sold the sauce to the Oldfield company," he said, handing the telegram back to her.

"I did. Villa Hortensia." She nodded.

"Good. Good for you."

"It's for us, Louis."

"I didn't have anything to do with it."

She watched as her husband angled the eggs onto the toast and took a bite. "We're not in competition. We're a team."

"Whatever you say." Louis chewed slowly.

"It's not whatever I say. It's what's true. Now, what is true for you?"

"That we are what we are. We keep on living."

"And that's good enough for you?"

"What choice do we have?"

"We have all the choice in the world. We have opportunities. We can grow. We can change."

"If I didn't know you were a teetotaler Baptist, I'd think you were drunk."

"I need to confess. I'm not exactly a teetotaler. I like a glass of wine from time to time."

"Good to know, Hortense."

"But I've not had any today. I'm as clear as I can be. We can create anything in this life, Louis. We can be whatever we want to be. Have what we want. It's all there for us. For you."

"You've lost your mind. What opportunities are out there for me? What opportunities have there ever been?"

"We can make things, Louis. I proved that with the sauce."

"Nobody ever wanted anything I made. All I ever did was clean up after people and the messes they made. I had ideas, but nothing would come of a colored man's ideas because a white man always had a better one. And if he didn't, he just took mine."

"Until now."

"For you."

"For us. Are you proud of the sauce?"

"It's yours. I'm just standing behind you as I always have. That's the world I live in."

"We stand together. At least, that's how I saw it. You worked hard. You're a deacon in the church. You're an important man."

"I don't need to go through all of this with you."

"I'm your wife."

"That doesn't make you right."

"Oh, Louis. It's fine with you for us to just keep going on the way we have been, isn't it?"

"Marriage lasts until death. It's in the Bible," Louis said with conviction.

"Somewhere in there it also says that *He came so you would have life and have it more abundantly.* Well, what we've been living is famine. *Lack.* This isn't working, Louis."

"What do you mean?"

"I know everything. I saw you with the widow."

"I had a church meeting." He shrugged.

"There was no congregation, Louis. Just a kiss on the street corner. But let's put that aside, because it's not the reason for what I'm about to do. It's just another fact in a long line of them that adds up to your truth and mine."

"Hortense . . ."

"Louis, let me talk. I have tried for over forty years to make you understand that you are worthy. I even dressed you. I bought you an Italian suit, I pressed a cotton shirt with French cuffs. I bought you a silk tie, made in England and sold at Wanamaker's. Couldn't afford it, so I put it on lay-away. Took me seventeen months to pay for it. You remember that, don't you? I saved up and bought you a car so you might drive down the street and feel like somebody."

"I appreciated what you did."

"I raised our girls and educated them. Sat at this table and did their homework with them every night when I couldn't keep my eyes open. I taught our daughters skills—both of them can iron silk without leaving a press mark, and last I checked, Maxie can type a hundred and four words a minute, and you know, she got the long fingers, and even Mary, with more effort, can type ninety-two words a minute. They are miracles. And you gave them to me. And every day, I say a prayer of gratitude for you, for them."

"I love our girls."

"I know you do. And I took care of your mother. I took her into the house to live with us and treated her with the respect I gave my own mother before she passed. I washed your mother's hair and set it once a week faithfully and took her every Sunday for services at the Everwood AME Church and every Wednesday night to Bible study, even though that wasn't my church and that wasn't my Bible group."

"She appreciated it."

"I changed out her church hats with every season—straw in the summer, felt in the winter. I placed silk rosebuds on the band in the spring and clusters of green pearl grapes in the fall so she might know that she was special and that her hat backed it up. Whenever she got a compliment on her hat, she'd turn and wink at me. I didn't do this for me, I didn't do it for her, I did it for you."

Louis pushed his chair away from the table.

"Now, I'm not saying you're a bad man. I don't know what all you did when you left this house. I didn't question who you were with and why you were with them and I never asked, not because I wasn't curious but because the answer would have meant I might have to do something with the knowledge. And the truth is, I was tired. I had enough with my job and taking care of this house and our family. But now the girls have moved out, they are on their way with lives of their own, your mother is gone, and it's just you and me. And I am neither happy nor unhappy, I am on that island of nothing where dreams aren't born but they don't die either. They just aren't. And that's not living. You might be fine in neutral, but I'm not."

"I'm sorry, Hortense."

"I accept your apology. And please accept mine. I'm responsible here too. I thought we could pick up where we left off before we had the girls. But now I know that youth isn't waiting for you on the other side of wisdom."

"It's not." Louis put his head in his hands.

"In Roseto, I learned a few things about myself. I learned I could think on my feet, get myself out of hot water. And around here, I've been wading in lukewarm since I had Maxie. That's right. That long. And it wasn't your fault. Once I made you over, I needed a new project. I didn't realize it then. I figured a new project would present itself—and when the children were cooked, well, I had nothing on the worktable. And in Roseto, I learned how to make gravy. Not our gravy. Not brown gravy. But gravy the Italians make. So I'm going into business with the Oldfields. And because I stayed with you for all these years and you blessed me with two fine daughters, I'm going to give you half of whatever I make. If I can, as a farewell gift, make you rich, it would be my pleasure. But as your gift to me, you must pack up your things and leave this house. It's time for you to be with someone who loves you. It's time for you to share a bed with a woman who faces you when you sleep. Do we have an understanding?"

"We have an understanding." Louis wiped a tear away.

Hortense had never seen Louis Mooney cry. Never once. Not when his lung was pierced by a falling window when he was working the odd job, not when she lost the baby boy in 1916, not when his mother died or when he was laid off from the railroad. Today, of all days, he cried. But he wasn't sad; he wept tears of relief, the kind that come after a dry spell, when rain falls after a long drought and the sky opens up and drenches the fields, saving the crop that saves the village, that saves the country, that in turn saves the world. It was like that with Louis in that moment. He was on the brink of happiness before it was too late, before he died without knowing it could be his.

Hortense got off the bus in Manhattan at East Sixty-third Street and Madison Avenue. Nicky had promised her that Quo Vadis was easy to find. She looked down at the business card he had sent in her birthday note.

As she descended the steps of the bus, she passed a small group of colored ladies, domestics in uniforms, on their way home from work. Hortense nodded at them in recognition. They returned the acknowledgment.

She pushed through the front door of the restaurant and into ancient Rome. The walls were covered in hand-painted tile mosaics, a series of Doric columns separated the tables, and red velvet wallpaper framed the arches.

Hortense waited at the maître d' stand. Inside, a sea of white faces looked up at her, taking in her hat, gloves, and coat, and finally her brown face. Hortense patted the gold brooch on her collar as the maître d' returned. "I'm here to meet Mr. Castone."

Gino, one of the owners, surveyed the reservation log. "I don't have a Mr. Castone on the reservation list."

"But he invited me here for dinner at seven o'clock."

"Yes, I did!" Nicky bounded through the restaurant and joined Hortense. "She's with me," he said to Gino.

"I'm sorry, sir, she asked for a Mr. Castone. I didn't recognize the name."

"That's my given name," Nicky explained.

"Let me show you to your table." Gino smiled and escorted

Hortense and Nicky back to their table. Gino helped Hortense into her chair.

"If you're no longer a Castone, what do you call yourself now?" Hortense asked.

"Nick Carl."

"Sounds like the first and middle of a name, not the entirety of one."

"Carl is for Carlo, our old pal the ambassador."

"Why do you want to be reminded of him? He almost ruined you. Or you him. I can't remember." Hortense chuckled.

"Either way, he changed my life."

"Almost ended mine."

Nicky laughed. "The Ambassador changed everything. When we went to Roseto, we got out of the car, and they loved us and they didn't even know us. It's a lot like being on television."

"They only accepted me because I was with you," Hortense reminded him. "I'm a bad actress."

"Not true. You were very imposing on your own. I have a feeling they were on to me from the beginning, but they wanted to believe I was the ambassador, they needed him. He was coming all the way from Italy to honor them. People need to feel important."

"They do indeed." Hortense thought of Louis, and that made her eyes fill with tears.

"Are you crying?"

"No. It's the onions."

Nicky looked around. "There are no onions here."

"I said it was the onions. It's the onions."

"Mrs. Mooney, I've never seen you cry."

"I've been known to weep here and yon. I've had some sadness. Some misery." Hortense opened the menu.

"The food is good here."

"I think your friend Gino thought I was here to apply for a job in the kitchen."

"Well, you're not."

"Funny thing. I could work in that kitchen now. I know my way around Italian cuisine."

"Years around the Palazzinis."

"You could say that, but not really. I stayed to myself over at the garage, except for the times I took care of you at the house."

"You took care of me?"

"Yes, sir."

"Was I a good kid?"

"Better than your cousins. I thought those boys would end up in prison. They would not follow instructions."

"What do you remember about my mother?"

"She was a lovely person." Hortense closed the menu. "Very kind. I would say she was the prettier of the two sisters, and had the better figure. Jo leans to the stocky, if you know what I mean. Your mother was more graceful. And the face—she had a very sweet countenance. And good teeth."

"Do you remember when she died?"

"It was a long illness. You know, when an illness goes on and on, you don't think that the person will pass. She fought hard because she didn't want to leave you behind. That was her only worry. You were everything to her."

"Where was I when she died?"

"You were in the room with her."

"I was?"

"You had a day bed in her room. Do you remember that?"

Nicky nodded that he did.

"You were asleep. It was night, almost morning. Mrs. Palazzini called me because she didn't want to leave the children alone when she went with her husband to take your mother to the hospital. I went right over. When I got there, Mike and Nancy had arrived. Her boys were all over the place, one slept on the couch, the other two on chairs. You slept through everything. I went upstairs when they took your mother out of the room."

"They left me there?"

"I was with you. And when you woke up, you asked for her. And I didn't know what to tell you, but I could see, even though you were only a little boy, you knew. So I told you the truth, that she had passed but she was in heaven, and now she was everywhere."

"Did I believe you?"

"I don't know. Did you?"

"I guess I had to."

"So I picked up a book and read to you. That made you feel better."

"I wish I could remember more." Nicky straightened his necktie.

"Your mother did come to see me at the office a few months before she passed. She said she was looking for her sister, but I knew better. She needed to talk to me alone. She knew that I did the books, so she wanted to make sure that you got everything you needed. She gave me her bank account number. And I took all the information down, and she sat with me awhile, we talked about my girls. She was interested in them too. When she got up to leave, she said, 'Mrs. Mooney, I know this is asking a lot, but will you watch out for Nicholas?' That's what she called you. She said 810 Montrose was a zoo, and she was afraid you'd get lost in the commotion over there. And I told her that I would."

"And you have."

"Why else would a sane woman agree to pose as Eleanor Roosevelt's attaché in Roseto, Pennsylvania? I only did it because I promised your mother I would look out for you."

"Here I thought it was because you believed in my acting skills. Do you drink?" Nicky offered Hortense the wine.

"The occasional nip."

Nicky poured Hortense, then himself, a glass of wine. They toasted and sipped.

"Have you met a nice young lady from a good family yet?"

"I can't do two things at once."

"Work and a social life?"

"No, nice lady from a good family. It's either one or the other, never both."

"I saw Peachy DePino. She had her baby. A boy."

"Good for her."

"I didn't recognize her. A lot of baby weight, even though the baby was in the pram." Hortense shook her head.

"I can't imagine Peachy heavy."

"You don't have to. You can see it plain. Of course, some of it's baby and will come off, and the rest is cannoli filling. According to your cousin Mabel."

"I'm happy for Peachy."

"I told you that would all work out. Every heel finds its shoe."

"You never said that. You just said don't marry her."

"Same thing. You ever hear from Mamie?"

"No."

"But you made it all square with her, didn't you?"

"I did."

"Would you like to see her again?"

"I got her to her destination."

"When she got there, did you have any feelings for her?"

"You never forget the person that healed you."

"Or the one that made you rich. Minna was an angel. And I guess now that she's gone, there's no need to go back to Roseto. I have no reason, no excuse. Well, maybe I'll slip down and go to the cemetery sometime. Italians and Baptists think that's important, so I'll do that."

"Why do you think she gave you the recipe?"

"I don't know. I think about that sometimes. She believed that the most important thing was—" Hortense rapped on the table, "*This.*"

"*La tavola.*" Nicky toasted Hortense with his wine glass.

"Right. Minna said anything of importance in a family happened right here."

"So this is a good place to bring up my problem."

"How can I help you?"

"I'm making money."

"Where's the problem in that?"

"I didn't think about getting paid, when I got on television. I just thought about the job and loving the work. And it turns out that being happy brought the money."

"Minna told me that one leads to the other. Happy leads to money but never money to happy."

"Money can bring out the worst in people."

"It can. When money is the goal. When Minna died, she left all her money to the church. Nobody had any idea how much she had, but it was a lot. She kept it in a bank in New Jersey. She felt if anybody in Roseto knew she had a few bucks, they might treat her differently. So she never told them she was rich. I thought that was odd. Why not be proud of the money you earned? So I went to the library to see if they had a book on the subject. I wanted to understand how to keep my head if I got rich. Now, when I go to the library, they don't let us into the Main Branch stacks, we have to go in the back to a room designated for colored folks. We don't get a good selection. But sometimes they trip up, and a good book gets through and I grab it."

"Good for you."

"Anyhow, I found this one book, the story of the richest man in Araby. He was a sultan. You know, with a silk tent and a harem. He lived in a desert so vast you needed full sun or a full moon to find anything in it. In the middle of that desert, he had a palace. A palace so huge you couldn't count the rooms. People would visit and get lost in there and show up years later. That's how vast the inside of this cat's palace was! Everything inside was made of something rare from some exotic island or foreign land. Elements like fine marble, hand-painted enamel, tiny mosaic tiles made of turquoise and jade. He was so rich, he even had a gold toilet. Gold seat. Gold flushing handle and chain. Gold lid. A golden commode. I sat with that thought for a while. And I thought what it might be like to be so rich that you think you need a gold toilet.

"Common sense tells us that even if a man has great power and genius and cunning and possesses all of the treasures of the Orient, the last thing he needs is a gold crapper, because shit is shit. There's no way to make it into anything more. But rich people believe they are better than you and me, and therefore everything they make is more important than it actually is, including their own dirt. Now, you keep your wits about you. You remember where you came from, and you'll be all right. And if you don't need all that money you're making, give it to somebody who can use it."

"I think I can do that."

"There's a lot of need out there."

"I'm sure there is."

"You have an old friend in dire straits right now."

"I do?"

"Calla Borelli has to sell the theater."

"When?"

"Soon. I hear it's going up for auction. Poor kid."

Nicky held the door for Hortense as they left Quo Vadis.

"I can get the bus back to the Port Authority from here," Hortense said.

"You're not taking the bus." Nicky motioned for a black town car to pull up to the curb. "You get a royal coach, Mrs. Mooney."

"Do tell."

"I always wanted to do something nice for you. I never got you that Lilly Daché hat."

"There's still time," Hortense teased, "This isn't enough, but it's something." Hortense reached into her handbag and gave Nicky a jar of Villa Hortensia Fine Italian Tomato Sauce. "This is the very first jar of my tomato sauce. See there? It has a gold number one on the lid. I had that put there just for you. You can use the sauce—just save the jar."

"It's a knockout." Nicky held the bottle like a treasure.

"The label is something else. I had an artist render the canal and the gondola. That's the real Villa Hortensia right there on the label. I think Minna would like it."

"Why wouldn't she? It's Italian." Nicky smiled.

"Do you ever think you'll come home to visit?"

Nicky was glad it was dark out, so Hortense wouldn't see his face flush with shame. "I have such a crazy schedule."

"I know. But it would mean a lot to your aunt. You're one of her own, and you're the only bird that ever flew out of that nest. I think it traumatized her."

"They come up for the show. We have dinner."

"It's not the same. She wants to *do* for you. She wants to make the bed for you and do your wash. Press your handkerchiefs. Cook a good meal. Have the whole family around the table telling stories until it's too late to do anything but go to sleep. That's the only gift you can give that lady. The gift of you."

"I'll do my best, Mrs. Mooney."

"I know you will."

A group of middle-aged women in hats and gloves tiptoed up behind Nicky. "Mr. Carl?"

Nicky turned to them, smiling warmly. "Yes?"

"We're your biggest fans!" the ladies shrieked.

Hortense laughed.

"Could we trouble you for an autograph?"

"We never miss *Love of Life!*"

The women began to snap open their purses to fish out pens and scraps of paper. They spoke over one another, in harmony lines of commentary about *Love of Life*, characters they liked, others they didn't, and was Artie the cabdriver going to end up with Alice the nurse? Nicky tucked the jar of tomato sauce under his arm as he signed his name. His most ardent fan, a cheerful woman who was built like a packing box and dressed in a beige wool suit, pulled Nicky close and kissed him on the cheek.

Nicky turned to Hortense and winked. "Don't wait for me, Mrs. Mooney."

"All right. I know this thing has a meter." Hortense nodded as the driver opened the door on the town car for her.

"Excuse me, ladies," Nicky said as he handed the pen to one of the fans. He went to Hortense and embraced her. Hortense hugged him for a long time, realizing she had never, in all the years of knowing Nicky, ever taken him in her arms since he was a boy. She made up for all the years in that moment by holding him closely and tightly.

Hortense gave Nicky back to his fans and slipped into the car. The driver closed the door behind her. She rolled down the window, wanting to say something more to Nicky, but the gaggle had consumed him once more. There is no fame like the fame that comes from being on the television set. When you appear in someone's home, you belong to them.

As the car pulled away, Hortense turned to look back at Nicky.

"Do you need to go back?" the driver asked her.

"No sir."

"You looked like you forgot something."

"I didn't forget. But it can wait."

"You can always call him," the driver offered.

"Or I could send him a telegram."

"Do people still send telegrams?" The driver looked at her in the rearview mirror. All Hortense could do was smile.

As the town car pulled into traffic, Hortense removed her gloves and hat and placed them on the seat. She smoothed her hair and opened her purse, removing her handkerchief, a gift from Jo Palazzini. In the corner, Jo had embroidered "HM" in glorious purple whipstitches in honor of her retirement. Hortense saved this handkerchief for church and special occasions. Tonight had been a very special occasion.

As Hortense's eyes filled with tears, she dabbed them with the handkerchief. What she wanted to tell Nicky could wait, because it would always be true, because it always had been true.

Hortense Mooney loved Nicky Castone as though he were her own son. It's not that he had replaced the one she lost, but the time she spent with Nicky had made the loss of her own son bearable. She wanted him to know that he had healed her.

And, like all good mothers, Hortense had prayed for Nicky's happiness more than her own. She could see that he had finally found the thing he loved to do, and he was happy. It filled her heart to bursting.

Nicky walked back to his apartment, carrying Mrs. Mooney's jar of spaghetti sauce. He moved through the revolving door, past the white-gloved doorman, and took the brass-trimmed elevator to the heavens, the twenty-first floor. He entered his apartment.

Ralph Stampone had decorated it in black, white, and silver in the Art Deco style, sparing no expense. Every surface gleamed, reflecting the view out the floor-to-ceiling windows of the bridges of the East River that Nicky had driven across daily as a cabdriver. He often shook his head in wonderment that his first home in the sky reminded him of his humble start.

Nicky put the jar of sauce on the counter of his modern kitchen. It was outfitted with all the latest equipment, which he hardly used. Life as a bachelor was sad that way. He could make anything he desired in that kitchen but it was no fun eating alone. He loosened his tie and took off his jacket. He hung both in the closet, which was full of the latest shirts, ties, and suits from Bronzini's, where all the men who worked in television shopped for their clothes. He rearranged the marble ashtray, the sculpture of gold-leafed Capri coral, and the small stack of velvet-covered Shakespeare plays that Ralph had artfully arranged on the black lacquer coffee table, before he picked up the phone.

"Aunt Jo? Did I wake you?"

"No, not at all. Are you all right?"

Nicky chuckled to himself. If he wasn't all right, the last person he would alarm was his aunt. "I'm fine. I was thinking of coming down this weekend."

"You mean it? Everyone would love to see you."

"If the family gets any bigger, you'll have to move to another city."

"Isn't it wonderful?"

"It is. Now, listen, Auntie. Don't fuss."

"Of course not."

"And don't tell anybody."

She squealed in delight.

Nicky hung up the phone. He went to the window and looked out over the city. He smiled to himself as he looked down and saw rows of yellow cabs cluttering the black streets. The cab, once his life, his job, and the way he moved through the world.

He had a spectacular view. This cityscape was exactly what he had pictured in his dreams when he was living in the basement on the Lower East Side. But tonight, as it lay before him, dazzling in its sharp, black lines, frosted glass windows, and angled rooftops, even New York City wasn't enough—or perhaps it had been plenty, and Nicky had simply had his fill. Whatever the case, the answers were no longer here, in the stacks of black buildings floating in the clouds high in the night sky or even on the streets below, where if a young man was lucky enough, he found himself a part of things.

The secret of life, the joy of everything, lay elsewhere. There was little wonder in the way the moon rose behind the skyline and over the East River, as though it were a pearl loosed from a string of them. There was so much beauty, but it did not belong to him any longer.

It was time to go home again.

12

Nicky drove through the familiar streets of his old neighborhood in South Philly in his custom Ford convertible, painted the color of a stick of Dentyne gum. It was fully loaded with whitewall tires, silver chrome enhancements, and a dove-gray leather interior. A car for a star.

When Nicky turned on to Montrose Street, his heart sank. Aunt Jo had failed to tell him that there was a street fair blocking the house and garage. He squinted, trying to figure out how to navigate through the throng.

But it wasn't a street fair or a holiday. It wasn't the anticipation of a parade going by, with neighbors standing on their porches awaiting the spectacle. These folks were waiting for something else entirely, *someone* else: Nick Carl, their own Nicky Castone, who had left South Philly to seek his fortune and found it on the television set in New York City. Many had left South Philly to make it big, and some disappeared down the drain, but Nicky had put a stopper in it, filled the tub with gin, and was floating on top, with the rest of the winners from the neighborhood, including Buddy Greco, Gus Cifelli, and Al Martino.

Nicky was embarrassed by the attention but also moved by it, as his family and neighbors turned out to welcome him home, waving small American flags. He felt overwhelmed as he drove his car at a crawl through the crowd. The familiar faces gathered around, reaching for him, whistling, applauding, and blowing kisses, as though it were Palm Sunday, he was you-know-who, the small American flags were green branches, and his Pontiac was a donkey.

Aunt Jo stood on the steps of the porch of 810, her family behind her, the small army with which Nicky had locked steps all of his life. Of course she had not followed his instructions. Why would she? This celebration was as much about her love for her family as it was for Nicky, because when one Palazzini made it big, they all did.

Nicky parked his car outside the Borelli Theater in the same spot where he used to park his bike. He pushed the stage door open to find his fellow actors in costume, ready to perform the matinee. The company swarmed around him. He was the beacon, the Saint Malachy of this band of players, the one who made it out, made it to New York, survived, got cast in a television show, and was exalted in the art form, and no longer had to work two jobs in order to act in a show. He made his way through the house and out into the lobby, where Rosa DeNero was eating a doughnut in the ticket booth.

"How's the house?" Nicky asked her through the ticket window.

Rosa dropped her doughnut. "Nick Carl."

"Just plain Nicky to you, Rosa."

"I cannot believe it." She ran her fist delicately over her bottom lip to remove the powdered sugar.

"It took a television soap opera for you to believe in me?"

Rosa nodded in awe.

"How many tickets have you sold?"

"Thirty-three."

"How's the mez?"

"I haven't sold a seat up there this entire run." She leaned close to Nicky through the glass. "The days are numbered here."

"What do you mean?"

"Everything is falling apart. Tax man came through. Or maybe it was a plumber. We're not sure. All we know is that there's no money to fix anything and no money coming in. It's just too much for one woman to handle. That's all I can say."

"Did you ever get that washing machine?"

"I did. But now I'm saving up for the dryer."

"When one dream is realized, there is always another."

"Oh brother, that's the truth." Rosa went back to her doughnut.

Nicky took the stairs down to the basement, where he found Hambone Mason standing on a stool as Calla mended the hem on his tunic.

"Nick, old chum!" Hambone threw his arms around Nicky.

"Hambone, old rum!" Nicky held his breath until Hambone released him from his grip. "You old gin hound," he teased.

"Only on show nights." Hambone winked. "A little cheer keeps me clear. Can't remember my lines without it."

"You're good to go." Calla patted Hambone on the back. He grabbed his ruff, snapping it around his neck as he climbed the stairs to the wings.

Calla rolled the empty rack into the hallway. "Welcome back, Nick. Are you going to stay and watch the show?"

"Evidently I have my choice of seats. Anywhere in the house."

"What's that supposed to mean?"

"You haven't sold any."

"We've sold thirty-three seats."

"Big deal."

"It is to me." Calla went back into the costume shop and began clearing the worktable.

"You're in over your head, Calla."

"How would you know?"

"Simple arithmetic."

"Don't you have an accountant who does that for you?" Calla queried. "Can you still do math?"

"Can you?" Nicky shot back.

"Let's see. You took off for the big city, went on the television, began making big money, and who's heard from you? Oh, there was that article in the paper that showed you in your new digs. Art Deco. All shiny. Leather couch. A big painting by some modern artist, and lamps that look like upside-down feet."

"Actually they're modernist Italian."

"It doesn't matter. They look like feet."

Nicky shook his finger at Calla. "There it is. The old bait and switch. You make all this about me and my deficiencies, so it's not about the theater and how you've bungled this enterprise and driven it into the ground like those pipes they're laying over on Wharton."

"I don't know what you mean." Calla plunged the needle into the pincushion.

"The place is falling apart."

"I hope you didn't drive in from New York to tell me that." Calla grabbed her notes and went up the steps. "Because that was a waste of gas."

"War's over. No more rations."

"It's a waste of your time." Calla grabbed a basket of props and went up the stairs.

"I'm beginning to think so." Nicky followed her. "I have my own problems, you know."

"Sorry to hear it."

"Doesn't sound like it."

"Look. I have enough to do, enough to worry about without a swell-headed television star coming in here and looking for sympathy for I-can't-imagine-what. I am doing what I can do here. I was in the red when Dad was alive. And it's only gotten worse. I got an offer on the building, and I turned it down. You see, for me it's about keeping the theater going, the history, the legacy, the family line. It's not about the money. If I wanted to be rich, there are ways."

"You could marry it."

"Aren't you a modern man?"

"I can be."

"Just not right now. Just not with me. *Ever.*"

"You're tough."

"Circumstances made me this way. If you must know, I'm trying to find someone to buy it who will let me rent it so we can continue our work."

"What work, Calla?"

"The plays of Shakespeare. Performed in repertory. Year-round. With a permanent and professional company in residence."

"Reaching an audience of tens. Sometimes an audience in pairs."

"You can't hurt my feelings by being rude."

"This is a business, you know."

"Oh, should we try and get sponsors? Like television? Lux soap? Lucky Strike cigarettes? American Steel?"

"It's worth exploring." Nicky followed her through the theater.

"Ugh. You've become a snob. The driver is now being driven."

"I'm going to ignore your jabs. You think you can continue to put out a product however you want, and just because *you* decide it's good, the audience should show up just because you say so. That makes *you* the snob, Calla."

"I don't have a fancy apartment decorated by some snooty guy named Ralph in the Sunday magazine of the *Inquirer*—"

"It was syndicated by the AP!"

"I don't even know what that means, and I don't care."

"Associated Press."

"It's telling that you live on the twentieth floor."

"Twenty-first."

"High up in some glass building. Your feet haven't touched the ground since you went on the television. You aren't a real person anymore. You forgot the groundlings. I live among them. I am one! I create for them!"

"You had your picture in the paper with the mayor."

"That was months ago."

"Still, you have a connection to the hoity-toity. Why don't you ask Big Frank Arrigo to get in here and fix this place? He knows plaster guys and marble people and Sheetrock installers."

"I don't ask for favors."

"You should start."

"You too? What is it with you guys? If a woman isn't needy, you can't relate to her? What's wrong with a woman who can run the show?"

"Nothing, if she can actually run the show."

"You know what, Nicky? I don't need this. I don't need you coming around here, telling me what to do when you haven't lifted one finger to help."

The cast clustered in the wings as Calla trudged across the stage and kicked open the stage door. The afternoon sun threw a bright beam of light across the dark stage. Nicky stood in it.

"You can direct as well as anyone—any man. But you are not good at bringing in money. That's a different skill. Your father didn't have it, and neither do you."

The cast, stunned at Nicky's barb, inhaled a collective breath. Their eyes turned to Calla, who they were certain would explode. Instead, Calla looked at Nicky. She put her hands in her pockets calmly.

"Maybe he didn't. And maybe I don't. But we are devoted to our work. We stay here, we do our best, and we don't give up. We believe that South Philly deserves a live theater that mounts the classics. We don't run away, because there's a certain nobility in serving people. I don't expect you to understand this, because you've made other choices."

"Hold it right there, Calla," Nicky protested.

Calla held up her hand. "Instead of badgering me with questions, I have two for you. Who's seen you? Who's heard from you?" Calla pointed to Tony, Norma, Josie, and Hambone, who kept their eyes on the stage floor. "Has anyone?"

Nicky looked over at his old friends, who would not look him in the eye. He had thought about calling Tony and having him come into the city to see the show and meet Gloria, but he hadn't done it. He knew that Norma would have loved to participate in a weekend workshop at the Abbe Theater, but he had never sent her the flyer. Hambone would have enjoyed watching the soap, and Josie would've glided for months on one postcard of the Statue of Liberty with a message that read *Hope you and Burt are well.* But he hadn't sent it. He hadn't done any of those things. Thinking about them was not the same as doing them. He was a lousy friend.

"You forgot the people that made you. This theater gave you your break." Calla looked up into the fly space overhead, where the lines of the cables looked like delicate silver spider webs. What a grand place, if you let your imagination build it so, but Nicky Castone didn't get it.

Calla continued, "Sam Borelli's theater. How kind of you to come back to honor my father by insulting him, calling him a bad businessman."

"He would agree with me."

"He's not here to defend himself."

"Why can't you admit you need help?"

"If I did, and I don't, you'd be the last person I'd ask."

Rosa DeNero peeked through the stage curtain. "Excuse me. It's time to open the house."

"Open the house, Rosa." Calla called off, "Places everyone." She turned to Nicky. "We have a show to do."

Calla kept her hand on the handle of the stage door. Nicky walked through the beam of light and out the door, into the afternoon sun and out onto the loading platform, as Calla closed the door behind him.

"She told him," Hambone whispered to Tony.

The cast took their places behind Hambone and Tony in the wings, looking like a box of crayons in their velvet costumes.

"What do we do now?" Norma said, clipping on rhinestone ear bobs.

"Those lips that love's own hand did make, Breathed forth the sound that said 'I hate,'" Tony whispered.

"What the hell does that mean?" Hambone squelched a bourbon burp.

"It means we won't be seeing Nicky around here anymore," Norma said.

Nicky lay in his old bed in his basement room at the Palazzinis'. He wasn't nostalgic for his basement room any longer. He found out he no longer missed the scent of the spaghetti as it dried, or the sweet tomatoes as they were canned. This was no sanctuary. He no more belonged in this room than he did behind the wheel of Car No. 4. His old life was hanging in somebody else's closet now; he had outgrown the shoes, the pants, and the cap. Nick Carl no longer fit in Nicky Castone's clothes or his bed or his old life. It felt odd.

Nicky lay on top of the coverlet, shirtless, his belt loosened, and the top button of his trousers undone. His stomach was distended from Aunt Jo's twelve-course meal, which ended with a round of prosecco followed by a hit of homemade limoncello and a *cin cin* of Uncle Dom's bitters that had done nothing to settle his stomach, and in fact, had only made his bloat worse.

Nicky was his own definition of fat and lonely and unlovable. As he drifted off to sleep, he imagined climbing the road to Roseto Valfortore, which unlocked the door to his dreams. He would count the stones until he could no longer, until he had reached the top of the mountain. He hoped to wake in the morning with some direction.

Calla adjusted her hat in the reflection of the window outside Frank Arrigo's construction trailer on Wharton as the sun set behind the city. She had spent the day consulting every bank, builder, and real estate agent in town regarding the theater, and every one of them told her that Frank Arrigo was the man to see. Their romance had ended poorly and abruptly, but Calla put that aside as she had nowhere else to turn as the secretary ushered her into Frank's office inside the trailer.

Frank looked up at Calla, warmly, at first, surprised to see her. When he remembered his feelings, his eyes narrowed.

"Congratulations on your wedding." Calla smiled brightly.

"Thanks. We're very happy."

"And that makes me happy."

"I always wondered what did."

"Frank, you're the best businessman I know, and I'm in a rough spot with the theater. I'm looking for someone to buy it and lease it to me until I can buy it back."

"Why would I do that?"

"You'd make a profit when I bought it back."

"Or I'd lose my investment entirely."

"I wouldn't let that happen."

"Calla, there's a reason the banks won't loan you money. You're a very bad risk. You persist in keeping a business open that doesn't make money. At best, here and there it breaks even. A private business is not going to partner with you if a bank, with all the resources in the country, wouldn't do it."

"But you know me. You know I'm not a risk."

"I'll tell you what I can do."

"Okay."

"I'll buy it from you now. Outright. We'll set a fair price. But no theater. I want the lot."

"I don't want to do that. I didn't want to do that when I was going with you and I don't want to do that now."

"Then I'll wait for the property to go to auction—which, at the rate you're going, it will—and I'll buy it for pennies on the dollar. I want you to remember we had this conversation."

"I'm not likely to forget it."

Calla stood. She was sorry she had put on her best hat and gloves for this.

"Good luck, Frank," she said as she left his office. He said something to her as she went out the trailer door, but she didn't hear him; the metal steps were noisy as she climbed down to the ground.

Frank Arrigo said *You'll be back*. He was a man who always had to have the last word. What he didn't know was that Calla hadn't heard him—but it didn't matter, she wouldn't be back. She would find another way to save Borelli's.

Calla took a long walk after meeting with Frank. She stopped to pick up a sack of fresh cookies from Isgro's and, eating them as she walked, she gave a lot of thought to her situation at the theater. She actually laughed when she saw *Freddie Cocozza was here* written in chalk on the sidewalk. Only the old-timers knew Freddie became Mario Lanza. She stopped and looked in the window of Ye

Old Apothecary, where they had a display of White Shoulders and Golden Shadows in their glistening bottles before heading back to the theater.

Calla exhaled as she pushed through the stage door and made her way down to the costume shop. She flipped on the light and gasped.

Nicky was sprawled out on the worktable.

She recoiled. "What are you doing here?"

"I couldn't sleep. Why the good hat?" Nicky rolled over on one side and rubbed his lower back.

"I had a business meeting."

"How did it go?"

"I don't want to discuss it."

"Poorly, then, I take it. I realize now, years later, that the mattress at 810 was bad from the first moment I slept on it. I didn't know because I didn't have anything to compare it to. I'd love a cookie. Thanks." He took the bag from her and fished out a chocolate and vanilla checkerboard and ate it.

"Why are you telling me this?" She grabbed her cookies back.

"I wanted you to know I didn't sleep well last night. Did you?"

"If this is your roundabout way of apologizing—"

"I'm not apologizing. Why would I apologize? Why would anyone be sorry about telling the truth?"

"Then let's shake hands and part friends. I've got work to do. There's plenty of places in South Philly where you can pass the time. Go to the Casella Social Club and get in on one of your cousin Gio's card games."

"You're a cold cookie. You're impossible. Unfeeling, actually. You turn on and off like a garden hose. And not one of those nice ones with the sprinkler feature that goes back and forth like a windshield wiper. You're an ice cold gusher. You have to be right. You don't listen to reason. You know everything about everything. What am I doing here?"

"What *are* you doing here?"

"I don't know. I have a good life in the city. I like my routine. I live in the sky. I get to see clouds float by where I used to see feet shuffle by. Shoes. I use to see pigeon toes, now I see pigeons fly by. At night, I see stars. The moon."

"Ugh."

"Yes, sister. And I'm free. I can stay out all night on Fridays and drink with my friends after the show tapes. We blow off steam. We laugh. Carry on. I answer to no one."

"Well, I do. I answer to this company of actors. I listen to the audience, dwindled as it is, as you've pointed out. I listen to my gut, and that has failed me. I try and listen to any voices from the other side that might offer some direction, but my mother and father, ostensibly in heaven, are not speaking up, and all I hear is the banging of the pipes that need fixing on the mezzanine floor. We live different lives, Nick, but what I don't understand is why you came over here to remind me what a failure I am. *Again.* You must take some glee in that, which makes you sadistic, which means that your success has made you not humble but proud, and turned you into one of those men that likes to tell the rest of us why we're failures, as if we don't have the talent you possess, when in fact it's not about talent at all, it's about luck. Sheer luck put you where you are. Talent, yes, that's a factor—when luck appears, you need it. But without the luck, all the talent in the world doesn't matter."

"You really believe that?"

"I'm living it! I went to Frank Arrigo. I asked him to buy the place. I made him an offer. And he turned me down. He said he'd wait for the auction. He'd get a better deal that way. What are the chances that the only business in town that wants this building happens to be a man I used to see?"

"An old flame you put out with a fire hose. You shouldn't have gone over there. That's my fault."

"No, it's mine. I thought he was my friend. But you see, he

didn't get what he wanted from me, so that makes me the enemy. Men have a crazy way of moving through the world. You don't do things their way, it doesn't get done. I will never understand it. Ego before progress."

"He married Peachy. Who knew that bookkeeper was Joan of Arc, and her cause was slaying me to get to Frank Arrigo?"

"Shut up, Nicky. She's over you, and so am I. I'm down to the last of my money. I asked my sisters to bail me out, and Portia said no—she was done supporting this theater. Helen—you know, she's pretty smart—she said, 'Calla, when are you going to stop trying to redeem Dad's life? When are you going to realize that he never made it because he was chasing a silly dream?' And I said, 'Is that what you thought when you watched him from the mezzanine? I thought he was astonishing. I was fascinated when he worked with the actors. When he blocked the play. When weeks later the sets rolled in and the lights came on, and the costumes appeared, and a world was unveiled right before our eyes. There was nothing but a dark space, and suddenly it was filled with life. Who does that? Who can do it? Not an ordinary person but an extraordinary artist! My father! Our father! Perhaps in heaven!' My sisters thought he was a crackpot. They didn't appreciate how he searched for meaning and tried to create work that mattered. All they knew is that there was never enough money. Mom never had what she needed. The house was never repaired. We wore hand-me-downs so the actors could have new costumes. We had to work the box office and scrub the restrooms and seat the patrons. We had to get up early in the morning before the sun came up and hang posters throughout South Philly, hoping that they would help sell some tickets.

"All my sisters remember is the worst of it—like when Dad burned the bad reviews. And they looked down on him for getting bad ones in the first place as though it was his fault. And when he got good ones, they weren't enough. He couldn't win. He was being judged all the time. How can an artist survive that? Well, we can't always. We quit."

"This isn't really about art, Calla."

"That was my dad's life."

"Yes, it was. But this theater is just another family business. Some people cut lumber, some people make pants, and others drive cabs. Your family made shows."

"Not anymore. I'm done."

"What will you do?"

"Maybe I'll work for the Philly opera company. I can do crew work. Sew costumes."

"Crew? You're a director."

"It didn't work out."

"So you'll just quit?"

"It quit me."

"I see. The scribes and pharisees of the American theater got together and took a vote and ousted you."

"None of this is your problem. Thank you for listening to me. I told you some things I haven't told anyone. I guess I thought no one wanted to hear them. But it seemed like you did."

Calla looked down at her clipboard. She removed the pencil and began to tap it against the board until the sound drove Nicky to gently take the pencil from her.

"Are you hungry?"

"Do you think that's why I can't think straight?"

"Yes I do. You can't eat cookies and think big thoughts."

"Too much sugar"—Calla sighed—"brings crazy ideas and a fat fanny."

"I'm trying to get as thin as I was when I came out of the army. The television camera adds some pounds. But right now I don't care. Before I go back to the city, why don't we have a cheesesteak? In honor of our long friendship. What could it hurt? I promise not to be critical of you. Let's eat. Why not?"

"Why not?" Calla smiled.

"I haven't seen your teeth in a while. You have a smile."

"I'm keeping it under wraps until something good happens."

"Might happen sooner than you think."

Calla locked up and soon followed Nicky out of the theater. Nicky helped her into the passenger seat of the cab and closed the door behind her, then went around the front of the car. Calla shielded her eyes from the street light as he moved through it. It was just a momentary thing, but he seemed to disappear in the light, and while she heard the click of the driver's-side door and felt the body of the car rock gently when he sat in the seat, she had a moment of believing Nicky gone, and that made her think.

Nicky picked up two cheesesteaks at Sal's window as Calla cleared a spot on the outdoor table, where he soon joined her with their dinner.

A woman of sixty sitting across from them, her blue-gray hair set in tight curls, was chewing her sandwich when she recognized Nick Carl from the television set. A grin spread across her face like a pat of butter melting over a hot pancake. The soap opera fan reached up and adjusted the small saucer hat on her head, so the button adornment might face out properly. She got up and went to their table.

"I was wondering," she said, flirting with Nicky.

Calla took a bite of the sandwich and nodded. "Yes, this is Nick Carl from *Love of Life*."

"I knew it!" the lady said. "I love you on the show. Will you sign something?"

"He'd love to. He's not hungry at all," Calla said through a bite of the sandwich.

Nicky shot Calla a look, then smiled politely at the fan. "Of course."

The woman fished in her handbag until she found her check-book. She snapped the fountain pen off the jacket. "Here," she said excitedly. "Make it out to Ethel. That's me."

"A check?"

"No, no, just your autograph."

Nicky followed her instructions.

"Thank you. The girls at the Aster and Posy Garden Club won't believe it."

"Well, you won't have to worry about that. Now you have proof we met." Nicky handed the lady the autograph and pen. Ethel backed away, elated. "Thanks for that." Nicky took a bite out of his sandwich.

"You must have the ladies throwing themselves at you con-stantly, now that you're famous," Calla said.

"Here and there."

"Is it like Roseto?"

"It's got its similarities. When I was a big, phony ambassador with a cheesy accent, heavy on the parm, the women liked me because they thought I was important. Nick Carl is just another invention. Neither of those fellows is real."

"I know the real Nicky Castone."

"Keep the details to yourself. It will kill my love life."

"No kidding. But, it'll cost you. The next time the AP wants the story, you tell them to call me."

"What would you say?"

"A lot. Do you ever hear from Mamie?"

"No." Nicky's face flushed. Calla really did know everything about him, and he wasn't so sure that was a good thing.

"Would you like to?" she asked innocently.

"Mamie came into my life and showed me what was missing. Whatever I lost, she found. She married the beat cop and had a baby. She's happy. All my exes are happy. "

"Good for them."

"How about you?"

"I'm always going to be alone."

"Don't tell the AP that. They won't think you're a credible interview."

"Why not?"

"Because you're not going to be alone."

"I wish I had your confidence."

"So what were your plans when I go back to the city tonight?"

Calla shrugged. "I was going to check the want ads."

Nicky made a face. "Sounds like fun."

"See what's out there," Calla said positively.

"What *is* out there?"

"Right now? I don't know. I saw an ad. There's a new coat factory going up in Germantown."

"Do you mind if I offer some advice?"

"Please do."

"The want ads are never a good way to go when you're looking for a job. I know that from my hack days. I used to clean the cab at the end of the shift, and people always left their old newspapers in the back seat. Two observations: very few people ever finished the crossword puzzle."

"Fascinating."

"I thought so. And the want ads—will make you feel unwanted. You're not somebody who can be described in three lines."

"I'm not?"

"So you shouldn't spend time looking through them."

"I don't know how else to look for a job."

"You already have one."

"Nicky, the theater has to close. I've run out of options."

"All but one."

"Don't hold back. I'm listening."

"Me."

"Keep your money, it's a losing proposition. Even the loan sharks turn away when they see me coming."

"I believe in you."

"I could never take a dime from you, knowing what I know about the debt, the repairs that need to be done, and the audience that we'd have to build to put the theater in the black. It's impossible. But thank you for wanting to try."

"I don't want to give you any money."

"That's wise." Calla patted his hand and went back to her sandwich.

"I want to give you *all* of my money."

Calla took another bite of her sandwich.

"Calla, did you hear me?"

She nodded. "You're out of your mind." She took a swig of birch beer from the bottle. "What does that even mean? All of it. Are you dying? Do you have a bad kidney or something?"

"Could you please stop eating for one moment?" Nicky took her sandwich and put it down. He moved the bottle of soda. "I want to be your family." Nicky leaned across the table and, taking Calla's face in his hands, kissed her.

When his lips touched hers, the sound around them became louder, more distinct. She could hear the radio inside Sal's, the roar of a truck engine as it went by, a sprinkle of conversation across the way, staccatoed with laughter from behind Sal's window. It all made a kind of music that she had never heard before. She forgot all about the sandwich, hungry now for Nicky's kisses.

"Excuse me, Mr. Carl. This is my friend, Viv. She watches *Love of Life* too. She's your biggest fan."

"I'm in the middle of something here," he said without opening his eyes, before kissing Calla again.

"I can see that. But we're kind of in a hurry. Viv has a sodality meeting at her church and is on a tight schedule."

"I'm in charge of the cake and coffee," Viv said firmly.

Nicky stood and extended his hand. Viv and her friend were petite Italian ladies in their late seventies. Separate, they were demure; together, they were a pair of tire irons. "It's a pleasure, Viv."

An electrical current of desire went through Viv, almost sparking. "My, you're tall."

"I was fully grown by my eighth birthday."

The ladies looked at one another. "I'll bet." Viv nodded. "Will you sign my collection envelope? It's all I have."

"As long as I don't have to fill it."

"Oh, you don't."

Nicky signed the back of Viv's tithe envelope from the church of Saint Thomas Aquinas.

"Thank you! This will never wind up in the collection basket now!" The ladies tottered off like two squirrels sharing a single nut.

"What happens now?" Calla sat back and folded her arms.

"That depends upon your knowledge of Shakespeare."

"Quiz me."

"What happened in Act four, scene three of *Twelfth Night*?"

"Sebastian and Olivia marry."

"So, we find a priest. That is, if you'll marry me."

Calla Borelli looked into Nicky Castone's eyes. They were at once as blue as the water off the shore of Santa Margherita, a place she longed to know, and as gray as the floorboards on the porch at the old house on Ellsworth Street. He was, in an instant, all the places she dreamed of and the only home she'd ever known. He was the past, and he was the *now*—the elusive moment her father tried to explain, which could only exist in the theater when the actor and the audience are one. But Nicky was also the love she had hoped for, and waited for, even when she believed it would never be hers. Calla had no idea her true love would appear in her life first as her friend.

Calla didn't want to be a wife and marry like her sisters or her mother; she didn't know how. She didn't want to change her name, and give up her father's, as though he hadn't lived and didn't matter. If she had been born her father's son, she would have carried it proudly. Why did she have to sacrifice Borelli because she was born a girl? Calla wanted her own life, one that could grow with another, like the dual twists of the lilac's trunks as they wrapped around the drainpipe over the stage door, the ones she could never cut, afraid somehow, that if she did, she would sever beauty itself from the theater she loved.

"Why would you want to marry me?" she asked him.

"Honestly? All the other girls I asked said no."

"How many did you ask?"

"Fourteen."

"Is that all?" Calla asked.

"Not enough?"

"You have a national audience."

"I don't read all the fan mail."

"Maybe you should."

"So what do you say?"

"I never let myself think this might happen."

"Why not?"

"I didn't want to be disappointed."

"So now you don't have to be. Ever again. What do you say? I'm hanging here like that flat on the stage wall. The one where the pulley never works right. One nudge in the wrong direction and I come crashing to the floor impaling Hambone to the prop table."

"How are you going to explain this to all the other women?"

"Calla Borelli, you're the only woman I've ever been sure of."

"I'm broke."

"I've been broke."

"I have debts."

"We'll chip away at them."

"I'm bossy."

"I know."

"I won't change."

"So henpeck me."

"I think I know it all sometimes."

Nicky nodded. "More often than not."

"I cut my own hair."

"That will stop."

"I can't see myself in the beauty parlor."

"You'd better."

"I've loved you all along, Nick."

"You have?" He was intrigued. "How long?"

"Dad was directing *As You Like It*. Spring season, nineteen forty-eight."

"Nineteen forty-six."

"I'm not good with numbers."

"This explains the problem with the bank."

She ignored the comment. "And you came into the theater. You were very thin. Like all the guys back from the war. And Dad asked you what you wanted to do, and you said, 'Anything but act.'"

"I don't remember that."

"And later Dad said that you were the first person that ever walked into the theater that didn't want to be an actor."

"I've done all right, Calla."

"It wouldn't matter to me if you hadn't. You're my best friend."

Calla put her arms around Nicky. She meant it. She believed in Nicky Castone in ways that her mother believed in her father. Calla would love him always, but she didn't want to give up her own dreams for that great privilege. How could she ever tell him this? She couldn't. So instead she kissed him; she kissed his cheeks, his nose, his mouth, and as her lips grazed his, she let herself stay in the best moment she had ever known: the one that lasts a lifetime.

Nicky rapped on the priest's door of the rectory with his left hand and held on to Calla's hand with his right.

A young, fresh-scrubbed priest, wearing a new Roman collar and black cassock, answered the door.

"Father Rodo?"

"He's on retreat."

"Are you the priest on duty?"

"Yes."

"Father, what's your name?"

"Father Berry."

"Beautiful name. Sounds like summer. Father, Miss Borelli and I want to be married."

"You have to come and meet with Father Rodo, and for six weeks the banns of marriage have to appear in the church bulletin."

"We don't have time for that."

"Those are the rules."

"Father, I implore you, as a Roman Catholic from my first squawk to my last confession, to please marry us immediately. Calla is a Catholic in good standing at Our Lady of—"

"Good Counsel," Calla finished the sentence.

"You see, we're very devout."

"You have to follow the rules." Father Berry recognized Nicky.

"Nick Carl. Father, I am Nick Carl on *Love of Life*. I'm from South Philly."

"No kidding." Father Berry grinned.

"Do you think you could help out a native son?"

"And daughter?" Calla added.

"I'm sorry. The rules are, as you know, set in Rome. There's no wiggle room."

"None?"

"I could call Father Rodo if it's an extreme situation."

"I assure you, it's extreme."

"Do you have rings?"

"Yes," Nicky lied.

"Come in."

Nicky fished his key chain out of his pocket. He turned and ripped the keys off the loops, pulling two loops from the key chain as Father Berry went into his study. Calla shook her head. They waited until Father Berry emerged a few moments later.

"I can't marry you. I'm sorry. Father Rodo says it's impossible."

"But nothing is impossible with God!"

"In this instance, unfortunately it is."

"Tell him—and I'm sorry to tell you this, forgive me—Miss Borelli is going to have a baby. We're already on the road to Bethlehem, Father. If you understand what I mean."

Father Berry's face lost all color. "I understand. That's a different situation. I'll be right back."

"I'm not having a baby," she whispered.

"You will someday." Nicky and Calla waited for the priest to return.

"Come with me." Father Berry showed them the way into the chapel.

Calla, in her best hat, and Nicky, in his tight belt, were married by Father Berry before the small altar at Saint Mary Magdalen de Pazzi, at the foot of a stained-glass window, which in the light of the full moon threw shades of blue on the happy couple and the nervous priest. The priest blessed the rings without judging the cheap wire. Calla and Nicky took a moment to tighten the wire around their ring fingers before they kissed.

"I hope you'll raise the baby Catholic," Father Berry said solemnly.

"Dear Friar, you have my word," Nicky promised.

Nicky and Calla kissed on the sidewalk outside the church.

"Where do we go?" Nicky asked her. "Montrose Street is a bus station."

"You've never asked me where I live."

"Where do you live?"

She smiled. "It's your home now, too, Nick."

"Are you a good cook?"

"A better baker."

"I'll take it. I've got two more grommets on this belt."

Nicky was surprised when Calla guided him back to the theater. She flipped on the work lights and instructed him to follow her as she climbed the ladder in the wings to the crawl space above the stage.

She took his hand as she led him across the grid to a small door about five feet high, which she pushed open and ducked inside. He followed her in.

When Nicky stood inside the room, it was dark. Calla moved through the space, turning on small lamps that threw pink light onto the floor. Her home was an enormous room, beautifully appointed with the best furniture from her parents' home, including a big four-poster bed, a dresser, and a large easy chair, covered in an afghan her mother had made. The kitchen was a simple sink and hot plate.

Calla went to the far wall and pulled a rope, not unlike the one that made the stage curtain rise and fall. As she did, a canvas tarp pulled away to reveal a glass ceiling, a skylight, a set of paned windows on the roof of the theater.

"What do you think?"

He kissed his wife.

"We used to play in this room as kids. This is where they stored the flats," she explained.

Nicky held Calla close. "I would have liked to give you a big fancy wedding."

"This was sweet."

"What about the dolls on the cars and the cookie trays?"

"Not important."

"The confetti?"

"I don't need all that."

"What about a diamond ring?"

"Someday, maybe."

"Ah, there *is* something Mrs. Castone desires."

Calla kissed her husband's lips, his eyes, his cheeks, his neck, and his hands. As they undressed, she said *Don't peek!* for old times' sake, but they laughed, which was more important than anything that had come before or after their vows. Nicky lifted his wife off the ground and carried her to their bed under the stars.

Calla pulled Nicky close, thinking he belonged there, that he always had.

Nicky wanted to make up for all the time they had lost, that he had squandered, living a different life without her. He had found his Beatrice; she had emerged from the pages of *Tales from Shakespeare* in a cloud of gold satin and now she was his. It had been so obvious that he hadn't seen it. That night he vowed never to leave her, and she believed him. Calla made some promises to Nicky too, ones she would keep all of her life. Destiny had snuck up on them, claimed their hearts, secured their souls, and flown them as close to the moon that night as the heights of Borelli's Theater would allow. Calla Borelli was no meltaway, she was a keeper. And Nicky Castone? He was an orphan no longer. He would never be alone again.

Hortense Mooney almost got off at the wrong stop on the crosstown. Out of habit, she was going to cross on Chestnut as she had done all those years for work, but today she had business on the other side of Broad.

She adjusted the collar on her Nettie Rosenstein coat, which she had bought at a trunk show, knowing she needed a good cloth coat for her business meetings. Using the window outside Joella's Bakery as a mirror, she pulled the brim of her cloche hat just so over her eyes, exactly as the saleslady had demonstrated.

She took a deep breath when she walked under the dazzling red, white, and green awning of the Pronto Taxi & Limousine Service at 113 Fitzwater. Mike Palazzini knew how to make an entrance on his shop; he had flair, that was for sure.

Hortense pushed the entry door open, stepping into a waiting area. To her right was a floor-to-ceiling glass window; to her left, a long red patent-leather bench. Beyond the glass was a fleet of cabs in a garage three times as large as Palazzini's. Hortense squinted, and noticed a lift, where a team of mechanics was working on a car elevated in mid-air. This was a first-class operation—not that Hortense was surprised.

"Mrs. Mooney!" Mike Palazzini entered the waiting area from the door that connected it to the garage.

"Mr. Palazzini, it's been a long time."

"I was young." Mike clucked. "I miss being young."

"We all do."

"You haven't changed." Mike Palazzini was sharply dressed in a navy blazer, white slacks, a blue-and-white striped shirt, and camel suede loafers. "How have you been?"

"Busy."

"My brother keeps you hopping."

"I don't work there anymore."

"What did he do?"

"Oh, no, it was nothing like that. I had an opportunity to start my own business."

"No kidding."

"All my years with you paid off. I make spaghetti sauce. I have a deal with the Oldfield company."

"You must be rich."

Hortense lowered her voice. "I didn't buy this hat on lay-away."

"Congratulations! Why not? This is America. Why can't a dispatcher become a mogul?"

"Don't forget I was also a Western Union telegraph operator."

"That was after I left."

"That's right."

"Why did my brother put that in the garage? It never made any sense to me."

"When Mrs. Palazzini sent all four boys off to the war, she vowed that she would never answer the door if an officer came with the worst news. She wanted to get the news before they did, so she asked her husband to put in the telegraph office."

"And they all came home."

"That's right."

"You know I lost my Richard."

"Terrible. I'm sorry."

"What can you do?"

"Nothing. Not a thing. Just pray." Hortense patted his shoulder.

Mike found his pressed handkerchief in his pocket. He wiped away a few tears. "I cry about that kid every day. Here I go. The old waterworks."

"You always will, you know."

"I guess."

"I came to see you about your brother."

"Is he all right?"

"I think so."

"Is he sick?"

"The man is in a constant state of dyspepsia, but I don't think that'll kill him."

"So he's okay."

"I think you should take him off the island." Of all the Italian expressions Hortense had learned from the Palazzini family over the years, the one that remained with her was the concept of *the island*, the place you put people when you had a falling-out and weren't speaking to them.

"He put himself on the island," Mike said defensively. "He doesn't talk to me. I'm the one who's on the island."

"Well, whoever put the other on the island, it doesn't matter now. What does matter is that there's a wedding reception, and I've been asked to deliver this invitation to you and Nancy and your boys and their wives." Hortense reached into her purse and gave the envelope to Mike, who opened it.

"These are tickets to a show."

"Partly. There's a party after the play. That's the wedding part. Now, if you need more, you just use my name at the box office at Borelli's, and they'll give you whatever you need."

"Nicky got married?"

"Yes, he did."

"But he's on the television in New York City."

"Yes, but he's come back to Philly. Married a local girl. Calla Borelli."

"Is there a nuptial mass?"

"They were married at the church by the priest in the chapel."

"Oh, one of those." Mike whistled. "Shotgun."

"No, *not* one of those. They just didn't want a big fanfare."

"Who doesn't want a big fanfare?" Mike scratched his head. "Does my brother know I've been invited?"

"This is from Nicky."

"I always felt bad for that kid. No father. No mother."

"He's done just fine."

"Jo mothered him, I guess." Mike shrugged.

"Nicky had many mothers." Hortense stood to go. "I hope you can make it."

"I'll ask Nancy. She's the boss."

Mike watched Hortense as she walked out onto Fitzwater. The bus pulled up, and she climbed aboard. He shook his head. Mrs. Mooney had worked for Dom too long; she had picked up his tight ways. Why would a titan of business take the bus? She should have her own car and driver. Maybe he'd ask her about that. Maybe she hadn't thought about it. Maybe Pronto could provide such a service. Why not?

The curtain call for *The Taming of the Shrew* was an additional scene to the raucous comedy in the play proper. Calla had directed Petruchio (Nicky) to chase Katherine (Norma) up the stage-right aisle and down the left until he caught her; she had the rest of the cast pair off and chase one another. Tony Coppolella chased Josie Ciletti in the mezzanine aisle while the remainder of the cast fanned out onstage. The audience went wild; the play earned the first standing ovation that any play directed by Calla Borelli had ever received.

The set was an exuberant Elizabethan wedding village painted in cotton candy colors, bright shades of yellow, green, and pink with a bright blue muslin sky; modernist papier-mâché clouds swayed beneath the canopy of blue. Tonight it would also serve as the setting for Calla and Nicky's belated wedding reception. Every cousin, friend, and neighbor had been invited to the celebration. Gloria Monty and her husband, Robert F. O'Byrne, had driven down from New York City. Ralph Stampone and Mary and Mark Silverberg drove in too, not wanting to miss a moment of the launch of Nicky and Calla's new chapter.

As the curtain fell, the family made the party onstage.

The cousin-in-laws along with Calla's sisters Helen and Portia flew into action with the crack efficiency of a good prop team as they set up the party. Nonna was wheeled center stage in her chair as guests lined up to greet her. Mabel threw the lace tablecloth on the work table while Lena centered the flower arrangement and the candles. Tony rolled in coolers of A-treat soda and beer. Josie handed the cast members baskets of fresh-wrapped sandwiches to disburse. Nino brought the punch bowl in from the wings, Elsa followed with the cookie tray, and Gio pushed the wedding cake in on a cart. Soon, the guests filled the stage and the rest of the cast filtered in from the wings.

Hortense Mooney climbed up the steps to the stage, leading the ladies from her church auxiliary. Her favorite thing to do with her money, after spoiling her daughters, was to treat her friends from the church to bus trips and cultural events. The ladies enjoyed *The Taming of the Shrew*, but mostly, like everyone else, they were thrilled to see Nicky, who was on television.

Backstage, Gloria and Robert knocked on Nicky's dressing room door.

"Open up!" Gloria banged on the door.

Nicky threw the door open and embraced them. "Gloria! You made it! Robert!"

"We decided we're not taking a train every time we want to see you. You have to come up and do the show again."

"And give up all this?"

"We'd love to have you back," Robert said. "Lux soap is insisting on it."

"Please consider it," Gloria said. "The play was magnificent, and so were you! The theater was packed."

"My wife put my face on the poster with the subtitle 'Star of CBS Television's *Love of Life*.' She figured she could sell out the house, and she did."

"So business is good?"

"We're getting there, breaking even, which is better than bleeding red."

"Let's get you back on our show. You can do both."

"You got it, Gloria."

"Great. We're on it." Gloria gave Nick a big hug. "I think I need you to come back on and kill off a few people. Or not. I just miss you."

"You know she means it." Robert embraced him too.

"We're going to have to drive back tonight, but we had to see you."

"I can never thank you enough, both of you."

"Don't thank us. You're just plain old-fashioned good, my friend," Gloria assured him.

Nicky watched Gloria and Robert go, and thought how lucky he was to have met them, and how once you meet your angels, they never really leave you, even when you leave them.

"Hey Nick." Tony poked his head out of his dressing room. "Hambone brought you a gift."

Hambone Mason emerged from the dressing room in a smoking jacket, carrying a bottle of vodka. "The wedding punch needs a kick, I understand."

"What are you waiting for, Hambone?" Nicky laughed. "Spike it!"

Nicky followed Hambone up to the stage where he found Calla directing the guests to the buffet table. Nicky swept Calla into his arms.

"Do you like my dress?" she asked. Calla twirled in the bright yellow taffeta gown. "It's the only yellow gown I could find. I look like a lemon."

"No, you're Beatrice." Nicky kissed his wife. He whistled to get the revelers' attention as Josie went through the crowd with the traditional white satin bag, collecting wedding gifts of cash. The sack, *La Boost*, was filling up fast. Josie encouraged the guests to contribute with both her words and her cleavage.

As the cast, their friends, and the family gathered around, Nicky saw Hortense and her church ladies, standing in the wings. He went to Hortense, took her by the hand, and brought her center stage. Leaving her with Calla, he went back to the wings, gathered the church ladies, and brought them into the spotlight too.

"I have to thank Mrs. Hortense Mooney. Please raise a glass. I lost my mother, and my Aunt Jo became my second mother, but God didn't think one mother was enough, so he gave me a third mother, Mrs. Mooney. No woman ever looked out for anyone like she looked out for me."

"*Cent'Anni.*" Hortense raised her glass, and the guests followed suit. "It means a hundred years of health and happiness," she explained to her church group.

"Best dispatcher. Irreplaceable," Dom grumbled. "Had to go and make gravy and get rich."

"The American dream, honey," Jo said softly. "Enough to go around."

"I'd like to toast my wife, Calla." Nicky raised his glass.

"A fine director," Tony shouted.

"Relentless but kind," Hambone chimed in.

"To Calla!" the Palazzinis toasted.

"Who would like the floor?" Nicky raised his glass. "We have a lot of actors here—this could go all night. And we have enough punch to take us to the matinee." The company cheered.

Mike Palazzini edged through the crowd, excusing himself, until he made it to the center of the stage. Aunt Nancy, her sons Micky and Tricky, followed him.

Silence fell over the crowd as Mike stood across the stage from his brother.

"What are you doing here?" Dom asked Mike.

"We were invited." Mike stood with his feet about six inches apart. He twisted the gold ring on his hand.

Dom and Mike stood facing one another, their wives beside them and their families behind them. Nicky and Calla looked at each other. The guests knew the story of the feud, but it was rare to see one dramatized on this stage that had not been written by Shakespeare.

"I invited them," Nicky admitted.

"But I was the messenger. I went over to Fitzwater to deliver the invitation."

"You too, Mrs. Mooney?" Dom felt betrayed.

Hortense shrugged. "I knew Mr. Mike wouldn't throw me out."

"We want the families to be together again, Uncle Dom," Calla said.

"I think it's a good idea, Dominic," Jo said quietly.

"Did I ask you, Joanna?"

"You did not. But I'll say it again."

"You don't have to. I think it's a good idea too, Dominic," Mike said.

"Did you see the play?" Dom asked Mike gingerly.

"We sat up in the nosebleeds with the colored folks," Mike admitted.

"Hey," Hortense said. "We liked our view."

"It's not bad, Mrs. Mooney," Mike agreed.

"I like to sit up high." Nancy Palazzini looked lovely in a sapphire-blue satin cocktail dress with a matching bolero. Her hair was tinted red; her makeup and nails, as they always had been, were a study in perfection.

"Good to see you again, Aunt Jo, Uncle Dom," Micky said. He was handsome and well turned out like his father, with the same head of thick hair.

"Same goes for me." Tricky was shy and didn't like to speak in public, but everyone knew his heart. He was trim and well manicured, like his mother.

Dom made a circle on the stage floor with the toe of his old black dress shoe.

"I'm sorry about Ricky," he finally said to his brother, Mike.

Mike's eyes filled with tears. "What are you going to do?"

"We gave him up for a good cause," Nancy said. "But we live with the loss every day."

"Not easy," Mike said quietly.

"No, it isn't." Nancy put her hand on her husband's back. "But we cope. Jo's letter got me through."

"You wrote her a letter?" Dom asked.

"I can write letters without permission from you."

"Not when they're on the island."

"You can get mail to the island, Dominic." Jo raised her voice.

"Since when?"

"Since I mailed it and it arrived and it was read. All right?"

"Watch your tone, Joanna!"

"I will not! Especially when you're behaving like a jackass."

"Can't argue with her there, Dom." Mike opened his hands to them.

"You're on her side?"

"I always liked her better than you."

"Now the truth comes out."

"And none of it matters," Nancy said, gripping her alligator purse so tightly by the handle it seemed it might snap off. "All we are is what we've lost. And you boys"—she looked at Dom and then at her husband—"know we've lost a lot."

"It affected all of us. We miss our cousins. Even though we always had our seats together at the Phillies games," Dominic admitted.

"You did what?" Dom was stunned.

"Ricky, Micky, and Tricky, and Gio and Nino and me. We went to the games together. And when Nicky got old enough, we brought him along too," Dominic confessed.

"That's insubordination." Dom wiped his face with his hands.

"Evidently, they even have sports on the island." Jo sipped her punch.

"We would've done it anyway, Pop. We're family. You don't just throw people out like paper plates." Nino put his arm around his father's shoulders.

"We have so many good memories. We'd go to Wildwood Crest

in the summers. Uncle Mike would blow the horn when we passed the bridge with the burning torches."

"You remember that, Gio?" Uncle Mike smiled.

"And Pop, you taught us how to fish. You drove the boat when we water-skied. And you took us on all the rides." Gio looked at Dom.

"Because I had a weak stomach. I still do," Mike admitted.

"You always looked so beautiful in your bathing suits. And your caps always matched," Jo said to Nancy with admiration.

"What can I say, I love fashion."

"Nothing wrong with that," Jo assured her.

"And when we came in from the beach, you had dinner ready. Every night," Nancy said appreciatively.

"It was my pleasure," Jo said. "I'm allergic to the sun. I'm not allergic to pots and pans."

"Thank God for that," Dom said.

Nicky took Calla's hand and joined his uncles, his cousins, and their wives. "There's something I wanted to tell you."

"Please say you're coming back to drive Number 4." Dom put his hands in the prayer position.

"No, I've found a new calling, Uncle Dom. When you become an actor, you learn a technique, and it requires you to use your memory and feelings. And early on, when I first started taking classes, I couldn't stop thinking about Ricky. He was the one among us that had the soul of an artist. He loved the opera. He read books. Not comic books."

"Books with hard covers." Micky nodded.

"He was nuts for the theater. Broadway. He loved to go to a show in New York. He was always begging me to take him into the city for a show," Mike remembered.

"Ricky had class," Gio said. "That's the only word for it."

"It was nice that one of us had it," Tricky offered.

"He was my boy that appreciated the finer things," Nancy said quietly. "But the finest of all were his friendships. He would be happy tonight."

"To Ricky." Nicky raised his glass.

"*Cent'anni,*" Calla said as they touched their glasses.

"No more fights!" Dominic raised his glass.

"*Mazel tov!*" Elsa clinked glasses with her cousins-in-law.

Calla raised her glass. "To my sisters and my brothers-in-law!" Helen and Portia raised their glasses with their husbands.

"*Salute!*" Mike tapped his glass with his brother Dom's.

Hortense tipped her glass to Hambone.

"Refill?" he asked.

"A smidge." Hambone filled Hortense's glass.

Two policemen pushed through the crowd.

"Officer, we're having a party. If we're blocking the street, we'll clear the cars," Nicky promised them.

"The cars are fine," the officer said.

His partner scanned the crowd. "We're looking for Giovanni Palazzini."

"You are not serious." Mabel turned to her husband and smacked the back of his head. "We're at a wedding reception."

"Is he here?" the cop wanted to know.

"Of course he's here. The entire family is here." Mabel offered her husband up like a Swedish meatball.

"I'm over here, Officer." Gio raised his hand.

Aunt Jo stepped between the cops and her son. "I'm sure there's been a mistake."

"Is this your mother?" the cop asked Gio.

"Yes."

"Mothers. Vessels of hope." The cop shook his head. "Mr. Palazzini, we need you to come down to the station with us."

"The station?" Mabel moaned. "Will there be cuffs?"

"You guys, don't let this throw you. Carry on with the party,"

Gio said as his hands were clicked into the handcuffs. Gio was led out the stage door and into the squad car parked in the alley. Mabel followed them into the alley.

"Where are you going?" Aunt Jo asked Uncle Dom.

"I gotta bail him out."

"You can't leave me here alone."

"Stay and enjoy." Dom raised his hands and addressed the group. "Enjoy the party. All will be well. I'll spring my son and return to the festivities."

"I saw this coming in 1939," Hortense shook her head.

Mike looked at his nephews. "Should we follow him?"

Calla stood at the window of the Fourth Precinct. There were more cars representing the Palazzini family parked in front than there were official police vehicles.

Nicky emerged from the jail with Gio and Uncle Dom. "We got him!"

"When God closes a door, He opens a window!" Jo exclaimed.

"But not wide enough that I could jump out of it." Gio rubbed his wrists.

Mabel burst into tears and she embraced her husband.

"I won't gamble anymore, honeybun," Gio promised.

"And I'm going to pretend to believe you."

The family shuffled out of the police station and into their cars. Mike went to Dom. "How much did that set you back?"

"I didn't pay."

"Who did?"

"Nicky used *la boost*."

Mike shook his head. "That's bad luck."

"I couldn't stop him. It was a bag of cash when cash was called for."

"It's still bad luck."

"Hey. After all these years, I'd call it good luck—Nicky and Calla collected enough to spring him."

Calla rolled over in bed. She'd woken up to the scent of bacon frying, eggs being scrambled, and buttery toast.

"I have the best husband."

"It's always a good idea to stand next to Gio when you want to be head of class."

"Poor Gio." Calla sat up in bed.

"Good thing we had *la boost*. Cash at the ready is evidently a requirement in night court."

Calla got out of bed and went to her husband. She put her arms around him. "I could stay here forever."

"We can't."

"Why not?"

"I bought a house."

"Nicky, I don't want a house."

"I know."

"I want to live right here. You love this place too, don't you?"

"This is very bohemian. We're theater people, so good for us. We're like jazz. Or the beat poets. We live in the crawl space of the theater. What could be more romantic?"

"I want to keep things simple."

"I know you do."

"I got a bad taste when my sisters divvied up my parents' stuff. I don't want a life of material things."

"We won't need much in this house that I looked at."

"Is it small?"

"It's not too big."

"I don't like ostentatious."

"I understand. Why don't you eat your breakfast? Get dressed, and I'll show it to you. We still have time to wiggle out of the deal."

"We do?"

"I'm never going to do anything to make you unhappy. Except maybe buy the wrong house."

When Calla and Nicky jumped into his car, she looked back at the theater. She told herself she would look at the house Nicky found, politely thank him, but she had no intention of ever leaving Borelli's. It was her heirloom, her lamp, clock, crystal, and formal set of dishes, the living meaning of the lives of her parents. She was one with their memory whenever she was inside the theater.

Nicky drove up Broad Street, remembering his days as a hack, and how he'd slow down at corners, hoping for a fare. The reflex remained, and occasionally caused him some aggravation when he tapped the brakes at a green light when a corner fare was imminent, even though he was no longer in the business, and there was no meter inside the convertible.

Nicky took a familiar left turn and slowed down. Calla sat up in her seat. She looked at him, the street, and the row of houses.

"You're not serious, are you, Nicky?"

Nicky pulled up in front of 832 Ellsworth Street and stopped the car. The gray porch still sloped. The flowerbeds were still lousy. The walkway had a crack in the concrete that was a few feet long, with a chunk missing at the gate. The wood planks on the porch needed paint, and the whole house needed new windows. The elm tree in the side yard had died of blight; where there once had been bright green branches, there were now gray antlers.

"But the house sold."

"I bought it back for you."

Calla buried her face in Nicky's neck.

"Come on, let's go inside."

"I can't."

"It's all yours."

"I'm afraid if I open my eyes, it will be gone."

"And I'm afraid if we don't get to work on this old barn, it will fall down from neglect."

Calla opened her eyes. Her home was where it had always been, from the day she was born. She had lost it, when it seemed she had lost everything.

"You must really love me," she said.

"You'll never know." Nicky kissed her. "We're home."

Epilogue

There was an oak tree shading the lot on Montrose that had caused the Palazzini brothers their trouble in 1933. So many dead branches had been cut away through the years to save the tree, its thick trunk was scarred with flat circles where the saw had severed the limbs. But somehow the mighty oak had survived, and there were plenty of new branches with bright green leaves and nut pods that shook like beads as the wind blew through.

Dom and Mike stood on the sidewalk, surveying the lot that had caused the rift that led to the fight that marooned them on the island.

"I passed this lot every day, you know," Dom said after a while.

"It gave me pleasure to know it."

"I'm sure it did."

"But not anymore."

"Why now, Mike?" Dom looked at his brother, who in his opinion had held up pretty good for a man of his age. Maybe there was something to living it up and enjoying life that put a glow in a man's cheeks and a certain pep in his deliberate step. Maybe vacations were good for people; maybe rest and a proper period of relaxation shored them up for the hard work that awaited them when they returned. Whatever the case, Dom could see that the years had blown past his brother, barely ruffling that thick white hair. The same had not been true for him. Dom wore the years with more lines on his face than the bus map of Philadelphia.

"I started thinking about Ma." Mike kicked a small pebble with his shoe, away from the lot and into the gutter in the street.

"Yeah?"

"I got these daughter-in-laws—nice girls, don't get me wrong, but it's all about their families, their holidays, their mothers. I'm a check-cashing service. I might as well sit in a glass booth and disburse funds all day instead of sitting in my lounger. The men don't matter so much as life goes on."

"I get you," Dom agreed.

"Maybe it's for the best. I thought Ma was more important than Pop. Didn't you?"

"I don't know. Pop had problems, so I don't know if I can answer that. But Ma, she was a lady. We had nothing, you remember, but she made it seem like we had everything. She made Pop out to be a hero, like one of the Knights of the Round Table. He had sacrificed everything to come to America to provide for us. He was building bridges."

"We thought he personally built America by himself, that he alone made transportation possible." Mike smiled. "A welder with a union card."

"You got to give him credit. Pop was brave because he worked high in the air without a net. And he sent every penny home to her. That stuck with me."

"He missed her too, Dom."

"You think so?"

"How could he not?"

"He had enough lady friends after she died."

"He was lonely," Mike reasoned.

"You always made excuses for him."

"I probably always will."

"That's all right. Everyone deserves a good defense." Dom buried his hands into his pockets.

Dom looked around the lot. He remembered when his father had purchased it for a song, a nickel, a pittance. No matter. The lot was a steal. Their father had a grand scheme to own Montrose Street, with both sons beholden to his power and wealth. Domenico was a journeyman, but he schemed like a king. He had big American dreams like a Rockefeller, but possessed enough self-recrimination to punish his sons for his own shortcomings. Instead of being circumspect, he was envious, even of his boys and their relationship, so he broke it. It was he who planted doubt between them, and allowed it to fester. Two against one never works in any competition, so the old gambler hedged his bet so both sons would remain loyal to him instead of each other. They did. But now, they were the only players left at the table. Neither Dom nor Mike had anything to prove.

Mike reached into the breast pocket of his coat and removed a blue envelope, folded and sealed. "Here's the deed."

"You keep it."

"What?" Mike was stunned.

"You keep it. I got enough real estate."

"Are you kidding me? You wanted it, now I'm giving it to you, and you won't take it?"

"How much is it worth?" Dom reached into his pocket, pulled out a pack of matches, and picked his canine tooth with the edge of the cover.

"I don't know," Mike answered honestly.

"No appraisal?"

"No." Mike was confused.

"Haven't called Bones Bonocetti?"

"Why would I call him?"

"To find out what the lot is worth."

"I don't care what the lot is worth, Dominic."

"Maybe that's why it's so easy for you to part with it. It holds no value for you."

"What?" Mike felt steam rising from his collar.

"You got a parcel in your real estate portfolio, and you don't know its worth? What are you? An idiot?"

"Dom, I'll knock you to the Parkway." Mike backed up as if to slug his brother.

Dom took a step back, shuffling as if to avoid a punch. "Hey, hey, take it easy!"

Mike saw the glint of a tease in his older brother's eye and dropped his fists. "You son of a—"

Dom chuckled. "I'm playing with you."

"And I fell for it." Mike massaged his chest. "I thought you were serious. My blood pressure. Mary Mother of God help me."

"You'll be all right." Dom smirked and walked onto the lot. "Come on."

Mike followed his brother.

No matter how old a man grows, the boy he was slumbers within him, taking up a corner of his soul where he once occupied the sum total of it. There are times when the sleeping boy stirs within the man, roused by the niggle of an old score that needs settling, or jolted awake by a sudden burst of physical strength that galvanizes his body in its ferocity. The old man will even experience the unexpected ripple of sexual desire that does not pass, but must be acted upon, until he is satisfied and satisfies the object of his passion, the latter lesson learned from a place of experience. In the man's memory, he is never old and will never grow old. He is neither father or son, but just a boy, who time cannot own.

When the brothers reached the middle of the lot, Dominic stopped and looked up.

"Lot of sky here."

"Until they build up Broad. All you need is one ten-story building, and your sky is shot," Mike commented. "Hey. What am I supposed to do with this?" Mike waved the deed folded neatly inside the blue envelope, which was the exact color of the sky that day.

"Put it in your pocket," Dom said quietly.

"You're a piece of work." Mike shook his head. "All that time, lost for nothing."

"It wasn't for nothing."

"How do you figure?"

"I had a kid brother who left me, stood on his own two feet, and built his own business. He built it so well, he almost ran me out of mine. Now, that's a success. Had we stayed together, you never would have reached your potential."

"You got smart in your old age?" Mike joked.

"My wife came up with that one."

Mike bit his lip. "You really won't take this lot?"

Dominic put his hands in his pockets. For a moment, he thought he might take the lot. He still had some ideas, a dream lying around here or there that might be realized if he massaged the situation just so. He thought of things that he could do before his life was over that might be a challenge met, or even just a fun enterprise for his amusement and profit. But none of Dom's potential schemes mattered much when he weighed them against time he might spend with his brother. Those imagined moments, just the two of them, as they were in the beginning, happening anew, seemed priceless to Dom. They could become just a couple of kids again, figuring life out. This seemed like a pretty good segue to the inevitable dirt nap, the final good-bye, the eternal snooze after the anointing of the sick was administered on whatever dark day it happened to fall for either of them.

Dom decided he didn't want the lot after all. But he did need to tell his brother what he had hoped all those years ago, so Mike might understand why they had a falling-out in the first place. So Dom looked down at the deed and said, "I just wanted you to offer it to me, Mike."

Mike stood holding the deed, thinking Dom was a little nuts. If money was the cause of every split in every Italian family since the Etruscans, Mike had just found out why. Money loaned from family was validation; given, it was encouragement; shared, it was legacy; and when denied, it meant you had not measured up. You had not contributed enough. You had not made the family proud by the course of your actions, the details of your business plan, or the depth of your personal need. Money given could be a prize, but withdrawing it was always a punishment. Money was symbolic. If you made a lot of money, you knew something; if you held on to it, you were worth something. If you couldn't do either of those things, you'd be better off becoming a priest.

It had taken Mike almost twenty years to understand what Dominic meant to him. Mike learned, without his brother in his life, that their relationship was fundamental, even when it was flawed; even when they were inept and inarticulate with one another and brought the worst of themselves forward, they still needed to be loved and to love one another. Mike felt lucky that he had figured out that he loved Dom more than he hated his brother's limitations. With that realization came redemption. He opened his arms wide. It was as if a hundred black crows flew out of his chest and up into the sky until they were specks of ash over South Philly. He let it all go, the broken promises, the anger, and the determination to change his brother; it all was gone. Mike swore he could hear their wings as they departed toward heaven, releasing the years of resentment, and making the space for forgiveness.

Mike would mail the deed to his brother later. Or he'd leave it in secret with his sister-in-law, Jo. Or maybe he'd will it to one of his great-nieces or -nephews on Dom's side for their Confirmation day or a wedding. Mike would come up with some way to move the chips to Dom's side of the table without his brother's knowledge. Mike slid the deed back into his pocket. "If you won't take the lot, you have to let me do one thing for you."

"What's that?"

"Buy you a suit. You dress like an undertaker."

Dom scowled, but before the impulse turned to anger, he chuckled.

"What's so funny?" Mike wanted to know.

"That you think you could take this"—Dom modeled his body—"and improve it."

Mike was going to argue the point, but gave up. He laughed. Soon, Dom was laughing too. In the time that it took for one brother to tell a self-deprecating joke and the other to hear it, they were at peace once more. The dark days were over. Dom and Mike were together as they once had been in a place that they had tried to forget because it was easier to hate than to love. But love was so much better. It had only taken, what? Five? Ten? Twelve? Twenty years? It didn't matter. Now they remembered. Now they understood. Now, they knew.

Postlude

A woman bent over the telegraph machine and tapped out the message coming in over the wire in code. She spun in her chair and typed out the telegram swiftly and accurately on the manual typewriter, a licorice black Olivetti.

She pulled the message from the carriage, attached it to the letterhead, folded it neatly, and slid it into an envelope. She went to the window and pushed open the bright blue shutters. The telegraph office in Alberona filled with the midday sun that reflected off the golden walls of the piazza. A group of young boys sat on the steps of the colonnade.

"Andiamo, Federico!"

The boy, around fourteen, came running. The woman handed him the telegram out the window. He jumped on a bicycle pulled from the clutter of them parked under the window, stuffed the envelope in his shirt pocket, and was about to pedal off when the woman shouted to him: *"Il tuo cappello!"*

She tossed his cap out the window. He caught it and put it on his head.

The boy pedaled through the town and out onto the main road. He took a turn and began to pedal up the hill to Roseto Valfortore.

The hillsides were covered in white blossoms over fields of green. The landscape looked like the finest swath of Fortuny velvet, the deep green embossed with lighter shades of mint where the sun fell behind the clouds into shadows on the peaks.

The boy stood up on the bike, taking the rake of the steep hill in long strides. His lean form threw a long shadow on the road, which was inlaid with smooth stone that had neither a groove nor a crack in it. In these ancient hills, this particular road was easy to navigate; it was smooth in the modern fashion, with gutters to funnel rain down the mountain without flooding the pass.

As the boy rounded the top of the hill, the fig trees that grew in abundance near the entrance of the town sprouted citrine buds that would bloom and grow into sweet fruit.

Carlo Guardinfante stood on the balcony outside his bedroom, holding his newborn son. The sweet scent of the roses blooming on the village walls drifted through the air. Everything, as far as he could see, was fertile, rich, and ripening under the warm Italian sun.

The piazza below was crowded with Rosetani shopping at the outdoor market. Fruit of every kind, fresh fish from the Adriatic, flowers from neighboring Foggia, fabric from Prato—it was all displayed under bright canopies for the locals.

Carlo looked beyond the piazza. The new road from the village down the mountain to the main highway was traveled with such frequency that Carlo ordered traffic signs made and requested that a carabiniere be assigned to deal with the traffic as it flowed into and out of the village. No longer isolated, the Rosetani were part of the world again.

From his window that morning, Carlo could hear the music of ordinary conversation, Rosetani bartering and laughing as they shopped. It reminded him of what life was like when he was a boy, and he was pleased. His own son would know the childhood that he had known.

The boy in the cap pedaled up to the entrance of the villa. He hopped off the bicycle and spun the chimes on a wheel next to the front door. Soon the houseman opened the door. The boy tipped his cap and handed the old man the telegram. The old man dug in his trouser pocket for a coin. He found it and gave it to the boy. The boy thanked him, jumped back on his bicycle, and coasted down the hill.

Carlo watched the boy glide down the road effortlessly like a gray feather floating in a gentle breeze.

"Bring the baby, Carlo," Bette called out.

"He needs fresh air."

"He needs milk."

"He likes the balcony."

"I'm his mother. Bring him to me."

Carlo smiled and did as he was told.

Bette was propped up on pillows in their bed. She extended her arms. "Come here," she said. Carlo handed the infant to Bette. She nursed him.

The houseman slipped the telegram under the door.

"Father DeNisco said to tell you the baptism is set for Sunday." Carlo pulled the coverlet up to his wife's waist. He went around the bed and propped up the pillows behind her so she would be more comfortable as she nursed the baby.

"Are you sure about his name?" Elisabetta wondered as she looked down at her son.

"I like it. Don't you?"

"Very much. But it has never been used in our families, and tradition says the baby should be named after your father. His name should be Carlo."

"I like Nicolo," Carlo said. "Nic is very modern."

"Nic sounds American." Elisabetta smiled. "Not that I mind."

"Our son should be as generous as our friend Nick Castone."

Carlo picked up the telegram and opened the envelope.

"Bad news?" Elisabetta asked him anxiously.

"It's from Nick and Calla."

He read aloud:

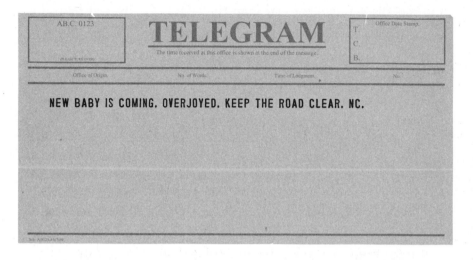

> **TELEGRAM**
>
> AB.C. 0123
>
> The time received at this office is shown at the end of the message.
>
> Office of Origin.   No. of Words.   Time of Lodgment.   No.
>
> **NEW BABY IS COMING. OVERJOYED. KEEP THE ROAD CLEAR. NC.**

"Wonderful news! I will write to them," Elisabetta said.

"See? You worry too much, and you worry for nothing."

"I can't help it, Carlo."

"When the baby arrives, I'll invite them for the summer." Carlo was delighted.

Elisabetta nursed their son as Carlo curled up next to his wife on the bed. When the baby had had his fill, she placed him tenderly in the soft straw basket on the bed next to her. She draped her arm around it, protecting her highest dream.

The afternoon sun, the color of a ripe apricot, cut a ribbon of light across the polished floor. Elisabetta thought to get up from the bed, close the sheer draperies and the doors, but she was tired, the bed was warm, and the air was sweet. The scent of the fresh fields in *la primavera*, blossoming and green, wafted over them. She settled back on her pillow instead.

A warm breeze stirred the old wind chimes on the balcony, making a sweet tune that lulled the father, the mother, and their baby to sleep.

Acknowledgments

Michael Anthony Trigiani (1903–1968) was a good and in all ways a glorious man. My grandfather taught me how to tie my shoes, play checkers, and eat soup properly. When I was punished for being a troublemaker in kindergarten at Our Lady of Mount Carmel School, my penance was to appear in the school Nativity play as the lone girl shepherd and wear a burlap sack, but my grandfather, who owned and operated the Yolanda Manufacturing Company (in Martins Creek, Pennsylvania) with my grandmother, was having none of it. Instead, he made me a gorgeous purple satin tunic. Knowing the costume might incite the peevish nun, he walked me into the school the night of the performance and charmed her. I remember his hand in mine that cold night, when he took what could have been a moment of humiliation and turned it into something beautiful and empowering.

Grandpop came from a big family (four boys, five girls). His parents emigrated from Roseto Valfortore, Italy, to Roseto, Pennsylvania, at the turn of the twentieth century. He began as a machinist in a pants factory, and worked his way up to managing it with my grandmother, until they went into business for themselves. His education took him to the eighth grade, but later he took courses to complete his high school diploma. He was four-teen years old in 1917 when a miracle occurred in Fatima, Portugal, which had a profound effect on him. His faith fueled his aspirations to make his hometown the best it could be. He locked arms with his friends to build two parish schools and a ballpark in Roseto. After years of serving on the town council, he was elected chief burgess (mayor) of Roseto in 1942. He was a director of the First National Bank of Bangor, Pennsylvania, from 1951 until his death, a feat for the son of Italian immigrants, but one that confirmed his composure, steadfast business sense, and role as a community builder.

While I have written extensively about the women in my family, I never meant to give my grandfather short shrift. He was at ease in the world, and possessed an innate elegance, which the Italians call *sprezzatura*. He worked side by side with his wife, Viola, who easily owned any room she entered—or could clear one when she was displeased. His love for her made him a feminist, and he was proud of her accomplishments and ambition; so much so that it was *her* name over the door of the factory they owned together. His family and friends relied on him; in times of trouble, it was he who showed up and took care of the broken-hearted, or just the broke. He died not long after he made me that costume, but even having known him for a short time, I'm certain he set the needle of my moral compass. I try to live right so I'll see him again someday.

I am delighted to be published by the great, hardworking, and visionary team at HarperCollins, led by two wonderful leaders: Brian Murray and Michael Morrison. I am in awe of my brilliant editor, Jonathan Burnham. He is a writer's dream. He has exquisite taste, the ability to press like a good coach when necessary, and he supports the work in every way to make it the best it can be. Thank you, Jonathan! Doug Jones is a superb leader and I rely on his vision and team to put the book into your hands. Thank you Emily Griffin, who works hard, sparkles, persists, and has the countenance of the aforementioned saints. Jonathan and Emily's right arms: Mary Gaule, Amber Oliver, and Jennifer Civiletto get kisses from Carlo, too.

Kate D'Esmond is tireless, wise, and a joy, a publicist with panache. Tina Andreadis is a Greek goddess who rules all media on behalf of authors with warmth and affection. In publicity and marketing, thank you Leah Wasielewski, Renata Marchione, Emily VanDerwerken, Leslie Cohen, Katie O'Callaghan, Jennifer Murphy, Mary Ann Petyak, and Tom Hopke Jr. Virginia Stanley, director of library marketing, calls and I get on the plane. She is the queen of the libraries and my dear friend. Thank you Amanda Rountree and Chris Connolly.

Robin Bilardello designed the spectacular cover art; every detail bursts with life. Thank you to the design and art team: Leah Carlson-Stanisic, Fritz Metsch, Joanne O'Neill, and Sarah Brody.

The team that works around the clock to serve our readers, providing books to independent bookstores, chains, online, and to libraries in every manner and format to serve you, is amazing: Mary Beth Thomas, Josh Marwell, Andy LeCount, Kathryn Walker, Michael Morris, Kristin Bowers, Brendan Keating, Carla Parker, Brian Grogan, Tobly McSmith, Lillie Walsh, Rachel Levenberg, Frank Albanese, David Wolfson, and Samantha Hagerbaumer.

The paperback team, Mary Sasso and Amy Baker, are phenomenal. Thank you Tara Weikum, my great YA editor; the video team, Marisa Benedetto, Lisa Sharkey, Alex Kuciw, and Jeffrey Kaplan. The sublime audio book was produced by Katie Ostrowka and read by the incomparable Edoardo Ballerini. Thank you Danielle Kolodkin, Natalie Duncan, and Andrea Rosen in our speaker's bureau and special markets.

Over at WME, I am represented by the petite and gorgeous tornado Suzanne Gluck. Thank you Andrea Blatt, Clio Seraphim, Clarissa Lotson, Kitty Dulin, Eve Attermann, Alicia Gordon, Sasha Elkin, Becky Chalsen, Jonathan Lomma, Evan Morse, Joey Brown, Tracy Fisher, Alli Dyer, Cathryn Summerhayes, Elizabeth Sheinkman, Fiona Baird, and Siobhan O'Neill.

Nancy Josephson has been my agent and guiding star since the start; I adore her. Jill Holwager Gillett, we are back together again and not a moment too soon! Thank you Sylvie Rabineau, Rehana Lodge, Ashley Kruythoff, Ellen Sushko, Graham Taylor, Will Maxfield, Michelle Bohan, Joanna Korshak, Chris Slager, Liesl Copland, Alli McArdle, Amos Newman, Lauren Denielak, Kathleen Nishimoto, and Hilary Savit.

The Glory of Everything Company is a small but mighty team. Thank you Sarah Choi, you're a star. Hannah Drinkall, who has energy and pluck and patience; Doni Muransky, we still have the glow from your time here. Thank you Matthew Hong, the great designer, and Jean Morrissey, my gifted and generous partner. Our summer interns rocked the West Village; they are stars of tomorrow in writing, editing, marketing, publicity, and art—thanks and love to Oona Intemann, Emilie Kefelas, Kenneth Marciano, Arden Batista, Olivia Olson, Ashley Murray, Jania Perez, Paula Ubah, Fiona Hines, Carrie Klein, and Amy Dworsky.

Deep gratitude to the dazzling Nancy Bolmeier Fisher, executive director of the Origin Project, and Linda Woodward and Grace Bradshaw. Thank you for your wisdom Richard Thompson, Bryna Melnick, Helen Rosenberg, Donna Gigiliotti, Larry Sanitsky, Gina Forsythe, Katherine Drew, Maya Ziv, Kim Hovey, Ian Chapman, and Suzanne Baboneau.

If you must choose one friend in your life, make it Bill Persky. If you must choose two, add Joanna Patton. They gave me (Saint) Judith Kelman and Visible Ink; which shored up my soul.

The story of Roseto in the late 1940s was told to me by Ralph Stampone, Jack Parillo, and Mamie Ciliberti. Cousin Gary Stampone provided photographs; cousin Joe Peters confirmed who the folks were in the pictures. Caroline Giovannini was a font of info on all things Rosetan. Cousin Ben Tartaglia, the son of the Mary "Mix-Up," helped with the details of life in South Philly, as did fellow native Gina Casella, fabulous president of AT Escapes. Samantha Rowe, research assistant, cracked Morse code, ladies' hats, and historical Philadelphia for this one. Brandy Carrao Piche and Jack and Pat Carrao of Chicagoland gave me their family tree to pick and prune with love. The grace notes of heroism in wartime came from cousin Tommy Falcone, Navy Seaman, 2nd Class, who died at nineteen when the USS *Franklin* was hit on March 19, 1945. First Lieutenant Michael J. Cleary and Army Specialist Richard D. Naputi Jr. were killed in Iraq on December 20, 2005. Their heroic spirits fill these pages. Sister Jean Klene, thank you for your vast knowledge of Shakespeare, which I was so lucky to witness in your classes at Saint Mary's; you truly lit this spark, while Reg Bain threw a gallon of gas on it when I watched him expertly direct *Hamlet.*

Thank you Jake Morrissey, who reads early and often. I've come to rely on his sound judgment and high opinion. I have two fabulous brothers, but I am blessed with a third: David Baldacci is a great writer, but he also has the biggest heart on the planet.

In the Roseto and Big Stone Gap traditions, friendship is everlasting and more precious than gold. My evermore thanks to: Chris and Ed Muransky, Mary Pipino, Kristin Dornig and Tony Krantz, Candyce Williams, Robyn Lee, Dorothy and Bob Isaac, Pat Bean, Brian Balthazar, Jennifer Bloom and Andrew Kravis, Nigel Stoneman, Charles Fotheringham, Hannah Palermo, Christine Onorati, Matthew T. Weiner, Andrew Hauser and Emily Suber, Joe Rudge, Jacqueline Cholmondeley, William Watson and

Adelina Castro, Aunt Bunny Grossinger, Kathy McElyea, Lou and Berta Pitt, Doris Shaw Gluck, Dianne and Andy Lerner, Tom Dyja, Matt Williams and Angelina Fiordellisi, Christina Geist, Susan Fales-Hill, Charles Randolph Wright, Donna Diamond, Liz Travis, Betty Fleenor, Diane and Dr. Armand Rigaux, Monique Gibson, Sharon Ewing, Dan and Robin Napoli, Dagmara Domincyzk and Patrick Wilson, Gail Berman, Eugenie Furniss, Phillip Grenz, Joyce Sharkey, Spencer Salley, Robin Kall, Dana Chidekel, Tracy and Greg Kress, Cate Magennis Wyatt, Carol and Dominic Vechiarelli, Mark Amato, Mary Beth and Mike Allen, Meryl Poster, Sister Robbie Pentecost, Mary K. and John Wilson, Jim and Kate Benton Doughan, Richard and Dana Kirshenbaum, Marisa Acocella, Violetta Acocella, Emma and Tony Cowell, Hugh and Jody Friedman O'Neill, Nelle Fortenberry, Cara Stein, Dolores and Dr. Emil Pascarelli, Eleanor "Fitz" King and Eileen, Ellen, and Patti, Sharon Hall, Rosanne Cash, Constance Marks, Jasmine Guy, Mario Cantone and Jerry Dixon, Judy Rutledge, Jayne Muir, Father John Rausch, Mary Ellen Keating, Nancy Ringham Smith, Sharon Watroba Burns, Dee Emerson, Elaine Martinelli, Sister Karol Jackowski, Jane Cline Higgins, Betty Cline, Beth Vechiarelli Cooper, Robyn and Max Westler, Tom and Barbara Sullivan, Ninette Bavaro-Latronica, Brownie and Connie Polly, Catherine Brennan, Karen Fink, Beata and Steven Baker, Todd Doughty, Randy Losapio, Craig Fisse, Steve and Anemone Kaplan, Christina Avis Krauss and Sonny, Eleanor Jones, Wendy Miller Hughes, Becky Browder, Connie Shulman, Evadean Church, Miles Fisher, Marion Cantone, and Tom Leonardis.

Michael Patrick King, how lucky I am that you took that parking spot next to mine and your engine fell out and we fell in for life.

Ladies, I adore you and you know why, thank you: Michelle Baldacci, Cynthia Rutledge Olson, Mary Testa, Dottie Frank, Wendy Luck, Elena Nachmanoff, Dianne Festa, Joanne LaMarca,

Jackie Levin, Hoda Kotb, Kathie Lee Gifford, Christine Gardner, Sheila Mara, Rosanna Scotto, Mary Murphy, Whoopi Goldberg, Ruth Pomerance, Jenna Elfman, Janet Leahy, and Susie Essman.

I thank my husband and daughter for not changing the locks. You are my heart. Thank you to my brothers and sisters; their families and the fabulous Stephenson family. My mother, Ida, is still teaching me how to live, I am eternally grateful to her.

As I wrote this book, I mourned the loss of dear friends and family, who were once angels on earth and now enjoy their heavenly reward. God bless my beloved cousin Paul Godfrey; Mary E. Burton and her daughter Margaret Gallemore; Frank Pellegrino Sr., Rao's regal raconteur; Jack Hodgins, magnificent, award-winning innkeeper; Frank Delaney, divine storyteller, treasured friend, and Diane's true love; Bob Minzesheimer, irreplaceable book lover/writer, loving dad, and husband; Judy Parks Krafft, my fabulous aunt by marriage; Hortense Mooney, devout and joyful; Betty Matera, Al's shy and loving wife; Vincent Matera, the hilarious quintessential New Yorker, Marie's Italian stallion, and Rosemarie's perfect father; Robert Francis of Chisholm, Minnesota, the kindest and most gentle soul who ever lived; Rosalyn Angelini Mugavero, Roseto beauty, loving wife, mother, and grandmother; Rosemarie D'Alessandro, beloved wife and mother; Kenneth Ciliberti, perfect son and brother; Carol A. Ciliberti, wonderful wife and mother, Mitzi Thomas, dear friend, Jan Rohrs, good mother and friend; Joseph O'Connor, Trish's dear dad; Dr. Brownie E. Polly and Barbara Polly, lifelong friends; Brooklyn's Kitty Martinelli, bella mother and wife; Adrianne Tolsch, the hilarious, gutsy gamine, Bill Scheft's beloved wife; mentor Earl Hamner Jr., who cut the path in the Blue Ridge mountains so all the rest of us might follow; Miles Coiner, the hippest man in any room, director/writer/professor, and Mary's good husband; Kathleen Lang, Tom's wife, Kaitlin's mom, kind and generous, a fellow

Lizzie on the Arizona Women's Board; Frances Keuling-Stout, the madcap, original poet and Henry's true love; and Lisa Obry, a Saint Mary's girl from Jersey who was loyal, fun-loving, and the first in line to buy a ticket to any play her friend had written. And I would know: I was that lucky girl.

About the Author

ADRIANA TRIGIANI is the bestselling author of seventeen books, which have been published in thirty-six countries around the world. She is a playwright, television writer/producer, and filmmaker. She wrote and directed the film version of her novel *Big Stone Gap,* which was shot entirely on location in her Virginia hometown. She is cofounder of the Origin Project, an in-school writing program that serves more than one thousand students in Appalachia. She lives in Greenwich Village with her family.

ML   AUG   2017